Humble Warrior Tales

John Eudy

Contents

A Glorious Day in Hell

The Day Jesus Descended

Contents

PRELUDE

A SUDDEN AND TERRIBLE REALIZATION

The sounds of battle echo down a well-traveled Middle Eastern road. A loud “thunk” reverberates through a Roman Legionnaire’s chest before he falls to the ground. Everything goes silent.

Ioannes opens his eyes. The sky is no longer blue. The dust, stirred up by battle, no longer swirls around him. Instead, he sees an ethereal, almost post-twilight, sky. He looks out over a now silent battlefield. Only the dead are present; they lie on the ground around him. Time has stopped. Nothing is moving. There is no sound. The sky and land have turned a gray, muted color.

He turns his gaze downward, only to see his own 19-year-old body lying on the ground. Shock sets in as he stares at an arrow protruding from the seam of his body armor; his lifeless hands still clutch the pole bearing his legion’s standard. Ioannes looks up and around in bewilderment, staggering backward in disbelief. Dropping his head down again and raising his hands, he looks at his open palms. As he does, he suddenly realizes he is completely naked. He lowers his hands, instinctively covering his genitalia, and begins to look up with paranoia.

Without warning, a pair of callous hands grasp his forearms tightly from the rear and yanks them behind him. Simultaneously, a coarse, foul-smelling burlap sack is thrust over his head and pulled tight around his neck. Bits of twilight shine through the dark burlap while he begins to wrestle with his captors. Ioannes is unable to break free and soon feels metal shackles clamping shut around his wrists. He grunts as he feels the thrust of his captor’s heel against the back of his knees. Forced painfully to the ground, everything becomes silent once more.

A growling, guttural voice breaks the silence, "Heh, heh, heh. Another sinner for the pit!" Higher-pitched cackling emanates from all around him now. Ioannes, unable to see any precise details through the burlap, knows deep in his gut something terrible is about to happen.

Chapter One

Many Questions

Fierce fighting continues on an ancient Middle Eastern road. A Roman Centuria[1], holding their phalanx formation, repels raiders attacking from surrounding hills near the summit of a mountain pass. Near the front of the column of troops, there, in the middle of the phalanx, is a seasoned veteran named Cælius. Though he is only 27, he has seen battle before. This time is different, though.

A rage stirs in his breast, an old fury that resided in the darker corners of his heart. Quietly aware of its existence for years, Cælius has always thought he might appease it as a soldier but now rises uncontrollably to the surface. It makes his hands shake and his temperature rise. Sweat beads on his forehead run past his brow and drip from his chin. A low growl rumbles through clenched teeth. Throwing his shield and spear into the dirt, he suddenly breaks ranks and draws his gladius. His growling erupts into a blood-curdling war cry as he rushes madly toward an enemy raider.

The raider thrusts his sword at the Roman with his right hand. Cælius, in stride, steps to his right, avoiding the thrust, instinctively raises his left arm, hitting his opponent's forearm and knocking his sword hand upward. He then mercilessly runs his gladius upward into the enemy's chest. Cælius stands, holding the raider upright, impaled upon his gladius. He stares into his eyes, watching life leave his enemy. Finally, he lets go of the sword. His enemy falls to the ground; Cælius stands over the bloodied corpse, breathing heavily.

---

[1] 80-man unit

The unbridled wrath departs, and he slowly regains consciousness and senses. Both remorse and fear overcome him. He realizes he is not only out of formation and exposed, but a foreign sense of regret permeates his mind. Looking around the dusty, rocky area, he sees the bodies of the enemy littering the ground while a handful of raiders flee back over the ridgeline. Their retreat signals the end of the battle. Cælius takes a deep breath in relief.

Feeling calmer, he looks toward his Centuria's front and sees a missing banner. He pulls his gladius from the chest of his enemy, instinctively wipes the blood from the blade, and sheathes it. He rushes toward the banner carriers, parting other soldiers from their formation until he reaches the carriers. There, he sees his friend Ioannes lying on the ground. He drops to his knees, lifts the dead soldier's body, and places his back on his raised knee. He takes the banner from his lifeless hands and hands it to a random soldier within the formation. In a sad, almost tearful voice, he says, "My brother. Why must it be you to fall this day?"

Another Legionnaire moves up through the ranks to where Cælius is. Stopping next to Cælius, he observes in a dismissive tone, "Isn't that Ioannes? Is he not the one who refuses to fight? Why do you mourn him so, Cælius? His death is not a significant loss."

Cælius slowly looks up at the intrusive legionnaire. Angered and annoyed by his comment, he retorts, "We are all brothers, are we not?"

The Optio[2] approaches. Older and much more gruff, he barks out orders while physically moving soldiers in the direction he wants them to go. "You, get back in formation! You, help gather our dead! You, go help dig graves over there." He points to a sandy, gravelly area north of the road.

---

[2] Second in command of Centuria

He then stops and points to Cælius and the other legionnaire, commanding, “You two, strip that man of his armor and put it in the cart coming up. Afterward, take his body to the grave. Then clean up and get back in formation.”

Having given all his commands, the Optio returns to his previous station.

The two soldiers obey the orders and begin stripping the armor off Ioannes’ body. As they do, Cælius, who is looking down, reflects on a conversation he recently had with his slain friend.

* * * * *

It was a late day in Cæsarea Maritima. A soothing breeze was blowing in off the water. Having completed their tasks and given liberty for the evening, Cælius and Ioannes sit on the part of a rock wall facing the wind and the Mare Internum[3]. Low tidal waves splash at their feet below. The occasional gull squawks in the air overhead, and a bustling market can be heard in the distant background. Neither soldier has his helmet or spear; however, for safety’s sake, they still wear their armor and carry their gladius.

Ioannes looks down at the waves breaking on the sea wall below him. Cælius, sitting a couple of feet away, gazes at the open ocean. He is always mesmerized by the deep blue sea. Today, though, he has something to ask his young friend. “I’ve heard rumor, Ioannes, that you will not fight. That you lack the courage to kill.” He pauses for effect. “You march with the legion; you even carry our banner, but you do know you will never be considered a true Legionnaire unless you fight. We are rewarded in eternity for what we do in life. If you want to see the green fields of Elysium, you must overcome your fears.”

---

[3] Mediterranean Sea – (translated from Latin)

Cælius looks over at Ioannes, who keeps his head down, still observing the water splashing against the wall. Cælius grows slightly indignant, "Do you hear me, Ioannes? Soon, we will reach Hierosolyma[4]. Beyond that, we will claim territory, treasure, and slaves in Augustus Cæsar's name. Those people will not be submissive, either. You must find the courage to fight."

Ioannes turns to his right to look at his friend and mentor. Though they are far enough away from others, he still speaks in a low tone so as not to be overheard. Somewhat nervous, he is hesitant in his response, "I do not fear Bellum[5], Cælius. I simply have no desire to take a human life; I cannot bring myself to it. I am content in my humble service to you and other soldiers. I am happy to cook, serve meals, build roads, shore up fortifications, or whatever is needed. I am even more proud to carry the banner for the legion. I simply have no desire for violent conquest. I only seek to find the truth of God in my service and my travels."

Cælius, his chain of thought broken by Ioannes' words, turns to look at him with curiosity. "Ah, there it is again, your God. Tell me more about this god you've discovered."

Ioannes, realizing he mentioned God inadvertently, quickly turns his attention back to the waves below. He is reluctant to respond but, after an awkward silence, eventually faces Cælius again. "I can only say that I believe the God of the Iudæus[6] people ***is*** the one true God." He pauses and takes a deep breath before continuing, "I believe he is merciful, loving, and more powerful than the gods we Romans worship. His prophets of old accomplished such miraculous things with his aid and in his name. Moreover, we have yet even to receive his son, the Messias. It is for his sake

---

[4] Jerusalem (translated from Latin).

[5] "war" (translated from Latin)

[6] Jewish (translated from Latin)

that I do not kill and that I serve the legion the way I do. It is for him that I no longer indulge in the sins of the flesh."

Ioannes pauses again. He returns his attention to the waves lapping the wall below. In a soft tone, he says, "I, I have said too much. If you sincerely want to know more, and if I can trust you, my friend, we can speak again when we reach Hierosolyma."

Cælius is reflective. "Hmm." He begins. "You're a fine young man, Ioannes; I'll keep your secret for now. Maybe I will even give your offer of a deeper conversation some consideration while we march tomorrow." Cælius stands. "Well, you can sit here if you like; however, it has been a long journey thus far, and, unlike you, I **am** going to indulge in wine, women, and food. I'll see you back at camp later tonight, my friend."

Cælius collects himself and then turns to leave. He walks confidently toward the gate leading into the city from the sea wall.

Ioannes remains seated on the break wall. Thinking his friend and mentor is far enough away, he raises his eyes to the bright blue sky and prays to a God he barely knows, "Deus Meus, it is YOU I fear, and YOU I love. Grant me the strength and courage to do what is right."

Cælius hears Ioannes praying. He stops silently in his tracks for a moment and turns his head slightly to his left to listen to the prayer. When Ioannes is done, he mumbles a "harumph," turns his head back, and walks toward the sea wall gate.

* * * * *

It's night now, and the city celebrates. Soldiers and sailors indulge themselves in whatever pleasure is to be had. Cælius emerges from the cloth-covered doorway. He looks left and right as he adjusts his armor and gladius. Legionnaires solicit prostitutes on either side of the entrance to the lupanar[7]. Although he should be somewhat content, having slaked his lust, he has a somber look on his face. He glances up and down the alley before walking past all the revelers. Cælius rounds a corner to his right and strolls into the main thoroughfare. He turns left again and walks about a block before entering a tavern, searching for food and drink.

He spies a small table in the back, away from the bar and other partiers. He takes a seat there with his back to the wall. As if knowing what he wants, a server brings him an empty cup, a flagon of wine, bread, and a couple of figs. He gives her two coins, and she moves on. He pours the wine into his cup, throws back the first round, and then pours another.

He leans back in his chair, placing his left hand on his thigh while keeping his right on his cup. Cælius stares past the bar and out into the lively streets. *What is this feeling?* He broods. *Why do I find no pleasure in eating, drinking, or having sex? What is this empty feeling within me?* He contemplates this while slowly eating the bread and figs and sipping his wine.

He sets his empty cup down on the table. Intertwining his fingers in front of his cup and leaning his face toward his clasped hands, his firm chin hovering above his empty cup, he thinks, I come from a hearty, seafaring family *who never questioned the gods. Why do I question them now? Why does the idea of a single, living God bring such unrest to my heart and mind?*

Cælius looks down at the plate and cup in front of him. He surveys what little remains. "Maybe Ioannes will have an answer. I will speak with him when we reach Hierosolyma," he reassures himself.

Unlocking his fingers, he reaches for his flagon of wine and fills his cup. He takes a bite of the remaining bread and then

---

[7] Brothel (translated from Latin)

puts the cup to his lips. He throws his head back, gulping the entire cup of wine. He sets the cup back on the table and pours another.

* * * * *

The next day has come, and the legion marches along the Via Maris[8]. The ranks move along quietly. Many legionnaires are overcoming their previous evening's indulgences as they trudge along. Cælius is disquieted and agitated. His thoughts are plagued by thoughts of this God Ioannes speaks of. Although he doesn't understand why, he knows all the emptiness, anger, and unrest are related to his doubts and queries.

The soldier marching to his right quickly glances in Cælius' direction and sees the confounded look in his eye. "What troubles you, Cælius? What irritates you so?"

"Nothing!" He barks. "It's nothing."

The slightly offended soldier ignores the anti-social Cælius, who is happy to march on in silent contemplation.

* * * * *

Later that evening, the road-weary legion files into the Ioppe Citadel. Soldiers, tired from their march, break formation and head to various places within. Cælius does not speak to others after entering the citadel himself. Instead, he is of a single thought: find Ioannes.

Cælius comes across him, securing his shield and spear for the night. He walks up to Ioannes, grabs his shoulder, and urges him to turn around. Turning to face his friend, Ioannes sees he is upset about something. However, before he can say anything, Cælius says in a low, secretive tone, "I am

---

[8] Ancient road from Cæsarea to the Roman citadel in Ioppe

disturbed by this notion of a single, living God who involves himself in our daily lives, Ioannes. Tomorrow, we cross the Judean mountains. Once we reach our destination, you and I must speak about this in greater detail." Cælius turns and departs hastily before Ioannes can answer. Unsure of his friend's enigmatic statement, Ioannes spends the rest of the evening in prayer.

* * * * *

That was yesterday, before the ill-fated raid. Now, random soldiers lean on shovels, wipe dirt from their faces, and drink water from their skins. Their hard work digging a mass grave has been completed. Cælius and the other legionnaire lower Ioannes' body, stripped down to his tunic, into the grave. The other soldier climbs out while Cælius remains. His uniform is covered in dust and soaked with sweat. He takes a deep breath and kneels next to Ioannes' body. He removes two small silver coins from a purse on his belt and gently places them on his friend's eyes. "I hope your God has granted you entry into his Elysium, my friend. If not, this will pay for your journey across the River Styx."

Cælius stands and wipes the sweat from his brow. At that moment, an authoritative voice rings in his ears, "Cælius, you will not see my Elysium if you continue in your ways."

Startled, he looks around, but no one is near enough to speak to him. His heart beats rapidly. A shiver runs down his spine, and he cannot control the tears glazing his eyes. The voice speaks again, "It is time to seek a new path."

Deep down, he knows he has heard the voice of the one true God, and nothing else will ever be the same for him.

Chapter Two

A Soldier's Descent

Ioannes kneels on an old mountain road turned into a battlefield. He sees nothing with clarity for the rancid burlap sack covering his head. He can make out the sky, a strange mix of twilight and gray as if there were an evening thunderstorm, and bits of the dark tan and muted land. Shackles clink against the chain behind his naked body. He sees blurs of movement as his captors circle him.

A band of four short dæmons led by an exceptionally large fiend surrounds two humans. The larger demon points his axe toward Ioannes and another unseen soul and commands in a deep, snarling voice, "Chain them together and bring them along."

The little goblin-like dæmons rush about, pulling Ioannes to his feet and wrapping chains around his bare waist. The unnamed soul thrashes in resistance, pulling Ioannes backward. The Dæmon Captain unleashes his whip, cracking it against the flesh of the unnamed soul, who screams and curses as he falls, "Scum! Damn you, little freaks!" His hands are bound, and a burlap sack is pulled over his head as well. He kicks blindly at the goblin dæmons, who are violently grappling him, trying to make him stand up.

Ioannes can barely make out the back of the Dæmon Captain as he straps his axe to his back. He bends down to pick up the chain lead, shouting, "Get up and get moving! Or I will give you another stripe, you worthless sinner!" He snorts and then yanks the lead chain. Ioannes nearly loses his footing as he lurches forward. He strikes his foot on a jagged stone, slicing it. He stumbles but, not wanting to feel the sting of the whip, limps forward in pain.

Ioannes assumes the unnamed soul is one of the fallen raiders who attacked his Centuria, but he can't be sure. Quietly walking now, the slow-moving procession moves away from the battlefield on the road. Ioannes hears the shouts of dæmons capturing and chaining others around him, likely soldiers and raiders from the same skirmish.

As he trudges along, he begins to think, *I only wanted to find the truth of God. Was my lack of courage to fight and kill what led to this exile in the underworld? Or was it something worse? Did the one true God find me unworthy and send me here? What did I do to offend him so to be cast down?* His thoughts turn toward his youth.

* * * * *

The late afternoon sun warms the rolling green hills. Young Ioannes, dressed in a clean, white tunic, scampers across the verdant land of the quaint hillside vineyard. The 10-year-old boy weaves and wanders around rows of grape vines, occasionally plucking a cluster here and there from the vines and placing them in a small basket. Nibbling on one or two grapes as he walks, he tries to talk to some of the servants but is often shooed away as an annoyance. Eventually, he gives up and trots back to his villa with the basket mostly full of grapes.

Later in the evening, just after dusk, the young Ioannes sneaks out of his villa. He cradles a small but relatively full burlap bag and runs as silently as he can toward the servant's quarters. There, he stops in front of a wooden door at one of the small houses and knocks.

The door creaks open in short order, and the youthful Ioannes is greeted by a gruff, elderly man, who immediately crosses his arms over his small round belly. He tucks his bearded face down to give the boy an 'unwelcome' look. The youth is clearly not intimidated, however. He peers past the older man to see his wife and two children, one a boy about eight years old and the other a girl the same age as he is. They are reclining on cushions around a short Middle Eastern table.

Ioannes looks back up at the frowning father, who quickly opens his arms after a final scowl and gives a large smile, greeting him with a quiet but cheerful tone, "Aw, who am I fooling? Ioannes, my boy! Shalom! What are you doing out here?" The father glances outside the door, first left and then right. "You know you're not allowed here, especially this late."

"I know, but I wanted to bring you something."

"Ah, let's get you in where it's safe. Come in, come in." The man motions for the boy to enter. Ioannes swiftly takes his sack to the table, where the rest of the servant family happily greets him. The father again cautiously looks both ways outside the door before closing it.

Ioannes eagerly empties a loaf of bread, three peaches, and a small wadded-up tunic from his sack onto the little table. The mother reaches over to pat him on the head and caresses his cheek as only a mother can, "Oh, thank you, Ioannes. You're such a good boy!"

Taking the small tunic and the peaches with her, she gets up and enters the tiny kitchen area. Her husband comes to the table. Exhausted from working in the vineyard, he groans as he reclines to the left of the young lad. He motions for their guest to sit. The children scooch around the table so there is room for him to sit with them.

"Well, my boy!" He begins with an exhale. "Truly, you are a fine young man. God bless you." The father leans across the small table toward Ioannes and motions to come a bit closer with his finger. "In our language, your name is Yohanan. It means 'God is gracious." The man winks at him. "Indeed, he is, yes?" He then reclines at the table again, smiles at his children, and in a more jovial tone, says, "Yes, I think that's what we will call you from now on, Yohanan." His children smile in agreement.

Young Ioannes smiles, too, with an affirmed delight. The mother, who has put the fruit away for later, returns to the table with tea. She sets one more cup out for their guests and pours everyone a small amount. The father takes his cup in hand, lifts it to his nose, and breathes deep of its aroma. He exhales, "Ahhhh. It smells delicious, mother." He then happily sips his hot tea.

In his youthful impatience, Ioannes unexpectedly blurts out, "I would like to know more about your God. Would you be willing to teach me?"

The father sputters, nearly choking on his tea at the question. His children giggle at the sight of their father being caught off guard. He sets his cup down, brushes off tea from his beard, and raises his eyebrows in surprise. He clears his throat and says, "Hmmm... well now, that is a large and sudden request. What would your parents think if they knew I taught you such things?"

Ioannes shrugs his shoulders and looks inquisitively at the father, who, in turn, glances at the mother. She nods reassuringly, "Go on papa. Surely Adonai will smile on you for teaching the boy."

He turns back to face the young man and lets out a short sigh. "Well then, Yohanan, I suppose we could teach you a little bit. How about his commandments? Yes, let's start there." The father begins to warmly and patiently instruct young Ioannes and his own children. "The first commandment is to worship Adonai alone. We are never to worship any other false gods or idols. He is a jealous God who desires the attention and affection of his children..."

* * * * *

Time passes. Twilight gives way to the darkness of night, and Ioannes' mother becomes aware of his absence. She flings open the door of their villa. She is upset and is frantically looking for her son. He is not to be found in the house, so she races to the stables. He is not there either. She stops to think for a minute. Remembering his growing fondness for the servants, she rushes to their quarters.

She does not knock. Instead, she barges into each house, one by one, until she finally bursts into the Iudæus family's home. A startled Ioannes whips around to see his angry mother glaring at him. Driven by both fear and anger, his mother scolds him. "There you are. What are you doing out at night and in here, no less? Come with me. Now!" Ioannes's Mother storms over to the table and grabs him by the wrist. She pulls him to his feet and drags him out of the quarters. Ioannes looks back to the father, who lovingly smiles while shrugging. The young man waves back to him before disappearing around the corner.

* * * * *

Ioannes, the man, ponders this memory as he stumbles down this new, unseen path into the underworld. *What the Iudæus servants believed always struck me as true. They led me to believe a living God who loved and cared for them was better than any Roman god. The Roman gods seemed to want to use humanity for their selfish whims and desires.*

He remembers secretly visiting his favorite Iudæus family over the years. They taught him about the prophets of old and of a coming Messias, one who would save his people from slavery, tyranny, and oppression in this world and the afterlife. He was drawn to the Messias, and he thinks, *Although I never became fully Jewish, I wondered if he would save me too.*

* * * * *

Years later, a teenage Ioannes, now 16 years old, is seated at the dinner table, eating supper with his family. Ever the brash young man, he talks about his conversations with the servants. He tries to express his understanding of the Ten Commandments and the Messias as it was taught to him.

The discussion is visibly uncomfortable for his parents and siblings. His brother and sister eat quietly with their heads down, and their father looks distantly concerned. Ioannes, in his naivety, speaks in a semi-joyful voice, uninhibited but still respectful: "...I think the commandments are just, and I'm fascinated by their Messias."

Ioannes' father interrupts dismissively, "Give no credence to such lies, son; you should ignore the servants and their nonsense! There is more than one god, and you need to start paying attention to them, or you will find yourself cursed." The room falls silent. Everyone, including the dejected Ioannes, quietly eats the rest of their meal.

* * * * *

Ioannes feels the tug of the chains and hears his captors goad him along. He thinks back to how he came to serve in the legion. He recalls his parents' disapproval of the Iudæus' beliefs, his subsequent rejection of the Roman gods, and his quiet internalization of the one true God's commandments. He remembers the hunger for the deeper truth, which had been cultivated within his heart. As Ioannes grew older, he also grew tired of his father's chastisement and squabbling with his family over his persistent belief in Elohim.

Once he entered manhood, he left home to serve in the Roman Legion. This would allow him to expand his knowledge of God and find the truth. So, at the age of 18, Ioannes joined the legion and left his home. Thinking it divine providence, he was overjoyed to find out he would be assigned to a garrison headed for Hierosolyma.

However, he quickly learned to guard his faith and never openly professed to be a follower of Elohim as a Roman soldier. Though he hoped privately that following God's commandments might still grant him entry into Elysium one day, he dreamed of walking near the living God under the blue sky of his Elysian Fields, feeling the eternal light upon his face. *Instead, I find myself here*, he thinks to himself.

The procession moves along an ancient, wide, well-worn stone road leading downward into a desert-like valley and ending at a cave entrance on a barren mountainside. Though he cannot see it, the valley resembles a gaping wound in the land, like once fertile earth had been slashed open by evil.

Darkness permeates the foul-smelling burlap sack over Ioannes' head. Occasional glimpses through tiny holes show the surrounding environment growing more barren. The vegetation has dwindled. There are no trees or grass, only an occasional dried-up shrub or sickly-looking weed springing up between rugged rocks. The once star-laden sky has vanished, too. Now, an ever-darkening atmosphere blankets the procession as it makes its way toward the cave.

All is silent except for the shuffling of feet on the ground, the rattling of the prisoner's chains, and the goblin dæmon's raspy, high-pitched gossiping.

"These humans just don't comprehend it, do they? Romans, Arabs, Jews, Africans, they all fall. They're all ours." States the first dæmon.

One of them giggles and pokes Ioannes in the left shoulder with something sharp, "You hear that, **boy**? No Elysium for you. Hee, hee, hee!"

Ioannes says nothing. He keeps plodding forward instead. They enter the yawning maw of the mountain cave. Moist, stale air greets them. A massive rust-covered gate lay about 300 feet into the cavern. Moss and lichen-covered parapets of black and gray stone rise at each side of the gate. Water drips from rows of stalactites onto stalagmites, which run from the parapets to the cavern walls on each side. From a distance, the scene resembles a monstrous, salivating mouth. Fire pits glow orange-yellow from behind the rock 'teeth,' illuminating the scene and casting shadows.

The procession slows as it approaches the gate. With a deep, commanding growl, the Dæmon Captain calls them to a halt, "Stooooop! Fools." He loudly drops the chain lead on the ground and walks toward his captives. Sandaled footsteps fall heavily on the stone path as he slowly circles the unnamed soul behind Ioannes. "Shall I tell you what the sign over your head reads?"

The unnamed soul pulls defiantly at his chains and curses, "I don't give a damn what it says, filthy creature!"

"Filthy!?" He responds and rushes upon the shade of a man, punching him in the head. The unnamed soul immediately falls to the ground, the weight of his fall pulling Ioannes backward. The Dæmon Captain, who moves with inhuman speed to Ioannes' side, growls in Ioannes' ear, "What about you, wretch?"

Heavy though it is, the burlap sack over his head ripples with each exhale of the Dæmon Captain's putrid breath. He does not respond; Ioannes simply lowers his head, waiting to be assaulted. Dæmon Captain backs slightly away and begins circling his captives again.

The goblin-like dæmons pick the unnamed soul up off the ground, standing him back up. Dæmon Captain says in a slow, haughty cadence, "No guesses? Fine! I will gladly tell you what it says so you understand your situation. Though you cannot see them, we are at the Devorandum[9] Gate of hell. The beautiful sign over your head reads, 'Abandon all hope ye who enter here.'"

He stops in front of the procession, raises his arms, and says in a triumphant tone, "Welcome to eternal damnation, you pathetic fools! Ha, ha, ha!"

The clanking sound of iron and the high-pitched grind of rusty metal are heard as the gates open wide in the dank cavern. Dæmons manning the gate and the dæmon escort break out in cheers and maniacal laughter.

Dæmon Captain spits at the feet of his captives before bending down to pick up his lead again. With a yank of the chain and demonic laughter, the procession continues its descent through the Devorandum Gate and into hell.

---

[9] Devour, swallow, or gulp down (translated from Latin)

Chapter Three

Crossing the River Styx

The hell-bound procession has walked for some time. The scenery, if you could call it that, has changed. The road has narrowed and now winds toward a riverbank of jagged pumice, obsidian boulders, and a black sand shore. Sounds of wailing, screaming, and cursing are heard in the distance. The road draws closer to the dark, mud-colored water of the River Styx, which flows and glistens in the dim light.

A wooden ship, similar to a Roman hemiolia, has run up on the bank in the distance. It has a narrow draft and only one row of oars on each side. A makeshift gangway of hastily cut wooden planks extends from its deck just behind the bow to the gravel beach. Wailing and the sounds of whips cracking on flesh grow louder and louder as the procession nears.

Several goblin-like dæmons herd shades up the gangplank, whipping and beating them as they board. As Ioannes' procession draws near, Charon, the ship's captain and ferryman on the River Styx, arrogantly approaches the railing. He is a gaunt, older man with a long, unkempt white beard. Wiry arms protrude from his dirty tan tunic, and a small gray cloak hangs over his shoulder. He glares down over the railing at the Dæmon Captain and his captives. He offers an indignant greeting, "More for darkness and fire, I presume?"

Dæmon Captain snorts at his derision, "Of course! You will allow us to escort them, yes?"

"Hrmph. Throw them in the hold and come aboard." Charon mumbles, "Scurvy bilge rat, that one."

The Dæmon Captain reluctantly nods with false gratitude and then yanks the chain forward toward the gangway. Ioannes, still hooded, feels the wood underfoot, but before he can navigate his way, he is shoved from behind by one of the dæmons and stumbles up the gangplank.

Not able to see when he is at the top, he steps off the gangplank and falls on the hard, wooden deck, hurting his shoulder and head. Surrounding dæmons laugh gleefully before quickly seizing him and the one chained behind him. They shove them both toward the boat's hold.

Below decks is a burly creature whose features are difficult to make out in the shadowy hold. His massive, clawed hands reach for the two souls and forcefully pull them down inside the hold. There, he shoves them to the side of the hull to make room for more. It isn't long before the ship is packed full of captured souls. The burly dæmon exits the hold and loudly slams the wooden hatch closed.

The ship's hold is completely dark; Ioannes can see nothing but blackness. He hears the oars scraping the hull as they are extended outboard. Some plunk into the water, and some land on the gravelly shore. They scratch and splash, pulling the soul-laden boat out into open water.

Charon's raspy voice rings out, "Row damn you! Row!" A whip cracks, and the sound of the boat's keel scraping the rock on its way back out into the River Styx echoes briefly in the hold.

Above decks, wingless, seagoing dæmons skulk about. Dæmon Captain leans against the main mast and looks out over the muddy river. He growls at any crewman or other dæmon brave or naïve enough to come too close.

Hoping to instill despair into his cargo and get his scurvy crew working in rhythm, Charon sings a sea shanty (a variation of "Leave Her Johnny, Leave Her"). Holding fast to the rudder, he guides the ship to its destination while singing in a loud, gruff voice,

"The winds blew foul, and the seas ran high.
Leave her sinner, leave her.

We shipped up green, and none went by
And it's time for us to leave her,
Leave her sinner, leave her,
Oh, leave her sinner, leave her,
Oh, the voyage is done, and the winds don't blow
And it's time for us to leave her."

The dæmon crew joins in while handling lines, rowing, or working on other tasks. Their low tones make the shanty sound more like a dirge as the ship slowly plies the muddy waters.

"The old man swears, and the mate swears too,
Leave her sinner, leave her.
The crew all swear, and so would you
And it's time for us to leave her,
Leave her sinner, leave her,
Oh, leave her sinner, leave her.
Oh, the voyage is done, and the winds don't blow
And it's time for us to leave her.
The rats have gone, and we, the crew
Leave her sinner, leave her.
It's the time be-damned that we went too
And it's time for us to leave her,
Leave her sinner, leave her,
Oh, leave her sinner, leave her.
Oh, the voyage is done, and the winds don't blow
And it's time for us to leave her.
Well, I pray that we shall ne're more see
Leave her sinner, leave her.
A hungry ship, the likes of she
And it's time for us to leave her,
Leave her sinner, leave her,
Oh, leave her sinner, leave her.
Oh, the voyage is done, and the winds don't blow
And it's time for us to leave her."

The crew's song soon ends, and all is quiet except for the hull creaking, rhythmic oaring, and occasional shade moaning. Ioannes peers through a small hole in his sackcloth hood. He cannot see anything in the darkness but can hear muffled weeping.

Oh, my head and shoulders, he thinks. *Is that water or blood on my feet?* He wonders if this was how prisoners and slaves were treated after the Roman army captured them. He knows those who taught him about Adonai were slaves; *did they suffer in this way?* He thinks.

An intense sadness for them overcomes him, which in and of itself becomes an unexpected burden on his soul.

Somewhere in the hold, he hears a poor seasick shade vomit. He hears others around that soul commit violence against him. Doing his best to hold his own, his thoughts turn. He thinks about the words on the sign over the entrance to hell. *I refuse to give up hope, to give into despair. Since the Messias has not yet come, I will continue to hope he can save me from an eternity in the underworld.*

He turns his restricted view upward, then, seeing nothing but dirty, aged wood through the gap in his hood, leans back against the bulkhead: the boat pitches and rocks in the river currents.

May Elohim remember me here and be gracious to me on that day, he thinks, desperately clinging to his little flame of hope.

Unexpectedly, his thoughts turn to his friend Cælius. *I should have said more on the shore in Cæsarea. I should have spoken more boldly of God so that I might spare him from a fate such as mine.*

Ioannes lowers his head back down, and in the darkness, he whispers, "I hope God finds you, my friend before you suffer as I do."

Chapter Four

From Soldier to Sailor

A meeting is taking place in a private room in the Antonia Fortress. Cælius pleads his case with his Centurion, a weathered but fit man in his mid-30s. Because this is an informal meeting set in the garrison, the Centurion, proud but not arrogant, is not in full uniform, yet he carries himself upright as he walks back and forth. The Centurion's hands clasp a scroll behind his back, and his gaze is straight ahead as he paces. Though he seems annoyed by the request, he thoughtfully listens to what Cælius has to say.

Cælius stands still, at the position of attention, as he makes his request. He has thought deeply about Ioannes' words in Cæsarea, and they spur him on in his request to leave the legion and become a Marinus. "I cannot help it, sir, this longing to return to the sea. The call to make this change is great, which is why I request reassignment to the Praetorian Fleet."

"Yes, yes, I know, you love the sea; you've only said so 20 times. Cælius, you have pestered me with this request too many times, almost daily since we arrived in Hierosolyma." He exhales and continues, "You're right. I cannot understand why you would make such a request. What you're asking for, discharge from the Legion to serve in the navy, it's..." He pauses, "It's a demotion!"

"Yes sir, I know it is perceived as much, but I will still be serving Rome, just as a Marinus instead."

The Centurion stops in front of Cælius and turns to face him directly. He presents the scroll he has been carrying behind him, finally acquiescing, "Well, it would appear fortune smiles upon you, Cælius. I received word of a marinus on a ship in Cæsarea seeking the glory of becoming a legionnaire. An exchange then; him for you." The Centurion hands him the scroll.

Cælius, restraining his excitement, accepts it with courtesy. The Centurion places his right hand on Cælius' left shoulder. "He is already on his way. Gather your things. You leave immediately. You are to report to the Centurion on the Navis Prætoria Pax in Cæsarea in two days."

"Yes, sir! Thank you!"

"You're a good soldier, Cælius. Your actions in the ambush were noble. We will miss you." The Centurion releases his shoulder and then turns to walk away.

However, he turns back abruptly. Offering a brotherly and somewhat mischievous smile, he says, "Oh, and one piece of advice... don't drown." He offers his hand: Cælius clasps his forearm firmly, and the Centurion his. Upon release, Cælius strikes his chest in salute.

"May Neptunus protect you," The Centurion offers. Now get out!" he adds with humor, shaking his head.

Cælius rushes out of his office and goes to gather his things.

* * * * *

It's been two days, and Cælius is happily returning to Cæsarea by way of the Via Maris. He carries his shield and spear in his left hand. Slung over his right shoulder is a small bag containing a few personal items. He strides with purpose and anticipation as he nears the city.

It has been a great journey thus far, he thinks. *I cannot wait to reach the sea!* He has dwelt upon his friend Ioannes and his living God for much of the way. *How little I knew of them both. Yet, here I am, changing my entire life to honor my friend and seek out the one true God.*

So many emotions and conflicts tumble through his heart and mind. He wonders, *Have I made the right decision? Can I transition to life in the fleet after my service as a soldier?* Despite the uncertainty, Cælius has learned to trust his instincts, his intuition. Of course, he feels some trepidation; however, he is also confident he has made the right choice: to follow his conscience and discover the God Ioannes knew.

Cælius stops for a moment with the city in full view. Its sandstone buildings set against the blue sea are a welcoming sight. He lifts his head skyward, breathing deeply of the salty sea air carried by an ocean breeze. In the distance, he hears the dull roar of ocean tide crashing gently on rock and sand. Seagulls gliding in the sky above him lift his spirits. A youthful exuberance swells within him. He resumes his pace and enters the fledgling city with great anticipation.

He confidently walks through the bustling city streets and finds food and drink at a crowded market. He then finds a place to rest briefly to enjoy his small meal before heading to the harbor and his new ship.

Cælius walks along the deep-water harbor, noting minor work that must be completed before the port's official dedication. There are quite a few ships moored in the new harbor. Cælius stops to ask a man for directions. The man points toward a trireme ship moored nearby. Cælius approaches the sentries at the gangplank. He produces the scroll given to him by his former Centurion and is permitted to board the ship.

She is a beautiful two-tone, brown-colored ship. Her upper hull and superstructure are dark brown, while her lower hull is light brown wood. The two tones are separated by a white stripe adorned with ruby-red, round Parma shields. Adorned with golden wings and arrows and spaced perfectly down her side, the shields glint in the sun. A cheerful eye adorns her prow below the stripe while the ornate prow curls up to the stern. Her white sails are furled, and a polished bronze ram glints just below the water on her bow. She appears to be a majestic queen from a distance, wearing a ruby and pearl-laden crown and peering above the sea's surface to greet humanity.

On her stern is an arched, red and white striped ceremonial tent, which has been set up for dignitaries and official business. Cælius makes his way there and then stands at attention before a table in the shade beneath it. He holds his scutum shield in his left hand on the deck and his spear in his right, also resting on the deck, but with the spear tip pointing out to his right, away from the naval Centurion, who is seated behind the table.

The Centurion is similar in age to his previous one. He is clean-shaven and has a fresh haircut. Except for his helmet, which sits on the table, he is wearing the full regalia of his post. He quietly reads the orders on the scroll produced by Cælius, occasionally looking up at him. The ship's Optio stands just behind and to the left of Centurion. He inspects Cælius more closely.

The Centurion rolls up the scroll, lightly drops it on his desk, and stands. "Well then, Cælius," he begins, "I was a bit surprised to learn a legionnaire such as you would want to become a marinus. This is often considered a step down from your lofty position as a soldier of Rome." He states with some sarcasm. "Why have you made such a request?"

"I wish to be back on the sea, sir. I... missed it. If I may be so bold, my humble wish is to serve Rome in a way that will fulfill me, too."

The Centurion tilts his head slightly and raises his right eyebrow. He glances at the Optio, who gives him an expressionless look before moving around the right side of the table and to Cælius' left. He surprises the former soldier with a hearty laugh and a slap on the back. A little stunned by this move, Cælius turns his head to look at the Centurion. The Optio moves toward the desk, takes the scroll, and tidies up.

"Ha, ha, ha! Good answer. Welcome aboard Cælius! Truly, I am happy to have a battle-tested legionnaire such as yourself onboard. I have no doubt you will make a great marinus."

"Thank you," Cælius says cautiously. "I am not accustomed to such greetings. You are much too gracious."

"Ah, well, that's because you're used to legionnaires."

"If I may, sir, as you say, I have been on land for a long time. It may take me a while to get used to the movement of the sea under my feet again."

The Centurion pats him on the back again and laughs. This time, though, he steers him out of the tent into the open air. He teaches Cælius about the ship as they walk. "Come, let me tell you about our lady, Pax, explain your duties, and introduce you to some of your shipmates."

Walking slowly in the sun, the ship's captain continues, "She is both a diplomatic vessel and a cargo ship. Our squadron, Classis Alexandrina, makes its home berth in Egypt. We were sent here to Cæsarea Maritima for the dedication of the deep-water port, which the Iudæus King Herod built; his tribute to Augustus Caesar." His gregarious nature revealed, he winks at Cælius, denoting his pride in receiving the tribute on behalf of Caesar.

He continues his instruction, "Once all the pomp and circumstance of the dedication is over, we will embark upon our mission of escorting spice and grain shipments from here and from Alexandria back to Peninsula Italia. There, we sometimes pick up Legionnaires and transport them back here."

"Now, as you probably already know, most piracy has been quelled on the Mare Internum; they know better than to provoke the wrath of our fleet." Again, he pats Cælius on the back and gives him a nod of confidence. "However, you are here in case we do find them or any other threat."

"Now, as for your duties," he says more seriously. There are no roads or fortifications to build; instead, you will help maintain our vessel. She's a fine ship worthy to ply the waters of Neptunus! I expect you to defend her with your life and to help keep her seaworthy. As a matter of fact, you will be standing guard this very night. It will be an opportunity for you to get to know her."

They approach another Marinus standing near the seaward side of the ship with shield and spear in hand. He is roughly the same age as Cælius and is dressed in full armor.

"Ah, Marcus! This is Cælius, our newest marinus. He is our legionnaire transfer, so it should be easy for you to train him. You're both standing the watch tonight. Marcus, I expect you will familiarize him with the ship."

"Aye, sir. Come, Cælius, we'll start our rounds at the bow."

"Good man. Good man." Says the Centurion as he turns to take his leave.

The two marinus turn and walk toward the bow, talking. Marcus asks, "So, why the request for reassignment? There is already much speculation among the crew."

Cælius thinks it wise not to mention the answers he seeks about the Iudæus God. Instead, he provides the same reasons he gave his former and new Centurion. These explanations satisfy Marcus, too, as they begin the ship's tour.

* * * * *

Later that evening, Marcus and Cælius are standing near the stern on the seaward side of the ship. It's sunset, and there is a slight ocean breeze. Marcus asks, "I'm going below to make a round. You will be okay up here, yes?"

"Yes. I'll meet you at the bow ladder."

Marcus turns and walks toward the stern ladder leading below. Cælius lingers near the railing, staring out at the ocean. Glistening, blue waters gently rise and fall. White and gray gulls glide on salty ocean breezes in twilight skies. The once-white clouds have begun to turn different shades of vermillion, purple, and orange. After enjoying this simple beauty for a moment, he turns, crosses over to the port side of the ship, and then continues his patrol.

On the port side, a torchlit Cæsarea, flames twisting, flickering, and casting shadows against the white stone buildings. Like the last time he was here, there is revelry in the streets. He pauses near the gangway momentarily and nods at the sentries standing below on the dock. Gazing out at the city, he mutters, "Last time, I was the one celebrating. A part of me still wants to roam the streets for wine, women, and food. Hmmm...those habits will be hard to break, I think... It may be a long night. God, if you are indeed present, I ask you to guide me and quell the lust in my heart."

Marcus climbs the ladder and steps out on the main deck. "What? Did you say something?"

Cælius is a little caught off guard. "No, nothing. Just commenting on my new perspective of the city."

"Ah, yes." Marcus agrees. "I, too, would like to join in the revelry. Not tonight, I'm afraid. Not tonight." His voice trails off.

The two continue to stand their watch. They exchange stories of adventures and battles, talking about different towns and ports, faring sea storms and weathering dust storms, and life at sea and in the legion.

Chapter Five

Skewed Judgement

Charon's ferry runs aground hard and fast on the other side of the River Styx. It jolts as the keel slides up a gravel bank and meets with solid rock, causing some crewmen and demonic escorts to heave forward at the sudden stop. Charon laughs heartily as some of his 'passengers' fall before instantly changing to a foul mood. He curses, "Bloody rowers!" And shouts at everyone within earshot, "Get the damned off my ship!"

Dæmons rush the cargo hold, fling open the hatch, and gleefully pluck souls from below. Some are pushed indiscriminately down the gangplank, while others are led semi-orderly. Others are brutally cast overboard. Ioannes is one of those cast over the side.

Still hooded, he is drug out of the hold by the chains on his wrists, led to the railing, and then shoved over the side. He lands on the shore with his bare back on land and his feet in the water. He writhes in pain on the forsaken shore. The unnamed soul is cast over, making a large splash next to Ioannes.

Goblin dæmons fly over the rails. Flapping their leathery wings, they slowly descend and land around the two shades. Dæmon Captain strolls casually down the gangway to collect his quarry. The goblin dæmons stand them up, chain them together, and prepare them to be escorted down a rougher road into hell.

Dæmon Captain wrests the lead chain from one of the lesser dæmons and gives a yank, prompting Ioannes and his compatriot to follow. They limped out of the water and up the rocky beach, moving on to the next road.

Inland, the terrain changes. Gone is any feeling of moisture from the river. This new road is like a dry, desert mountain region. Rocks cast shadows from an eerie, gray light in the background. The group follows the winding road, their pace slowing as a line forms.

Ioannes cannot see the malignant outcropping of rock ahead, which is a small blessing. It's a kind of stone amphitheater. A makeshift platform has been carved from the dark brown stone in the center, with an archway leading downward into the further depths of hell on the left. A single demon reclines on a large curule chair in the middle of the platform. Perched in various places above him are gray-winged dæmons glaring at the souls passing through the judgment seat of hell. They glare at passing shades like gargoyles, waiting to devour any one of them who dares to escape.

Dæmon Captain is reluctantly patient as he herds his souls forward, grumbling and passively cursing until he reaches the front of the line. There, he stops his procession and waits to be called forward by the dæmon 'judge.'

Although his clothes are stained and soiled with ash and burn marks, the vainglorious judge is dressed in what were once the finest Roman robes. A civic crown crafted with small fig leaves encircles two smaller horns upon his head. He reclines lazily on an ornate curule chair carved from opaque bone.

A massive arm carved out of the stone above reaches out over him. Its hand grips a jagged and rusty iron scale. Both bowls, filled with flame, hang from soot-covered chains. The left bowl dips lower than the right one, denoting skewed justice and favoring the archway that leads downward.

It is easy to see that this judge fashions himself as a haughty Roman governor or a pompous senator. With an uninterested sigh, he lazily motions for the next sinner to come forward, sighing, “Bring forward the next offender.” Dæmon Captain grins, unchains Ioannes, and half-drags him to the platform. There, he quickly drives Ioannes to his knees. The wicked justice asks, “Are you not going to remove his hood?”

“He is not worthy to look upon this fine court.”

The judge sighs again. “Very well. Proceed with your accusations, dæmon.”

The Dæmon Captain begins, “This man is not only a terrible soldier; he refused to fight or take the life of his enemy. He did nothing in service to his ‘empire’ but carry a banner and cook meals. He is a coward!” He laughs heartily. “He was not a good son either, often disobeying his family’s wishes, rejecting our *beloved* Roman gods, associating with Iudæus slaves, and seeking out our enemy, the one, true God. He is a traitor to his family and is an unprofitable servant to the same living God he claims to follow. Ha! This wretch could not even openly commit to serving El Yisrael.”

There is a slight pause before Ioannes drops his head toward his knees. A sudden sense of guilt and shame overcomes him. He knows more of his sins; his iniquities, even the hidden ones, are about to be laid bare.

Dæmon Captain grins before continuing, “Oh, the things he did in his youth before attempting to serve his God. Unable to control his hunger, he stole food from a market. Unable to control his lust, he snuck out of his home to visit a lupanar, wantonly laying with prostitutes. Desiring to keep these and other sins hidden, he has lied. By his actions, he either allowed or brought evil into the world. Now, he thinks God will spare him and rescue him. No!” He spits toward Ioannes. “He deserves punishment.”

An uneasy silence fills the air. Dæmon Captain looks expectantly at the judge as he deliberates. Ioannes thinks to himself, *I am a liar, a thief, and a fornicator; indeed, the things*

I have done in my youth justify my sentence. Still, I hope, beyond all hope, that I have done more virtuous things in my adult life out of love for Elohim and that the Messias, the true judge of the world, might yet find me... even here.

The arrogant judge again waives his hand dismissively and moans, "I agree. Take him to Limbo for now. There, you can bind and abandon him until we decide which circle of hell best suits him. The lower-level scum will retrieve him at the appropriate time."

Dæmon Captain nods and then drags the hooded Ioannes back to be chained once more. His unwilling companion, the unnamed soul, resists being unchained at first. He has heard Ioannes' judgment and knows what is to come. However, he, too, is forcefully drug to the platform and driven to his knees. The false judge yawns with boredom, "And this one?"

The unnamed soul does not think he should be judged. Cursing loudly through clenched teeth, he insults, "Worms and maggots consume you!" Though hooded as well, he then lunges in the direction of the judge's voice. Startled, the judge gasps as he jumps to his feet.

The gargoyle dæmons rattle their wings and scrape claws on the stone above the platform, eager to descend upon the offender. Dæmon Captain instantly grabs the unnamed soul, throws him to the ground, and begins beating him.

The judge collects himself, raises his hand to stay the gargoyle dæmons, and then haughtily steps down from the platform. He moves close to the Unnamed Soul, "You dare?!" exclaims the enraged judge through gnashed teeth. "Take him to Limbo as well... for now."

Dæmon Captain restrains him, holding him down on his knees.

The evil magistrate leans down next to Unnamed Soul's ear and, in a vicious tone, hisses through the burlap hood. "I know which circle is suitable for you. I will contact your torturer personally, you disease-ridden criminal. I want to be there when he drags you, kicking and screaming, deeper into hell. You will wait in Limbo in anticipation of our arrival."

The judge gathers his dirty robes and strolls arrogantly back to his comfortable chair, proclaiming, "Now get him out of my sight and bring the next one before me!"

Satisfied with the outcome, Dæmon Captain drags Unnamed Soul back and chains him to Ioannes. Taking the lead chain, he gives a yank to let them know to move forward. They are then led through the archway like bulls to slaughter.

The gargoyles scratch at the rock and hiss as they watch the condemned pass through the arch, where everything darkens.

Chapter Six

Sailing the Mare Internum

It isn't long before the pageantry of the Cæsarea Maritima port dedication is over, and the crew of the Pax is finally underway to Alexandria.

Cælius stands near the bow as they head out to sea. He relishes the simple pleasures presented to his senses: the wind and ocean spray on his face, the sound of creaking oars splashing into the water and taking strain, the white sail unfurled and filled with the wind, and the awareness of a rolling sea underfoot. It brings back fond childhood memories of fishing near the coast with his father. This day, the day he returned to the sea, is the happiest he has been in quite some time.

Days at sea come and go. Yes, there is always work to be done, scrubbing the main deck, coiling lines, and watches to be stood, but life at sea is good, and oh, the sights. The Pharos Lighthouse, its great beacon calling out from miles away and rowing into Mandrákion Harbor where the Colossus of Rhodes once stood. Though he marvels at these wonders of man, his thoughts often turn to Adonai. *If man can create such wonderous things as these, what majestic things might the one true God be capable of?* He thinks. The growing thirst for knowledge of God completely changes his port calls over the next two years.

As his faith grows, his habits begin to change as well. Instead of seeking out the usual vice with shipmates, Cælius spends many port calls, especially in the Iudæa province, quietly seeking out teachers willing to instruct him in Elohim's ways. He learns different lessons each time, and the frequent escorts between Cæsarea, Alexandria, and Peninsula Italia afford him much time to contemplate this new knowledge.

It isn't always easy to find a rabbi willing to teach him, but he manages to connect with a handful who were happy to teach him God's commandments, how to pray, what the prophets of old accomplished, and the coming of the Messias. He even discovers a couple of Ioannes' former teachers.

While on another voyage back to Cæsarea, Cælius patrols the ship. He stops at the bow to feel the fresh sea spray on his face; to him, it never gets old. There, he reflects on the reason he became a soldier—for discipline and glory. Now Elohim has led me back to the sea, to my new life on this ship. *I must discern what he has in store for my future.*

The change in his behavior is not lost on his shipmates either. He becomes aware of a slight mistrust forming among the other marinus. As Cælius turns and walks astern, he moves past Marcus and two other marinus standing next to the mast. They watch him go by silently and begin speaking again after he passes. Cælius cannot hear what they say. He is still too deep in his thoughts.

He ponders a predicament: *Legionnaires and Marinus are supposed to be loyal to the emperor and no other. That loyalty is usually demonstrated by offering a sacrifice to him if promoted to the rank of centurion. This violates Adonai's first commandment and puts me in a dangerous position. The more I learn and the closer I come to God, the greater the danger of being found out. I could be thrown into the ocean and left to drown if my centurion, optio, or other marinus knew of my ongoing conversion in faith.* Cælius looks over his shoulder toward the sea as he walks.

His secret port call activities and cloistered life onboard the ship are mostly tolerated as eccentric, though, and life at sea goes on a bit longer without issue... for the time being.

* * * * *

On this day, the ship is moored in the port of Andriake in Anatolia. Most of the crew goes ashore and walks up the road into Myra. Marcus, Cælius, and a couple of newer marinus are standing on the main deck, discussing their plans for the evening. The two new marinus are younger than Marcus and Cælius. Cassius is 20, and Felix is only 19 years old.

Marcus states, "We will sail for Seleucia Pieria tomorrow and then on to Cæsarea. Since we don't have watch tonight, I say we all head into town to indulge in the pleasures of wine, women, and feasting. What say you?" He asks as he gestures to the group.

Cælius responds, "Thank you, Marcus, for the invitation, but I think I'll pass." Cassius and Felix look curiously at him.

"You haven't been out with us in a very long time Cælius, surely you miss the revelry?" Inquires Cassius

"Why do you hold yourself apart from us?" Asks Marcus. "You think yourself superior because you were once a Legionnaire?"

"No, not at all. I only prefer a smaller meal close to the ship and a respite. Truly, I appreciate your invitation, but I wish to enjoy a quieter evening before we sail tomorrow."

Snubbed by perceived rejection, Marcus shrugs his shoulders and turns to the other two marinus, "Come on then, who else is going?"

Cassius, "I'm in. Let's get into town before the rowers do."

Felix, "I need to stow my gear. Head on in, I'll find you."

Marcus huffs, turns, and heads for the gangplank; Cassius walks with him. Cælius watches them leave. Felix, still politely observing Cælius, asks abruptly, "I know I haven't been onboard as long as you and Marcus, but I can see there is something different in the way you carry yourself compared to the rest of the crew, Cælius. You certainly have a pride in you but are much too humble and kind for a former Legionnaire. We're all just trying to figure out what has brought this about in you."

Cælius turns to look at the young sailor. He offers a smile of gratitude with a pat on his shoulder, "Maybe one day soon I will tell you the source of what you see in me, young man. Now, you better hurry off, or your shipmates will drink the wineskins dry before you get there."

Felix nods and then goes to ready himself for a night ashore.

Dusk has overtaken the Andriakian Harbor. Cælius cloaks himself in a plain, cream-colored toga, covering his uniform. He acknowledges the sentries as he steps off the gangplank onto shore and pulls a length of his toga over his head. He looks around and then begins to walk toward a small housing area toward the back of the port, which is downhill from the city of Myra. As he walks through a tiny market, two Roman soldiers with red togas concealing their identities begin to follow him.

Cælius stops at a house and knocks. An older, bearded man dressed in a simple tunic opens the door. The old rabbi smiles at him and then motions for him to come in. Cælius again briefly looks around; he does not see the two soldiers standing down the alley.

He enters and then closes the door behind him. The two soldiers watching him from a distance remove the togas from their heads and are revealed to be Marcus and Cassius. Marcus puts his hand to his chin and strokes it, "Hmmm? I wonder whom Cælius meets with?"

Cassius is agitated and frustrated from having to spy on a fellow marinus instead of reveling in town. "I told you, it's no one. Let's go, Marcus. I want wine and women."

Marcus snaps out of his contemplative stare and slaps his shipmate on the shoulder. "You are right, young man. I have held us up far too long. Let's see what this little town has to offer us, yes?" The two turn and head toward Myra.

* * * * *

The next day, the Pax, which is at full sail, plies through the waters surrounded by the other ships in the squadron. Cælius stands near the rail, staring out at the deep blue waters glistening under the bright sun. He hears footprints and turns to see Marcus casually approaching him. "Quiet night, then, Cælius?" he asks.

Cælius turns to look back out at the sea. "Dinner with old friends. It was nice to see them again."

"You have friends in Myra? How is that possible?" Though he seems calm, Marcus's voice is accusatory.

Cælius' response is guarded, but he remains honest. "They were good to a legionnaire brother of mine when we marched to Cæsarea a couple of years ago. Since we were in Andriake, I thought I would pass on good tidings. They offered dinner, and I could not refuse."

Marcus steps closer to Cælius with a suspicious and slightly irritated look as if to warn or threaten him. The exchange, however, is abruptly interrupted by shouting from the stern of the ship.

Having just rounded the Carpasian peninsula of Cyprus, the island can still be seen in the distance as the two men look astern. A dark, malevolent storm has come to life north of the peninsula. It is moving directly toward the squadron as if purposefully seeking them out. A massive gray and white squall line has already stretched out across the sky ahead of it.

Marcus turns back to give Cælius a hard stare. Their duties overtake their issues, and then they both run toward the main mast. They lash their shields and spears to it and then help other crewmen lower the main sail. High clouds move overhead, darkening the sky and creating an ominous shadow over the ship as they work.

Chapter Seven

Abandoned

The condemned procession emerges from a short, dark tunnel amidst sulfur vents. Yellow stains cover dark, blackish-red stalagmites, venting light gray smoke into a dark, almost black sky. The once smooth, wide road has become a more treacherous path. The ground is hot, jagged, and harsher. Ioannes and the Unnamed Soul are led down a twisting side trail away from other shades, moving downward. Everything is much darker here; an eerie firelight dimly illuminates the sky.

They only walk a short distance before Dæmon Captain abruptly halts in a small open area. He quietly points to two eyelets anchored in rock on the ground about 20 feet apart. He drops the lead chain and growls, “Stooop! We are here slaves.”

That is the extent of his courtesy, as he immediately shoves Ioannes to the ground on his belly and steps on his back with one foot. Goblin dæmons pull the chain from his shackles and connect them to an eye anchored in the black, gritty rock. Once chained, the goblin dæmons loosen his hood and step back.

Dæmon Captain reaches down and painfully yanks the burlap hood off his head, scraping his face as he pulls it off. He removes his foot from Ioannes’ back, who wearily rolls to his side and glances up to finally see his imprisoner. Dæmon Captain immediately strikes him with the back of his hand and then spits in his face.

Ioannes keeps one eye closed so the spittle will not run into it. He looks slowly around. After all this time, his captors are revealed. The smaller, goblin-like dæmons are all roughly

5-foot-tall with average human builds. They have bat-like wings on their backs, some tucked down and others stretched out behind them. Their skin color is a reddish/tan color; they are 'naked' but have no genitalia. The hair on their head is wild and matted, with two small horns protruding from their foreheads. They carry chains, shackles, or a slender, two-pronged, skewer-like pitchfork, which is as long as they are tall.

The Dæmon Captain appears black against the dark sky, but his skin has a blue shimmer. He stands nearly seven feet tall and is very muscular except for his pudgy belly. Red irises blaze through otherwise black eyes. A haughty smirk spreads across his battle-scarred face. He carries a large, cruel-looking, single-blade axe in his left hand while his right hovers over a Whip on his belt. He wears black and dark brown barbarian armor, with a black, spiked pauldron on his left shoulder. Small, ivory-colored horns protrude around his bald head like a spiked crown.

Through his grotesque smile, he hisses, "You think you lived a virtuous life, did you not?" A deep, guttural chortle slips past the yellowish, dagger-like teeth. "Heh, heh, heh. You are a sinner. God does not love you, worm."

With a sudden, swift motion, he pulls the whip from his side and cracks it across Ioannes' side and back, splitting his skin. Ash, stirred up from the whip, immediately mingles with the blood and stings.

Ioannes wails in both physical and spiritual pain. "Deus meus[10], why have you forsaken me?!"

"Shut up! God is the one who sent you here, fool." He swiftly kicks Ioannes in the head. "I told you to abandon hope." He takes pleasure in watching his victim roll to his side in pain. "Go on wretch, despair, for you are a great sinner who

---

[10] "My God" (translated from Latin)

does not deserve to be in the presence of God. There is no rest, no peace for you here."

Dæmon Captain grinds his hot, sandaled foot into the open wound on Ioannes' side, making it open further and burn more fiercely. He laughs with hearty satisfaction. All the other goblin dæmons skulking about in the shadows join in with their incessant cackling. Ioannes curls up on his side on the bare, black stone, the shackles cutting into his wrists. Dæmon Captain waives a dismissive hand at him. "Bah! Leave the whelp to his despair."

He then turns his sights on the Unnamed Soul. A vicious grin spreads across his face again as he stares down at his prey. He motions for the goblin dæmons to bind him to the ground and remove his hood.

Dæmon Captain places his axe on the ground and secures his whip while they carry out his orders. Once he can see, the still-angry Unnamed Soul kicks at one of the smaller dæmons. The Dæmon Captain pounces on him without a word, unleashing his fury and beating him severely.

Afterward, he stands upright and takes a step back, breathing heavily from his assault. The Unnamed Soul is barely conscious, lying limp on the ground. "Truly... [pant] I... [pant] enjoyed that." He reaches for his axe and then motions to his squad of dæmons to go. He secures his axe to the armor on his back, kicks ash at Unnamed Soul, and then turns to leave. "Let's go find more! HA, HA, HA!"

The demonic band walks away. Ioannes stirs. He wipes the blood, saliva, and ash from his swollen eye using his forearm and then painfully rises to his knees to survey his surroundings. The hellscape is brought into full view.

There is no sky, just black, stale air. Billowing, gray clouds, moving fluidly like a shadowy, turbulent thunderstorm, fill the space overhead. The rock, too, is a black and burgundy color. The only light comes from a red-orange glow of what looks like several lava flows emanating from a lake of fire or cauldron of lava near a vast chasm. Glowing embers and big flakes of gray ash fall sporadically from the ebony tempest. The landscape resembles a slowly erupting volcano seen just after dusk.

Ioannes glances at his counterpart chained nearby but can only see his back in the firelight. Unnamed Soul suddenly twists and turns with rage as a large, burning ember lands on him. He curses through gnashed teeth as it burns his skin. Ioannes whispers, "Oh, Adonai, how long must I remain here? Will you come for me? Or will you allow me to be dragged deeper into the pit? Deus meus, salva mea[11]."

[11] "My God, save me." (translated from Latin)

Chapter Eight

Drowning in Sin

The wicked tempest churns and boils, moving swiftly toward the squadron of ships. Ahead of the squall line, the sea turns violent. Waves rise and fall, breaking across the bow and tossing the Pax about like a piece of driftwood. Shouts of fear erupt when the gale force broadsides the ship with such power as to push it into the crashing waves. Rowers have manned their oars and worked desperately to keep the ship stable and plying forward through the angry sea.

The ominous white squall line, highlighted by the ark green and gray sky behind it, blows over the ship, blotting out the sun entirely. An eerie feeling fills the hearts of Cælius and other crewmen, who keep glancing out past the bow, watching the blue sky disappear behind the shadowy, turbulent edge of the storm. Lightning flashes furiously overhead, crackling and sizzling. A massive boom of thunder sounds. It shakes the ship's planks before rumbling across the dark, rain-laden sky. The thunderclap bursts the clouds, releasing a torrent upon them.

Having secured all the equipment he can, Cælius rushes forward to the port side of the bow edge to brace himself. Marcus is already there, clutching the starboard rail and shouting a fearful prayer, "Oh Neptunus, we beg you, calm the waters! Save us from this tempest."

Cassius and Felix join them as the boat pitches and rolls in the swelling sea. The Pax crests a massive wave and dives, bow first, into raging waters. Ocean spray crashes over the bow and soaks everyone gathered there.

Cælius, calmer than the others, instinctively calls out but not to the Roman god Neptunus… "Adonai, I fear your wrath.

Please, Father of us all, spare this crew from your anger; save us from this tempest."

Suddenly, the same trepidation the young Ioannes had in Cæsarea overcomes him. He knows he just prayed out loud. Cælius looks up toward Marcus and the others. Water pours from their faces as their stares meet. Lightning flashes and thunder rumbles. Still clutching the rail, Marcus shouts, "You! This storm is your fault! You have forsaken the gods and brought the fury of Neptunus upon us!"

He turns to the other two marinus and orders, "Throw him over the side! His death will please Neptunus, and he will calm the sea."

Cælius turns and slides his right foot, opening his stance and bracing his back against the rail. Marcus, Cassius, and a hesitant Felix cautiously move toward their shipmate. Gripping the railing with his left hand, Cælius instinctively reaches across his body and places his right hand on the handle of his gladius. He does not wish to fight his fellow countrymen but knows he must defend himself if necessary.

There is no time for a confrontation, though. The bow begins to rise as the ship moves up a large wave at an angle. Cælius notices the faces of the marinus approaching him grow pale. Cassius points at something behind him and shouts something inaudible. Then, he and Felix rush back to their side of the railing. With gladius in hand and standing just in front of Cælius, Marcus freezes in terror.

Cælius looks over his shoulder and sees the unthinkable. A rogue wave has turned the Victoria, one of her sister ships in the squadron, sending it straight toward the Pax. Her ram will undoubtedly sink them. Cælius grabs the railing with both arms and braces for the impact.

The Victoria slams into the side of the Pax, breaking her main mast. Its ram pierces the hull just behind the corvus[12]. The impact thrusts the Pax sideways into another wave. Cælius nearly loses his grip from the shock of the collision.

The hull splinters and brakes, and rowers below deck scream in horror. The massive wave they once plied crashes down upon the damaged deck, completely splintering the ship in two. Water floods inward, and the ship quickly breaks apart, sinking into the stormy deep. Utter chaos ensues as crewmen fall or jump into the raging sea.

The bow of the ship, which Cælius held firm to, turned downward due to the heavy ram on its prow. It raised into the air, giving Cælius enough visibility of the wreckage around him. He noticed Marcus was gone, swept into the sea. The two younger Marinus were jumping blindly into the water.

He spots a large chuck of hull nearby and leaps toward it, plunging into the briny waters. He quickly surfaces, swims through debris to the chunk of wood, and pulls himself up on the makeshift raft.

Catching his breath and looking around, Cælius sees the Victoria capsize under the weight of the wave that broke the Pax in two. He also notices several crewmen bobbing up and down in the stormy waters, desperately trying to keep their heads above water. Some rowers cling to bits of their paddles, while others frantically search for something buoyant to grasp. He knows he must save them.

Searching for something to help, he spies a length of rope trailing from the piece of hull he lay upon. He grasps it, pulling all of it up to his raft. He ties off the tethered end, making sure it is secure. Discarding his belt and gladius into the ocean, he ties the loose end around his waist.

---

[12] Naval boarding weapon near the bow.

He is about to jump in when an unexpected thought enters his mind. He remembers his friend, the Andriakian rabbi, and the lesson of the previous evening. Cælius learned about God's willingness to cleanse the Assyrian commander Naaman of his leprosy in the Jordan River.

Deep down, he was envious of Naaman. He, too, had hoped to make a pilgrimage to the same river one day to be cleansed of his iniquities in its waters. He wonders if the Mare Internum will do now instead.

Momentarily dwelling on this thought, a sense of calm overcomes him. He turns his eyes skyward. Rain falls upon his face. "God in heaven, is this to be my baptism? Might I be purified in these waters? If so, Adonai, grant me the strength to save as many of my shipmates as you will. In this, I trust in you."

He returns his focus to the turbulent sea and searches for the closest man. Taking a deep breath, he dives in. He swims stridently to the first man. Bobbing and sputtering, he shouts, "Grab onto me! I will pull you to safety!"

Without a word, the rower quickly obeys and grasps the collar of his armor. Cælius uses the line to pull them both back to the raft. Once the rower is safe, he swims back out for another and then another. In all, he pulls four of his shipmates to safety.

Fatigue, however, is setting in. When he goes out for a fifth, exhaustion overtakes him. The weight of his breastplate and waterlogged clothes pulls him downward. Not only is he unable to reach the fifth sailor, but he also struggles to keep his head above water.

Fear of dying causes panic. Choking and gasping for air, he flails about in the choppy water before finally sinking beneath the waves, unseen by the ones he saved. He tries desperately to hold his breath but cannot. The saltwater fills his nostrils, causing him to gag and breathe in more. His arms and legs fail; he has no strength left.

He looks toward the surface, still tethered to the debris but sinking deeper. He hears the muffled sounds of screaming, timber bursting, and thunder rumbling across the sky. Those he saved are too weary to notice him. Fleeting thoughts pass through his mind. *Is this... Is this what sinners drowning in the great flood experienced? Was this... their final view... of Noah's ark?*

His vision blurs. He barely recognizes the bolt of lightning flashing across an unreachable sky. It sheds just enough light to silhouette several feet and legs surrounding the makeshift raft he is tethered to. Then, there is nothing more, no sound, no sight, no thought, only the silence of the darkest deep. The once-blue waters of the Mare Internum have swallowed him whole.

Chapter Nine

Cursed Waters

The hellscape comes into focus—blue-colored lightning streaks through the distant volcanic maelstrom above the lake of fire. Ioannes rests on his legs in a kneeling position with his head down. The cut on his left side, from the dæmon's whip, has cauterized but is still raw. Dark purple bruises cover his body, and blisters from falling embers have risen in various places. He has only enough chains to sit or rise to his knees; he cannot stand.

He raises his eyes to the distant, churning fires; great wailing noises echo across the barren landscape. They are drowned out only by his thoughts: *how long have I been chained here? How long have I listened to sounds of violence, of wailing and weeping?* The once-youthful features of his face have sunken. His lips have split and cracked; he licks at them to no avail. His throat is parched; not even his saliva can ease the dryness when he swallows.

He begins to look around slowly and aimlessly, thinking, *this abandonment, this torment, and pain, it is maddening. The temptation to despair, to give in to the darkness, weighs heavy on me. Thoughts of hopelessness that there is no way out of this place constantly plague me.* He feels disorientation setting in. *How long have I been here? Days, months, years?* He sighs out loud. *There is no knowing in the scope of eternity.*

Ioannes continues to search his surroundings when he realizes Unnamed Soul is sitting on his buttocks with crossed legs and looking in his general direction. He seems to be peering through Ioannes to some far-off place. His face and body appear far worse than Ioannes'. Scars covering his face and torso long before coming here cover his face. His appearance is quickly overlooked as Ioannes perks up at the prospect of a conversation.

"How long do you think we've been here, friend?"

Unnamed Soul's head turns ever so slightly, and his intense focus lands on Ioannes. He shouts through clenched teeth. "Friend?! I am NOT your friend! Were you not listening? We've been sent here for eternity. Time no longer matters. Stultus[13]!"

His irritation, hatred, and contempt are palpable, reflected in his body language and words.

Ioannes is taken aback by it but maintains his calm demeanor. Desperately trying to keep his sanity in the tumultuous surroundings, he continues the conversation, "I know you think me a fool. Though I cannot explain why, I still have hope Elohim or his Messias might still save me, us before we descended any further."

Unnamed Soul snorts in derision, "You have hope? You're even dumber than I thought. I would kick you myself if I could reach you. Shut up. Leave me alone."

The Unnamed Soul uncomfortably turns his body and fixes his gaze on the black pit in the distance. Defeated and dejected, Ioannes drops his head in sadness. The distant wailing and churning fires once again fill his ears.

* * * * *

Somewhere close by, a large greenish-brown river flows uninterrupted. Its black sand banks bear no vegetation, only boulders of volcanic pumice and the intermittent spire of jagged obsidian. Small, blood-colored whirlpools swirl here and there, streaming out burgundy eddies into the putrid waters. Unseen fires give a dim glow to the sky overhead.

---

[13] Stupid or fool (translated from Latin)

Several bodies are floating in the river, and Cælius is among them. He floats on his back with arms outstretched. Only his torso and head ride above the surface; everything from his stomach is underwater. He opens his eyes to the dark sky. He immediately realizes he is drifting, completely nude as it were, in the foulest of warm, muddy waters. Thinking he is still drowning, he flails about in the water before trying to swim without direction.

Coming to his senses, he stops to tread water and spits the foul-tasting liquid from his mouth. *Wait, where am I swimming to?* He thinks. Mourning and crying from all directions reach his ears. He scans the water for others, finding many. Some are treading water like him, some are trying to swim, while others float belly up. He murmurs to himself, "What is this place?"

Then, floating by him, groaning, is the fifth rower he tried to save from his ship, the one whom he had drowned while trying to save. An awful feeling quickly fills the pit of his stomach and his mind races. *Is this? Am I in the underworld? God did not grant me purification in the stormy waters of the Mare Internum? Why am I in this river? If I am bound for Hell, this cannot be the way. There is a road into the underworld; one must pay the boatman to cross the River Styx into the afterlife.*

He pauses as he realizes the truth. *Wait! Is this the River Styx? Is this how those who die at sea enter the afterlife?*

Fear grips him. Cælius searches anxiously for a haven, again mumbling to himself, "I must get out of this horrible water." He spots a place downriver where he can get out and try to gain his bearings. He uses the current in his favor as he swims toward it, doing his best not to get any filth in his mouth or nose. Small eddies push and pull his body, driving a deep sense of urgency to reach the bank.

Just as he nears the shore, a frenzy breaks out downstream—frantic splashing and screaming spread upriver like a tidal wave of sound. Cælius does not turn to see what causes it.

He closes in on the small pocket of black obsidian. The water shallows, and underneath him is thick, gritty mud. It oozes under his feet and hands. Rather than trying to stand and walk through it, he stays low, pulling his naked body through the squelchy, water-lapped mire toward the bank.

There, he quickly and quietly pulls himself up on the flat stone. Sharp spires of volcanic glass form giant claws; he feels like he is sitting in the palm of some monstrous stone beast. However, the spires provide some protection from which he can catch his breath and see what is causing the madness in the water. Breathing heavily, Cælius cautiously peers around one of the spires.

Three trireme ships are working their way up the river ahead of a massive, gray fog bank. The fog bank rolls like the squall of the ill-fated storm that brought him here. However, it appears to follow the ships slowly and does not overtake them. It also blankets the river and banks so he cannot see beyond it.

Some lighter, wispy fog dances around the glistening black hulls at the ship's water line. Separated by a green, scaled stripe, like that of a giant serpent, the upper part of their hulls is blood red, not black. Ragged, ebony oars reach out into the water like the legs of a centipede. Great black sails with scarlet stripes billow in an unfelt wind, likely spurred on by the wicked fog.

On the prow of each ship is a great angry eye peering out into the desolate riverscape as though it is looking for fresh souls. A great open maw lined with massive spear tips for teeth is just above their massive, rust-colored rams but below their evil eyes. Though it does not burn the ships, an ominous fire churns within those mouths. Orange and yellow tongues of flame lick the sides of the vessels as they move upriver, their salivating trail of black smoke mingling with the billowing fog to their sterns. Their prows curl upward into the shape of great, brown horns with rusty chains as rigging running from the foremast to the main mast, all the way back to the stern.

The ships stop and pull in their oars. A variety of grotesque, barnacle, and seaweed-covered dæmons carrying large boathooks, tridents, and nets man the rails. They rhythmically beat their tools on the main deck and railing, chanting and cheering in unholy synchronicity with the drumbeats echoing from below decks. Their sound reverberates through the water.

An unseen, deep, and raspy voice booms upriver, echoing along the cursed banks, "Call forth this new beast…this Kraken. Let it whet its appetite on these shades. Let us witness its power before we release it upon the world of the living."

At his command, a giant demon steps forward on the lead ship. He carries a great horn, curved like a mouflon, except much larger. He steps to the bow and sounds the horn; its deep guttural bawl sends ripples across the surface of the river of the damned. Then, the crews fall silent in anticipation of what is to come.

Though it continues to flow, the water begins to churn and bubble, like water in a hot cauldron. Random souls here and there suddenly plunge beneath the roiling waters. The source of their disappearance is quickly made known. Large tentacled arms clutching their prey burst through the river's surface. The men and women in their grasp wail, curse, and flail about as they are painfully whipped through the air and slammed down on the decks of the wicked ships. The demonic crews descend upon those souls, binding them and thrusting them below decks.

The unseen monsters' tentacles entangle those who try to swim away. Some make it to shore only to be ambushed, chained, and beaten by ghoulish hordes patrolling the banks. Others swim directly toward the ships out of fear of the creature below or the roving bands ashore. The demonic crews howl in delight as they plunge their boathooks into the water, yanking their fresh catch of shades, screaming, and cursing out of the foul waters.

Cælius sees something unexpected then. He considers a panic-stricken Marcus swimming toward him.

"Help!" he screams between gurgles. "Help me!"

Before Cælius can react, Marcus plunges backward beneath the murky waters. Only seconds later, a slimy tentacle breaks through the surface of the water, with Marcus dangling helplessly in its grip like a worm in a man's grasp.

The beast's massive brown beak rises slowly above the waterline at the center of the river. Opening and closing, it makes a loud clacking sound as it prepares to feast. The creature's glowing red eyes are visible below the surface of the muddy river. The Kraken holds several other souls overhead like grapes about to be devoured.

It begins releasing its victims, who plummet into its mouth. As soon as it releases a shade, its tentacles plunge beneath the water, searching for fresh souls to devour. Finally, it finally drops Marcus, who screams as he falls into the mouth of his tormenter.

Cælius has seen enough. He ducks behind the obsidian spire and hides on the banks of the River Styx. He is out of breath, and the vile water drips from his head and body, forming a puddle around him. He is naked, alone, fearful, and full of regret.

Whispering to himself, "What do I do? I drowned in sin before the Messias could save me."

Courage comes to him. *I must resist the temptation to give up. I must evade these monsters as long as I can. Since the Messias has not yet come,* he thinks, *there may still be a chance to be saved... even here.*

He retreats from the water's edge and hides behind the rocks. Cælius looks skyward, but there is no sky nor star in the black, stale air to gain his bearings. He is trapped. Sounds of violence, carnage, wailing, and weeping ring out. Just then, a strange movement draws his gaze toward the waters at his feet, to the mire in front of where he sits.

Cælius leans over, straining to investigate the water in the dim light. Something swirls in the mud and river foam. It moves like a snake. He spots a small tentacle, and then more appear. He scuffles back to the rocky bank as the tentacles creep up on the obsidian stone toward him. The monster to whom they belong slowly rises out of the murky water.

It appears to be a twisted, more sinister siren of legend. A woman's naked torso, but with the hips and legs of an octopus. She is brownish-green, making her almost unnoticeable in the water. Her matted, bladderwrack seaweed hair covers her scaly, green shoulders and breasts. Oversized black eyes, like that of a shark, lock onto Cælius; she peers at him with a predator's gaze. Her slimy tentacles slip up and around his legs; there is no escaping her grip.

Raising her arm, she points a long, bony finger toward him. "You cannot hide from usss, Cæliusss." She says with a gurgling hiss.

The foul creature opens the gaping maw on her long face, exposing her rotten teeth. A narrow, forked serpent's tongue swishes as she begins singing her sinister and painful song.

Contrary to earthly sirens, she is not seducing Cælius. Instead, she calls out to dæmons patrolling the shores. She bids them come and take him. Cælius closes his eyes, covers his ears, and screams, “Deus meus, salva mea!”

Chapter Ten

What the Damned Saw

Ioannes stares upward into the darkness from his knees. He searches for an answer to his condition, wondering when or if the remnant of hope he holds onto might give out. Without any explanation, his body freezes in this upward-looking position. A vision of events unfolding on the Earth above fills his mind, and he forgets his place. Instead of a hellscape, he sees a garden at night.

The moonlight casts shadows in the light mist, dancing through a grove of gnarled olive trees. A man kneels alone among the trees. He prays to Adonai, whom he calls "Father." He prays with his entire being. Blood mingles with sweat from his brow. The man is in agony. Ioannes hears his words, "O, my Father, if it is possible, let this cup pass from me; nevertheless, not as I will, but as you will."

The vision fades to another image of the man standing in the garden, surrounded by others. A squad of Iudæus soldiers approach, led by a man who is not a soldier; he is dressed like the others. This man, leading the soldiers, greets the man in the garden with a kiss on the cheek. Again, Ioannes hears the man, "Judas, you betray the Son of Man with a kiss?" The Son of Man is immediately arrested and beaten while the rest of his friends fly into the night. This vision fades to another.

This Son of Man is chained and bound; he has been assaulted. He stands before a court of Iudæus Pharisees and is surrounded by many people making false accusations. Ioannes can see them gesturing and speaking, but what they say is inaudible.

The Son of Man remains steadfastly silent. The high priest steps forward and says something, but Ioannes cannot hear his words. Only the answer of the Son of Man reaches him. He speaks calmly and with authority, "You have said so. But I say to all of you: From now on, you will see the Son of Man sitting at the right hand of the Mighty One and coming on the clouds of heaven."

The chief priest tears his robes and wails at this response. The other priests spit on the Son of Man, while some strike him and mock him before taking him away. Then blackness.

Ioannes intuitively recognizes the setting of the next vision: the Antonia Fortress next to the temple mount.

Light from the early morning sun illuminates the room where the Son of Man now stands. He is alone with a Roman Governor, who questions and studies him. Again, the Son of Man remains steadfastly silent until he gives a last response, "You say rightly that I am a king. For this cause, I was born, and for this cause, I have come into the world that I should bear witness to the truth. Everyone who is of the truth hears my voice."

Ioannes' heart begins to beat rapidly. Hearing only the Son of Man's voice in these visions, he begins to think he is witnessing the Messias himself. He watches the Roman Governor send him away. His vision blurs again.

The Iudæus King, Herod, who commissioned Cæsarea Maritima, strolls into his palace court. By the color of the light, Ioannes knows it is still morning.

Chains lead the Son of Man to the court of the king, who is initially excited to meet him. The king fervently questions him and makes a request of him. Here, the Son of Man says nothing; he does not speak a word. As a result, the king and his court mock him before sending him away.

The vision fades back to the Roman court. The governor makes a declaration. Soldiers seize the Son of Man, and the vision fades.

Ioannes is released from his paralyzed state. He drops his head into his hands. Shame overwhelms him. He whispers, "Deus meus, what are you showing me? Is this the Son of Man on whom all my hopes are pinned? Is he the Messias?"

He hears the scourging in the background. Ioannes covers his face with his shackled hands, flinching with each crack of the whip and each strike upon the Son of Man.

He becomes aware that he is not the only one to see these visions. Each time Jesus is marked with the whip, each time he is struck, dæmons and evil souls scattered throughout the darkness cheer. The roar is loud, as though it comes from a packed coliseum.

Ioannes looks up again, his face a messy mix of tears and ash. He thinks to himself, *Again, I see the innocent man suffer, scourged, and beaten. Who is this man that he would endure such abuse for those he called friends, brothers, and sisters? Who is he that dæmons would cheer so at his torture?*

A clear vision comes back. It is mid-day. A small dishonorable group of a garrison of soldiers hides the Son of Man away in an anti-chamber somewhere in Antonia Fortress after the scourging. He sits shaking in a corner, trying to suppress the pain of his beating.

The legionnaires are supposed to prepare him for Pilate. Instead, they ridicule him. They smack his face and pluck hair from his beard. They wrap a scarlet cloak around him and brutally fix a crown woven from thorns upon his head. They mock him by bowing to him. They spit at him and call him names, all of which are inaudible.

Somewhere in limbo's volcanic darkness, a lesser dæmon squeals with giddiness, "Now these are my kind of soldiers!"

Ioannes hears this and, searching the dark landscape, exclaims in defiance, "How much more can this Son of Man take? He has done nothing to deserve this!" He looks up again to see the Roman governor, standing with the Son of Man on the outer steps of Antonia Fortress. He has already offered a choice to the crowd. They rejected the Son of Man, and the governor released a criminal who was seen entering the crowd.

After their accusations, the governor grows uneasy with the mob and, half leaning toward the Son of Man, quietly questions him one last time. Ioannes still cannot hear what is shouted by the crowd or inquired of by the governor.

The Son of Man, shaking from pain, looks the Roman in the eye to tell him, "You could have no power at all against me unless it had been given you from above. Therefore, the one who delivered me to you has the greater sin."

In the darkness of limbo, a chant begins to grow. Dæmons and condemned souls alike add their voices to the mantra of the earthly crowd, "Crucify him! Crucify him! Crucify him!"

Ioannes leans his head down and moves to cover his ears, but a sudden hush falls over Limbo. The only sound is the lava churning in the cauldrons. He doesn't know what has happened. Curiously and cautiously, he looks up.

In the distant area, just over the black pit, the vast chasm, hanging in midair by his throat, is the traitor Judas. He had despaired and hung himself. Now, he hangs from the very noose placed around his neck with his own two hands. All eyes watch the soul of this traitor descend into hell. With an eerie, flame-colored light on him, the hanged man slowly sinks through the dusky, ash-filled air toward the distant pit.

Chatter hisses, and noise increases as the traitor descends, climaxing when he nears the threshold of the abyss. There, both dæmons and sinners curse him and hurl stones at him. They scream, "Traitor! Liar! You will suffer!"

Judas cannot wail or scream because of the noose tied around his throat, but he does gnash his teeth and flail about wildly as he tries to defend himself from the stones. However, he promptly slips into the chasm's depths near the lake of fire and is out of sight. Just as quickly as it started, the scene ends.

Then, a different shout from somewhere in the black hellscape, “Guilty! Guilty!” A raucous cheer goes up as though some gladiator had won a great victory. Jesus has been condemned and sent to be crucified.

Ioannes watches the Son of Man bear a heavy cross down the crowded Via Dolorosa in Hierosolyma. The burden is tremendous, and he witnesses him stumbling and dropping his cross. He falls atop it in exhaustion and struggles to return to his feet. Some, out of hate and others out of adoration, call out his name, Jesus.

Soldiers continue to scream at him and whip him until he reaches locus Calvariæ[14]. There, Jesus falls to the ground with his cross. He is stripped of his garments and then dragged on his back to place him on the cross, which is lying flat on the ground.

A legionnaire carpenter advances with hammer and nails in hand. He kneels next to Jesus’ hand, which is already stretched out and tied by his wrists. The carpenter holds a nail to Jesus’ palm with his left and raises his hammer with his right.

Ioannes cannot bear to watch any longer. He falls prostrate on the hot, black rock, burying his face in his hands. He knows what comes next. He weeps as he talks to himself, “This innocent man, the Son of Man, has already endured much. Whipped, beaten, and suffered more than I. He was led out to his death as I have been led here. He is nearly as naked as I am, too.”

The ping of hammer on nail resonates through the bare landscape of hell, echoing off the volcanic terrain and inciting dæmons to a disgusting ecstatic cry. They shout in a frenzy

---

[14] Place of the Skulls – (translated from Latin (AKA Golgotha)

with each hammer blow while Ioannes utterly sobs with each one.

Ioannes yells uncontrollably, “No, stop this! He does not deserve this!”

A lesser dæmon rushes out of the black wasteland and kicks Ioannes in the ribs, knocking the wind out of him and rolling him onto his side. The fiend stands over him, exclaiming in his bloodlust, “Shut up, sinner!

The hammer strikes another nail while the dæmon strolls confidently back in the direction he came from, disappearing in the darkness. Ioannes reaches for his side. The pain in his ribs is nearly unbearable.

The hammering is done. Everything is still in Limbo—Ioannes labors to catch his breath in the silence. In time, he lifts his tear-stained face to see Jesus being raised on his cross.

Racked with pain, he hangs in the hot sun. Criminals flank him on their crosses. To his surprise, Ioannes hears the taunts of the first criminal, “If you are the Christ, save yourself and us!”

As well as the retort of the second criminal, “Do you not even fear God, seeing you are under the same condemnation? We receive the due reward of our deeds, but this Man has done nothing wrong.” Then, with great humility, the second criminal pleads to Jesus, “Lord… remember me when you come into your kingdom.”

“Amen…” His voice is broken. “I say to you, today…” He labors. “You will be with me in Paradise.”

Ioannes witnesses Jesus' mercy. A flicker of hope appears in his weary eye. Short of breath, he whispers, “Truly, he must be the Messias.” He continues to watch the unfolding scene on earth with great anticipation.

Still hanging from the cross, Jesus is broken, exhausted, and at his end. He looks skyward and exclaims, “Father, into Your hands I commit my spirit!”

Those in the first circle of hell watch as Jesus breathes his last, dying on the cross. A raucous cheer erupts, as loud as 20 filled coliseums. In the distance, a lesser dæmon shouts joyfully, “What a glorious day in hell!”

Ioannes merely falls prostrate in sorrow. However, the merriment of the damned rapidly subsides. All fall silent and still; a great hush blankets the underworld.

Chapter Eleven

The Appearance

The Siren's song has stopped. She no longer twists her tentacles around Cælius. Things have gone eerily silent. The strange moment causes him to open his eyes in a squint and slowly pull his hands away from his ears.

Though still in her slimy clutches, the Siren pays no attention to him. She is distracted by something happening downriver, some unknown place beyond the fog. He slowly turns his head to see what she is looking at. It is then he notices two winged dæmons out of the corner of his eye. They are standing just above and behind him on the higher part of the riverbank.

Similar to the goblin-like dæmons but a little bigger and browner in color, they, too, have stopped in their advance and are staring downriver. Something is causing a great hush to descend upon the river and making every hellish creature stop in its tracks. Even the waves have begun to flatten. There is an odd feeling in the air, as though there has been a collective deep breath before they plunge beneath the waves.

* * * * *

Ioannes rises painfully to his knees, trying to see what is happening around him. The sound has been completely sucked out of the air; it is an eerie and uneasy calm until... 'KRA-BOOM!' A deafening thunderclap shakes the ground. It startles Ioannes, who instinctively reaches to cover his ears and ducks his head. The sound wave reverberates through his chest before rumbling across the muffled black sky, breaking the uncomfortable silence.

After it passes, he returns his gaze skyward. Just above the volcanic maelstrom in the blackest sky is a point of pure, twinkling white light. It burns brighter than any star in the earthly night sky, brighter than any flash of lightning or burning ember in the hellish atmosphere. It begins to expand into the shape of a giant round orb.

At first, the yellow-white orb appears like the sun, as seen through an ash cloud of an erupting volcano. Unlike the sun, it is encircled by a spinning band of golden fire, sparking as it spins around the orb. This flickering band releases a great wind that blows the ashen clouds away in all directions.

Then, in the bright circle of white light, a figure appears, the silhouette of a man. He seems both far away and near at the same time. He stands upright with his hands extended slightly outward from his sides.

Though it is hard for Ioannes to distinguish the figure's details, his appearance throws all of hell into a panic. Throughout the darkness, sounds of fearful scurrying like a field of rats trying to hide from a great, golden hawk. The skin of any demon unfortunate enough to have the pure light land upon him burns. They scatter and run, seeking shelter among any shadow they can find.

* * * * *

Cælius, who was already looking downstream, curious as to what captivates the attention of the winged dæmons and the siren, hears the same massive thunderclap. Though it is farther away, it is still more potent than the ones in the tempest that sunk his ship. It rumbles across the pitch sky and echoes along the rocky banks.

He sees the same single point of pure light, which twinkles before expanding into a giant orb. The same great wind blows upstream, dispersing both smoke and fog on the River Styx.

Though he is far from it, Cælius can still see the shape of a man in the light of the orb. He was not blessed with visions of the Passion of the Christ, yet his soldier's intuition tells him this can only be one thing: the arrival of the Messias. Cælius knows only he could appear in this way. He becomes visibly excited, like a child who sees his father returning home after a long journey.

Sounds of chaos near the light spread outwardly in all directions. The figure in the light has indeed plunged the denizens of hell into widespread panic.

* * * * *

Light displaced evermore shadows. A new dawn rises over the desolate hellscape. Ioannes watches as the unseen becomes visible; volcanoes, lava flows, and even the distant pit can now be seen with more clarity. This new dawn is not welcomed by all, however.

A deep roar erupts from the chasm in opposition to the light. It shakes the landscape in view, including the ground Ioannes is chained to. Rocks tumble and shake as the ground quakes. A voice filled with rage, defiance, and contempt screeches, "No, Son of the Most High, these souls are mine! I will not part with a single one!"

All sound, even the echo from the voice of the devil himself, is quickly muted as Jesus begins to speak. Though none can see him speak, all can hear his voice. It is soft but robust, comforting but with authority. His speech is in perfect cadence and pronunciation. "Silence. You will have only what my father wills you to have. I am here for the just who went to sleep before I came. I am their shepherd, and they will know my voice, for I am the way, the truth, and the life."

Ioannes, who is already on his knees, notices the unnamed soul and all of Limbo by the sound of it, bending a knee to the Messias. As Jesus commanded, all is silenced.

The shape of the orb begins to change. From it, light stretches out above, below, and to the left and right, forming the shape of a cross. The overall effect of the beams of light resembles what will one day be known as a monstrance, with Jesus at its center.

With a tremendous explosion, the most brilliant white light, gold around its fringes, bursts forth from the orb. The gold fringe appears to shimmer, sparkle, and crackle before expanding outward and descending all around. Ioannes quickly realizes it is not a normal, shimmering light but that each light is alive. Angels, each one invading the underworld. They are sent out to find the just who await salvation.

As the holy legion descends in all directions, Ioannes notices the figure in the orb growing in stature. Though his silhouette is still dark, light shines through holes in his hands and feet.

* * * * *

The Siren unconsciously relaxes her grip. Cælius is on his knees along with the dæmons behind him. He sees the angels descending. He watches in desperation, hoping they will come to the River Styx. Unfortunately, they do not appear to be doing so. He grows desperate. Wrestling completely free of the stunned Siren, he jumps to his feet and, waving his hands, shouts like a castaway, sighting a ship nearby, "Elohim! I am here! I am here! Do not forsake me, Lord. Please!"

His screams shake his would-be captors from their confusion. The first shore dæmon jumps down the bank and strikes him with a cudgel in the back of the head. It knocks him down, belly first, on the smooth stone between the Siren and the sharp spires. He falls on one of her tentacled arms, too, both hurting and insulting her.

Enraged, she quickly winds all her large tentacles around his torso, securing his arms. She wraps a smaller one around his neck and squeezes his throat. She brings her horrid face close to his, which is turning red from strangulation. She gives him a nasty smile before she reaches around his shoulders and places her jagged fingernails near his spine. She then drags them outwardly to his shoulders, tearing his flesh while laughing with delight. "You hurt me. I hurt you."

Cælius winces in agony. She leans back toward the river, loosening her grip. His arms are now free, and he falls to the ground, gasping for breath. He looks up at the wicked siren. She licks at the blood on her fingertips with a morbid pleasure before gurgling a hiss of contempt, "Now, get off me, sssinner!"

The dæmons, standing between Cælius and the bank, watch her assault with satisfaction. He placed his palms on the ground shoulder length apart. With searing pain, he weakly lifts himself. The Siren pulls her slimy tentacle out from under him.

He lets himself down and reaches to wipe the muddy water from his face. Before he can, though, the dæmons waylay him. The first one grabs him by the hair on his head and pulls him back up to his knees. Standing behind, knee in Cælius' back, he bends down to chortle a growling whisper in his ear, "They're not coming for you. You, shade, are not even in hell yet!"

He flings Cælius back down on the rock. Like the blackness of the water that took his life, despair consumes him. He feels as though he has been cast off on a small island somewhere near Greece and must watch his ship, captain, and crew abandon him. He feels bewildered and lost.

The first dæmon keeps his knee in Cælius' back while the other dæmon grabs his hands, bringing them behind his back. This time, he does not resist. He only wonders if his past sins were too great to be forgiven. He doubts his worthiness to be rescued by the Messias. *He will not come for me; I am lost. Adonai has judged me unfit for salvation and sentenced me to hell to be forever tormented.*

* * * * *

Closer to Ioannes, the silhouette, still illuminated by the sun-like orb, continues growing. It becomes easier to see the figure. It **is** Jesus the crucified who stands in the light.

Ioannes' face changes from awe and curiosity to surprise and uneasiness. He unknowingly murmurs, "Wait, is he coming toward me? How can this be? Surely, I am not worthy of the Messias, the Son of the living God. What do I do?"

Awestruck, Ioannes watches Jesus' approach for a moment longer. The Messias is clothed in the purest white linen, and he walks on a billowing white cloud, which gracefully descends toward him.

Ioannes is visibly nervous, lightly shaking with trepidation. His heart pounds faster with both fear and hope. Sitting on his feet, he bows his head low, almost to his knees, again murmuring, “Might I be blessed by he who conquers death?”

Though he is on his knees, the unnamed soul holds his head high in arrogance and pride. He leans toward Ioannes slightly, whispering in a low voice, “Shut up, stultus, and listen to me! Don’t you recognize the adversary? This is an elaborate trick to lull you in. He is Lucifer, the Morningstar; don't be tricked by his light or appearance. Our time has come. He is here to take us deeper into the pit, to greater punishment. Don't trust him!" The shade straightens himself back up in defiance.

Ioannes keeps his head bowed but his eyes open. There are no footsteps, as Jesus sets no foot in that forsaken place, yet the light around him gets much brighter. He knows the Messias draws near. In a voice as firm and soft as a devoted father speaking with love to his young child, Jesus calls his name, "Ioannes."

Ioannes shutters. It is impossible to keep the tears of joy from his cheeks at the sound of Messias' pure voice. Yet, still hiding his face in his ash-covered hands, he responds with fear and humility, "I am here, Lord."

He removes his hands from his face and clasps them tightly at his chest. He continues through a parched throat and split lips, "Domine miserere nobis[15]. Please, Lord, have mercy on me."

Ioannes' heart thumps against his chest. His body still racked with pain, aches with the rush of blood pulsating through it. Tears stream uncontrollably from the young man's eyes, making his face a black, muddy mess. He finds it hard to breathe and sob at the same time—his body trembles.

Jesus crouches down to meet him. He reaches out and places his hand gently, yet firmly, on Ioannes' shoulder. In that instant, everything changes. The prostrate soldier is calm and unafraid. He no longer trembles; he is still. He takes a deep breath and, based on his previous visions of the passion, focuses on the image of Jesus' face in his mind.

The Messias speaks to him. "My child. I know you. I have seen all you have done in the belief of my Father, the one true

---

[15] "Lord have mercy" – (translated from Latin)

God. Though they were slaves, you gave food and clothing to the ones who taught you my father's commandments. From then on, I watched you seek out the truth; although you may not have known it was me you sought, me you fed, me you clothed, and me you served.

You were gifted with the vision of my passion and my sacrifice. You cried out for me; now, I am here for you. Will you trust in me? Will my grace be enough for you? Do you accept the gift of salvation I offer?"

Ioannes answers without hesitation, "My Lord, though I feel I have been no servant of yours and therefore am not worthy of you, yes, still, I trust in you with all my heart. The grace you offer is more than enough for me. Truly, you are the Messias, the Son of God, and I humbly receive you."

With his head still down, Ioannes does not see the joyful smile on Jesus' face. The Lord draws a slow, steady breath and exhales upon the humble soldier. His exhale moves through Ioannes' hair and down his back, blowing soot and ash from his body. The shackles click open and fall from his wrists, which are still clasped together at his chest. His burns, wounds, and bruises disappear; his skin is cleansed and made whole.

Immediately following this, he hears the rush of enormous wings. One from the legion of angels hovers just above and to Ioannes' left shoulder. His wings beat rhythmically, making a whoosh sound with each flap.

Jesus removes his hand from Ioannes and stands. Wind from the angel's wings blows away the ash and filth around them. Then the angel lands on the ground next to Ioannes, his sandaled feet lighting quietly on the ground. He folds and tucks his translucent wings behind him.

The angel appears as a perfect copy of a man in his early 30s but somehow more elegant; his skin radiates holy light. He has no discernable race; he appears to be mixed between

Africanus, Asian, and Caucasian. Upon arrival, he bows to Jesus.

The angel wears a deep blue leather breastplate trimmed in gold. His armor is set against a light gray tunic, and a golden belt wraps his waist. A golden scabbard holds an ivory-handled gladius at his side. His sandals are the same golden color as his belt and the trim on his armor. He holds something made of cloth in his hands, which he transfers to his belt behind his back.

He reaches down, takes Ioannes' hand, and lifts him to his feet. He is several inches taller, so they are not entirely face-to-face. The angel pulls the cloth from the belt behind his back and unfolds it. He swiftly clothes Ioannes with a pale blue linen robe and then wraps a golden sash around his waist. Once he is done, he smiles at Ioannes before slightly dipping his head and motioning with his left hand toward Jesus.

Ioannes turns reverently toward his savior, who, standing on a cloud, is slightly elevated and looking down on him with unfathomable love. His eyes blaze forth in a deep copper color as though they were made of molten metal. Divine light emanates from his face, from his entire being. An overwhelming sense of undeniable joy fills Ioannes' heart and soul, and a wide smile spreads across his face.

The Lord says, "The faith and hope you clung to has saved you Ioannes." He takes a step closer, continuing, "I still have much to accomplish here and in the world above. Go now to paradise. Great joy awaits you there."

Jesus pats him on the shoulder and offers an encouraging smile, "I will be in my Father's house soon after I fully accomplish His work. For now, you must go further up and further into my kingdom."

Jesus turns to move throughout the forsaken precipice to the abyss, claiming others as he claimed Ioannes, who lingers with the angel for a moment. Together, they watch evil souls and dæmons flee as the Magnificent One brings ever-expanding light to Limbo and joy to those who awaited his coming.

The angel turns to Ioannes and officially introduces himself: "I am Præsidiel. Come, my friend, as our Lord said, it is time to leave this forsaken place."

He stretches out his white, translucent wings, reflecting God's holy light. He gestures to rise and then places his arm around Ioannes' back, beneath his shoulders. The two ascend toward the perfect orb of light still spiraling in the black sky.

Ioannes observes thousands of similar angels rising into the light with them, each accompanying another soul. In the darkness of hell, they first appear as glinting points of light, but their glory is evident as they all move closer to the orb.

"See, our Lord comes for his servants and prophets of old, as well as others who believe in him and follow the commands of Elohim. He is the good shepherd who seeks out his lost sheep," informs Præsidiel.

Ioannes has no words; he quietly smiles. He thinks back to the moment Jesus died on the cross, how the dæmons cheered as if it were a great victory for them. It was not that moment, no. It is this moment, the moment of the Messias' appearance in hell, the salvation of those God still loves and has not forgotten, and the ascension of the just into His kingdom, that made it a **truly** glorious day in hell.

The chasm between the threshold of light and Limbo increases exponentially. Ioannes' vision remains locked on the oscillating orb of light, his emotions swelling with youthful anticipation of the world to come. Quickly forgotten and fading rapidly in the distance is the hellscape from whence he came, where another shade is being taken in the opposite direction.

There, a horrible, twisted creature clutches the ankle of the hate-filled, unnamed soul. It drags him across the jagged landscape toward the edge of the black pit. His wrists are still bound in irons, and being drug on his belly, the soul's outstretched hands reach out beyond his head. His fingers rake through loose gravel and rocks, desperately trying to grasp onto something, anything that might pause his unwilling journey downward.

The pompous demon who fancied himself a judge follows at his side, antagonizing, kicking, and spitting on him. He delights in the soul knowing he is bound for darkness and fire.

Once bound in a field of black pumice, the two men have finally departed for their eternal destinations. One is taken to paradise; the other is left to his destruction. Ioannes has already forgotten most of his earthly life; instead, he is enthralled by the prospect of Elysium. Unnamed Soul, however, will be forever reminded of his sins and is repulsed by his prospects. Ioannes blinks as he passes through the gateway into blinding white light.

* * * * *

Cælius lies on his belly, hands bound behind his back. He shakes his head, trying to get the filthy water from his face. He looks up to his right, and the hideous face of the Siren glares back at him, a disturbing smile upon her wretched face.

The two dæmons are standing between him and the rocky bank behind them. The first one says, "Pick him up. Since he's already on this side of the river, we'll take him straight to the judge."

The second shore dæmon grasps Cælius by the right arm and yanks him up. Once he is on his feet, the other demon grabs his left arm. Together, they drag him up the bank to higher ground. The fallen warrior finally gets a clear view down the River Styx. However, in the distance, there is an unexpected sight. The Messias is coming toward them.

Jesus walks just above the surface of the now calm water; the small cloud under his feet keeps him from touching its filth. His light illuminates the river valley as he walks with a steady pace, full of purpose. He is already ahead of the raider ships and strides directly toward them. The dæmons see the Son of God, too. They drop their prisoner at the sight of him and scurry off. The Siren gasps, turns, and plunges back into the mire.

Cælius, stunned, watches in awe from his knees as Jesus approaches. However, he suddenly becomes conscious of all his sins. Out of fear and shame, he does something foolish, so very 'uncharacteristic' of a well-disciplined soldier. Hands still tied securely behind his back, he quickly and clumsily stumbles back down the bank to the rock on which he crawled out of the river. He kneels behind the spires and hides in his shame.

Cælius mutters, "My sins, I never completed the purification ritual. Murder, lust, selfish pride, more than that... How foolish am I to think I could ever be worthy of the Messias? How foolish am I to think salvation would come to me on the banks of the River Styx? Think! What am I to say? What am I to do?"

Wisps of cloud move around the spire and fill the area around him. He falls prostrate, knowing Jesus has come.

He hears his name. "Cælius," calls the Messias.

A shiver runs down his spine. It is the same voice he heard the day he buried his friend Ioannes. His nose stings as he tries to hold back the tears welling up in his eyes. He is desperate to control his emotions. Though he still hides his face in shame, he responds faithfully, "I... I am here, my Lord."

"Why do you hide from me?"

"I saw you coming and was fearful. I am a great sinner, Lord, and I am ashamed." He pauses briefly, slightly lifts his head, but not high enough to look at Jesus, and then boldly says, "I saw your angels descend into the underworld, but not here. I thought... I thought, surely, I was lost... condemned."

Jesus stands in front and to the left of Cælius. Just as he did with Ioannes, the Messias squats down before the former soldier and sailor. With the greatest compassion, he reaches down, places a hand under Cælius' chin, and gently lifts his face so they might see each other. "Peace to you, Cælius."

Cælius looks up into his molten copper eyes. His smooth bronze skin radiates the purest light, and his dark hair and thick beard are clean and oiled. His features are soft yet firm. Jesus looks upon him with profound love, as a father does for his child.

A peacefulness enters the heart of Cælius as Jesus releases his chin and begins to speak to him. "Did you not call to me?"

Cælius answers with longing eyes.

The Savior continues, "You are right to admit your sins. However, you were not in the world when I taught. If you were, you might understand that my love, my mercy, is not something to be earned through the completion of any ritual. True salvation is a gift to those who believe in me. Baptism is an outward sign offered by those who accept my gift."

He pauses for a moment. Cælius knows he cannot hide his thoughts from the Son of God, yet a visible love and mercy shine forth from Messias' face as he speaks. "I taught this lesson to those who could hear. Let me also ask you. Suppose a shepherd has a hundred sheep and loses one of them. Does he not leave the ninety-nine in the open country and go after the lost sheep until he finds it? And when he finds it, does he not joyfully put it on his shoulders and return home?" He pauses briefly to let the questions sink in. "Do you understand this parable, Cælius?

"Yes, Lord, I think, I hope, I understand. You are the good shepherd, and I hope... beyond all hope... that maybe I am the lost one you seek."

Jesus laughs with delight and stands up. Cælius remains on his knees but sits on his legs, listening to the great teacher. "Amen, I say to you, I love your unshakeable hope, your optimism. I have seen your works, Cælius, both good and evil. I know the sins of your youth, your sins as a soldier, and your sins as a sailor. However, I also know you repented and amended your life when you began to seek out my Father, the one true and living God. Your optimistic will to continuously ask, seek, and knock in search of the truth has always pleased me."

He smiles. "I also know you willingly laid down your life for your shipmates. There is no greater love than that: laying down your life so that others may live. I, too, laid down my life so that others may have eternal life. I paid the price for all sin, and I have the power to forgive those who trust in me. So, Cælius, do you believe that I have the power to do this? Will you accept the gift I offer?"

Cælius looks deeply into the eyes of Christ, knowing full well who he is. Desperately trying to restrain the tears in his own eyes, he lifts himself to one knee, hands still tied behind his back, and confesses, "Truly, you are the Messias. I am sorry for my sins with all my heart. If you are willing to forgive, my Lord, then yes, I gladly trust in you. Your grace, your mercy, is enough for me."

Jesus smiles. "Your sins are forgiven Cælius, your faith has saved you."

At the very sound of Jesus' words, Cælius' bonds are instantly loosed. All the water, mud, and filth fall from his body. Even the wounds on his back are healed. His strength is regained. He, like Ioannes, is set free, cleansed, and made whole.

Still on bended knee, but now with hands freed, Cælius rubs his wrists. He then bows his head and strikes his breast with his right hand, offering Jesus a soldier's salute. After this, he looks up at him again.

Jesus smiles and motions with his right hand to look downriver. Coming quickly toward them out of the distant, volcanic wasteland is a brilliant angel, one of the hosts who held open the orb of light.

His enormous translucent wings beat harmoniously, moving him swiftly through the dark sky. He swoops slightly upward at the water's edge on the other side of the spires. The wind from his wings blows gently on them as he lands on the high bank. He bows to Jesus and then extends his hand down to Cælius.

They clasp forearms, and the Angel lifts him up the rocky bank. He then reaches behind his back and pulls out a pale blue robe. He helps cloth Cælius with it and then ties a golden sash around his waist. He smiles and places a hand on Cælius' shoulder. "There. That is better."

Jesus rises up the bank on the cloud. Cælius turns to face him. Jesus smiles. "I am pleased you called to me, Cælius; however, I still have much to accomplish here and in the world above. It is time for you to enter paradise now. You will find great joy there, and we will meet again very soon," he smiles. "After I have fully accomplished my father's work," he says.

Cælius slightly bows his head and lightly strikes his breast in salute once more. Jesus turns back toward the forsaken, hellish landscape from which he had initially appeared. Again, his stride is swift and purposeful as he departs them.

Cælius turns to face the Angel, who says, "Come. As the Lord commanded, let us leave this cursed shore for the white shores of Elysium."

Without haste, he stretches out his white, lustrous wings. He places his right arm under Cælius' left arm, wraps it around his upper back, and gestures upward. They began to ascend swiftly toward the orb of light in the distance.

Cælius disregards his former surroundings as they fly above the River Styx. Dæmons still scurry about its banks, hiding from the light of Christ. Frightened souls willingly crawl aboard the ships of the damned, bound for hell. Even the tentacles of the unseen monster plunge back below the blood-stained waters.

As the Angel climbs toward the orb, the distant landscape of hell comes into sight, but Cælius pays it no mind. Charon's ferry is seen pushing ashore and beyond that, what looks like a desolate, volcanic wasteland.

Cælius, his eyes fixated on the light, sees none of it. The great chasm opens between hell and the gateway. The empty, black void engulfs all the features of the underworld. The angel smiles as they prepare to pass into the blinding white light, "Hold on."

Chapter Twelve

A Discovery in Heaven

Everything on the other side of the orb is much brighter and more vivid. All the colors seem far more brilliant. An angel carries a man with his arm around his back. They light on a soft, verdant, grassy outcropping. The angel folds his wings and then speaks, "Welcome to Paradise Ioannes."

"Thank you, my friend." Ioannes closes his eyes and lifts his face to the sky, soaking in its warmth. He re-opens them, slowly surveying the lush, sprawling domain. He takes a deep breath and exhales, continually marveling at the landscape.

Fields of tall grasses, meadows filled with colorful flowers, and deep green forests with various flowering and fruit-bearing trees. Vast, rolling hills surround the meadows and woodlands. Streams of the clearest water flow from vast, snowcapped mountains rising behind the rolling hills and wind in various directions.

A fresh, cool breeze ruffles his robe and Præsidiel's wings as it carries floral scents throughout the vast lands of Heaven. "Even the fabled Elysian Fields cannot compare to this," acknowledges Ioannes. Præsidiel laughs.

As he observes, Ioannes thinks; *creation has not only been remade but is laid out before me. I find the prospect of seeing and knowing my savior in this place all the more than exhilarating.*

In the distance, a great, gleaming city sits majestically upon a hill. It is how he always envisioned the picturesque Jerusalem. Its tan and white stone buildings beckon new arrivals to enter through its wide gates and wander its sacred streets. Millions of stars and even other worlds are visible in the sky above it. The sky itself fades from a bright blue to twilight and on to starlit heavens beyond the luminous city. From the city flows a pure river, clear as crystal. Just below the city, a massive tree straddles the river. Ioannes can make out twelve different fruits in its lush canopy, one of which appears to flash with lightning trapped inside.

He observes; *here, there will be no more darkness, no more weeping and gnashing of teeth, no more war, no death or despair. I see only life, love, truth, and joyous discovery laid out before me, just as he promised.*

Ioannes turns to Præsidiel, who can easily read the unbridled joy and curiosity on his face. The angel smiles, tilts his head in a slight bow, and motions toward the road leading up to the city on the hill with his left hand. Ioannes feels like a child being released into an ethereal playground. Ioannes nods back in gratitude while lightly striking his breast in salute. He takes his first step into the Kingdom of Heaven.

He begins up the road toward the city, reflecting as he walks; some *might call those of us redeemed from the precipice of hell the 'just pagans' of the world... Me? I am happy to have been called by our Lord at all. Truly, I am content in having all of eternity to express my gratitude and eternal thanks for the sacrifice, mercy, and grace of our Lord Jesus the Christ.*

* * * * *

Ioannes walks with a slow, steady, joyful, and observant look in his eye. He follows the well-laid, stone road toward the gleaming city on the hill. The road is perfectly hewn out of the hills, rising toward the city. It is lined by outcroppings of rock with small grasses and blue squill flowers popping up between the stones. Small fig trees and patches of purple lavender also adorn the road.

Beyond it, on the right side, lay beautiful fields of green wheat. A light and fragrant breeze moves across its surface, and the grass sways and moves like waves on the water. Further up, on the left side of the road, a relatively lush olive tree has grown between tan boulders.

Though Ioannes continues to observe his newfound surroundings, smile, and greet others moving up the road with jubilation, he keeps his focus on the olive tree. As he grows closer, the true detail and beauty of the tree stand out. Its massive, brown trunk twists and turns upward as though it has been dancing and twirling in the presence of Elohim for thousands of years. Ripe green olives fill its leafy canopy.

Ioannes approaches to touch its trunk and, out of the corner of his eye, notices a subtle, less traveled trail branching off from the road. His curiosity is peaked.

He stops, climbs on one of the boulders near the tree, and rests momentarily. He observes the path and its destination from the elevated position. It runs parallel, albeit much more winding, toward the city on the hill, meandering between the main road and a pure stream. A long row of enormous eucalyptus trees lines a portion of the winding path ahead. Beyond that, a short waterfall cascades over a small rock face, not far from where the brook branches off from the river of life flowing from the city. The sparkling clear waters splash beautifully on the tan rocks below.

The trail and the stream call to him, inviting him to follow it onward and upward. He wonders aloud as he looks around, "Surely, I am not the only one to notice this path?"

Many other men, women, and children from every race and culture, even some he has never seen, move with much excitement up the road toward the city. Each person in heaven easily understands all languages, and he cheerfully waves and greets a family (a father, mother, and two young daughters) as they pass by his lofty perch upon the rock.

Another man approaches. One dressed in a way Ioannes has never seen. Ioannes observes him closely. The Chief wears light tan pants from animal skin; leather-like tassels run down each leg's side. He has a long-sleeved cloth shirt, blue in color, over which is an ornate breastplate made from two columns of tiny bones. Feathers tied to the ends of leather tassels adorn the bottom of it, and a silver disc in the middle. For all his ornamental dress, the Chief wears no shoes or sandals.

On his head is an opulent headdress. The blue band with orange designs woven into it stretches across his forehead. On each side are decorated red discs, on which two white feathers hang. Rising from the top of the band and encircling his head like a halo is 30 to 40 feathers. Each one is white with a black tip. The shaft of each feather is wrapped in tan leather and red string and fixed to the thick blue headband.

Long, jet-black, braided hair protrudes down from under the feathered headdress and rests on each of his shoulders. His dark brown facial features are rugged, and he has a solid warrior's build. His stride is proud and happy yet purposeful as if he were seeking the soul of another who would be there. The Chief raises his hand when he greets Ioannes, smiling, "Háu kola."

Ioannes immediately understands it to mean "Hello, friend." He returns the greeting in kind, "Salutate amicus."

Still sitting upon the boulder, he curiously watches the Chief pass by, saying, "What an interesting man. I hope to meet him again."

Returning to his previous thoughts, he turns his eyes skyward, where angels of all types are seen flying to and fro in the clear, deep blue sky. Some have a human form, some are made of pure light, some have six wings, and some have less.

He looks down at the rock upon which he sits and, for a fleeting moment, has a single thought, a regret, which he expresses softly: "I wish I had told so many more about the Messias, especially my friend Cælius. I pray God might save him from the fires of hell, too."

A warm, scented breeze rustles the olive leaves, and the thought vanishes as quickly as it comes. The wind blows toward the side path, directing his attention there. The sound of the babbling stream reaches his ears. Like a siren, it calls again to him.

Without hesitation and with confidence, Ioannes slaps his thighs and declares, "It is decided then, I will follow the path less trodden."

He hops down, places his feet on the new path, and sets off on the trail with the enthusiasm of a young boy.

Having walked a good distance up the new path, Ioannes nears the eucalyptus trees he saw from the boulder. The trail comes close to the stream, so he stops kneeling at a little sandy bank and dips his hands in the cool, clear water. A rainbow trout darts upstream and draws his eye further up the trail, where he notices the first large eucalyptus tree to the right side of the trail.

A man is sitting on a grassy outcropping between the trail and the tree, leaning against the trunk of the fragrant tree. The man's gaze is fixated on the water flowing in the stream. Ioannes whispers to himself, "There is something familiar about that man, the way he stares at the water. I know I have seen that look before."

He stands and continues up the path to greet the man. To his great surprise and delight, he realizes the man is a friend and fellow legionnaire. Genuinely excited, he quickens his pace. Nearly running, he shouts and waves, "Cælius! Cælius, my friend!"

Shaken from his contemplative stare, Cælius turns to see Ioannes rushing toward him. He jumps to his feet and, raising his arms, exclaims, "Salve, frater meus![16]"

Ioannes runs off the path and up the grassy outcropping with hands outstretched. They meet with a brotherly hug, patting each other on the back, and then pull away to look at each other. Cælius keeps his hands on the younger Ioannes' shoulders, who is filled with excitement at finding him.

Ioannes says, "I worried I would never see you again, my friend."

"Oh, but I had a feeling I would see ***you*** again, brother."

Still stunned to find his friend and mentor, Ioannes babbles with youthful exuberance, "I… I don't know what to say. I am overjoyed to see you." A curious look suddenly comes over his face. Forgive me, but how did you come to this place?"

"Ha, ha, ha. Calm yourself, little brother. I am here because of you. If not for you, I may never have learned about our Lord Jesus, the Messias."

"Indeed! Did he save you, too?" Ioannes realizes what he has just asked. What am I saying? Of course, he must have. He is the way!"

"Yes, my friend, he is the way, the truth, and the life. I do not have the words to express just how grateful I am for his mercy."

Cælius releases Ioannes, but they continue to stand, conversing, on the grassy outcropping under the faint shade of the eucalyptus tree.

"Truly, as am I," begins Ioannes. "Of all the ways leading to the city on the hill, though, I find you here."

"An angel brought me to the trailhead by the olive tree. He suggested I follow the path along the stream, and so I did."

---

[16] "Hello, my brother!" (translated from Latin).

Cælius states. “Well, until I came to this beautiful eucalyptus tree. Here, the beauty of this place interrupted my thoughts. I have seen so many shorelines and waters since you and I last spoke. I sailed the deep blue waters of the Mare Internum and swam in the blood-stained, muddy waters of the River Styx.”

Ioannes interrupts, “Wait, you were in hell too?”

“No. No, I never made it that far. Our Lord saved me while I was stranded on the river’s bank. The horrible things I saw there before he came...” Cælius’ voice trails off as though he is already forgetting his time in the underworld.

“Anyway, that is why I stopped here. I have never seen such crystal-clear water as this. I was drawn to its purity. I took a refreshing sip and then rested, contemplating the unfathomable mercy and love of our savior, Jesus. I was thinking of words to express my gratitude and love. Out of the hundreds, no thousands, of souls I saw in the underworld, how he could be so gracious to save one such as me...” His voice trails off a bit.

“After all I have seen, I was content to rest peacefully under the tree in the presence of Elohim.” Cælius slaps Ioannes on the shoulder and grins. “Until I heard your voice, that is. A very pleasant surprise indeed! Now I am here with you, my brother, who started me on the path to God so long ago.”

Before Ioannes can respond, the familiar sound of angel’s wings beat overhead. Slowing his descent, the angel lands on the trail ahead of them.

Both exclaim simultaneously, “Præsidiel!”

The two men look at each other with joyful surprise, realizing then that Præsidiel had served as each of their escorts into paradise.

Præsidiel folds his wings and raises his hand to greet the two men, "Dominus vobiscum[17]!"

Ioannes and Cælius, being former soldiers, strike their breasts and bow their heads in salute, saying in unison, "Et cum spiritu tuo[18]."

Then, without hesitation, each man takes a turn clasping Præsidiel's forearm and shaking their new friend's hand.

The angel asks, "What a glorious little spot, yes? I thought this would be a wonderful place for you two to reunite. Ioannes, I knew you wouldn't resist the adventure of the side trail." Præsidiel winks at him in jest. "Have you had a moment to share your stories and the glory of our Lord Jesus' saving grace?"

"I had only just begun. I have not yet heard Ioannes' tale. Join us?" Asks Cælius.

"Unfortunately, no. I came to retrieve you, my friends. Our Lord's work is nearly complete. He will be returning soon. All the heavenly hosts are preparing for his coronation."

Præsidiel motions for them to accompany him as he starts up the trail toward New Jerusalem. "Come. Come, you can recount your tales on the way. We can relive the love and mercy of our magnificent creator as we go to his feast. Time to go further up and further into His glorious kingdom." The two former soldiers follow happily.

* * * * *

Upon reaching the city on the hill, Præsidiel presents Ioannes and Cælius light blue tunics with white linen togas, which is more suitable attire for the upcoming coronation and feast. He then escorts them both into an indescribably lavish Romanesque banquet hall.

---

[17] "The Lord be with you!" (translated from Latin).

[18] "And also with you!" (translated from Latin).

Elaborate tapestries hang from high walls, supported by massive, ornate pillars. High, vaulted ceilings are covered with frescos honoring the Holy Trinity. Many tables fill the hall. Some are short, Middle Eastern tables, while others are long, European-style tables. A magnificent bounty fills each one.

Some souls recline at table, others sit in tall chairs, while still more stand in joyful conversation. The blending of peoples and cultures from all over the world is striking. The great hall is filled with gleeful chatter praising God in the highest.

Angels escort souls to the hall and help them find a place at the table for the celebratory feast. Præsidiel shows Ioannes and Cælius to seats at a long, low table. Both men look around at others coming to sit. One such soul is the Chief, whom Ioannes met at the crossroads.

He carries his headdress under his arm at his side. Ioannes jumps up to meet him, “Hello again, my friend. Please excuse my earlier manners; I am Ioannes. I was hoping we might meet again.”

The Chief smiles, but before they can have a conversation, a loud click is heard: the latch of a large door.

Every angel, every soul, grows silent. Those who were reclining or sitting now stand. All eyes turn their attention to the two enormous, opulent marble doors at the end of the room as they swing open.

The purest bright light shines through the gap, filling the room with God’s holy light. The silhouette of Jesus appears in the light. He raises his hands, and the light shines through the holes in them. He declares, “Welcome, good and faithful servants! Welcome to the joy of your Father’s house!”

GUARDIAN OF THE LIGHTNING SEEDS

Contents

Prelude

Fruit of the Tree of Life

Fire crackles and embers rise swiftly and gently to the starlit night sky. Firelight dances around, casting shadows on the surrounding trees and rocks. An old chieftain and a young man sit silently on opposite sides of the fire. Though weary, the old chief sits up straight and still, his legs crossed in front of him. He stares at the fire. His once blazing, brown eyes are fixated on the tips of the flame as they dance in the night sky. The jet-black hair of his youth has turned almost silver but is still clean, neatly braided, and rests on each shoulder.

Many seasons have come and gone for him. He has walked many lands, seen the profound beauty of Mother Nature, and fought against the darkest of evils. Etched in the wrinkles that now cover his brown-skinned face is the wisdom of his age, the experience of a good life. His old fingers lay gently upon the weathered spirit stick across his lap. The short staff has deep and long burn marks at its base with strange markings (蛍 雷 光) near its top. An enormously long and mysterious black feather with a blue tip and a white edge all along its inner vane is tied with a leather strip from the top of it. The feather is as long as the spirit stick itself.

"The embers dance like fireflies," the chief says softly and slowly. "They remind me of another time. They remind me of my brother-friends, the Hotaru-Raikō[19], and my quest as a young warrior. The embers also remind me that my time here

---

[19] Pronounced ho-tar-oo rheye-koh - (Horaru is firefly and Raikō is lightning, translated from Japanese).
Not an actual word combination in Japanese, this is author's name for these unique characters.

is at an end." His old eyes focus through the fire onto the young man sitting across from him, who listens with an open mouth and gleaming eyes.

"It is your time now, Elu[20]. You have completed your rites of passage into manhood and must take up the mantle of protector when I go."

"Of the lightning seeds, Grandfather?" He says a bit eagerly.

"Yes. Those and your tribe. You have learned the sacred value of both. We are unique amongst other tribes. Our history and our charge to protect the lightning seeds make us so. You are a man now, Elu, and if you are to be wise, you must know the full history of our tribe and how we came to protect the lightning seeds."

Chief Hania pauses for a moment. "Let me take you back to the beginning."

* * * * *

All life comes from the Great Mysterious One. He set Father Sun and Mother Earth in the sky and blessed their union. The undying warmth of Father Sun entered the bosom of Mother Earth, who conceived both flora and fauna. The Great Spirit poured out all his goodness into the land, the water, and the sky. Then he created the first man. In the beginning, First Man was good and was at peace in the unspoiled lands. Though he lived in harmony with beast and plant, he was lonely. Little Boy Man was created, and First Man became Elder Brother.

Elder Brother was content in teaching and guiding Little Boy Man from infancy to manhood. All the animal tribes loved Little Boy Man because he was friendly and kind. He, in turn,

---

[20] Name means "full of grace."

learned their ways and language. They were all happy until the evil spirit came.

Unk-to-mee, the spider, the troublemaker, the deceiver, saw Little Boy Man grow in wisdom and ingenuity. He feared man would be the master of all animals. So he convinced all the animal tribes to turn against man. Unk-to-mee brought war upon the earth, forever dividing the trail between man and animal. Elder Brother saw this treachery and gave Little Boy Man bow, arrow, war club, and spear. With these weapons, he easily repelled his enemy. Soon after the defeat of Unk-to-mee, Boy Man entered a second battle, this time with the elements.

In autumn, Elder Brother and Boy Man prepared a warm tent and stored food for the winter. So much snow fell that winter that only the tips of man's teepee poles could be seen in the cold snow. The fierce and famished animal tribes finally came to kill Man, but they were stopped by Father Sun, who melted the snow, causing a great flood. Elder Brother and Young Man rode out the flood waters in their birch bark canoe while only a few animal tribes were saved. In the end, man had finally conquered animal and withstood the elements.

The Great Spirit was disturbed by the wars and violence, however. As punishment, he denied Elder Brother, Man, and all the animal tribes access to the tree of life, the fruit of which gives eternal life to those who eat of it. The tree of life grows from the light of the creator himself. Its trunk of light once grew in turquoise-laden rocks. Its branches danced and spun in many upward directions. Its canopy was the clouds, which, like the seasons, changed colors each day with the sunrise and sunset. Fireflies with dark bodies, burgundy heads, and gray wings danced in the lush, grassy fields around it, flashing their bright golden lights in gratitude for both the life they had been given and for each other's company.

The tree bore the most amazing fruit in those days, round and lightning filled. They sparkled in the canopy. Unfortunately, it was ripe with fruit when it became forbidden. The Great Spirit sent his servants to harvest the lightning seeds from it. Then he placed fierce, winged warriors around the tree so man could not return to it. The great tree remained dormant until the price for man and animal transgressions was paid.

Many seasons passed. Peace returned between the descendants of Boy Man and the land they wandered. Knowledge of the tree and its location was lost to them. However, the creator, who still loves his children, sought a relationship with Man again. He looked down upon his creation and saw our ancestors. He was truly pleased with how well they lived in harmony with the world. Because they were honorable, peaceful, and just, he entrusted the lightning seeds to our clan as a sign of confidence. The winged warrior who brought them instructed our ancestors to keep them safe and hidden. Planting them was forbidden. The creator said he would come back for the seeds one day. He would sow them and, at the appropriate time, harvest a bounty of fruit to be given to his faithful children so they might live forever.

Before even First Man, there was another mighty winged warrior, a servant in the Great Mysterious One's presence. His name was Lucifer, which meant light bearer. He witnessed all the creator made but took no pleasure in it. Envy and resentment blackened his heart. He wanted the creator's power and title—to rule over Father Sun, Mother Earth, and all of creation. Lucifer rebelled but could not defeat the creator. He was cast down, plummeting from the sky to the underworld like a bolt of lightning. He lost all his light as he fell, becoming the bearer of darkness instead. He was forever exiled from the spirit lands.

Brooding in his emptiness, the evil spirit contemplated ways to corrupt Man and the lands he inhabited. He used Unk-to-mee to sow mistrust among the animal tribes and start the first wars. After the flood and over the ages, he sent disease upon the land and into the animals. He poisoned the waters and the fish that swam in them. He corrupted the spirits of weak men—teaching them evil magic and instilling selfishness, jealousy, and hatred of their brothers and sisters in their hearts. In time, he learned about the gift of the lightning seeds to our ancestors. From then on, his desire to steal them was insatiable. The evil spirit wanted to grow his own perverse grove rooted in the rotten soil of his hell, twisting and corrupting their fruit. The fruit from his trees of ruin would bring death, destruction, and damnation to all who ate of it.

The evil spirit searched for many moons before learning the lightning seeds were hidden deep in the heart of our dwellings at Mesa Verde.

Chapter One

Thief in the Night

Many generations of warriors guarded the lightning seeds, keeping them safe and hidden. Tribe members knew each warrior's identity because they were always given names of a powerful element like *Sacred Wind* or *Rain Bringer*. Their dress was always adorned with some elemental symbolism too. Over time, however, their number dwindled, and the defense of the seeds became complacent; relaxed. In time, they fell under the care of Chief Ouray[21], who felt the lightning seeds were hidden well enough and that his tribe had more significant worries than the creator's seeds. Besides, his son, Notah[22], was preparing for his rites of passage into manhood.

As is tradition, Notah's mother gave him over to his father at the age of eight to begin his warrior training. His grandfather passed on the knowledge of the seeds to him at the age of ten. He also taught him tribal history, traditions, and even a little humor. Notah's uncle taught him how to navigate the land, hunt, and fight. His father taught the boy how to understand the moods of Mother Nature, how to forage from her bounty, and trade with other clans and tribes. He also instructed Notah on diplomacy—how to keep peace and prepare for war. The inquisitive youth listens attentively to their instruction with reverent silence.

Notah is an average fifteen-year-old. He is a wiry youth, full of energy. He keeps his hair braided, always wearing a simple cloth headband to keep his hair back and the sweat

---

[21] Pronounced oh-rey. The name means "the arrow" (Also the name of a great Ute Chief circa mid to late 1800s).

[22] Pronounced no-tah. The name means "almost there."

out of his eyes. Although patient, he is eager to complete the eneepee (vapor bath) and enter manhood. But, unbeknownst to him, his trial will be more extraordinary than anyone expects.

The evil spirit had sent his minor servants, who came in many forms, to test the tribe's reactions and resolve. Finding their defense of the seeds lax, he sends his most cunning servant, Lost One, a skinwalker, to steal them. Lost One comes as brother coyote, the trickster, on a night with no moon. He slips quietly into their dwellings and past sleeping tribesmen. His acute sense of smell sniffs out the prize. He quickly finds the sacred room and opens the creaking door just enough to slip past. In the darkness, the seed's white, subtle glow emanates from the most ornate, bowl-shaped basket Notah's ancestors had ever weaved.

Lost One approaches the basket. He removes the leather bags he carries over his back with his mouth and sits them beside the table where the basket rests. He awkwardly stands on his hind legs, reaching for and grasping the basket with his front paws. He clumsily pours the contents into the bags and then tosses the basket into the corner. He doesn't notice the seed that falls, landing in the sand beside his pack. He covers the flaps of the bags and then, using his long nose, part the backs of the bags and slips through the arch so they once again rest on his back. When he turns to leave, his paw twists more sand on top of the dropped seed, hiding it.

He nudges the door open, widening the gap enough for his now full packs to fit through. As Lost One cautiously slips past the door, a young brave, woken by the scuffling sounds, notices the coyote coming out of the forbidden room. He raises his torch to get a better look and sees the packs on the large coyote's back and his odd eyes. They do not reflect light the same as a regular coyote. Instead, they look like a man's eyes. The courageous young warrior knows something is wrong. Though he fears the skinwalker, his courage is stronger. He draws his knife from its sheath and rushes toward the coyote. Lost One quickly exits, angered by his discovery. The brave gives chase, yelling a loud war cry to wake the tribe. Unfortunately, it is not long before he loses sight of the wily coyote in the darkness.

Several tribesmen search the grounds for the coyote but to no avail. He has already made his escape in the dark, moonless night. It is nearly daybreak when Chief Ouray inspects the forbidden room where the seeds are kept. He opens the door and stands with sadness at the room's desecration. He knows he has failed the creator but does not know what to do next. He bends down to pick up the discarded basket when a glint of light catches his eye. He scoops up a handful of sand with the remaining seed in it. Blowing the dust from his palm, he stares at the luminous seed glowing there. It has been years since he has taken the time to look closely at one. It is the shape of a maize kernel but with a thin, translucent outer skin. Tiny arcs of lightning flash within its soft white shell, making it flicker. It is more beautiful than any precious stone.

He decides to plant the last seed in a moment of fear and doubt. He thinks if he can bring a new tree to fruition, he can replace the lost seeds and avoid any calamity descending upon his people. But, unfortunately, many generations had passed since the creator's emissary had visited the tribe, so the chief, in his momentary weakness, did not think the growth and harvesting of a single, small tree would be noticed.

Chief Ouray calls for the tribal healer, Wounded Crow, and the elders to don their ceremonial dress and gather at the foot of Mesa Verde to conduct a rain dance in the early morning. Notah is not invited to participate in the dance; however, since he has begun the rites of passage into manhood, his father instructs him to come close and watch. The elders, and other respected tribesmen, gather around a small, open patch of land. Notah sits near a sage bush on a little hill near the site. It is both close and high enough that he can see the ritual in all its ceremony.

The Chief and the healer stand on opposite sides of the dry patch of land. Ouray approaches the center with the glowing seed in hand. He gently plants it there before moving back to the edge of the outcropping. A drumbeat begins slowly. The two men step toward each other, back, and then turn. They begin to dance slowly around the seed. Rhythmic chanting accompanies the circular dance. Wounded Crow's dance purifies the land, while the chief calls for life-giving rains.

The patch of ground appears to take on a light tan color as rain clouds move slowly over the cliffs. The tribe continues their rhythmic drumming, chanting, and dancing until the first drops of cool rainfall. The ground turns darker with saturation. Then, sizzling, sparkling, and crackling, a small piece of light breaks through the surface of the sand. The elders continue the ritual. Crooked light shoots skyward like slow-moving lightning.

Unlike normal lightning, though, it does not give way to the thunder that follows typically; it stays connected to the ground. A small white fire burns around the base of its trunk. The bolt grows outward. The blazing tree forms branches of static white light. Storm clouds are caught up in the limbs, forming the tree's canopy. Wounded Crow, spirit stick in hand, and Chief Ouray continues dancing around the edges of the flashing trunk. Arcs of the purest white light randomly connect with the healer's staff, leaving burnt streaks on one end. *It is working*, thinks the young Notah observing with wonder. *The seed is producing an enormous tree*.

Without any warning, the tree implodes with a mighty thunderclap. An outflowing ring of sound reverberates through Notah's chest and knocks him and everyone else to the ground. Elders, tribesmen, Wounded Crow, and Chief Ouray are all thrown several feet away from where the tree of lightning once stood. Even a few pine and juniper trees nearby are toppled by the soundwave. Notah wipes the settling dust from his eyes. Presently, the sky is completely clear again. Standing on the glass-like ground at the center of the open ground in the tree's place is a mighty winged warrior.

He is easily two heads taller than the tribe's tallest warrior. He is of a race Notah does not know. His arms are crossed, and his enormous, brilliant white wings stretch upward to his right and left. He wears a deep blue armor (the likes of which Notah has never seen) over a light gray shirt. His belt is gold, with a long sheath hanging from it. *Is this the legendary "Wind Walker" who visited my ancestors?* Wonders Notah, still wiping the dust from his eyes. The visitor unfolded his arms, tucked his wings against his back, and walked swiftly toward Chief Ouray, who kneeled on the ground in reverence after raising himself out of the dirt. It will be the only time Notah, or any other tribesman, sees his father kneel.

The angel stands over the chief momentarily before sternly saying, "Do you know what you have done, Ouray? Did you think it was you who brought the rain? No! It is the Great Spirit who sends the rain when you dance. Did you think he would not notice why you asked for the rain; or what you were trying to do? Were you not told that planting the lightning seeds was forbidden? Seeds from the Tree of Life were yours to protect; they are neither yours to plant nor yours to reap from. You have disobeyed the Great Spirit."

Chief Ouray has no words. He turns his head downward in regretful silence. Wind Walker takes a deep breath, leans down, and lifts him from the dirt. His tone softens, "My friend, you have lost all of the lightning seeds," he said with great sadness. "You were not vigilant; you let a thief take them from your home. The Creator is disappointed and justifiably angered," he pauses.

The chief humbly lifts his head. "I know now I have done a great wrong, Wind Walker. I have broken my tribe's ancestral treaty and will accept my fate. I ask only that he does not curse my people."

Wind Walker sighs. "The Creator is merciful. You shall not die, nor shall your people be cursed." He pauses again in uncomfortable silence. "However, because you have shown such open disregard for the trust he put in your people, you must make amends. Here, in Mesa Verde, your people have become unbalanced. So, your tribe must leave this place and never return. It is time for your people to travel with the seasons once more. It would be best if you trusted in the land to know that your people will be provided what they need to live. Accordingly, you will be blessed with a vision of a land north of here. You will lead your people there. Furthermore, you must send your only son" –without even looking in his direction, Wind Walker lifts his mighty arm and points to where Notah hides among the sage– "Notah to recover the seeds without delay."

Notah drops down to the ground in shock. He stares at his father, who turns his head toward the boy, then down for a moment. They both know they cannot argue or sway Wind Walker if they are to keep the tribe safe. The task would not only be just punishment for the chief's misdeed but would become Notah's rite of passage into manhood. Though he does not show it, the boy pushes his fear deep down. The uncertainty and great unknown of the task weigh heavily upon him.

Chief Ouray looks back up at the angel. "It will be done as you say."

"Chief Ouray," Wind Walker reassures, "I know you have been preparing Notah to become a man. You have taught him properly. He knows your people's kinship with the land and animal tribes. You have taught him how to fish, hunt, forage, and clothe himself. You have taught him how to fight and to survive. You have taught him to see the sacred spirit in all things. Still, I see the concern in your eyes." Wind Walker makes a long pause. "He will not go alone. I will call warriors from the Hotaru-Raikō clan to accompany him." The chief looks inquisitively at the angel.

Wind Walker turns toward me. He motions with his hand. "Come here, Notah." The chief's son stands and approaches with fearful respect. He feels like a small child standing amidst giants. Wind Walker leans toward him. He places his mighty hand on the youth's shoulder, saying in a low tone, "You have little time; Lost One is swiftly moving west. Retrieve your bow, a full quiver, knife, netting, and blanket. Fill a pack with two water skins and two days' provisions. Return here as soon as you are finished. Go."

Notah runs as fast as he can to his dwelling in Mesa Verde. His mind races as fast as his legs carry him. He does not question the instructions; instead, he obeys willingly because he knows the task will be completed for his tribe, not just himself. Nor does he think to pause and take a last look at his home, even though he knows deep down it will be the last time he sees it.

"Chief Ouray, tell your elders to prepare your tribe for the journey," instructs Wind Walker. "They are to take only what they need to survive, no unnecessary possessions. You will leave on the second sunrise from today." The chief turns and walks calmly to where the elders had gathered. They are close enough to have overheard Wind Walker, but the Chief gives them more detailed instructions and assigns specific tasks. They nod in silent agreement and return to the rest of the tribe.

Only Chief Ouray and Wounded Crow remain with Wind Walker until Notah returns. They stand in silence, listening to Wind Walker. "If Notah is successful, your tribe will return to its nomadic life, moving with the seasons and flowing with the land again. You will be blessed with descendants who will create new, beautiful baskets to keep the seeds safe and hidden." So much of the day has passed. Notah realizes Father Sun is already past his peak when he finally returns.

"Good," says Wind Walker as he approaches. "I will call the Hotaru-Raikō now." He faces west. The sun still shows brightly in the clear blue sky. He raises his left hand and says in a loud but low octave, "Detekuru[23]!" His voice echoes down the canyon. He then turns back toward Notah, leaning down slightly, and gives him instructions for the journey.

"Notah, you are to journey to the place called Tomesha[24]. You know of this place, yes?"

"Yes," he answers.

"An old dead tree still stands in the desolate basin there. You will know it as soon as you see its petrified remains. At its base is an entrance to the ancient underground city named Shin-au-av[25]. The one you know as Lost One stole the lightning seeds and travels now to hide them there. You must enter the cavernous city, which has been claimed by wickedness, find, and retrieve the seeds. I have called the Hotaru-Raikō to aid you in your journey."

He pauses momentarily, then directs, "Along the way, I want you to weave a basket of sweet, agave fibers to carry the seeds in. You may include other plants, but the basket must be something worthy to hold such a prize, something you can carry on your back too."

Wind Walker looks up and points at the sky. Then, in a very somber voice, he says, "The evil spirit plans to lay claim to the seeds when the next full moon rides high in the sky. You, son of Ouray, must accomplish this task before it rises. Do you understand?"

"Yes," Says Notah.

---

[23] Pronounced day-tay-kir-oo—"come forth!" (translated from Japanese).

[24] Ground afire, roughly translated from Shoshone aka Death Valley.

[25] God's land or Ghost land," roughly translated from Paiute.

"Use the tracking skills you were taught to pursue him there." Continues Wind Walker. "He is following the north side of the Old Age River[26]. You, too, should stay on the north side to avoid enemy tribes to the south. You must swim across Aha Kwahwat,[27] where it meets the Old Age River. After that, you should be able to pick his tracks back up on the north side of Aha Kwahwat. Stay out of the Great Canyon. When Aha Kwahwat turns south, you will continue due west thru Red Rock Canyon and across the eastern side of the Mojave to the Black Mountains. There you can enter Tomesha thru the Old Queen's Pass[28]."

A low humming sound slowly builds in the western canyons. Notah sees Wounded Crow search the horizon out of the corner of his eye, but Wind Walker pays neither him nor the sound any attention. Instead, he stands upright again and, looking deep into Notah's eyes, says, "Remember what your clan has taught you, young brave. Travel wisely. Keep sight of Brother Eagle in the sky. Not only will he help guide you westward, but he will also serve as a messenger between you and the Great Spirit. If you need help, ask. The creator will send it." He smiles at the chief's son and then turns his eyes westward.

Those gathered listen to the sound of buzzing growing louder in the valley. Father Sun sinks lower in the crisp spring sky, turning a dark orange as it settles between the mountains to the west. Coming down out of the dusky sky are many small white lights. At first, they look like a swarm of small stars, swerving and flickering as they move through the river valley. They travel up the ancient riverbed, swirling about like fireflies until they get close. Though they move like them, Notah's keen eye sees they are not fireflies. He catches

---

[26] Aka San Juan River

[27] Aka Colorado River

[28] Aka Dante's view

a short glimpse of them as they hum past. The Hotaru-Raikō appear human in form but fly on insect wings. The swarm rises into the pink and purple sky before landing on the cliff edge over Mesa Verde.

Wind Walker goes to a nearby cottonwood tree. One of the swarm breaks away and comes down to greet him with a bow. Although only 8 to 10 inches tall, the Hotaru-Raikō are clearly a warrior class. Their leader dresses in armor unfamiliar to Notah. Every part of his body is covered except for his eyes and hands. Upon landing, he tucks long insect-like wings behind his back while simultaneously untying a long, decorative, dark red rope holding his metal helmet and face mask on, both of which are dark red. He removes them, exposing his pale-colored face, places them at his side, and then bows again, lower this time, to Wind Walker.

When he stands, Notah quietly inspects his armor. Much of his chest, shoulder, waist, and leg armor is made of overlapping pieces like scales on a snake. Almost all of it is black. Parts of his leg armor glint white in the twilight, almost like a firefly. He wears a sleeveless, thigh-length overcoat over his armor. It is dark gray and trimmed in white. Running horizontally through his dark belt are two long swords. He has all the coloring of an actual firefly but is human in appearance.

The tiny warrior speaks with Wind Walker in a language unknown to those present. Wind Walker turns to look at the young brave while the warrior keeps his attention on the angel. "Notah, come here." The young brave immediately walks to his side. Wind Walker motions with his right hand toward the strange warrior. "This is Takeda Kenshin. He is Daimyō[29]; the Hotaru-Raikō's leader. You will show him much respect." Notah nods in silence.

---

[29] Pronounced die-eem-yo—"feudal lord" (translated from Japanese).

He returned the introduction, "Takeda-san, this Notah. Son of Chief Ouray. His name means "almost there."

Takeda quickly inspects the young brave, then lets out a half grunt, half laugh. "Hrmph. We will bring him the rest of the way, Oyakata[30]," His words catch Notah off guard. Instead of being somewhat insulted by his tone, he is in awe of understanding what he said.

Wind Walker looks down at Notah and, probably because of the stunned look on his face, lets out a short chuckle. No one had ever heard him laugh before. "Ha, ha. I know you will, my friend. I know you will. Go, prepare your samurai and ashigaru[31]." He then turns to me, smiles, and says, "From now on, you will understand his language, and he yours. This is so you can accomplish the task at hand. Takeda Kenshin is a seasoned warrior and a good leader. Learn from him as you have learned from your tribesmen. They may not be as big as you, but you can trust him with your life; he will defend you."

He places his hand on Notah's shoulder. "You will learn about each other on your journey. Your people and theirs share many traits and customs. The Hotaru-Raikō are uniquely suited to this journey as they, too, are used to living between wilderness and water. If you rely on each other, you will succeed, Notah. Also," he says, slightly adjusting the leather strap of the brave's quiver, "when the time comes, the creator will send his spirit to you so you may be strong of heart. Now, say farewell to your father; it is time to leave."

He goes to his father, Chief Ouray. The son does his best to show no fear. His father places his hands upon his shoulders, looks deep into his eyes, and affirms, "I know you will make amends for our tribe, my son. I have faith in you.

---

[30] Pronounced oh-yee-ah-kata—"master" (translated from Japanese).

[31] Pronounced ah-shee-gah-ru—"Japanese foot soldiers."

When I see you again, you will be a man." He pats his shoulders and then releases him.

Notah turns to leave, but Wounded Crow, who has been silent the whole time, calls out to him. The young brave turns back to see the tribal healer holding out his spirit stick, which he used during the rain dance. "Notah, take this with you. It will protect you."

Wounded Crow approaches and slowly places the short staff into Notah's quiver. The boy turns around to face him. "You have been preparing for manhood and your vision quest." He pauses. "This journey will fulfill all the tasks which will initiate the dream. When you return to us, I suspect you will have found your purpose and the answers to many questions. We will offer a pipe of gratitude when you return. Go now." He turns and walks back to stand at the chief's side. Notah looks one last time at his father, who smiles back, then holds up his hand in farewell.

All the Hotaru-Raikō have already left the cliff top and are flying west toward the setting sun. Only three of them stayed back, the Daimyō and two others. They hover a short distance in front of Notah. Takeda has tied his helmet and his fierce mask back on. He takes his spear from one of the other warriors and then motions to follow them, saying, "Yuko[32], Notah-kun."

---

[32] Pronounced yee-koh—"let's go" (translated from Japanese).

Chapter Two

Journey with the Hotaru-Raikō

Notah is dressed lightly and has little to carry, allowing a swift journey. He wears sturdy leather moccasins, leather pants, a cloth breechcloth tucked over his belt, and a lightweight buckskin shirt. His folded blanket lies over his right shoulder and is fastened in place with a second belt around his waist. This belt holds his knife, waterskins, and a small food pouch. His simple leather quiver and bow case also straddle his right shoulder.

After departing Mesa Verde, Notah follows the canyon as far south as he can in the dark that first night before finding a safe place for them all to rest. Still adjusting to each other's company, the group travels in relative silence the next day. A young brave is customarily expected to go out into nature alone as part of his rite of passage into manhood. This journey is different, however. Notah observes the Hotaru-Raikō carefully. His new companions are unlike anything he has ever seen in nature before. They watch Notah, too, trying to learn from his habits, tracking skills, and more. The silence that pervades the party is not due to mistrust; rather, it is a sense of unfamiliarity driving their quiet observation of each other. Deep down, they all know that trust is something to be earned over time.

The young brave knows the land north of Old Age River well. He follows the wash south to Wounded Hand River[33], which flows directly west into Old Age River. There, he can move quickly along the valley floor and out into open, flat lands where he can run slowly and steadily. He makes stops

---

[33] aka Mancos River

when necessary, but with the ability to fly, the Hotaru-Raikō easily stays close to him.

This journey is quite different from others he made with his father and uncle. Those trips had a simpler meaning, often hunting or trading expeditions with other tribes. They traveled slower then. He was taught to harmonize with Mother Nature and understand her movements on each trip. His father and uncle would constantly ask him questions about natural events to see if he could identify plants, animal tracks, water sources, weather patterns, etc. Confidence in his survival skills gives him peace, but the coming conflict to regain the lightning seeds gnaws at the back of his mind.

* * * * *

By the evening of the second day, the group exits the valley and enters the flat land west of Mesa Verde. They set up a small camp there just before sunset. Notah takes the time to point out edible plants to Takeda and his samurai, ensuring they can eat when they need to along the way. Only a tiny sliver of a moon is in the sky that night. Most of their light comes from a small campfire. Notah quietly nibbles on the pine nuts from his pouch and observes the star trail in the night sky. He wonders if it leads to the great beyond, to the spirit lands.

Sasaki Nakamura comes to sit on a tall stone by him. He says, "We notice you say very little, Notah-kun."

"I was taught it was better to listen and to watch if one wants to learn," replies Notah politely.

"Very good," he agrees, "I am Sasaki Nakamura. I am samurai." He gives a slight bow. "Thank you for showing us the cactus flower."

"You're welcome, Nakamura-san." Notah pauses. "Did I address you correctly?"

"Yes," Says Sasaki with a smile. The two go on to have a short conversation, which is watched by all, making them more comfortable with one another.

* * * * *

The next day, Notah washes in the river just before daybreak. He then stands upright and thanks Father Sun, who rises over his old home in the east. The bright rays warm his body and help him dry. He collects his gear, makes sure the fire is fully extinguished and scattered into the earth, and then departs slowly. He travels slowly at first. Although he could follow the winding Wounded Hand River to Old Age River, Notah decides to turn northwest and quicken his pace across the flat ground to save time. The party reaches what Notah believes is the Old Age River valley as the sun starts to set.

The next morning, they wake to cool spring air. A chilly dewfall blankets the camp, letting them know they are close to the river. Remembering Lost One would be traveling this way, and knowing he is a skinwalker, Notah begins to watch for mixed animal and human tracks as they travel west. If he can find cougar or coyote tracks interchanging with human tracks, then he will know he is on Lost One's trail.

Notah explains to the Daimyō and his samurai, Sasaki Nakamura, and Hatano Yoshimoto, how to look for the tracks and what they looked like. Sasaki and Hatano then pass the details on to their ashigaru.

It isn't long before one of them finds human tracks leading up to one side of a small stream, a tributary to the Old Age River, and coyote tracks departing the exact opposite side of it.

Lost One must have stopped to drink, rest, and change into a coyote to pick up speed. Thinks Notah.

The ashigaru split into two bands, each one led by one of the samurai. Now that they know what to look for, they alternate days searching and tracking Lost One's prints, which helps Notah travel confidently. Working together to track the enemy also builds further trust and confidence among them.

* * * * *

Old Age River turns south slightly before returning north into a large bend. There is high, flat ground between a tributary and the Old Age River. After the bend, the river turns south again before flowing west and running into Aha Kwahwat. Notah decides to leave the river valley to travel southwest straight across that higher ground. Since the river might be slightly higher from spring flooding, crossing well north of the confluence will be easier at a narrower bend.

He soon finds a suitable spot between a northern tributary and the confluence. The water is swift but not too deep. If it were summer, this section of the river would be a simple, deep-water fording. Notah points out a narrow crack in the canyon rim on the western side of the river leading back up to higher ground[34]. "That is where we can reach the high, flat ground again," he says. Takeda agrees to lead the ashigaru to scout the path up the canyon. Sasaki and Hatano volunteer to stay with Notah as he crosses the fast waters. The Daimyō directs warriors in his party to carry Notah's bow, full quiver, blanket, and clothes over the river. They will keep everything dry. He is grateful for their kindness too. He strips down to his breechcloth and moccasins while a few ashigaru collect his gear and head across the river behind Takeda.

Notah heads upstream a little way because he knows the water will carry him downriver as he crosses. He stops on the bank and casts a stick upstream. He then observes how fast

---

[34] See Hole-in-the-Rock, Utah

the rushing water carries it past. He wades in. The water is cool and refreshing. The deeper he goes, the more he can feel it push against his legs. He knows he will be swept off his feet once he is chest-deep. He pauses waist-deep in the water for a moment. He looks up to see Sasaki and Hatano hovering ahead; they nod to give him confidence.

He looks downstream, once more targeting his goal, before plunging into the river and swimming. The water instantly carries him away like the stick. He swims slightly into the current as strongly as he can, but it feels like he is going downstream faster than he is crossing. He fights against the swift water. Determined to make it across, he concentrates on his strokes and breathing when he can. He puts all his strength into it.

Although only two or three minutes have passed, Notah feels like he has been struggling against the current for a long time. He is running out of energy quickly. His arms and legs smack the water like brother beaver's tail when warning strangers. The samurai call out, letting him know he is near the bank. He quickly lifts his head to get his bearings before dropping his foot. Relieved, he feels the ground below. However, it is still too deep to walk, so he makes a final push, half swimming and bouncing on the riverbed. He is finally able to stand in the river. He is breathing heavily; his arms and legs are weak, and he can barely stand against the rushing water.

Notah ascends the bank slowly, stopping thigh-deep in the river. With his hands at his waist and water dripping from his entire body, he bends over to catch his breath. He stands back upright and looks around. He has gone past his goal, but not too far. He trudges onto the dry riverbank, turns, and flops down upon his rear in the loose gravel. He is exhausted. The samurai land close by. Sasaki says, "You did well, Notah-kun."

Notah, still breathing hard, nods in gratitude. "Now you know what it is like for us to fly into a strong headwind." And the two samurai chuckle. "Kuru[35], the clan waits for us at the top of the pass." They take wing, and Notah slowly rises to his feet and follows them up the bank toward the gap in the canyon wall.

* * * * *

Notah, exhausted after crossing the river, decides to make camp early. He collects his blanket, bow, quiver, and clothes. He thanks the ashigaru for safely carrying it to the canyon wall's top. Finding a small pinyon pine tree, he removes his wet moccasins and breechcloth and hangs them over its branches. He places his dry blanket over his shoulder and wraps his knife belt around his waist, using the blanket to cover himself while his clothes dry.

He takes a few moments to observe his surroundings. *This will be good hunting grounds for rabbits, and for foraging,* he thinks to himself. It has been five days since he left Mesa Verde. He knows they are a third of the way there, so he decides to rest for a full day and restock his provisions. Fond memories of tribal rabbit drives come to mind; times when his people would congregate, socialize, dance, play games, and tell stories. He wants to share this joyous part of his culture with his newfound friends. He lets Takeda know his plans to rest and hunt.

A while later, after his clothes have dried and he is comfortably dressed, Notah goes down into a small ravine to string his nets between two small shrubs. He gathers the Hotaru-Raikō and explains how their ability to fly and speed will help chase rabbits into those nets. "We must be quick and

---

[35] Pronounced koo-roo—"come" (translated from Japanese).

wily, like brother hare," he says as he draws the image of their tracks into the sand.

Notah teaches the ashigaru how to find them before sending them out on scouting parties. While they hunt, the Daimyō and two samurai help Notah forage for wild spinach, cactus blossoms, and other edibles to share.

The ashigaru find and enthusiastically funnel three rabbits toward the netting; Notah joins in the chase. Just as the wild hare enter the nets, one of the squad leaders, whose name is Hasegawa, gets distracted. He flies into the side of a branch and tumbles down into the net. Not noticing him, the rest of the ashigaru quickly pull the corners of the net together. Notah jumps on the netting, quickly gathers the loose ends, and cinches them tightly. Hasegawa is now amongst the captured hare bundled on the ground. Notah, still holding the netting down, sees him and yells, "What are you doing? Get out of there! I cannot kill them until you're out of the way!"

Hasegawa grabs onto one of the rabbit's ears in the chaos. The ear immediately flops downward. He cannot hold on to the soft fur and begins to slide. The rabbit kicks at him with his hind foot, knocking him off. Now loose in the netting, Hasegawa is pummeled by the frantic rabbits. He tries desperately to fight back, although he doesn't know what part of the rabbit he is fighting. He avoids their sharp teeth, but his kicks and punches do not affect the rabbits. All the while, the net tumbles, twists, and turns while fur flies out.

Hasegawa is kicked hard in the stomach and decides to give up the fight. Escape quickly becomes preferable; however, he is sandwiched between two of the rabbit's sides. He reaches up and grasps the netting. Two ashigaru fly to the top of the net and reach for him. They grasp his arms and pull him partway through the mesh, but the pole holding the banner on his back gets caught, preventing them from pulling him out. The rabbits kick and jostle the netting. Finally,

Hasegawa lets go of his friends and finds himself pinned sideways against the net. He scoots his lower body around and pushes his feet through an opening. His friends fly down to grab hold of his feet and yank him awkwardly through. They all land in the dusty sand; their uniforms are entirely disheveled and covered in rabbit fur.

Notah quickly clubs the rabbits, killing them. Then, a little short of breath, he stands and looks down at Hasegawa and his two friends. They're busy wiping sand and fur from themselves. Takeda, Hatano, Sasaki, and the other ashigaru, who had watched everything unfold from the branches around the netting, laughed wholeheartedly at the trio. Notah, taking a second to think about what just happened, lets out a chuckle too. He sets his club down, offers his hand to them, and says, "Ah, you did well for your first hunt, little brothers."

Hasegawa, looking up in humble uncertainty, accepts the gesture. Notah slings the rabbits over his shoulder with his other hand and raises Hasegawa in his palm. The humble warrior collects himself while riding in Notah's hand back to the camp.

Later, at the little river feast, as it came to be known, Notah gives solemn thanks to brother rabbit's sacrifice, that they might all be nourished. He then prepares a meal for his new brother-friends, the Hotaru-Raikō. After the meal, Takeda, Hasegawa, and a few others eat nectar from the flowering cacti while Sasaki and Hatano spar with others using wooden sticks. Those around the fire tease Hasegawa, who openly laughs at his misfortune of being caught with the rabbits and fighting with them. Notah laughs, too, and says, "It is customary to receive a new name when a warrior achieves a great feat. To me, Hasegawa will always be known as 'Wrestles with Hare.'" Notah smiles fondly at his new friend, Hasegawa.

"Goi sa reta[36]," confirms the Daimyō in a deep voice.

Hasegawa humbly answers, "Hai[37]." Then, they both begin to laugh.

Notah and the rest of the ashigaru join in. Word of his new name spreads quickly among the rest that evening. They all held that night in high regard, recounting and laughing about the event throughout the rest of the journey.

Notah's laughter subsides as he looks up. He observes the simple but elegant waxing crescent moon low in the dark, starlit sky. He has made good time so far. However, the distance is great, and there is still much to be done.

* * * * *

It was early morning on the sixth day of the trek. They again wake to cool, spring air. A wet, chilly dewfall has extinguished the fire, and the cool morning air is invigorating. Notah rekindles the fire from still-warm coals buried under the ash. Takeda, Hatano, Sasaki, and a few others gather around to warm themselves for the coming day's journey. Notah has taught his brother-friends something of his heritage but realizes he still has much to learn from them. So, with much eagerness, he asks, "Daimyō, I have so many questions. Will you teach me about your tribe? Where did you come from? How did you come into service of Wind Walker?"

"Hmph," grunts Takeda warming his hands by the small fire. "So many questions, Notah-kun. However, if you agree to let me ride on your shoulder, I will be your sensei[38] for today's journey."

---

36 Pronounced go-ee-sah-reh-tah—"agreed." (translated from Japanese).

37 Pronounced hi-ee—"yes." (translated from Japanese).

38 Pronounced sen-say—"teacher" (translated from Japanese).

Notah readily agrees, gathers his things, and breaks camp. The party heads southwest on the high ground overlooking the river in the valley below. The Daimyō lights upon the blanket over Notah's right shoulder. He sits with his legs hanging in front of Notah's shoulder and supports himself by holding onto the bow sticking out of his bow case and quiver. It proves to be a comfortable place to be as they travel.

Takeda tells him the history of his people:

"We were there, in the beginning, when the first man was sent out of the garden into the earth. My clan once danced in the lush, grassy fields around the great, white Tree of Life. We brewed the most delicious tea from the leaves that fell from it. This is what gives us our long lives. We often celebrated our existence, lands, and love for Kami[39], the one you know as the Great Spirit, with elaborate tea ceremonies. But unfortunately, it was our pride and our quest for the perfect cup of tea that led to our downfall. In our pride, we made a shimmering, white tea from new leaves on the Tree of Life.

"What we did not understand was that it was Kami who made the leaves fall for us. We had no right to pluck them from the tree. We dishonored Him by taking what was his and not respecting the gift he already gave us. He was offended, and we were disgraced. But, like your father, he showed us mercy. Instead of casting us down as he did the evil spirit, he only sent us out of the garden to serve our smaller cousins. My clan was sent to a land called Nihon[40]. We pledged our lives in service to our Hotaru cousins to make up for our poor judgment. We became warriors and guardians in the court of a great Hotaru lord. Our cousins do not have human forms like us but still have many of the same customs.

---

[39] Pronounced kahm-ee—"God" (translated from Japanese).

[40] Pronounced nee-hohn—"Japan" (translated from Japanese).

"Eventually, we came to live and serve on the south, and more sunny side, of the Fukui castle moat. The water there is shallow, and the lotus lilies grow large and luxuriant.

The Lord of the Fireflies, whose name is Hi-o, lives deep in the heart of one of the great pink flowers. He has only one daughter, the lovely princess Hotaru-himé. She gave us the name Hotaru-Raikō because our light is white like lightning instead of the soft, golden glow they possess. While still a child, the princess was kept safely at home within the pink petals of the lily, never even going to the edges except to see her father fly off on his journeys. At least one of my samurai and two of my warriors always accompanied him to keep him safe.

"Every night, the fire glowed in Hotaru-himé's body. Her light grew brighter and brighter until it was as mellow as gold. Her light illuminated the lotus like a paper lantern in a globe of coral. She waited dutifully until she was of age, then her father said, 'My daughter is now ready, she may fly abroad with me, and when the proper suitor comes, she may marry whom she will.'

"So Hotaru-himé flew with her father in the twilight sky among the lotus lilies of the moat, then into rich rice fields, and at last far off to the western meadows. We proudly escorted them whenever she went for a crowd of suitors always followed. She had the remarkable power of attracting all the night-flying insects to herself; however, she cared not for their attention. Although she spoke politely to them all, she encouraged none.

"Upon her return, Hotaru-himé was arrayed in her most resplendent robes and set on the throne in the heart of the majestic lotus. There she awaited her suitors. The queen ordered us to keep them all at a respectful distance lest some foolish brute, dazzled by her light, should approach too near and hurt the princess or shake her throne.

"Suitor after suitor appeared, each in his own way, to woo the daughter of the King. Some were proud, some were humble, some were bold, and others meek. Some flattered or boasted, while others came with tears. Some sang to Hotaru-himé. Each offered his love, but regardless of their wooing, each received the same simple request, 'Bring me fire, and I will be your bride.'

"Each suitor, thinking he alone knew how to retrieve the fire she sought, sped away without telling his rivals. But none ever returned with fire nor won the princess's hand in marriage. Poor suitors! The lucky few only lost their antennae, scorched their shining bodies, or singed their powdered wings. Most perished in flame or oil. Their bodies lay black and cold the following day, dead from their foolish quests.

"Now, a young prince, who had recently ascended to the throne after his father's passing, ruled the north side of the castle moat and the fields beyond. His name was Hi-maro. He received word of the princess, her many suitors, and her request for fire. A noble and proper young firefly, Prince Hi-maro sent his emissary to King Hi-o, formally requesting permission to court his daughter. The king was pleased with the prince's courtesy and approved his courtship, with the single caveat that he, too, must fulfill his daughter's request for fire.

"Out of respect for both Hi-o and Hi-maro, I sent my two best samurai, Nakamura-san and Yoshimoto-san, whom you have met, and four of my bravest ashigaru to escort the Prince. They kept him and his glittering battalion safe from the frogs and toads in the moat. The night of his arrival saw the lotus palace aglow with the golden light of his army, yet their glorious blaze still paled next to the regal splendor of Hotaru-himé.

"Undaunted, Hi-maro entered the court of Hi-o. He opened his shell, filling the room with red, orange, and yellow lights, which danced on the walls of the lotus like the light of a fire. Driven by the passion in his heart for the lovely princess, the prince possessed a light, unlike any other Hotaru. The changing colors of his abdomen, like that of a flame, instantly attracted the eye of the princess. He approached her and humbly offered his hand for the dance. She eagerly but politely placed her hand in his and then looked to her father for approval."

Takeda pauses for a moment. "I was standing behind the throne that night overseeing the court. I saw what the king saw; Prince Hi-maro brought the princess the unquenchable fire of true love. There was deep happiness in her eyes and a glow upon her supple face. Hi-o nodded his approval with much satisfaction. The prince wooed the princess that very night and before he departed for his own kingdom, she agreed to marry him. They were married by the light of the next full moon, and their two kingdoms became one. A great peace came upon the tiny kingdom.

Soon after, Wind Walker called for us. It is Kami's desire for us to complete this great quest with you. By helping you retrieve the lightning seeds, we too may redeem ourselves in his sight."

"Thank you for the story. I am grateful to have you with me," says Notah. "I am still very curious, though; what are the weapons you carry? Why do you wear such ornate armor? What do the symbols on the poles your warriors wear on their backs mean?"

"Hrmm," grumbles Takeda, shaking his head, "so inquisitive. I will tell you more, but you must have patience, young Notah-kun. Let us enjoy this conversation."

"Yes, sensei," replies Notah.

"The long spears we carry are called jumonji yari, and the swords, long knives as you see them, are our uchigatana. Their blades glow white, with blue steel edges, because they are blessed with light from the Tree of Life. They can cut through any darkness or evil. Although they look like staffs because they are unstrung, some of my ashigaru carry a yumi or longbow. At camp, they sometimes train with a bokken or wooden sword."

"Our armor," Takeda continues, "is made in the typical fashion of all Nihon warriors with one exception, we wear the colors of our cousin, the Hotaru. The metal plates sown into our haidate, or thigh guards, will also glow with the same light as our blades at times.

There are ten ashigaru with poles holding banners attached to the backs of their armor; these banners are called sashimono. The design is far more ornate than you might find in Nihon." Takeda leans toward Notah's ear and whispers, "But we are not from Nihon." He sits back upright and smiles, "Squad leaders wear Sashimono. The squad leaders have five men each and follow the directions of their samurai. We are a small army of fifty-three warriors."

"The symbol is a beautiful, Kenshin-san. But what does it mean?" asks Notah.

"The sashimono is not only our clan symbol, but it also tells our story. The white banner represents the white of the Tree of Life, the light of Tengoku, or as you call it, the Spirit Lands. It is held to the pole by golden loops to signify our connection to our firefly cousins. A great mountain with a torii[41] on top to show we were once blessed and lived a higher calling. The lotus at the bottom of the mountain is our new home. It is all surrounded by the rising sun of Nihon." Takeda stands up on Notah's shoulder, holding his bow for stability.

---

[41] Pronounced tohr-ee—"gate" (translated from Japanese).

“We practice what is called Bushido, or the way of the warrior,” continues Takeda. “It is a code of honor and ideals that dictate our way of life. We are loyal to the creator and those placed over us by him until our death. We train in the mastery of martial arts, weaponry, and warfare, but also honor, duty, self-discipline, and self-sacrifice, tempered by wisdom, patience, and serenity. So what you see, Notah-kun are warriors, but we are more than that.” Takeda pauses and then, in a surprisingly soft yet proud voice, says, “We are also craftsmen, blacksmiths, farmers, artists, poets, monks, and teachers.”

“Thank you, sensei.” Notah, contemplating all that he has learned, is finally quiet. Takeda bows slightly and then stretches his smoke-colored wings out. He slowly takes flight and goes to speak with his samurai.

Wind Walker was right, thinks Notah, *my people, and the Hotaru-Raikō share so many qualities.*

He and Takeda will enjoy many more friendly discussions along the way, which make each day’s travel go by quickly. A deeper bond grows between them. The young brave’s confidence grows, and he is more determined to complete the task for the Great Spirit, his tribe, and his new brother-friends.

* * * * *

After crossing Aha Kwahwat, they continue to follow it southwest for three days. Notah knows the river makes many large, southward bends before returning to the northwest. After three days, he turns away from the river, taking the high ground due west, which saves valuable time. He reaches the north side of the great canyon in one day. There are several springs there. The expedition replenishes its provisions and continues due west until they reach the place where the Aha

Kwahwat flows south. Directly north of this southward turn is a place called Black Mesa. The Lowlands between feel like a natural gateway toward the desert.

Notah stops at the riverside to rest and refresh himself. He spots tracks that change from coyote to human and back to coyote there. The tracks are old and faded, but they are easily recognizable. The find lifts his spirit. *Lost One stopped here, too, before moving on.* He thinks to himself. *The Paiute people told of a large, lush spring northwest of the river bend called Painted Ground*[42]*. We can travel there for rest and provisions before winding through Red Rocks Canyon and crossing the desert to the Black Mountains.*

* * * * *

They traveled around the spring's southern side and made camp just west of it. Notah hunts for small game and fills his water skins in the spring, while the Hotaru-Raikō gather cactus and mesquite tree flowers. Later, Takeda, Sasaki, Hatano, and other ashigaru sit on rocks close to the campfire. Like warriors often do, they sip nectar and regale each other with stories from past adventures or battles. Of course, they also laugh about Hasegawa's battle with the netted rabbits. Notah greatly enjoys listening to all their tales; he learns much from them.

Everyone eats to a full belly, and things quiet down when Wrestles with Hare asks Notah for one of his people's stories. He happily obliges. "We will reach Tomesha in two moons," says Notah, "it is a desolate place now, but... it was not always so. I will tell you the story of how it came to be called ground afire." Only the crackling of the fire is heard as Notah begins his tale.

---

[42] aka Tule Springs

"According to an ancient legend, Tomesha was not always the dry, barren place it is now. The valley was once fertile and incredibly beautiful. Fresh water springs were many. A majestic lake filled the valley, surrounded by giant mesquite trees and lush vegetation. My ancestors settled around spring pools and meadows on the highlands. They grew many crops of corn, beans, squash, and sunflowers. They harvested mesquite seed pods, gathered pine nuts, and roamed the surrounding mountains, hunting deer and antelope. Their connection to the land was strong.

"In those days, they were called the Timbisha and were ruled by a beautiful queen. But she was vain, demanding, and desired a palace of her own—one greater than anything her neighbors to the South had ever built. So she ordered her people to build a palace. She forced them to transport magnificent stones and timber to the building site to construct it.

"Early on, the Timbisha worked hard to please their queen. They dragged and hauled stone and log over long distances. Considering it their duty, they did not complain because royalty was sacred. However, as the years passed, the queen feared she would die before the palace was completed. She became more and more demanding, even insisting that her family work alongside the rest of her tribe. Gradually, they became a tribe of slaves. The queen lashed their naked backs if they slowed during the noonday heat. She even flogged her daughter when she thought the girl was working too slowly.

"The princess dropped her load of stone upon being struck and turned on her mother, cursing her and the kingdom she sought to build. The princess then sank to the ground, overcome by heat and exhaustion, and died. Only then did the Queen realize how greed and obsession had corrupted her. She became painfully aware of how she had enslaved her people, subjugating a tribe rich in family values with a love of nature. Her remorse and insight came too late, however. The land also turned on her, punishing her for her wickedness and short-sightedness. The sun grew hotter and brighter, causing the plant life to wither, the lake to dry up, and the animals to flee.

"The once fertile valley was soon a scorched desert. Many Timbisha fled—those who stayed died of starvation. Eventually, only the queen and her half-finished palace remained. She was struck ill with a fever. She died alone in the parched valley with no one to soothe or care for her. Her empty palace crumbled, its stone and timber reclaimed by Mother Nature. It is said that spirits of the old warriors still haunt the land protecting weary travelers from the evil she allowed to consume the land."

His tale finished, Notah is keenly aware of the silence. The ashigaru contemplate the story. Takeda gives Notah a slight bow in gratitude for it. Notah warms himself by the small fire in the chilly night air for a short time and then returns to weaving his lightning seed basket. He looks up at the moon; it is more than half full now. They are running out of time.

* * * * *

Shadows dance on the valley floor as the sun turns the western sky gold, orange, and purple. The red and tan striped rocks change hues in the fading sunlight. Finally, they have all reached the other side of Red Rocks Canyon. The ground is leveling out, but it is also heating up. Notah thinks it better to rest now, sleep, and then wake up early to cross the desert under a darker, cooler sky. A little more than half full, the white moon rises between two peaks on the eastern mountains in the blue-gray evening sky.

He finds an old, twisting pinyon pine tree to make camp nearby. He places his blanket there and leans his quiver, bow, and mostly finished basket against the tree trunk. Notah makes a small fire and draws close while the rest look for good spots to rest. Though hot now, nights can be chilly under the dark wilderness sky. He returns to the tree, allowing others to close in on the fire. He leans against the sturdy trunk and stares up at the starlit sky. It has been a little more than two weeks since they departed.

He busies himself by crafting a round lid for his slightly elongated, almost cylindrical, basket. He has lined the inside of it with the rabbit pelts he cleaned. They will keep seeds from falling out and their light from showing when he travels. Next, he weaves a decorative medicine wheel on the lid using different parts of agave and other plants. Takeda approaches slowly on foot, climbs a rock near him, and sits, watching him work. "What design do you weave into the lid, Notah-kun?" he asks.

"It is called a medicine wheel." He continues to work as he speaks, "The sacred mysteries are contained with it. The outer circle of the wheel represents the outer boundary of the Earth. It represents the continuous pattern of life and death, the path of the sun and moon, and the shape of other parts of our culture.

The horizontal and vertical lines represent the sun's path and man's path. Where they cross is the center of the Earth. Man is at the center of it all. We strive to find balance and a connection between our physical, emotional, mental, and spiritual sides. We also strive for a connection to what was, what is, and what will be.

The East or red side represents the beginning, the ending, and the renewal. It represents the sunrise, the blossoming of spring, a light in the darkness—maybe the blossoming of a lotus flower?" He smiles at Takeda. "It is typically associated with the spirit world of light, of returning to our origin.

The South or yellow side represents the peak of the sun's journey through the sky. The South receives the most light. It is responsible for the growth and flowering of all living beings. It also symbolizes our inner child, our core wounds, and the rediscovery of wonder.

The West, or black side, is a place of sunset, the return of light to the dark. It is the autumn of our time, the end of our growth. The West symbolizes a place of transition, the shadow within us that requires introspection and confrontation." Notah stops for a moment and reflects outwardly.

"I believe this is why the Lost One took the lightning seeds west to hide them in the deepest part of the land in the darkest place. This is also why we must return them to the East." He continues weaving, contemplating, and speaking softly to Takeda.

"The North or white side represents a cold place of night, the winter of our growth. One must be strong in logic and beliefs if he is to survive his 'internal' north." Notah stops weaving and stares at the cross in the middle of his lid. Something catches and keeps his attention fixed upon it. He does not consider the four directions, colors, or spirit animals. Instead, his thoughts and eye remain on the cross at the wheel's center.

"There," he mutters, "in the cross lies the purpose of the Great Mystery."

A lone cloud passes in front of the moon; its shadow covers Notah. A shiver runs down his spine, and an unexpected sense of doubt and fear clouds his mind. He looks solemnly at Takeda and says, "I am not sure if I can do this. I have made the journey, but can I complete this great task? What if I fail? My father? My tribe? Will I survive, or will I die?"

Takeda sees the sudden fear in his eyes. "Death in this world is not to be feared, Notah-kun," Takeda reassures him. "The Hotaru-Raikō know, without doubt, Kami will not condemn us to oblivion if we love him. Therefore, we trust and serve him with the knowledge that when our time here is done, he will bring us to Tengoku. He will bless us with peace and joy. He will grant us an eternal and peaceful existence in the fields around the Tree of Life. Have no fear, Notah-kun. You are strong. You see the sanctity in all that surrounds you. I do not think it is time for you to meet Kami yet." Takeda stands, opens his wings, and then flies slowly up before Notah. He reassures him, saying, "Besides, I promised we would bring you the rest of the way." He then gives him a nod and a smile.

The cloud moves away from the moon, and a pure beam of moonlight falls upon them. A warm sensation fills Notah's heart; his spirit is lifted. He smiles at Takeda. "Thank you, sensei."

A sense of confidence fills him. He suddenly sees the world in greater detail, crisper and clearer. The light emanating from his friends seems brighter. The sudden change in emotion and senses makes him wonder, *This feeling...is this the helper Wind Walker promised?* As if he knows the young brave's thoughts, Takeda bows slightly to Notah and then motions for him to join them at the fire.

They rejoin Sasaki, Hatano, and the rest of the ashigaru. Then, in a more serious tone, Takeda says, "Notah-kun, if we are to be victorious, we must know our enemy. So tell us all you know about this skinwalker, this Lost One, who guards the entrance to Shin-au-av."

Notah's exuberance leaves him. The expression on his face turns sad. He hesitates to speak, "We are only to whisper these things. We are normally discouraged from sharing such stories outside of our tribe. However, since it is the Lost One we all go to face, the story must be told." He takes a heavy, deep breath. "Long before I was born..." He pauses, "Lost One was once a member of our tribe. Legend says he was a skilled healer too. Unfortunately, he was consumed by jealousy and corrupted by an unhealthy desire for power. More than that, he wanted to control nature, not simply to harmonize with her. He wanted to control his people too. Lost One's brother was a great leader of our people. Not only was his brother brave, noble, and wise, he was a good father and husband. He rose like the sun in the elder's eyes, and they planned to choose him as their new chief. Lost One learned of their plans, his heart darkened even more, and he sought out unnatural magic. He was caught haunting our ancestral burial grounds, looking for ingredients to make corpse powder to use on his brother. As a result, he was cast out of the tribe by the elders, while his brother was elevated to Chief. Lost One learned of a secret society in his bitter wanderings, a group of witches who served the evil spirit. They could shape-shift into many animals; he coveted this power."

Notah is saddened, even ashamed, to tell the rest of the tale. "Unfortunately, the power of the skinwalker comes at a heavy price—the blood of a family member. He was readily prepared to betray his brother too. On the night of a full moon, he slipped quietly into his brother's dwelling. There he silently slaughtered his brother's entire family. The Lost One collected two water skins of blood from them all. He escaped without notice and took the blood, along with three skins, a coyote, cougar, and bear, back to the witch's cave to complete the ritual in secret.

He acquired the supernatural power he sought and now serves only himself and the evil spirit. When in human form, Lost One clothes himself with bear skin leggings, cougar skin breechcloth and belt, and a coyote skin hood. He transforms into the animal he wants based on the task at hand. Needing stealth and speed, he came as a coyote to steal the lightning seeds.

There is only one way to tell him apart from other animals—his eyes. Lost One's eyes appear human in animal form, and when light is shined on him, they do not glow. Instead, they will turn bright red like a man's. His eyes will look like an animal's when he is in human form.

It is said that Lost One, and all skinwalkers, are hard to kill. No brave has ever fought him and lived to tell the tale. We would need the assistance of powerful medicine to turn the skinwalker's evil back upon him." Notah exhales. "Sadly, we are without such power, and I think trickery is our only way."

"Ie[43], Notah-kun, we are not without power," rebukes Takeda. "We have Kami with us always. We have but to ask him, and he will help us. However, I agree with you; some trickery and distraction are in order." The group spends the next hour formulating a plan until Notah reminds them of the pre-dawn departure. At that, they all get some rest under the chilly starlit sky.

* * * * *

It always grows colder right before dawn; that night was no exception. The cold air wakes Notah. His blanket had slipped down around his waist in the night. He is not drowsy, though; his mind is sharp. Though the moon had set, and the stars still illuminated the sky, a pre-dawn glow highlights the eastern ridge. It is time to go. He rouses Sasaki and Hatano, who go on to wake the Daimyō and the rest of the ashigaru. The group breaks camp hastily and heads west in the cold air. The terrain is primarily flat, and the sun rising at their backs makes it easier to follow the retreating night into the western horizon.

---

43 Pronounced ee-yay—"No" (translated from Japanese).

The time before dawn, when nature awakens, is a spiritual time. The cool air, the vast, open sky, and brother coyote howling and yipping; keep their minds alert as they travel the dusty, sage-covered lands. Near black silhouettes of Yucca trees[44] stand tall against the fleeting, dark-blue sky. Notah always imagined them to be giants plucking stars from the heavens.

Beams of blazing golden-orange sunlight shine down on the valley floor as the sun crests the mountains behind them. Notah stops, turns to face the light, raises his arms to his sides, and greets Father Sun. He welcomes the warmth and light. Even the smallest ritual and prayer bring a balance back to his spirit, giving him the confidence to continue. They remind him of his people, and he finds comfort in that.

Notah sets off on a slow run to make up time once he has better visibility. The group crosses the first half of the desert before the oppressive heat builds up. However, they slow their pace to conserve energy once it starts getting hot. Stopping briefly for rest and shade as they pass north of Shadow Mountain, some ashigaru stumble upon dusty tracks from Lost One. Brother Eagle also appears overhead, confirming they are traveling in the right direction. The land levels out again, and they quicken their pace after resting. Each warrior can sense the closeness of their goal; no one wants to stop. Before long, the Black Mountains appear on the horizon as the sun sinks low in the sky.

They make a final push to reach the Old Queen's Pass before sunset. Notah stays well back from the ridge upon arrival so as not to be seen in the fading light. The setting sun would cast its bright yellow-orange light on the eastern ridge where they are, alerting anyone, or anything, in the valley below to their presence. He plans to come back to the

[44] aka Joshua trees

ridgeline the next day when it is more advantageous. Right now, it is better to make camp, rest, and eat.

Notah leads them all back to the open plateau, away from the ridgeline. There, they build several small fires so there will be less concentrated light, and so any breeze will carry the smoke east, away from the valley. Everyone breathes a collective, relaxing breath. They have completed the long journey here. Though exhilarated to reach Tomesha, the war party is genuinely exhausted. It is agreed that they need a good night's rest, food, and time to prepare for the battle. They eat flowering cacti and roast cactus pads over their small fires. Notah, Takeda, Sasaki, and Hatano plan to climb up the ravine to the peak behind Old Queen's Pass the next day.

Chapter Three

In the Valley of the Shadow of Death

Notah stealthily climbs the ravine to the cold, naked peak behind the Old Queen's Pass. Takeda, Sasaki, and Hatano fly up one at a time to avoid attracting attention. Notah lay on his belly while the three Hotaru-Raikō, only about ten inches tall, were easily concealed, standing or kneeling next to the rocks. Then, in a moment of immature, nervous levity, Notah nudges Sasaki saying, "It's easier for you to go unnoticed, huh, little brother?" Takeda gives him a firm look, and he knows to be more serious.

Down in the barren valley stands the shell of an ancient, twisted old pine tree, just as Wind Walker said. No longer wood, it is now a petrified, black, and rust-brown color. Its misshapen branches look like flames frozen in time. At its base is an opening, a large black hole in the cracked, scaly ground. Lost One, in his gangly human form, stalks the tree's fossilized remains.

Not only do Notah and the Hotaru-Raikō have the high ground, but they are also upwind, which conceals their observation and approach. Besides his shape-shifting skill, the skinwalker's only advantage is that he could see them coming down the mountain pass. Because of this, Notah suggests they wait until dusk to descend, just after the sun sets behind the mountains and the moon rises. Takeda agrees. He will send his army north to fly down a wide gully they spotted in the mountainside and then approach the enemy. Lost One should be distracted by their lights in the shadowy twilight. Then Notah can descend the ravine directly in front of them and south of the Old Queen's Pass. He will be well concealed there as long as he stays low and quiet.

The Hotaru-Raikō will draw Lost One away from the tree so Notah can slip through the entrance to Shin-au-av. Then, Takeda, Hasegawa, and another will accompany Notah into the underground passages to help light the way. They plan on hiding in Notah's basket during the approach so the skinwalker will not see their light. Everyone agrees on this plan and then heads back to the camp to wait for nightfall.

* * * * *

Notah has never been to war. He sits on his blanket under a small pinyon pine in quiet contemplation while inspecting his bow. A warm breeze stirs the sand. He is acutely aware of the hush that has fallen over the camp. He looks around and sees the ashigaru sharpening their blades, adjusting their armor, or sitting quietly themselves. Sasaki and Hatano move around the camp, checking their warriors. The Daimyō, sitting on his feet in the seiza position with his palms on his upper legs, is in deep meditation. Notah fights off an emotional upheaval, a nervous disquiet. He closes his eyes and breathes, trying to slow his rapid heartbeat and racing mind. He puts down his bow and empties his mind of everything except what he has learned from his tribesmen, his new little brothers, and Wind Walker. He thinks of the journey here and all the sights along the way. In his mind, he seeks harmony with Mother Nature and the blessing of the Great Mystery.

Time passes. Notah has calmed his mind and spirit. He no longer fears; he accepts whatever fate the Great Spirit plans for him. With eyes still closed, he breathes in deeply and exhales slowly. Somewhere in the wide-open sky, a war eagle[45] screams. He opens his eyes to the faint moon riding just above the distant mountain range in the blue-gray heavens. It is time.

---

[45] aka Golden eagle

* * * * *

Notah's party started down the ravine while the rest of the ashigaru moved toward the northern gully. The army is much swifter and cannot begin their assault until the light has dimmed. Notah takes only the basket, bow, quiver, and knife. He has smeared soot from the fire on his face and hands to keep his skin from shining in the moonlight. At the bottom of the now-dark ravine, he sets the basket on the ground and removes the lid. Takeda, Hasegawa, and another warrior flew down with him. They climb comfortably into it the basket while he holds it still. 'Wrestles with Hare' lands in the basket and whispers, "Hrmph, trapped again with usagi[46]." They all give a low chuckle.

"I will keep you safe, Wrestles with Hare," whispers Notah. "Are you ready little brothers?"

"Hai," whispers Takeda. Notah closes and secures the lid before gently swinging it up on his back. He secures the ropes over each shoulder and sneaks onto the flat sunbaked mud. He walks as stealthily as possible, for as long as possible, along the mountain's base. To the north, he sees many white lights swarm down into the valley and watches for the skinwalker's reaction.

Lost One has taken notice of the swarm and realizes they are a threat. He falls on all fours and takes the form of a cougar, which gives him exceptional night vision and quiet prowess. Notah sees him crouch and lay his ears back.

He has taken the bait, thinks the young brave.

Lost One rushes out to meet the invading army, exposing the entrance.

As soon as the Hotaru-Raikō are close enough, the kyudoka[47] let loose a volley. Their white-tipped arrows look

---

[46] Pronounced oo-sah-gee—"rabbit" (translated from Japanese).

[47] Pronounced key-you-doh-kah—"archers" (translated from Japanese).

like tiny stars falling through the night sky. They strike their target like porcupine quills, but their sting only angers Lost One. He jumps, like a cat catching a bird in mid-flight, and plucks one of the ashigaru from the sky with his paws. He lands on his feet with the warrior in his mouth. Although his claws have already done their work, he bites down to ensure the warrior's death before tossing him aside. The tiny warriors encircle the skinwalker, striking with their yari and uchigatanas. The beast growls, then hisses when one of them cuts deep into his shoulder.

Notah seizes the opportunity, running as swiftly and quietly as possible toward the old tree. His moccasins are usually quiet, but the parched salt-laden ground crunches underfoot. He feels the basket rhythmically swaying from side to side on his back as he runs. Inside it, his companions brace their backs against the walls with their legs so as not to be jostled around too much. Notah takes his focus off the tree for a few seconds to observe the battle. He wants to make sure he will be able to reach the tree.

Lost One stops his attack. Hearing the crunch of Notah's footsteps, he perks his ears up. He wheels around quickly. He sees the young brave running toward the tree in the moonlight. He knows he has been tricked, and he is furious. He lays his ears back while giving a loud growl. The skinwalker ignores the ashigaru and charges toward the tree instead. Running at full speed, his head does not move; his eyes are locked on his prey.

"Oh no. He sees us," says Notah. "Hold on, little brothers." He gives up trying to be silent and runs full bore toward the tree, his feet now loudly crunching on the crusty ground.

Focused on his destination, he glances North to see the cougar's silhouette approaching rapidly. He's unsure if he can make it in time but runs with all his might anyway. *It's going to be very close.* He thinks.

Notah gets within a few feet of the entrance before Lost One arrives. The beast leaps at Notah in full stride, his paws out and claws extended. Notah dives head-first into the course dirt. The cougar flies over him, missing his target. He lands on his front paws first, which drag in the salty ground, causing his back end to whip around.

Notah jumps back up on his feet. He knows he is within reach of the entrance but keeps his attention on the skinwalker, who growls viciously. Saliva drips from his teeth and tongue as he advances toward his quarry. Notah, standing sideways and staring into the red eyes of the accursed cougar, inches toward the hole in the ground, feeling for its edge in the dirt with his right foot. His heart beats rapidly. He suppresses the fear rising in his stomach as he places his hand on the handle of his knife.

Suddenly, the Hotaru-Raikō swarm around both sides of the tree, shouting battle cries. Their weapons streak past in the moonlight as they drive toward Lost One, who stops in his tracks. Lost One looks over his shoulder at the advancing army. Notah realizes this is his only chance. He turns, finds the opening, and jumps down into the entrance to Shin-au-av.

He lands on the solid ground below and enters the ancient underground passageways immediately. His new surroundings are dark. Notah reaches out and places his right hand on the tunnel wall, feeling his way deeper into the alien world and out of Lost One's sight. He knows the ashigaru above will keep him from being followed, so although his heart still races, he slows his pace. The rock wall feels strange on his fingers. The stone is smooth and slightly rough, not jagged, but not polished. Once he deems it safe enough to stop, Notah removes the basket, sets it on the ground gently, and removes the lid. "I am sorry for the rough ride, Sensei. We are in the tunnels now."

Takeda says nothing. He and the other two promptly collect themselves and fly up and out of the basket. Hasegawa's sashimono glows with pure white light, illuminating their surroundings like a torch. Takeda draws his sword. The light from it and the other two warrior's yari add to the light.

While they climb out, Notah removes his bow and quickly strings it. He then places it on the ground, secures the basket lid, and swings it back over his shoulders. He picks up his bow, removes an arrow from his quiver, and nocks it on the string. Holding the bow and arrow with his left hand, he pulls a lump of charcoal from his belt with his right. He offers it to Hasegawa. "Here," he says, "we can mark the walls as we move down into the tunnels. The marks will help us find our way back out."

"Hai," replies Hasegawa. He takes it and makes a mark on the wall to the right.

Although Shin-au-av once belonged to an archaic race, it has since been overrun by monsters, demons, and corrupt souls. They haunt its once-sacred passages guarding one of the last entry points to the underworld. However, it has also been said that a few brave Timbishan spirits keep the old queen and others from returning to the world. Through all these thoughts, it suddenly dawns on Notah that he has no idea how to find the lightning seeds.

Seeing the worry on his dirty face, Takeda reassures him, "Because our light comes from the tree of light, our blades should grow brighter as we near its seeds. So we will light your way, Notah-kun."

Shrieks, weeping, grunts, growls, and other unknown sounds echo through the endless, black passageways. Only the light from the ashigaru illuminates the tan stone around them. They pass connecting tunnels, which Notah is unable to see down. He cannot tell from which direction the different sounds come. Nevertheless, he suppresses his fear and follows his brothers closely.

A strange faint bluish glow radiates from a tunnel ahead. Weapons at the ready, the party approaches cautiously. They turn the corner and discover the spirit of a Timbishan brave, standing resolutely as though he were expecting them. He cannot speak but communicates with the young brave using hand signals Notah recognizes. The spirit offers to guide them through the underground corridors. Notah signs back, gratefully accepting the offer.

The journey down the winding rock tunnels is a long and difficult one. They do not know how long they have been in the dark passageways. Hasegawa runs out of charcoal right before the narrow tunnel opens into a vast underground room. The Timbishan spirit nods at Notah, who thanks him using sign language. The blue-hued spirit then dissipates as though a wind scattered him.

They enter the room to find a narrow rock bridge arching over a bottomless black canyon. On the other side is an amphitheater-shaped cavern. In the back of it is a stone altar, on top of which sits a black, bowl-shaped basket. A bright blue-white glow emanates from the top of it. The Hotaru-Raikō's weapons glow brighter, which means the basket must contain the lightning seeds. Unfortunately for the band of warriors, coiled around the base of the unholy altar upon which the lightning seeds rest, is the legendary and dreadful Unhcegila[48].

Her massively long, scaly body slithers slowly around the prize. Dark red spots all down her otherwise rust-colored back shimmer eerily in the luminescence of the lightning seeds. Two long, ivory horns protrude in an upward curve from her skull just behind her eye sockets. A short row of

---

[48] Horned Serpent of Lakota legend.

smaller horns juts from the top of her viper-shaped head. Her black eyes appear as voids within the sockets while white pupils glow from their center. Her long, forked tongue darts in and out of her mouth with a slight hiss as she smells the air.

She knows the enemy has come. She raises her head and opens her gaping maw with a louder hiss upon being disturbed. A smoky, fog-like mass escapes the sides of her pitch-black mouth as two rows of needle-shaped fangs spring forward.

Notah stops at the chasm's edge, which keeps him out of Unhcegila's striking range. He is unsure if he can kill this beast but takes a deep breath and raises his bow.

Takeda and his warriors fly swiftly across the canyon and dangerously close to the right of the serpent, distracting it. There is no hesitation in her. She strikes with lightning speed, wholly devouring one of them.

Takeda and Hasegawa retreat safely out over the chasm to regroup. Unhcegila moves her head back and forth, spewing out the black mist. The cavern darkens, and the bridge is obscured from sight.

The black fog clouds Notah's vision. He loses confidence, lowering his bow. Unhcegila uncoils from the demonic altar and slithers toward the bridge under cover of the mist.

Takeda can see all this happening and yells to shoot her, but his voice is muffled in the dark fog. "She is on the bridge! Shoot her now, Notah-kun!" screams Takeda.

Notah cannot see her crossing the bridge. She is within striking distance. The snake raises her head in the black mist, opening her mouth for the kill. Notah takes a deep breath and exhales. He remembers his uncle's hunting lessons, how the instincts of animals have a sinless purity about them. He also knows to trust his instincts. He calmly raises his bow, aims, and believes his arrow will find its mark. Notah lets loose his arrow. It whizzes through between her needle-like teeth and strikes Unhcegila with a loud thunk in the roof of her mouth.

She twists and turns, violently slamming her heavy body on the stone bridge as she thrashes about. Then, turning back toward the seeds, she whips her enormous tail around, unexpectedly hitting Notah in the chest, knocking him backward and off his feet. Unhcegila returns to the chasm edge on the other side of the bridge.

Notah quickly returns to his feet, draws another arrow, and aims blindly through the obsidian haze black mist. He still cannot see the serpent. Takeda and Hasegawa realize this. They fly down into the chasm and then slice upward, their blades disbursing the dark mist. Their upward flight causes Unhcegila to raise her head again.

Notah now has a clear view of her across the bridge and through the fog. He does not hesitate; he lets loose the second arrow.

Notah does not know that when Wounded Crow placed his spirit stick in his quiver, he also quietly blessed his arrows. The medicine arrow Notah let fly finds its mark. It penetrates the weak spot on her torso, behind which lies her heart.

Unhcegila hisses and writhes in pain. Her serpentine body flops feverishly on the ground at the chasm's edge. The great serpent is dying. She tries to raise her head for one last instinctive strike. But, instead, her limp body slips from the edge pulling her down into the chasm. The battle is finally over. Unhcegila is no more.

Takeda turns and bows toward Notah. He and Hasegawa fly to either side of him. They light his way as he cautiously traverses the arched bridge. He then humbly approaches the altar.

Grabbing the rudely crafted black basket, he slowly lifts it and lowers it to the ground. Notah sees the lightning seeds with his own eyes for the first time. They are not quite what he expects. They are large and kernel shaped-like maize, yet translucent. He is mesmerized by the tiny lightning sparking and arcing inside each of them; they seem to pulse with life. Finally, Takeda and Hasegawa come close; their armor and weapons glow brighter.

"Hurry, Notah-kun, pour them into your basket," directs Takeda.

Notah is shaken from his awe. He removes his basket from his back, setting it on the ground next to the black one. He removes the lid and places it upside down to catch anything that might spill over. He then pours the seeds into his fur-lined basket, making sure to collect every single one.

"Yoi[49]," praises Takeda. "Now cover them, and let's get back to the surface."

Notah tightly secures the lid of his basket. The glow from the seeds is gone, and the cave is dark once again. He swings the basket around his back and runs his arms through the straps securing it over his quiver. The seeds are surprisingly light. He collects his bow and stands. With disgust, he kicks the ugly black basket into the chasm.

Takeda and Hasegawa light their way back over the narrow bridge. Notah pulls another arrow from his quiver, nocks it, and starts toward the tunnels without looking back. They find Hasegawa's last marking on the wall and follow the marks back the way they came.

* * * * *

Nearly halfway out of Shin-au-av, a demon long forgotten startles them. The hideous Dzoavits[50] unexpectedly charges the group from an adjoining tunnel. Nearly naked, he wears an old, tattered, and filthy breechcloth. Long, dirty, and thin

---

[49] Pronounced yoh-ee—"Good" (translated from Japanese).

[50] Demon ogre of Shoshone legend.

hair has grown from his head to his ankles, covering his pale skin. Behind the unkempt hair, large, round, yellow eyes glow in the darkness.

Sensing the creature is about to strike, Hasegawa zooms in front of Takeda to protect him. Dzoavits snatches him out of the air with his left hand. He tightens his grip, breaking off his sashimono and shattering Hasegawa's back. The ashigaru warrior screams in pain. His sashimono and yari fall to the ground. The ogre shoves Hasegawa into his gaping mouth full of rotten teeth. They hear his muffled screams and a horrid crunch as the demon ogre consumes him, armor and all.

The tunnels are dark and shadowy; Notah does not see Dzoavits swipe at them with his right hand. As a result, the ogre slashes through Notah's shirt and into his left shoulder. Notah grits his teeth and groans from the four claw-like cleave marks left by its sharp fingernails. The young brave spins back to his left to face the monster while instinctively unsheathing his knife with his right hand.

Takeda, who dodged the second swipe, swoops down to the ground. He sheathes his sword and picks up Hasegawa's yari. With both hands on the pole, he zooms up into the air between Notah and the ogre, screaming with a vengeful fury. His armor and the yari blade glow much brighter, temporarily blinding the ogre. He buries the spear in the yellow eye of Dzaovits, who screams in pain.

The ogre swats blindly at Takeda, striking and slightly wounding him. Notah ducks his flailing arm and then buries the blade of his knife between the monster's neck and shoulder. Dzaovits turns to escape, stumbling over the rocky ground. He screams in agony, groping blindly at the knife handle as he staggers into the black tunnel.

They both know it is a mortal blow; he will not return. Takeda flies down to pick up the now lightless sashimono of Wrestles with Hare. He removes the cloth from the pole, folds it, and tucks it into his belt. He and Notah pause for a minute. They mourn silently for the briefest of seconds.

Stinging from their wounds, the two return to the entrance. The sounds of battle are loud and close. They sneak cautiously toward the exit, only to find the skinwalker standing in front of the opening. Lost One has returned to his tall, gangly human form and stands with his back to the tree. Although he does not see them, he is too close to the exit for them to escape. He has many cuts on his skin.

The battle to keep him out of Shin-au-av must have been intense. Thinks Notah.

Then from below comes the shouting of evil spirits as they scurry and scuffle in the passageways. They are coming to the surface in search of the seeds. Notah knows he is stuck. He must decide which evil to face.

An unexpected pink and orange light shines briefly through the Old Queen's Pass and across the sky. It disappears as fast as it came.

"Day is breaking; how long have we been down here?" Whispers Notah.

Above all the chaos, somewhere in the distant unseen sky, is the cry of the war eagle. A simple peace comes over Notah. He takes a deep breath, leans back against the rock, and says quietly, "Brother Eagle, please tell the Great Spirit we are trapped. We have the seeds but cannot escape the tunnel. We need his help."

A shorter, fainter screech is heard as if in answer to his prayer.

The sounds of demons and evil spirits draw closer. Takeda looks at Notah. Though he remains calm, there is still uncertainty in the young man's eyes. Takeda grunts with an almost fatherly acknowledgment, "hrmm." He nods at Notah, draws his sword, and turns to face whatever might be coming up the tunnels.

Though it is hard to see much of what is happening above, Notah turns to watch for an opportunity to slip past the skinwalker. Dark storm clouds roll in, obscuring the morning light. He can no longer make out what is happening.

A flash of yellow lightning streaks across the turbulent sky, silhouetting the skinwalker against it. The streak is not only followed by thunder but a deafening screech too. One so loud that it causes Notah to fall back against the rock and cover his ears.

Then a second massive thunderclap trembles the ground, shaking dirt loose from the edges of the opening. The boom vibrates and echoes down the tunnels.

The battle sounds above stop, and all eyes silently turn toward the Black Mountains. The skinwalker moves away from the opening, out into the open ground.

Notah and Takeda look at each other and then bolt as quietly as possible from the caverns. Notah lifts himself out and then passes to the left of Lost One before looking up toward the ridge. He is awestruck and slows to a walk. The great Thunderbird had perched on top of the mountain range itself.

Its massive talons move on the ridgeline, and large rocks crumble downward. Random beams of brilliant yellow and orange light slip past rolling clouds and shine on its black and blue-hued, feathery body. The legendary bird holds its body up with noble pride while its head looks downward to the basin with great interest.

Wind Walker stands to the right of the great bird. Though his stature is relatively large, his appearance resembles a field mouse next to a great war eagle. He can be seen pointing down toward them.

The great bird again calls out with an earsplitting cry, followed by a loud thunderclap, "Skreeee—ka-boom." The ground again shakes with its cry.

Lost One falls to all fours. His body convulses and contorts as he changes into a giant bear. He then roars out in defiance.

The Thunderbird wastes no time. It ducks its head ever so slightly, stretches its blue-tipped wings outward behind, and thrusts them downward, fully extended, lifting its massive black body off the ridge. Gale force wind whooshes down the slope, tumbling stone and bolder as if they were small pebbles.

Notah, and the remaining Hotaru-Raikō, fly quickly to shelter behind the petrified tree and prepare for the impact of the wind. It slams into the tree, breaking off some stone branches around them.

The Thunderbird swoops down the Black Mountain slope. Lightning streaks from the white stripes on its feathers, arcing between the rocky ground and the turbulent sky overhead. The storm follows it; a deluge falls on the slope behind the bird.

Lost One stands on his hind legs. Now 10 feet tall, he spreads its massive paws outward, preparing to fight. The great bird pulls up as it reaches the basin and arches its wings, slightly slowing its descent. Its talons, twice the size of the bear, swing out in front. It readies itself for the kill.

The skinwalker stands no chance against such a colossal bird but is defiant nonetheless. The mighty Thunderbird easily locks its grip around the bear with its left talon.

The bear desperately claws and bites at the reptilian skin and black bone claws without effect. The great bird rises through the clouds back into the pre-dawn sky. Feeling the bear trying to break free, it reaches over and pierces the skinwalker with his right talon. Crushed and speared, the bear lets out a final, faint roar and then goes limp.

Notah scrambles out from behind the tree. He sees the storm waters cascading down the mountainside and runs out onto the salt flats as fast as he can, followed by the Hotaru-

Raikō. The flood waters pour into the entrance to Shin-au-av. Demons and evil spirits below scream as the water washes them back to the depths from which they crawled.

He slows to a walk and then stops once he knows he is safe from the raging waters. He watches in awe as the waters weaken the ground around the entrance, causing the petrified tree's trunk to collapse into the hole. Salt and sand settle over it, forever sealing off the ancient city.

Notah looks to the ridge for Wind Walker, but he is gone. Instead, he looks down to see the corpses of several Hotaru-Raikō who had fallen in battle. Their broken bodies settle in the water pooling around the collapsed entrance.

The Daimyō and his samurai find and collect each fallen warrior. Notah unstrings his bow and slips it into its case. Then he stretches his arms out, saying, "Bring your brothers to me, and I will carry them to high ground. I will take them to be close to the sky again."

Takeda, Sasaki, and Hatano lay six fallen ashigaru across his arms.

Notah slowly and somberly carries them back up Old Queen's Pass to the very same peak they used to observe the valley before. There he solemnly buries his warrior brothers under stones. They place one of their sashimono poles at the head of the mound to mark the grave. Takeda names the peak Senshi no Maiso-chi[51].

Needing a moment of reflection, Notah walks slowly down the summit. He drags his feet on the sandy plateau. Fatigue is setting in. Not just physical exhaustion, but his mind, body, and spirit are all weary. He is sleep-deprived, has faced and overcome his worst fears, and now he mourns the loss of many good warriors. He undoes the braids of his hair

---

[51] Pronounced sin-shee-no my-ee-so-chee—"Warrior's Burial Ground" (translated from Japanese). Known today as Coffin Peak.

in mourning while trying to process everything that has happened in his young mind.

Then, on the ground, near where the Thunderbird had once perched, he finds a large black feather with a blue tip and a white stripe along its vane. He picks it up and looks skyward. Brother Eagle circles in the winds over the ridge. Notah wonders aloud, "Is this a blessing, a reminder, or both?"

No answer comes.

Still, he is grateful for his own life. "Thank you, Great Spirit."

Notah turns to see the rest of the Hotaru-Raikō flying slowly down from the peak. He meets them, and they all return to their desert camp to rest, eat, and mourn their losses. Notah removes his basket, leans against the pine tree where he left his things, and rapidly falls asleep.

Chapter Four

New Lands and the Feast of Manhood

Notah wakes a few hours later. The Hotaru-Raikō are stirring as well. The sun is low in the sky. The nearly full moon is already in the sky, and he is eager to leave Tomesha behind. He speaks with Takeda, who agrees that evening will be an excellent time to cross the hot desert. They all prepare for a shorter journey back to Painted Ground. Notah returns to the Old Queen's Pass and fills his water skins from pools of rainwater left in the ravine from the early morning. He gathers all his things and then leads the party east toward the rising moon. *It's always easier traveling with the sun on your back*, he thinks.

* * * * *

They return to the site of their first camp at Painted Ground. Notah goes to the spring to fill his water skins. A west wind had been blowing all day, a blessing to have at their backs as they traveled. He crouches beside the spring and notices the same wind blowing across the water's surface while he fills his skins. The water ripples like goosebumps on the skin, which move across the surface with the breeze. The tiny waves glitter in the sun. He watches as the breeze comes toward him on the water, waiting anxiously for it to reach him and soothe his hot skin. Those few moments are cool and calming. The simple beauty of Mother Nature restores his mind and spirit.

He decides to stay at Painted Ground until he can discern where his tribe's new lands are. His little brothers welcome the respite too. In his downtime, Notah asks the Great Spirit which direction he should travel. While waiting for a sign, the party hunts, forages, and refreshes themselves in the spring waters.

On the third night, Notah sleeps peacefully under the full moon. Powerful vivid dreams come to him. He dreams of flying on the brown feathered back of Brother Eagle. They glide effortlessly on the wind, traveling north, up and over the cliff at his old home in Mesa Verde. He raises his face to the blue sky before observing the ground rushing beneath them. The bottom drops out of his stomach as they suddenly swoop down through arches and around tall pillars of tan and red striped rock before rising up and over another plateau.

He recovers by fixing his eyes on the horizon. Behind them is the land of the sacred arches. In the distance, Notah sees fertile grounds by a flowing river winding through the great basin. A soft voice whispers in his mind, "Leave tomorrow for Seeds-kee-dee-Agie.[52]"

He closely observes the lush grounds in a valley around a river bend before his dream ends. Then, finally, he wakes peacefully in the still night. He sits up and looks around. The moonlight illuminates the land around the springs. He instinctively reaches for his basket, which is still safe at his side. Brother Owl calls in the still night, "Whoo-whoo, whoo-whoo."

Notah knows where he must go now.

* * * * *

It has been over two months since Notah left his home in Mesa Verde. Spring has changed to summer. On a sweltering summer afternoon, he stands on a plateau looking down into a lush valley—a river snakes through old rugged mountains past the fertile banks. There is a small village below; he knows

---

[52] Prairie Hen River (translated from Shoshone—a.k.a. Green River).

these are his people. He has been guided to this place by an unknown sense of direction, a gift from the Sustainer. He is happy and longs to see his people again, but he hesitates to descend the side of the plateau.

The last time he was with his people, he was content chasing lizards and playing boyhood games. This journey has changed him, however. He briefly reflects on his actions and experiences, the many indescribable things he has seen, and the friends lost along the way. He wants to return home but is not quite sure how to explain all that has happened. *Will my people believe my stories?* He thinks.

He wonders if he will finally be called a man, a warrior among his people. He went out into the wilderness, contemplated and communed with the spirit, invoked the blessing of the Great Mystery, and retrieved the sacred lightning seeds. He has done what a man should. He should be happy to be home—still, he lingers on the ridge.

He watches a tall, proud man walk up from the river toward the village. The man stops, raises his hand to cover his brow, and looks up to see Notah standing there.

* * * * *

Chief Ouray walks up the bank toward the village. He stops. Something catches his eye on the ridge above. He sees a man standing motionless, staring down into the valley and right at him. He puts his hand over his brow to block the sun from his eyes so he can see better. "Could it be?" He mumbles.

It looks like him but somehow different. He thinks to himself.

The man on the ridge turns and starts toward the newly trodden path winding down the side of the plateau. He carries a large basket on his back and is followed by tiny, flying warriors.

Chief Ouray's heart swells instantly, and he yells, "NOTAH!"

The tribe is startled by his outburst. Notah's name echoes down the canyon walls, and the tribe turns to see where their chief is going. Chief Ouray walks toward the hill and is joined by joyful people in welcoming their young brave home.

* * * * *

A celebratory feast of elk, deer, beans, squash, and pinyon nuts is prepared three days later. The morning before the feast, Notah goes before his father, Wounded Crow, and the tribal elders. He goes alone, bringing only his basket containing the sacred lightning seeds. The elders are sitting in a semi-circle around a new, ornate blanket, their backs against the cliff. His father sits in the middle of them. Notah sets the basket on the blanket in front of the council, removes the lid, sets it in front, and then sits on a rock a short distance behind it. The white light from the seeds brightens the alcove.

There is silence at first, but he soon recounts the details of his journey, what he learned from the Hotaru-Raikō, how they worked together to retrieve the seeds, how Lost One met his end, and about his dream—how the Great Spirit directed him to the tribe's new home. The council listens quietly and carefully to his tale. When it is done, they sit in contemplation for a short time.

Notah stares at the basket. The council of elders disappears behind the light emanating from it. His thoughts retreat inward. He dwells on the splendor of Mother Nature. He recalls all the stunning beauty of the painted desert, the freshwater of lush springs, the vastness of starlit skies, and Brother Eagle gliding boldly in the clear blue sky. In his mind, he sees the smiles and laughter of his brother-friends. He remembers their courage and Takeda's leadership. He laments the death of Wrestles with Hare and the others. He hears Wounded Crow's words echo in his mind again: "I suspect that when you return to us, you will have found your purpose and the answers to many questions."

Indeed, he has. In his heart, Notah knows his role within the tribe should be the protector of his people and the seeds. In this, he has faith that the Sustainer will help him.

Chief Ouray sees the somber and distant look on his son's face. He breaks the silence. "My son," he begins, while Notah intuitively rises, "you have journeyed far. You faced many evils and many fears, bravely fighting to recover what was lost. You have restored the honor of our tribe. I, Wounded Crow, and the rest of this council recognize you as a man this day."

Chief Ouray stands. "You are to take my place as the primary guardian of the lightning seeds."

He walks toward Notah and is followed by Wounded Crow, each carrying one pristine feather from a war eagle. Notah's spirit is lifted. He knows what comes next and humbly removes his simple headband, handing it to his father.

They each fix their feathers to it. Notah bows slightly, and his father places the headband upon his crown before stepping back.

Wounded Crow walks forward and speaks, "The elders recognize you as a man now, a brave warrior. We give you the name Hania[53]."

He produces a long ceremonial pipe and lightly presses tobacco made with the bark of the red willow into the stone pipe. He lights it and then holds it high in gratitude toward the sun, low toward the earth, and then toward the lightning

---

[53] Pronounced hah-nee-ah—"Spirit Warrior."

seeds. The aromatic incense swirls around them. Wounded Crow partakes and then passes to Hania, who follows suit. The ceremonial pipe then makes its way around to each of the elders, its wispy smoke filling the alcove.

There is silence as they all share the grateful moment. Finally, Chief Ouray announces, "We delayed this year's Bear Dance, Hania. But now our tribe is whole again. We have settled into these new lands for a time, our scouts have returned with food, and you have returned with the lightning seeds. There is no better time than now to begin the celebration." Ouray places his hand on his son's shoulder and says in a quieter voice to him, "I am proud of you, Son."

The council returns to the gathered tribe, ready for the feast. Hania is presented to the tribe by Chief Ouray. Everyone gives thanks for his return. Hania sits next to his brother-friends, the remaining Hotaru-Raikō. Over the next few days, a spirit of understanding descends upon them all, allowing each to understand their different languages. There is dancing, feasting, games, storytelling, and blossoming courtships.

Near the end of the ten-day celebration, Hania senses the time to say farewell to his new friends is near. He carries the spirit stick with him on that last day. Removing the small medicine wheel from it, he approaches Takeda, who is sitting on a tall stone. He presents the wheel to him. "Sensei, my friend, throughout our journey together, I would look at this medicine wheel and reflect upon its meaning. I have yet to understand why, but my eye continues to be drawn to the cross in the middle. It has a deeper meaning, and I will discover the truth of it one day. However, I offer this medicine wheel to you as a token of my gratitude and to remember the brotherhood we share."

The Daimyō graciously accepts the medicine wheel and bows to Hania. Then, he motions to his samurai, "Yoshimoto-san. Bring me Hasegawa's sashimono."

"Hai," answers Hatano. Both he and Sasaki rush out of the feast. They return promptly, carrying a small, folded cloth. Hatano approaches Takeda, who stretches his hands out toward him, and, with his head bowed, he offers Hasegawa's (Wrestles with Hare) sashimono to his Daimyō. Takeda gently takes it from him. Hatano and Sasaki then stand behind their lord and look toward Hania. Takeda reverently unfolds the banner with their clan crest, holds it up to Hania, and bows. Hania receives it and bows back.

Takeda says, "This is our gift to you, Hania-san. It has been a great honor to fight at your side."

The solemn moment is interrupted by a curious look on Hania's face. "Hania-san?" Asks Hania inquisitively, "I thought my name was Hania-kun?"

"You are no longer a boy. You are a man now. A warrior. You have earned our respect and will be known to us as Hania-san." Takeda then smiles somewhat coyly. "I told you we would bring you the rest of the way."

Hania gives a hearty laugh. "Yes, you did, my friend. Yes, you did." They all join the laughter for a moment. Then, looking at the sashimono and saddened by the loss of so many brave ashigaru, Hania's laughter subsides. With tears forming in his eyes, and with the utmost respect, he says, "Domo arigatogozaimashita[54], sensei." He offers a low bow which Takeda, Hatano, and Sasaki return. The bond they share as warriors and brothers will last forever; it can never be broken.

---

[54] Pronounced do-mo ar-hee-got-toe-go-zeye-ee-mah-sh-tah—"Thank you very much" (translated from Japanese).

A surprising look of shock comes over Takeda's face. He and his samurai hastily land on the ground and bow low. The celebration comes to an unexpected silence. Hania turns to see the towering presence of Wind Walker standing close by. Before Hania can kneel, the angel announces, "Peace be upon you all." He motions to all the Hotaru-Raikō. "Rise, my friends. Rise." He places his large hand on Hania's shoulder and smiles. "Well done, Young Brave! The Creator is pleased with you. You have restored his confidence in your people. He will bless these and all the lands your people travel."

Everyone remains quiet, listening to Wind Walker as he addresses the Hotaru-Raikō. "Kenshin-san, Hasegawa, and the ashigaru who gave their last full measure in this quest have returned to Tengoku. They once again fly in peace in the fields near the Tree of Life." Takeda bows deeply, saying, "Arigatogozaimashita Omo.[55]"

Wind Walker motions for the rest of the ashigaru to gather. "Kuru. Kuru." The angel continues once they have gathered around. "You have all done very well, my friends. Kami is pleased with you. He happily releases you to return to your families in the lush forests of Nihon. Iku, return to watch over your cousin, the firefly, until Kami's son comes for you." There is a sudden and loud buzz in the air as the small winged army cheerfully gathers their things and prepares to leave.

They all assemble with Hania one last time a while later. They offer a final bow before taking flight. Takeda turns mid-air, raises his hand high, and shouts, "Sayonara kyodai![56]"

Not only is it the last time he hears or speaks their language, but it will also be one of the saddest moments in Hania's life. It is a pain that only warriors who have journeyed together, fought and bled together, and have had to say

---

[55] "Thank you, Lord." (translated from Japanese).

[56] "farewell brother" (translated from Japanese).

farewell to one another can truly understand. He will miss them greatly over the coming seasons.

* * * * *

Now, legend has it that on warm summer evenings, the wakai josei[57] will gather with fans in hand to gaze out over lush, verdant landscapes spangled by hundreds of brilliant golden lights. There the hotaru meet to dance and attract a lover. Sometimes, around the outer edges of the fields where they gather, incredibly rare flashes of white light, almost like short bursts of lightning, can be seen. It is said these white lights emanate from tiny warriors who protect the hotaru from anyone or anything that would do them harm. The wakai josei share the legend of Hotaru-himé while they hope their own prince will "bring them fire."

---

[57] Pronounced wahk-eye jo-say—"young women" (translated from Japanese).

Chapter Five

Legacy

"Countless seasons have passed since then, Grandson. Our people have known peace these many years," says Chief Hania as he stands up.

Elu can see that his grandfather is weak and stands to help him if necessary.

Hania moves slowly around the fire and stops in front of him. He holds out his spirit stick. "This is yours now, Grandson."

Elu hesitates before lifting his hands and accepting the gift. Chief Hania smiles before slowly returning to his seat on the other side of the fire. He speaks as he goes, "My time is at hand, Young Brave. I have already given my meager possessions to our tribesmen, keeping only the spirit stick apart, which is now yours."

He carefully sits on his blanket and crosses his legs. Elu sits as well, examining his gift in the firelight. Chief Hania continues his instruction, "The markings you see (蛍 雷 光) carved into it are called kanji. They are symbols for the words, Hotaru-Raikō. Wrestles with Hare's sashimono is sewn around the stick above them. The giant feather is from the majestic thunderbird." He pauses. "You must remember this, Elu—you hold precious items in your hands, but it is not what you possess that makes you a man. Your actions are what makes you a man. Give thanks for what you receive from Mother Nature; her gifts, her bounty, are sacred. Take care of your tribe, harmonize with the land, and work to see the great mystery in all things. These are the actions that will tell others whether you are a good man or not."

Chief Hania pauses for a moment; he grows visibly tired. "Never forget, the evil spirit still searches for the lightning seeds. You are their protector now; they are entrusted to you for safekeeping. Remember, one day, you must pass on our story to the next generation. Our people must know the great responsibility entrusted to us. They must remain vigilant too."

Elu places the spirit stick on his lap and looks at him. "I will, Grandfather."

"Lightning itself is a beautiful thing, Grandson. When we see it, we know the Tree of Life is still alive and growing. The Sustainer sends the spring and summer storms to water the tree. The rain, thunder, and lightning are his way of letting us know he has not forgotten us and that he still loves us. He will let us climb its branches like children among the cottonwoods one day. We will climb happily all the way up into his spirit lands."

Chief Hania takes a deep breath and exhales. He looks to the sky and says softly, "I am tired. I have done my best—Brother Eagle, let he who brings the rains know I am ready for the spirit lands." He looks back through the fire at Elu, who watches him closely.

"I am proud of you, Grandson." Hania smiles at him one last time before slowly closing his eyes. His head dips downward. He gently slumps over. Chief Hania has breathed his last.

Elu jumps to his feet. Still clutching the spirit stick, he rushes to squat in front of Chief Hania. He places his hand softly on his grandfather's shoulder and straightens him back up. He can see that he is gone. Small tears come to his eyes. "Thank you, Grandfather." Elu moves his shoulder to his grandfather's, resting him against it with his head down. He places his arm around his back for a last lingering embrace.

Elu takes care to release his grandfather in a way that leaves him still sitting but with his head down. He slowly, remorsefully loosens the braids in his hair, letting it fall where it may. Still squatting, he turns to find and collects a small handful of warm ash with his free hand. He smears the dark soot across his forehead and down each cheek. The tiny tears make it look black on his young face. He lowers his head, allowing himself a moment of mourning.

The young man raises his eyes just in time to see lightning strike the ground several feet behind his grandfather. He witnesses the white-hot fire burn the rock for a split second before tucking his head down and tightly embracing his grandfather. The deafening thunderclap that ensues stirs the desert sand and shakes his whole body. Startled and a bit fearful, he manages to keep his calm. He looks up to see two sandaled feet on opposite sides of the scorched, lightning-struck rock. Elu lifts his head a little more to see a mighty warrior tucking his wings behind him and walking toward him. The angel glows, his wings lighting the night sky with subtle white light. He can only assume this is Wind Walker, the creator's messenger.

Elu stands, unsure of how to behave in his presence. Wind Walker is at least three heads taller than him and formidable in his appearance. He approaches Elu steadily, softly saying, "Hau kolá."

Elu's heart is beating fast within his chest. He does not know whether to stand, kneel, or bow. So instead, he humbly returns his greeting. The angel stops at the edge of the ring of light the fire casts. "I am Præsidiel," he says, "but your people know me as Wind Walker. I come with peace and good news, young Elu."

Elu kneels on one knee, asking nervously, "How may I serve you, Wind Walker?"

"Please, stand. May I sit with you?"

Elu looks up in surprise. He stands and motions to a place for him at the fire between him and his grandfather. Wind Walker smiles and steps into the firelight. He pauses to gently and respectfully lean Chief Hania's body back on the rock behind him. He crosses the chief's arms upon his chest and covers his lower body with his blanket. Elu's grandfather looks like he is sleeping peacefully under the open sky by the fire. "He is a good man," says Wind Walker, moving to sit upon a large stone. He relaxes his wings, their tips almost touching the ground on either side of him. He motions for Elu to sit too.

Wind Walker smiles as Elu sits down on his blanket. "Your grandfather walks the spirit lands with much peace and joy now." He pauses. "But I have been sent to tell you much more than that. I was sent to instruct you as I did Chief Hania, so you too will be an honorable chief—a noble guardian of the lightning seeds."

EPILOGUE

ENTERING THE SPIRIT LANDS

Chief Hania reclines against a smooth flat stone with his arms across his chest and eyes closed. All sound has fallen away. Everything, even the cool evening wind, is still. He takes a deep breath and exhales. A sense of peace and contentment moves through his heart as he does. Then a hand gently touches his left shoulder as if to wake him from slumber. In the silence, a soft voice says, "Hania, open your eyes."

He opens them to a starlit sky like no other; so much more to behold in it than when he was a boy. He sits up. A brilliant full moon appearing closer than usual gives light to his surroundings. The landscape appears in post-twilight darkness, a partial night. None of the landmarks are recognizable to him. To his added wonder, Wind Walker stands just in front and to his left. His wings, armor, and entire body shine with a light Hania is not used to. The angel offers his hand. Hania takes it and rises to his feet. Oddly, he feels younger and more vigorous. Wind Walker smiles and says, "Hello, my friend."

"Hau kolá." Still trying to grasp what is happening, Hania looks down at his clothes. He finds he is wearing clean light tan pants made from animal skin, with short decorative strips of leather running down the sides of each leg. He holds out his hands, observing the rest of his attire. He has on a new long sleeve cloth shirt, light blue in color, over which his bone breastplate, adorned with small feathers, lay. Hania lowers his hands and looks about in curiosity, asking, "What is this place?"

"You are in a place between creation and the Spirit Lands. This is the time of your reckoning, my good friend, when you will understand the deeper truth of the Great Mystery. All you have done will be revealed, and nothing is hidden before the One, the Son of the Great Spirit, our Lord Jesus, the Christ."

A blinding light appears to the left of Wind Walker. It takes the shape of a large oval. The angel immediately steps aside, takes a knee, and bows low. Suddenly overcome with a deep sense of humility, Hania, too, is compelled to kneel.

A silhouette appears in the light. "Peace be upon you, Hania." Comes the soft but authoritative voice.

A tall man dressed in the whitest of garments passes through the light into the moonlit world. He has long, wavy, brown hair barely touching his shoulders and a thick beard. His copper eyes blaze brighter than a war eagle who defends its nest. Hania feels ashamed to look at him but cannot shift his gaze away. Jesus approaches the chief slowly. As he does, he opens his hands outwardly. Light beams through holes in each of his palms and lands warmly upon the penitent chief's face. Unexpected knowledge floods his mind; he sees the passion of Christ and suddenly understands the cross inside the medicine wheel—the real symbolism of it. This knowledge moves him to sadness. Shame over his misdeeds causes him to remove the feathers woven into his hair and lay them on the ground at Jesus' feet.

"The Sacred Spirit was sent to you many seasons ago," says Jesus, crouching down to pick up the feathers. He looks Hania in the eye and says, "Ever since that day in Red Rocks Canyon, you have contemplated the cross and its true significance. That is why I gave you the knowledge of my crucifixion. Since that day, the holy spirit has strengthened you, guided you, and revealed certain truths, preparing you for this moment. Although you continued to live harmoniously with the land, you elevated your spiritual life.

You believed though you did not fully understand. Though your people care not for possessions, you cared for the seeds given to you by my Father. Though you, yourself, did not truly know him. You sought the truth of the Great Mystery. You did not know it was me you sought, however."

The Lord smiles at Hania, who sees a father's love for a son reflected in his eyes. Jesus continues, "I *am* the fulfillment of the Great Mystery, Hania. I am the way, the truth, and the life. None enter the Spirit Lands except through me."

He pauses for a second before standing back up. "Because you lived as I wish all men would, not bound to possessions, reverent of the gift of nature, and seeking the divinity of my father in all things, I gladly offer entry to you. Will you accept my gift, my grace?"

Hania answers without hesitation, "Yes, Son of the Great Spirit, I will." Unbridled happiness and warmth enter him. Though he still kneels, he cannot stop the smile from spreading across his face.

"I am pleased. Well done, my good and faithful servant." Jesus makes a motion for him to stand. "Please, rise."

Hania stands. Jesus motions for him to turn around, saying, "You faced true evil to save what is sacred, what is my Father's. You earned these feathers by overcoming your fear, trusting in the Sacred Spirit, and recovering the lightning seeds."

The Lord gently weaves them back into the chief's hair. When he is done, he pats him on the shoulder, and Hania turns to face him again. Jesus says, "Like your earthly father, I too am proud of you, Hania."

The light behind him expands. The angel stands quietly as Jesus turns to walk toward the gateway. He motions for Hania to follow, saying, "Come now, I think there are others who long to see you again." He passes through the light. Wind Walker smiles at his friend and then turns to follow the Lord.

Hania walks briskly toward the oval-shaped light and then through.

He emerges into a vast sunlit land. The gateway closes behind him. The three are surrounded by a far more colorful and brighter nature than anything Hania has ever seen. More magnificent than the desert in full spring bloom. More beautiful than the full moon rising over the sandstone mountains. More splendid than proud brother elk standing on a grassy hill.

He realizes he is standing on a wide stone path, one like he has never seen. He lets his eyes follow it. The road leads to a city on a hill in the distance. It reminds him of Mesa Verde, yet much larger and more captivating. Still adjusting to the brightness of this place, he reigns in his wonder, focusing on Jesus, who is to his right. The Lord says, "Do you see the great, white tree on the hill there?" He points to another lower hill to the right of the gleaming stone city, upon which grows a massive tree of white light. Hundreds of tiny, golden lights flicker in the tall grass around its trunk.

A youthful exuberance wells up within the chief's heart. "There are your brothers, Hania. Takeda, Wrestles with Hare and all the rest," confirms Jesus with a smile. "They have been awaiting your arrival with great anticipation."

Hania looks at him with unbound excitement, yet he cannot find words to express his gratitude.

The Lord laughs, "Ha, ha, ha! Go. Further up and further in with you. We will meet again in the great city soon enough."

Hania bows his head to Jesus and says, "Thank you, Great Spirit. Thank you."

* * * * *

Hania walks the wide road with a purposeful stride and deep joy. He contemplates the Sacred Spirit (the sustainer), Jesus, son of the Creator, and the Great Spirit himself as he travels. *These three make up the Great Mystery, and I now have all of eternity to ponder with awe and gratitude. I will forever be thankful for their love, help, mercy, and forgiveness—their great gift.* He thinks to himself.

At the moment, however, he desperately wishes to see his brother-friends again; how *I missed them!*

He leaves the road when it turns to the left toward the great city and steps out into the grasslands with his hands out to his sides. The soft grass feels good as it brushes his palms. He marvels at the tall, bright-green grasslands. The sprawling field leading up the hill is covered with it. A light and fragrant breeze moves across its surface, and the grass moves and sways like the waves on the water at Painted Ground. He stops momentarily to feel the breeze caress him and watch the grass dance.

From here, he looks up to the tree in utter amazement. Though it is made of lightning, it keeps its shape. Billowing, light gray clouds with white linings surround its silver-leafed canopy. Far behind it are enormous, snowcapped mountains. The tree stands out in stark contrast against their dark rocky bases.

The tiny golden lights of fireflies intermingle and dance with brighter white lights around the tree trunk. He can see the Hotaru-Raikō. They no longer wear armor or carry weapons; they are not needed here. Instead, they wear more formal montsuki haori hakama[58] as they celebrate everlasting peace. He lingers in the tall grass watching his brother-friends for a moment. Their perfectly choreographed dance is beautiful to observe.

---

[58] Essentially, Japanese formal dress.

Soon though, vigilant as ever, Takeda Kenshin spots his friend, and fellow warrior, standing in the field below. “HANIA-SAN!” He shouts. The Hotaru-Raikō stop dancing. An unexpected group cheer goes up. Then, swift as ever, Hania’s little brothers streak down the lush hillside toward him. Their wings buzz, and the white light of their clothes blazes bright like shooting stars just above the swaying grass.

A tremendous joy swells the old chief’s heart, and his eyes fill with tears of joy. Hasegawa leads the charge. “Wrestles with Hare!” Exclaimed Hania before running up the hill with all the cheerfulness of a child. Finally, he goes to meet his little brothers under the Tree of Life.

The truly brave man, we contend, yields neither to fear nor anger, desire nor agony; he is at all times master of himself; his courage rises to the heights of chivalry, patriotism, and real heroism. “Let neither cold, hunger, nor pain, nor the fear of them, neither the bristling teeth of danger nor the very jaws of death itself, prevent you from doing a good deed,” said an old chief to a scout.”

~ Charles Alexander Eastman

Legacy of Lightning:

Rise of the Hotaru Onna-musha

Contents

Chapter One

Kumo and the Jilted Suitor

Takeda Kenshin is the Hotaru-Raikō's daimyō. He and his kind are unique to this world: human in form but endowed with slender antennae, smoke-colored wings, and thin, yet sturdy, coal-black wing covers of a firefly. Although their eyes are dark ebony, they are almond-shaped instead of round, like their firefly cousins. Their skin is fair and pale, while their fine hair is long and black, like their antennae. Women wear their hair long and straight, letting their antennae flow backward with their hair, while the men often arrange their top knot so it rests between their antennae.

Long ago, the Hotaru-Raikō, as they are known now, once danced above the lush, grassy fields around the great tree of life. Unfortunately, they committed an act of selfish pride, which offended Kami, the one true God.

However, unlike Akuma, the traitor, who was cast down from Tengoku,[59] the hotaru were shown mercy. Though disgraced, they were sent out of the great garden to live in the land of Nihon. For hundreds of years, Takeda-san and his clan lived on the outskirts of human civilization, peacefully sharing the lands with man, who saw them as beautiful and benevolent creatures.

Always watching and studying, the hotaru learned much, even adopting some of man's customs and culture. In time, man began to develop the land and use natural resources. This created a divide between the two races and a wariness of the hotaru clan. As a result, they began to move, building their temporary settlements near the villages of men, but not

---

[59] Heaven (translated from Japanese).

close enough to be seen. If they happened to be discovered, the clan would move to the borders of another village.

During what came to be known as the Heian period, Takeda-san and his clan finally settled in the Echizen Province. On the sunnier south side of the Fukui Castle moat, there, among a dense thicket, lies an old, long-forgotten ishidōrō.[60] A verdant moss adorns its hand-chiseled roof, while mint-colored lichen blankets the pitted gray stone upon which the lantern rests. It likely illuminated a road or a path to an ancient shrine once, but the hotaru quickly dedicated it to God and made it the center of their village. Now, there is a well-worn path leading up to its simple openings where man's flame once dwelt. Long-bladed grasses gently reach up on either side of the ascendant trail like curved, oceanic waves crashing on a rocky shore. Though they could easily fly up to the shrine entrance, the Hotaru prefer to approach humbly on foot between the swaying grasses.

To the north of Fukui Castle, where man dwells, a military governor holds court in the fortified residence. He is a landlord for local farmers, and his retainers protect them.

Between them and the Raikō clan is a large moat; the waters gently lap the sandy shore leading up to the woodland undergrowth. The clan has built an earthen wall inside the thicket to surround their daimyō's austere, shinden-style estate.

The shinden (main hall) itself sits directly north of the shrine. Covered breezeways stretch out to tainoya (additional or guest houses) on the eastern and western sides of the main hall. Tea saplings grow in each rectangular enclosure between the tainoya and shinden.

Leading south out of each tainoya toward the shrine are two enclosed walkways called rō. As is customary, inner gates

[60] Stone lantern (translated from Japanese).

were built in the middle of each rō, which line up with the east and west outer gates in the earthen wall. On the southern end of the western rō is an enclosed pavilion with a view of the niwa, or courtyard garden, and the torii leading up to the shrine.

On the eastern side is a rectangular open-air pavilion, the best place to view both the moonrise and Mount Haku, or Hakusan, in the east. The uncomplicated aesthetics of Heian architecture lend to the natural beauty of the shinden estate.

The niwa between the shinden and the shrine is wide open. Here, beneath the towering shrine, the clan occasionally gathers for theater, kyūdō[61] contests, and Takeda-san's favorite sport, Sumai no Sechi, a precursor to

[61] Archery (translated from Japanese).

sumo wrestling. The object of the Raikō version of Sumai no Sechi is to grapple one's opponent to the ground, forcing them to their back inside a ring on the ground made of heavy rope. The real challenge is that neither opponent can open their wing covers; they are prohibited from flying. The daimyō, his samurai, and several trusted warriors watch intently, making wagers on the matches and getting slightly boisterous depending on the outcome.

Conversely, Harumi, Takeda-san's beloved wife, allows the children to play kemari[62] in the courtyard whenever the warriors are away. She prefers their laughter and merriment to wrestling.

Just past the shrine, the earthen wall surrounding the estate gives way to walls of woven willow branches, which protect the rest of the village. The rest of the clan has built their family homes in this area south of the shrine. Some built simple wooden houses with flared, thatched rooves, somewhat reminiscent of the older Yayoi architecture. Some elevated their homes on posts, while others combined stone and wood to build into the surrounding thicket. Entering through the southern gate, one would get a sense of a rustic, tranquil, and inviting village at one with the natural environment, as though it had been there for ages.

To the north, on the outer banks of the castle moat, where the water is shallow, the lotus lilies grow large and luxuriant. Once the cherry blossoms have run their course, Harumi can sometimes be seen sitting on a tall blade of grass rising out of the eastern corner of the earthen wall. She contemplatively stares across the lotus fields from that most excellent vantage point. She is captivated by the gentle and vibrant flowers dotting the field of giant green pads floating in the clear and gleaming water. Each flower subtly

---

[62] A game that resembles a combination of soccer and hacky sack.

transitions from a vivid pink tip to a pure, soft white bottom on its petals. Like the sun, bright yellow stigmas resting at the center of each flower invite the dragonfly and the bee to visit. She always finds peace watching life unfold on the moat.

In this idyllic setting, many of the Hotaru warriors became especially intrigued with the burgeoning philosophy of Bushido, the way of the warrior. Historically, the men of Nihon were fascinated by war and military valor. Though they lacked knowledge of Kami, the one true God, the island nation's people cherished the beauty of nature, reason, and self-discipline.

Additionally, though warlike in their nature, the people practiced a strict moral code; unnecessary killing, thievery, intoxication, sexual misconduct, and bearing false witness were strictly forbidden. Takeda-san and his people quickly see the benefits of Bushido in their pursuit of a disciplined and moral earthly life. They look for avenues to integrate the way of the samurai fully into their culture.

In this pursuit, they came to pledge their lives to the protection of their weaker cousins, the Hotaru no Chikyū.[63] It was Hotaru-himē, the daughter of Hi-ō, lord of the Hotaru no Chikyū, who gave them the Hotaru-Raikō name. She said the white light of their armor and weapons reminded her of the lightning that spans the earth and sky.

As a matter of circumstance, it was after the wedding of Hotaru-himē to her prince, Hi-marō, that Takeda-san became acutely aware of the fact that he has only one child, a daughter and that he has no male heir to take his place as daimyō. He is not alone in this observation either. A young warrior named Ishida sees this, too.

Ishida is a cunning warrior, not much older than the daimyō's daughter. Like her, he was born in this world long

---

[63] Firefly of the earth (translated from Japanese).

after the Hotaru-Raikō were sent out of the garden. Ishida sometimes displays a greater love for this world than he does for their true home. He harbors an unspoken envy of Takeda-san deep within his materialistic heart. He craves worldly titles and power. He wants to live in the palace, control the shrine, and lord over the clan. He knows if he can win the hand of the daimyō's daughter and marry her, he will become the heir apparent, eventually replacing Takeda. So, unbeknownst to anyone, Ishida secretly plans to court the seventeen-year-old Ashi.

Ashi is a clever young woman, highly observant of her surroundings. Within her kind and generous heart, she carries a quiet passion for Kami, a pure and innocent love of God. Because of this love, she has the gift of sensing others' auras. Unlike man, who primarily sees only physical expressions, the elder Hotaru and Ashi can see the internal light, or darkness, of others. Like her father, she is incredibly observant of her surroundings. It is on one brisk autumn morning at the village market; her talent changes the fortunes of many in her clan.

It is early, and there are few others around. Ashi browses the market for berries and mushrooms. She is alone. Ishida discovers her there. He stalks her as she peruses the grocer's baskets. His light is dim, and he wears the brim of his bamboo sandogasa[64] down over his eyes to not attract undue attention from others. Standing just behind and to her right, he draws close to her and offers a soft greeting, "Good morning, Ashi-san."

Ashi glances in Ishida's direction, recognizing him immediately. He smiles coyly when she does and says, "Utsukushii.[65] You are beautiful."

---

[64] Conical-style hat (translated from Japanese).

[65] Beautiful (translated from Japanese).

Normally, Ashi would keep her head slightly downward when one of the samurai spoke, but he is not a samurai yet. His words have also made her feel uncomfortable. The presumptuous compliment prompts her to turn and tilt her head slightly. He lifts his head, too, so she can see into his eyes.

She peers at him out of the sides of her own eyes, staring deeply into the windows of his soul. There is something dark and selfish in him. She sees lust and greed lurking in his shadowy light. She mutters in reaction to what she sees, "Ie!" Ishida instantly feels the sting of her sudden and flat rejection. He gasps before taking a half step back from her in shock.

Ashi realizes what she has just done. She never meant to say it out loud, but she deeply offended Ishida with that one word. Wanting to escape the situation, she quickly collects her items and then hurriedly leaves the market. Ishida looks around anxiously, feeling as though everyone in the village saw her rejection of him. Though it went unseen by all, a sense of shame still fills him. It is a feeling he does not like, and it quickly leads to anger.

He looks up the road where Ashi rushes to return home. She accidentally dropped one of her items. Another young warrior in training, Saitō Sōji, stops to pick up the package and politely hands it back to her. Although Ishida cannot hear what is said, Ashi is obviously grateful for Saitō's assistance. She hurriedly bowed before rushing toward the estate.

Saitō moved on as though he had done nothing. Jealousy and resentment swell in Ishida's heart and mind. He slips behind the market to angrily pace in the alley near the wall of willow branches. He is uncertain how the daimyō will react to his advances toward Ashi. Fear and anger lead him to take flight and leave the village. He flies through the forest in short bursts, moving from branch to branch, landing only long enough to brood on his malcontent.

Because of their size, the Hotaru-Raikō have few enemies and are usually free to move about the fields and forests unmolested. Not even man has trails in this area of the woods. So he continues to fly through the red, orange, and yellow autumn foliage, consumed by his selfish thoughts.

As he flies, he is not aware of the changes around him. The woods' usually bright autumn beauty gives way to a darker, more shadowy sky than usual. The air grows stale, quiet, and ominous, but he does not notice because of his self-absorbed brooding. Ishida does not see the massive web between two old, leafless trees swaying back and forth in the stale air. He flies headlong into it and is immediately trapped by the sticky silk.

Because the hotaru fly with their bodies upright, unlike birds that fly horizontally, nearly his entire body is stuck. Only his wing shells remain free. Ishida stays still for a few seconds, looking around cautiously. He has been trapped somewhere near the bottom half of the massive web. There are many discarded husks wrapped in webbing on the ground below, some the size of small birds. The air smells of death and decay. Even the slight breeze that sways the web cannot carry the stench away. Nothing is moving; there is no sound.

Feeling only a little confident that it is an old, unoccupied web, he tries to reach for the tantō in his obi.[66] Unfortunately, he cannot reach it or either of his swords. He yanks his right arm, trying to break the web to reach them, but to no avail. He rests momentarily on the web, which bounces like a trampoline. Then he hears it. One of the radial lines of the

---

[66] Belt (translated from Japanese).

web is plucked like the string on a biwa,[67] reverberating down to where he is.

Ishida remains as still as he can. There comes another pluck of the line, harder this time, making the capture web ripple. He senses an evil presence; he knows he is not alone. An uneasiness arises in his stomach. He knows he cannot escape but also knows he must reach his tantō or wakizashi[68] if he is to survive.

He struggles to free his right arm, shaking the web. He hears movement above and suddenly stops. He looks up to see a massive, dark body. Several red eyes peer down upon him. Panic begins to set in. If he does not free his hand, he will die a gruesome and dishonorable death.

He looks down to see how close his hand is to his tantō. The spider violently bounces the whole web, causing him to become even more entangled. Thoroughly ensnared, he knows he is about to meet his end. He grudgingly turns his eyes toward the shadowy figure above and finds that it has changed.

There are now only two red eyes looking down at him. The spider creature turned its body, and Ishida could no longer see its eyes. He can, however, make out the spindly, hairy black legs starting to move down the webbing. It casts a silken line into the tree canopy and swings away from the web.

Descending slowly on the sleek thread, a human figure begins to come into the light. He is surprised to see the delicate feet of a woman appear first. Then, the rest of her is slowly revealed in the light.

The woman is as big as he is. She has fair skin and long, ebony hair, which is somewhat disheveled. She wears a three-

---

[67] Japanese lute, a stringed instrument (translated from Japanese).

[68] Smaller sword, similar to the modern katana.

layer jūnihitoe.[69] The inner robe is a white kosode covered by a crimson hitoe robe. And then there's a final black uchigi or outer robe. It is all loosely tied together with a golden obi, which allows more of the milky skin above her bosom to be visible. The skinny, black legs protrude from her back and hold onto the strand she descends from. Ishida finds himself strangely mesmerized by this yōkai.[70]

Curiously, the spider yōkai does not race down the web to inject her venom. Instead, she moves slowly, seductively, toward Ishida. She immediately recognizes the crest on his kataginu[71]; she knows from where he comes. She reaches out with her hands to grasp the webbing around him, slightly pressing herself against him. "Well," she whispers, "who has come to visit me today?"

Ishida's eyes are transfixed on her round crimson eyes; he does not notice her gently breaking the webbing around his wings. He does feel when they are loosened, though, and instinctively lowers them.

"Mmmm," moans Kumo while she guides his wings under their ebony shells. "How delicate and strong," she whispers in his ear, secretly ensuring the excess webbing has locked his wings closed, preventing his flight. She then moves swiftly to his left side; he turns his head to find her.

She slips her hand just inside the edge of his kosode and slowly slides it down to his obi. Again, she groans, "Ohhh." Ishida is becoming aroused by her. She grasps the sheaths of his blades, gently removing them from his obi. "You weren't going to use these on me, were you?" she asks innocently.

"Īe," he answers humbly.

---

[69] Layered robes, a precursor to the modern kimono.

[70] Supernatural creatures or spirits often considered demons.

[71] Short sleeveless garment (translated from Japanese).

"Yoi,"[72] she says with a seductive smile. She lifts the swords and tantō in the air over her head, and one of her spindly legs takes them and secures them to the strand of the web she descended on. Now that his weapons are out of reach, she slowly cuts the strands of webbing from around Ishida. "I am Kumo." She pauses. "I have been waiting for you, samurai, for a long time." She stops and looks deeply into his eyes, expecting him to introduce himself.

"Ishida," he mumbles.

"Ah," she acknowledges as she returns to cutting the webbing. "I have need of a fearless samurai...Ishida." After she finished clipping the webbing on his left side, she rolled him over on his back on the web. He is now utterly helpless before her. Kumo lets go of the ensnaring web. She dangles gracefully in front of him as if floating in mid-air. Her jūnihitoe nearly slips off her left shoulder as she sways on the strand. Ishida ogles her as she pulls it back up. She sees the lust in his eyes. "Where do your loyalties lie, young Ishida? Who is your master?"

"I am rōnin, my lady."

"Are you not of the Hotaru-Raikō clan?"

"No longer. I would have my own clan," boasts Ishida.

Kumo senses this is her opportunity. "Yoi," she says with a grin as she touches his chest boldly. "Are there others you hold sway over, young warrior?"

"Hai.[73] A handful."

Kumo pulls herself close to Ishida, her robes again touching his. "I have a proposition for you, samurai." Her tiny white fangs glint in the light as she smiles at him. "Your old daimyō stands in the way of what I intend to accomplish. If you help me, I will install you as lord in his place." She puts

---

[72] Pronounced "Yoh-ee"—meaning "Good" (translated from Japanese).

[73] Yes (translated from Japanese).

her lips close to his ear. "If you bring those loyal to you to serve me, I will give you back your blades and everything else your heart desires. Will you do this for me...koibito?"[74] A lustful shiver moves through Ishida.

"Hai," answers Ishida obediently. In that moment, he is wholly given over to lust and greed. An unholy bargain is struck. Kumo snips the last strands of webbing and those holding his wings to his body. Ishida flies out in front of the web and turns to bow to his new master.

"You will find me in the forest between the Kutsuki Valley and the Saba Kaido in the Kyoto Province. Seek out my webbed palace in the beech tree at the center of the woods."

"Hai," he agrees. Ishida bows again and then flies back into the forest from which he came. Kumo continues to grin with wicked pleasure.

* * * * *

It was no coincidence that Saitō was near the market that morning. He is enamored of Ashi and hopes to glimpse her gliding through the village. Saitō is only a year older than Ashi. He is handsome and strong yet humble, studious, and hardworking.

Every morning, he rises, cares for his hygiene, goes to the shrine in reverence of God, prays for the souls of his parents, and then eats. He practices his swordsmanship and archery daily. His goal is to fly with the daimyō one day as one of his trusted samurai.

Unlike Ishida, however, Saitō does not see Ashi as a means to an end; instead, he sees the inner beauty of her heart, which radiates outward. He knows her way, movements, smile, strength, voice, and light; he is attracted to everything about her. Though he does not have much to

---

[74] Lover (translated from Japanese).

offer in the way of gifts, nothing that might win her hand anyway, he hopes she might notice his light, which burns brightly for her.

Although he was all too eager to help, he made a concerted effort to keep propriety in mind while in the public square as he helped her with the package she dropped when fleeing the market that morning. The last thing he wanted was to bring any shame upon her.

Her kind words and smile made it difficult for Saitō to walk away that morning. Speaking to her made his heart thunder against his chest, and he struggled to keep calm. After that brief encounter, he boldly resolved to request an audience with her father later that day. He was even more thrilled when he received word the same evening that his request was granted. He was to meet with Ashi's father the next morning.

* * * * *

Takeda-san finds Saitō waiting patiently in the chilly morning air at the eastern inner gate. He approaches him, and Saitō offers a deep bow., "Good morning, oyakata-sama."[75]

"Good morning, Saitō-san." Takeda-san returns a slight bow. Afterward, he waives his hand, inviting him into the courtyard. "Kuru.[76] Walk with me." He turns to stroll across the niwa. Saitō follows to his left. "I hear good things about you. Hatano-san informs me that you are becoming a skilled and proficient warrior. I also understand you assisted my daughter in the market yesterday. It seems your assistance and your respect for her have caught her eye. Now, here you are ...wishing to speak with me."

---

[75] Master (translated from Japanese).

[76] Come (translated from Japanese).

"Hai." Saitō swallows his throbbing heart into his chest and summons his courage. "It is true, I wish to serve as one of your ashigaru,[77] but more than that…"There is a brief silence. Only the crunching of gravel can be heard underfoot. "Though I know it is bold of me, I would ask your permission to court Ashi."

Takeda stops in his tracks. He looks into Saitō's eyes, who has also stopped and stands upright before him. Takeda sees both humility and courage in the young warrior. "Why do you seek my daughter's hand?" he asks in a firm, deep voice. He tests the motives of the young hotaru.

"Truly, it is the light of her heart that attracts me. Her outer beauty is reflective of her mind, her heart, and her grace. All I ask is the opportunity to win her favor. Nothing more."

"And if she rejects your advances?"

"I am still your loyal servant, oyakata-sama. My sword and my life are yours to command." He offers a humble bow.

"Hrmm," grumbles Takeda as he turns and quietly continues his stroll. Saitō raises back up and follows. They walk in silence toward the western gate. A large autumn leaf gently lands on the ground near them, but neither pays it much attention. They stop near the entrance. Takeda turns to face the young warrior. "Your request is granted, Saitō-san. I am pleased with your courage and your courtesy. I will allow you to speak with Ashi. I will inform her you will seek her out soon."

"Dōmo arigatōgozaimashita!"[78] Saitō responds, restraining his elation as he bows. Takeda-san bows slightly in return. Although Saitō exits the niwa calmly, he can barely

---

[77] Foot soldiers (translated from Japanese).

[78] Thank you very much (translated from Japanese).

contain his jubilation as he returns swiftly to his humble home.

Takeda takes a deep breath of crisp fall air and returns toward the shinden. *Is my shōjo*[79] *really of age? So much time has passed*, he thinks.

* * * * *

Ishida returns to Raikō Village two days after the incident in the market. He delayed his return, taking the time to plot his next move. He arrives quietly in the morning when most of the village still sleeps. Visiting a fellow warrior, he learns of Ashi's courtship with Saitō; the whole village is abuzz with excitement. Ishida asks his host to discretely call the rest of their closest friends to meet under the giant cherry tree east of the village in an hour. He stresses they are to tell no one. "While you do this, I must obtain a new blade."

Under the lilting orange leaves, the young warriors sit around a council stone. Ishida stands at the clandestine meeting. He makes his case for the eight other young warriors to leave the Hotaru-Raikō and embark on his quest for power and glory with him. He uses the courtship to convince his fellow soldiers that the daimyō does not care about them. "We will never be given status or power while Takeda is daimyō. He does not appreciate our skills or prowess as samurai. This is why we are not even considered ashigaru yet. I think he fears us." He pauses. "But I have found one who has the power to place me in his stead. "

The others listen contemplatively.

"When the time comes, I will need powerful samurai to control the clan. I ask you to follow me." He continues to

---

[79] Little girl (translated from Japanese).

stand in his place at the council, observing the others as they consider his request.

One of the eight, Takayama, breaks the silence. "What you are asking us to do is wrong. Kenshin-san is a just and fair lord. We owe him our loyalty, our swords—"

Before he can finish speaking, Ishida, in a fluid motion and without warning, removes a tantō from his obi and slices Takayama's neck. He falls backward, dying as he does.

The remaining seven are shocked by the swiftness of the assassination. They quickly understand that disloyalty to Ishida will end in death. Their weak, fearful minds succumb to the strong will of their new leader. They agree to follow him, forever leaving their homes and their families.

"Tie a stone around Takayama's feet and throw him in the moat," Ishida commands as he removes Takayama's blades, taking them for his own. He then slices a piece of fabric from Takayama's clothes. "No hotaru must know our plans," he demands as he wipes the blood from his tantō. The rest quickly carry out his orders while Ishida stares at the crimson-stained steel. Though blood-free, the cursed blade now glows red in the sunlight. The desire to hide his betrayal prompts him to hide the blade in its sheath quickly.

After they do their master's bidding, Ishida leads his new ashigaru south to Kyoto Province. There, over the long winter months, Kumo will poison their minds and corrupt their bodies in service to her and her alone. Like the cursed blade of their treacherous leader, the light of their weapons and armor fades from a pale white to deep crimson.

Ishida's lust for Kumo and envy of Takeda twist his mind. His hair turns a light gray, like the color of Kumo's webs. And he lets it fall freely, never again putting it in a topknot. He keeps his face covered in public with a red devil's mask; his antennae sheltered in the protective horns of the mask. Using her silk and the husks of discarded beetles, Kumo weaves a new, jet-black armor for him. She ties a golden rope over the crimson obi around his waist. The shell plates of his armor are triangular, sewn closely together, and overlap like a serpent's skin. The scales on his thigh armor are blood-stained and reddish brown. He takes pleasure in the fear his appearance instills in those who come across him.

Ishida and his soldiers form Kumo's new Tsuchigumo clan. She declares herself kōgō[80] and gives the title of daimyō to Ishida. With the makings of this new clan, she introduces them to her kaijū,[81] who will be the general of her army. She lays out her plan to unleash a legion of fierce beasts just like him from the abyss. The kaijū will be one of many generals leading these beasts to plague man and slaughter her enemies.

She regales her clan with the story of how she conjured the kaijū, how it provided the location of the gate to their realm, hidden deep in the forest, in a long-forgotten shrine at the base of Hakusan. She tells them the Hotaru-Raikō are the only thing standing in her way. Therefore, Takeda and his samurai must be destroyed. All she needs now is the perfect opportunity to implement her plans.

---

[80] Queen (translated from Japanese).

[81] Pronounced "k-eye-joo"—meaning "strange beast" (translated from Japanese).

Chapter Two

Unexpected Journey

Saitō visits Ashi almost daily for the next few weeks. On sunny afternoons, after his training is completed, they meet in the open-air pavilion. There, they talk, stare at the distant Hakusan, and sometimes watch the moon rise. On rainy or cold days, they meet in the warmer and dryer tsuridono, where he shares poetry with her, and she will occasionally play music for him. The light of their love grows brighter with each passing day. Takeda and Harumi are pleased with their daughter's budding romance and announce a spring wedding. They decree that those preparations will begin at the first sign of the cherry blossom.

* * * * *

Months pass. The days are growing longer, the sun warms the earth, the snow is melting, and all signs point to a waking nature. The moss on the shrine is turning a deeper green. The heavy wooden thicket has begun to bud, and the cherry tree blossoms are swelling. During an early morning walk in the niwa, anxiously inspecting the cherry tree, Ashi notices a light in the shrine above. Her father is there, speaking with a stranger. *It is much too early in the season for visitors*, she thinks. *Who could it be?* The stranger stands in the shadowy area of the old ishidōrō. The morning sun has not risen high enough to illuminate the shrine either. So, try as she might, she cannot make out the stranger's features. She conceals herself in the covered pavilion and quietly waits for a glimpse of the stranger when they come down the path.

Several minutes later, her father emerges from the shrine. He descends the path alone and in deep contemplation. Ashi looks back at the shrine, but it is empty. She waits patiently for her father to pass through the torii. "Good morning, Father," she calls sweetly.

Takeda-san stirs from his thoughts. "Ah, Ashi-himē," he replies. "My beautiful daughter."

Ever the bold one, Ashi asks him, "May I share in your thoughts?"

"Īe, not right now," he replies softly. "Iku.[82] Tell your mother we must all speak privately. I will meet you both in the main hall."

Ashi hurries back up the rō to the shinden to inform her mother, Harumi. Together, they prepare a miso soup to warm him. Takeda-san is grateful upon receiving it. They sit together and share their meal. Afterward, he lets them know the stranger in the shrine was a messenger from Tengoku. "I am to take two of my best samurai and two-thirds of our army and immediately depart on a mission in a faraway land. Also, and most regretfully, we must postpone your wedding, Ashi, until I return." He can see the disappointment in Ashi's eyes but continues. "Harumi, I leave the Raikō estate in your hands. Ashi is of age and is well trained; she is onna-musha. We will test Saitō while I am away. He must suspend the search for the eight missing students. I will make him samurai and give him the east tainoya to reside in. He will now serve as your liaison to the Hotaru no Chikyū."

"Hai," agrees Harumi. Though she understands and knows he will serve Kami faithfully. However, Harumi is saddened by the announcement. Something in her heart tells her she will not see him in this world again.

---

[82] Pronounced "Ee-kooh"—meaning "Go" (translated from Japanese).

Studying her mother's face, Ashi lets her emotions get the best of her. She uncharacteristically jumps up and runs to her chambers.

Stunned by her outburst, Takeda looks confusedly at Harumi, who nods and humbly directs, "Iku, husband. She needs you. Comfort her."

He gets up slowly and walks quietly to her room. Stopping outside her chamber, he lets his shadow linger on the rice paper door. He can hear her crying and politely waits for Ashi to quiet herself. Once she is still, he slides the panel door open. She has collected herself and sits on her feet in the seiza position on her tatami mat. Her back is upright, and her hands are folded in her lap. She sits quietly with her right side facing the door. Takeda enters and sits on the mat directly across from her. "Daughter?" he inquires lovingly. "What troubles you?"

She looks into his eyes. "Please don't go, Papa. I have a terrible feeling about this mission." She breaks protocol, lunges, and wraps her arms around him.

"Ashi-himē," he begins as he returns her embrace, "I must go. This task comes from God himself. I dare not dishonor him. You must have faith that all is done according to his will." He pauses for a moment to pat and rub her back gently. "Your mother, gentle as she may be, is also onna-musha; she will protect you with the ferocity of a mother fox for her kit. You also have Saitō now, who has proven himself worthy. Besides—"

"I don't want to lose you," Ashi blurts out.

"Saiai no musume,[83] it will be okay. Do you remember why God sent us here? To this island, closed off to the rest of the world? I wondered that for many years. The men of this land are feudal and warlike at times, yet the divine law of God

---

[83] Beloved daughter (translated from Japanese).

is written on their hearts. They see it in nature all around them, yet they don't know the Author of this law. They hold reason and morality on high pedestals and value the customs of their ancestors. I know Kami wanted us to learn from them, learn the way of the warrior so we might defend them against unseen evil in this land or"—he pauses as he again pats her gently on the back—"in faraway lands."

Ashi sits upright and stares deeply into her father's eyes. Her father continues to hold her shoulders firmly but gently for a moment. "You must remember, my daughter, I do not fear death. Neither should you. In death, we find our way...our way back to Kami. Dying for Our Lord while fighting evil or protecting the weak is honorable. Death is not to be feared. If it is my time, I will gladly give my life to bring glory and honor to God and our family." Takeda releases her shoulders, sits back on his feet, and places his hands on his legs. "You must be courageous, Ashi. I know you will find the strength to protect our clan in my absence and to defend those who cannot defend themselves." He offers a humble yet reassuring smile. " And, God willing, we will return so that I may bless your marriage to Saitō."

"Hai," says Ashi, sniffling. She does her best to put on a brave appearance. "I will be strong for you, Otousama."[84]

"Hrmm...I know you will, musume."Takeda takes his folded fan from his obi. "You always make me happy and proud. I will love you forever, in this world and the next." He offers the kind of fatherly smile that goes straight to the heart and soul of a daughter. She smiles back at him and quickly bows her head. Confident she will be okay, he gently taps her on the knee with his closed fan before leaving.

Takeda returns to Harumi, who has finished cleaning the table. "All is better, my wife, but you will check on her later?"

---

[84] Father (translated from Japanese).

She smiles and bows her head slightly in agreement. "Yoi. I go to make arrangements for the mission." Takeda leaves the shinden. He will be with his samurai for the rest of the day. Together, they gathered his army and prepared for the journey. Ashi spends her day pouring all her love into making a single kanji, a gift for her father to take with him.

Ashi's mother comes to check in on her and finds her making the kanji. She does not disturb her daughter; instead, she stands silently in the door's opening, watching her focus on its creation. A tear wells up in her eye when she glimpses the kanji. Harumi has always been proud of Ashi's exceptional ability to write elegantly in both masculine and feminine ways.

* * * * *

The moment has come to say farewell. It is not, nor has it ever been, easy for Harumi to see her husband off to conflict. She, too, feels this might be the last time she is with her husband. Harumi gets up early the following day to help him don his armor. It is a solemn but serene moment shared between them. She begins by sliding his kosode over his arms, draping it on his shoulders from behind. She moves quietly, lovingly, around to fold it in front of him. She does not look him in the eye but humbly and gracefully goes about her work.

Takeda looks down at this beautiful wife as she folds his kosode. He remembers long ago when he took Harumi as his wife after arriving in Nihon. As Saitō is drawn to Ashi, he too is drawn to Harumi's inner light. It is a gentle, soothing glow that captured and has kept his desire for hundreds of years. In their youth, they had many adventures that spanned most of the island nation of Nihon. Now, as a weathered daimyō and father, he relies on her to bring balance to his lordship of the clan and within his household. He knows he would be only a half-empty shell if he lost her. So it is in these quiet moments, when not a word is spoken, that he cherishes every touch of her hand as she slowly dresses him in the ornate armor. For Harumi, it is in this service that she shows her love and devotion to her faithful husband.

Later, the Hotaru-Raikō army assembles in the predawn glow, illuminating the courtyard. Ashi awaits her father just inside the southern doors of the shinden leading out onto the covered veranda. She bows low as he approaches, her mother just behind him. She holds up a scroll of rice paper for him. He stops and looks down lovingly at her. He then tenderly takes the scroll and slowly unfurls it. The word 愛(Ai, or "love") is delicately and beautifully scribed there. He scrolls the paper back up and returns her bow. She rises to see him. Takeda truly loves his daughter, and to show his love, he slowly tucks the scroll into his kosode, close to his heart. Not a word is said; none is needed. Father, mother, and daughter all know their bond—a deep familial love and devotion that is unbreakable. No matter what comes, their love can never be taken from them.

Takeda-san moves to the doors. Mother and daughter each slide one side open, presenting the great leader to his army. He steps out onto the top step of the veranda—his samurai bow low, followed by the assembled army, all in unison. The daimyō's heart swells with pride; he is inspired by the loyalty and confidence of his men. He offers a bow of gratitude in return. He then stands upright and lifts his wing covers horizontally, which signals that the time for departure is at hand. The white edge, which runs along each dark-brown cover, glints in the sunlight. His strong, smoke-colored wings unfurl in the rising sun. Emulating their master, the army also prepares for flight. The drone of their wings fills the niwa. Without a word, Takeda-san rises into the air and flies east.

His faithful army follows. They hold their heads up high, looking to the horizon with conviction.

* * * * *

In the Kyoto Province, Kumo grows impatient. It had been a long winter, and her hatred of men and hotaru deepened. Long ago, she was being driven north out of the Nara Prefecture. The men of Kyoto also discovered her true nature, causing her to flee further north into the dense woods. Seeking revenge, she found a way to summon a single kaijū. This monster told her of a legion of others like him, waiting in Abaddon to torment men and destroy their crops.

Now she sits on her throne of stag beetle husks, remembering its words, "They need only be released." Her spies have found the gate, her army is primed, and she is poised to release the devastating horde. Her long-awaited revenge is at hand; only the Hotaru-Raikō stand in her way. Kumo is overjoyed when word of the daimyō's absence reaches her. She is told two-thirds of their army has left Nihon. Their absence is the opportunity she has been looking for. She prepares her treacherous Tsuchigumo clan to travel to Hakusan. They are to arrange everything before her arrival there. She is eager to conduct the ritual and open the gate to the abyss.

* * * * *

Spring and most of the summer have passed. Late summer heat is already giving way to cooler temperatures. A village subdued by the absence of its warriors sits quietly by the placid waters of the Fukui Castle moat. A familiar sound, faintly at first, begins to infiltrate from the east. The distinct sound of humming perks up the antennae of the denizens of Raikō Village; they know that sound—the Hotaru-Raikō army returns. Villagers rush past the ishidōrō shrine to line the outer edges of the courtyard, eager to welcome home their husbands, fathers, sons, and brothers.

Keeping low to the ground, a steady stream of armored ashigaru follow their daimyō and his samurai. Takeda is used to a more significant greeting when he returns from much shorter excursions. Surveying the inner lights of those who welcome his return, he senses both joy and sadness in them. He wonders if it is because they see the returning army's numbers are fewer or if something has happened to his clan while they were away. Either way, something is wrong.

As soon as he sets his sandaled foot upon the gravelly courtyard, Takeda calls his samurai, Sasaki-san and Hatano-san, to him. Speaking quietly to them, he states, "Something is amiss. There is an unsettled feeling among our people. Discover what has taken place in our absence."–He pauses as he notices the widow of Hasegawa[85] seeking her fallen husband among the soldiers.–"Speak with the widows and children of the fallen. We must care for them in their mourning and provide for them in their need. My wealth is theirs. I would ensure they have anything they need."

Both men discretely exclaim, "Hai!" They reunite with their own families before going on to investigate what has transpired in their absence and consoling the families of the fallen.

Folding his wings under their hard shell, Takeda-san turns toward his home. Ashi is standing on the top step of the veranda, looking down at him with longing. He knows his daughter. He reads many things in her eyes; his return brings relief, joy, fear, and sadness. Ashi is holding back tears of distress, of a heavy burden. He knows she wishes to run to him but is restraining herself. Indeed, something terrible has

---

[85] aka "Wrestles with Hare" from *Guardian of the Lightning Seeds*

happened. Takeda looks around for Harumi, too, but quickly realizes she is nowhere to be seen. He walks toward the steps and greets her, "Konnichiwa, Ashi-himē. I have missed you, daughter." He stops at the top step and faces her. "Where is your mother? Why does she not come out to greet me?"

"Otousama," she begins, "I have grave news." Ashi is losing the fight to hold back her emotions. "Kudasai,[86] come inside so I may tell you." She bows, turns, and slides the door open for him to enter. Takeda enters, and Ashi quickly closes the door behind them. Seeking the security of her father's arms, she surprises him with an embrace. It is tender and heartfelt; Takeda returns it unreservedly. Comforted, she finally pulls back.

Takeda looks deep into her eyes. "Where is your mother?"

"Oh, Papa, Mother went to one of the onsen[87] on Hakusan to search for kuro yuri[88] weeks ago. Neither she nor her escort ever returned. I've been trying to keep everyone's spirits high, but the village knows she is missing. They fear the worst."

A sense of urgency wells up in Takeda's chest. He tells Ashi, "Have lanterns hung all around the niwa to help light her way back, just in case. Where is Saitō? Has he treated you well?"

"Hai, Papa, he has. He has brought much honor upon our house during your absence. He should be coming back from a visit with King Hi-marō and the Hotaru no Chikyū soon."

"Yoi. Send him to me as soon as he returns. Tomorrow, I will take him and a squad of fresh ashigaru to find your mother." He begins to walk toward his chamber. Ashi follows him closely. "While we search, I want you to work with the

---

[86] Please (translated from Japanese).

[87] Hot springs (translated from Japanese).

[88] A rare, chocolate-colored lily that grows on the slopes of Mount Haku.

other wives and daughters to prepare a small festival for the returning army. We will share the details of our journey at the feast." He stops, faces Ashi, and stares lovingly at his daughter. "It will give you something to do, Ashi, and will take your mind off your troubles and reassure our people." He offers a comforting smile.

"Hai, Otousama." "She knows he is right.

"Now, I really must bathe and put on fresh clothes." Takeda-san heads into his chamber and slides the door shut behind him. He hears his daughter rush off. Knowing he is finally alone, he sighs quietly. His already heavy heart sinks further into his chest, but he has never been one to give in to sadness. He removes his armor, bathes, and then puts on fresh clothes. He knows prayer is needed and goes discretely into the shrine to not only give thanks for those who returned with him but also pray for his lost wife.

Ashi finds out her father is in the shrine and sends Saitō to meet him there. Saitō eagerly wants to give a complete account of all that has happened when he arrives at the shrine, but Takeda-san informs him of the following day's mission instead and his role. "I understand you have brought honor upon my house, Saitō-san. You have made me proud. I look forward to hearing all that has happened while we travel tomorrow. For now, though, iku. Find Sasaki-san and Hatano-san. Send them to me here, in the shrine."

"Hai!" answers Saitō before bowing and carrying out his lord's orders.

While he waits, Takeda prays and meditates. His heart and mind are burdened by much: the loss of so many fine soldiers in the faraway land, his missing wife, and now an overwhelming sense of betrayal from someone within his clan. Again, the urgency to find his beloved and the truth of what has happened fills him.

His loyal samurai joined him a short while later. Though deep in contemplative prayer, Takeda knows when they arrive, he can feel their presence. He trusts only God and his family more than them. Sasaki and Hatano entered quietly and respectfully waited until he was finished. Without opening his eyes, he asks them, "What have you discovered?"

"Oyakata-sama, there are rumors of an unseen evil moving through the woods. The eight students never returned, nor were their bodies ever found. Much suspicion surrounds their disappearance. It is whispered they travel with the wicked shadow," informs Hatano-san.

"Hrmmpf," grunts Takeda. He says only one word, a name, "Ishida." He reflects on what Ashi told him about the greed and lust, the dimming of Ishida's light she saw in the market last year. Takeda feels he may be the source of this sense of betrayal. "Select a squad of fresh soldiers. They will accompany Saitō with me on a search party tomorrow morning." The daimyō opens his eyes and looks at his samurai. "Sasaki-san, Hatano-san, we will search for four days. You have earned the time to rest. Iku. Spend time with your families while we are away, but be alert." Both samurai share their gratitude and then get up to leave.

"Hatano-san."

"Hai, sensei."

"Kudasai, send your daughter, Yui, to keep Ashi company while she prepares for the festivities."

"Hai." Hatano-san need not ask why; he understands his master. He leaves silently while Takeda closes his eyes and returns to prayer.

* * * * *

The following day, Takeda-san leads Saitō and a squad of soldiers on the long journey to the first of two hot springs at the base of Hakusan. Though a lengthy trip, Takeda relishes returning to Nihon, flying through the mountain's lush forests. He reflects on memories of gliding up the mountain with his beloved Harumi. Before Ashi was born, they would playfully weave and dance around the beech, mizunara, and tochinoki trees. The smell of rain-soaked leaves and pine needles would fill his nostrils, while the warmth of sunbeams passing through gaps in the leafy canopy overhead would warm his body. Today, he is motivated by a concern for his bride.

During the summer, vast amounts of flowers bloom simultaneously on Hakusan's open mountainsides. Though he knows those blooms will be fading now, he longs to look upon those fields again and remember the first time he and Harumi emerged into the open-air meadows. Amazingly fragrant breezes would waft down from the summit. He recalls the awe-filled expression on Harumi's face, the brightness of her eyes, the first time they flew out over the sprawling fields. The picturesque meadow was one of the few places he could remotely compare anything on earth to what he knew of heaven. He delighted in watching his bride dip, dive, and waltz among those blooms. She danced up into the sparser alpine fields, stopping only to breathe deep of the small, delicate white and lavender hakusanfuro flowers, the deep-purple, daisy-like hakusankozakura flowers with their yellow hearts, and, his favorite, gozen-tachibana. Though their blossoms are waning, the beauty of what still blooms is not lost on him or his soldiers as they reach the alpine meadows.

He looks for the gozen-tachibana flower, which grows in clusters and is made of four small and delicate white petals surrounded by five or six pointy and verdant leaves. The beautiful floral star inspires him, but that is not why it is his favorite. It is his favorite because it produces a sweet, delicious, bright-red berry he likes to pluck and eat. The flowers are sparse today, and the berries have not quite ripened. The joy of nibbling on berries is not to be. His empty stomach growls at his heavy heart as the search for his lost bride continues.

They fly north and east to the Ichirino onsen first, hoping they might find her stranded there. Instead, they find no trace. They camp there for the night before traveling south to the spring near the small human village of Shiramine the next morning. There, inspecting the area around the onsen, one of the soldiers spots a piece of material. A tattered cloth torn from a robe clings to the broken branch of a shrub. The soldier collects it and hurriedly brings it to his master, who instantly recognizes the material. It belonged to Harumi, an uchigi he had given her years ago. He is devastated. The mountainside is silent; he hears only the wind blow. The depressing silence is pierced by the screech of a golden eagle in the quiet summer sky. He looks up to see the bird soaring in the pale blue heavens overhead. He thinks of his "big brother," Hania, in the faraway land and wonders if the bird is an omen or warning.

They begin to examine the surrounding area thoroughly. Not far from the onsen, they find a strange, oblong object covered in webs. It looks like the remains of a spider's discarded prey, but it is too large. Saitō approaches cautiously, removes his tantō, and slices through the web. He takes a step back; he is shocked at what he sees. All that remains is the husk of one of his fellow Hotaru-Raikō. The body withered and distorted, fills only half of the armor encased in the webbing. All the fluids have been drained from the victim, giving him a mummified appearance. Saitō covers his mouth and nose while sheathing his blade. "What could have done this, my lord?" He looks to Takeda-san, who is also inspecting the body. "There is no spider large enough to attack us in this way. What else could have done this?"

The daimyō breaks a stick off the nearby bush. He pokes at a black, tar-like substance next to the body. He scrapes at it with the stick, but it does not dissipate over the rock. It reminds him of spittle.

"Over here, my lord. We found another," calls another soldier. Several feet away, one more cocooned body is found.

"This must be the other escort," states Saitō. He sees desperation and anger rising on his master's face. He motions to the others. "Spread out! Keep looking for our lady."

"Saitō," says Takeda in a deep voice.

"Hai, oyakata-sama."

"Have two ashigaru burn these bodies. We will continue the search and then collect their bones for burial later."

"Hai," Saitō obeys. He passes the orders to two soldiers who set the bodies alight where they lie. He then joins the rest in searching for Lady Harumi. Takeda-san stands tall, one hand on his sword handle, slowly scanning the rocky mountain, the swaying meadows, and the forest's edge. He looks for signs of enemy movement or the haunting presence of yūrei.[89]

They search for a couple of hours while the bodies of the escorts are cremated but find no sign of Lady Harumi. Takeda recalls his troops from their search and tasks them with collecting any remaining bones of the dead so they may have a proper burial in their village cemetery. He moves up the mountainside to a rock outcropping, away from his troops. There, among the alpine flowers, he kneels in reflection and prayer. He remembers coming here years ago, relaxing in the warm waters while watching Harumi bathe. Takeda closes his eyes. He could still see water glisten on her soft, milky-white skin and her smile as she washed her jet-black hair in the hot spring waters. Instead of joy, however, the memory brings

---

[89] Ghosts or spirits (translated from Japanese).

him sadness. He can feel the loss of her light in the world. He knows deep down his wife's fate has been sealed by whomever, or whatever, did this. He prays to Kami for the soul of his wife and her escorts. He gives thanks for keeping Ashi and the rest of the village safe in his absence. Lastly, he asks God for justice, for the destruction of those who would kill in such a deviant and cowardly way. The daimyō returns to his troops afterward and then leads them back home.

The expedition returns to find Ashi and Yui have organized a wonderful feast. Saitō takes the bones of the fallen to the village priest, while Takeda goes silently to his shinden, speaking to no one. Ashi visits her father immediately after his arrival. She is the only one outside his expedition who learns the sad news. Though he genuinely loves his daughter, he gently asks her to leave. "Kudasai, musume, spend some time with Saitō; be with the one you love before you have to turn in for the night. You will need all the sleep you can get for tomorrow's festivities." He then walks contemplatively through the western rō and into the private pavilion. From there, he slips outside and goes up to the shrine for meditation. He stays until he is exhausted and then turns in for what will be a restless sleep.

* * * * *

The following day, the daimyō leads a procession of samurai, elders, and priests into the shrine to place the medicine wheel he received from Hania on the altar. There, he also reveals the sad news that Lady Harumi has been lost. "We will mourn her together tomorrow." He proclaims, "Today, let us rejoice in those who returned from our distant journey and honor those who gave their lives in service to Kami." Ashi joins him in leading everyone down into the courtyard, where they preside over the festival.

The returning warriors act out a play depicting the journey with the young Notah, who becomes the man known as Hania. They tell the story of how Hasegawa earned his new name, "Wrestles with Hare," and the honorable way he died. The troupe also performs a reenactment of the battle to retrieve the lightning seeds. Joy, laughter, and a deep sense of filial pride return to the village. After the play, a few young warriors compete in Sumai no Sechi for their daimyō, who observes with a heavy heart and burdened mind. Hiding these emotions, he congratulates the winners and fulfills his duty to his people by offering the much-needed festival. They, in return, prepare for the dance to honor the spirits of their dead. During the dance, Takeda-san sees something which brings him hope and happiness.

Saitō respectfully approaches Ashi, who sits near her father and offers a low bow to them both. The daimyō gives an approving smile and bow. Even though Takeda knows Ashi mourns the loss of her mother, he witnesses both of their lights brighten when Saitō reaches for her hand. A father watches his daughter dance with her betrothed from his seat overlooking the festival. Their bodies flash and glow with a brilliant radiance. Truly, he can see the bond and the love they share. The strong and deep connection between them brings him peace. As a father and a lord, Takeda-san knows he has chosen the right samurai to marry Ashi and is looking forward to grooming him to take over the clan one day.

The village enjoys feasting, games, and uplifting times well into the evening. Night settles in, and most slip into a restful night's sleep. A serene hush settles over the quaint village...until the early morning hours. Sometime around three o'clock, the distant sound of taiko drums is heard, echoing through the woods like far-off thunder. Muffled by a light fog, the rhythmic beats are faint initially but grow louder and faster. They wake Takeda and his samurai. Their tone has a ferocity, a malevolence, which puts village guards on edge. Then, before the location of the drums can be determined, they fall silent. Like the cry of the golden eagle on the previous day, the lord of the Hotaru-Raikō knows the drums are a foreboding sign.

Chapter Three

Death of the Samurai

After the drumming stops, Takeda-san immediately calls for his samurai. He also sends runners to consult the guards around Raikō Village and discern from which direction the sounds came. They all come back to the steps in front of the shinden. Takeda-san stands on the top step with Saitō on his left and Ashi behind him.

"The eastern guards report the drums seemed to be coming from the base of Hakusan, oyakata-sama," informs Sasaki.

Hatano reports, "The northern guards saw no activity in Fukui Castle, my lord. This means the sound was not in the frequency of man's hearing."

"Hmmph. Am I to have no peace?" grumbles an exhausted Takeda. "Sasaki-san, Hatano-san, prepare two squads of ashigaru. We will investigate the drums." The two samurai bow and immediately run to prepare.

"And me, lord?" inquires Saitō as he steps closer.

"Go to your tainoya. Prepare your armor. You will go with us."

"Hai," Saitō responds with eagerness.

Takeda-san turns to face his daughter. "Ashi, you are onna-musha. I leave the defense of the estate and the clan to you. I pray, daughter, that it will not be needed."

"Hai. Me, too, Otousama."She opens the door for him as he strides in her direction.

* * * * *

One of the eastern guards is among the ten warriors who gather in the niwa later. He will be their scout since he heard from which direction the drums came. The samurai inspect the men and ensure they are ready for battle while waiting for their daimyō. He emerges and, without hesitation, takes to the sky. The band of warriors quickly follows him out into the chilly morning air. Their brightly glowing armor and sashimono are striking against the black, predawn landscape. In the distance overhead, yellow fades to orange, purple, blue, and finally, the fading night sky. Ashi moves out onto the veranda. She watches the white lights move quickly toward Hakusan before disappearing in the wooded distance. She returns inside to dress formally and again fulfills her leadership role in the village.

* * * * *

It is midday, and Takeda is growing weary. The lack of sleep. The heartbreak. The continuous search in vain for the missing. He has only had a single day's rest. Death and ominous signs of something wicked are everywhere without any trace of who or what is causing it. He does his best to remain disciplined and to keep striving forward with what he believes to be the right course.

Today, his Hotaru-Raikō search the northern section of the Kuzuryu River basin, all the way up to where it meets the Takinami River. From there, they move east of the confluence to the foot of the mountains. There is an area where bones of ancient, prehuman beasts can be spotted. Takeda knows of a large beech tree to rest in near the site and leads his men there. All are happy to rest in the shade of the lush tree. They sip nectar from the lotus and nibble on the seeds from the flower's pods.

Resting on a branch further up from his ashigaru, Takeda hears the distinct screech of a golden eagle in the distant sky. He looks up just in time to see arrows raining down upon them. He sounds the alarm, but it is too late. The volley of arrows slays half of his warriors. Saitō, Sasaki, Hatano, and the remaining warriors draw swords and fly up to surround their daimyō. Fierce howls and screams fill the air around them—creatures resembling their kind, yet twisted, buzz through the air, cutting down every surviving Hotaru-Raikō. Hatano steps out on the branch, desperately trying to get a good look at the enemy, but is cut down by a blur and a flash of red light. His limp body falls to the unyielding ground below. Everyone—save Saitō, Sasaki, and Takeda—has fallen from the tree.

Takeda stands with his back to the tree while his remaining samurai hover just in front of him and to the left and right. The enemy disappears as fast as it came. An unsettling quiet permeates the shadowy canopy. Swords drawn, the three warriors keep their guard up. There is silence, an eerie stillness. Then they hear noise, something large crashing down through the canopy. A giant locust, longer than they are and just as tall as the Hotaru-Raikō, breaks through the leaves. It lands on the branch in front of Takeda with a thud. Its appearance is grotesque. Black, ink-like saliva drips from the sharp teeth protruding from his almost human-looking face. Takeda watches the saliva land on the branch and recognizes the consistency; it is the same as he found at the onsen. Wrath rises in his chest. "Kaibutsu!"[90] he screams, holding the tip of his sword outward toward the beast. Its white blade glows brightly as lightning in the shade of the beech tree. "You took my beloved from me!"

---

[90] Monster (translated from Japanese).

The locust lets out a guttural laugh as he opens his wing covers. His red-tinged wings begin to beat, and he rises slowly, hovering just over the branch. Takeda does not hesitate. He begins to charge, running along the branch. His eyes are locked on the monsters. Unfortunately, he does not see the scorpion-like tail uncurling from its back. Sasaki does see it from his position. He flies quickly in front of his lord to cut the tail but is not fast enough. Instead, the barb of the tail runs completely through Sasaki's abdomen, and its tip pierces Takeda's chest, injecting its venom into the daimyō. The monster whips his tail backward, discarding the samurai to the ground while watching the reaction of his actual target.

The light of Takeda's sword dims as he stumbles and begins to fall from the branch. Saitō swoops to his aid, catches him in midair, and begins to fly downward, away from the tree and down toward the river. An arrow from an unseen enemy in the tree is loosed; it goes through Saitō's wing but misses its true mark. The pain is agonizing, but he sputters on toward the water. Once over the river, he turns his body so that his unconscious master is above him, painfully folds his wings under their covers, and freefalls, plunging into the Takinami River.

The enemy loses sight of them, but it matters not to them. "They're dead, or soon will be," comes a sultry voice from the shadows in the trees. "Gather the bodies of the fallen beneath the tree. They can still serve me in death."

* * * * *

Three days passed, and Ashi feared neither her father nor her betrothed would return. Near the evening of the third day, Saitō is spotted by guards carrying her father over his shoulders toward the eastern gate. He is on foot. And one of his wings, damaged from the arrow, is sticking out from under its cover, dragging in the dirt. The guards announce their approach. Ashi, accompanied by other warriors, runs out to meet them.

"Your father..." starts Saitō, desperate for breath, "he is wounded...poisoned. Quickly, take him." The guards take their unresponsive daimyō and rush toward the shinden. Saitō, walking next to Ashi and dragging his feet, does not reach the courtyard. He collapses to the ground from exhaustion after passing through the outer gate. He is battered, bruised, and breathing heavily. Villagers come to help carry him to the eastern tainoya.

Once inside, servants immediately attend to Takeda-san. They removed his armor, bathed him, dressed his wound, and clothed him in a new kosode before placing him in his bed. The poison has taken its toll; there is nothing they can do to save him. Ashi stays with Saitō briefly while the servants care for her father. She helps treat his wounded wing while he tells her about being ambushed and about the monster that poisoned her father. He explains how they escaped and, using a lily pad as a raft, floated down the Kuzuryu River to Eiheiji. From there, they traveled the rest of the way on foot. Ashi can see he is exhausted. She calms him and quickly gets him to rest. She leaves to be with her father as soon as he is asleep.

Ashi enters his room, and all the attendants leave. She quietly slides the door shut and then immediately kneels at his side. With her hands clasped together on her lap, she leans to his ear and whispers, "Papa?"

Her father barely opens his eyes. He groans in agony as he turns his head slightly to see her. "Saiai...no musume," he labors to say. "I...I love..."—his voice trails off to a whisper—"you..." He exhales. Closing his eyes, he breathes his last.

Ashi stares down at him, stunned. She leans over his body, resting her head on his chest. Tears stream uncontrollably down her soft cheeks. She wants more time with her father. She does not know what to do or what to say. Instead, she cries. It takes a few minutes, but she forces herself from her sorrow and sits back up. She lovingly turns his head so he is facing skyward. She kisses his cheek and, through her tears, whispers, "Go in peace, Otousama. May you find Mother waiting for you in the fields of Tengoku."

Ashi feels lost and alone. Her mother is assumed dead, her body never recovered. An assassin has killed her father, and her betrothed lies injured down the hall. Their warrior ranks have been decimated. Standing, she collects herself. *I promised Father I would be strong*, she thinks. *I must honor my parent's memory.* She leaves her father's room and walks stoically toward the niwa. Sadness tugs her heart lower. Ashi covered her head with her uchigi, wrapping it around her so only her face showed as she walked out into the night air. She looks at the long band of twinkling stars set against the dark sky. She lets out an unconscious sigh and then enters the empty, gravel courtyard.

Although she loves Saitō deeply, her thoughts dwell upon her father. Ashi wanders the courtyard, desperately trying to collect her feelings and process everything. *So many dead.* The burden of leadership in such a desperate time falls squarely upon her shoulders—*so many expectations. I never anticipated being without my father's guidance so soon. How can I lead the Hotaru-Raikō now? Must we move again? We still don't know the source of the drums or the magnitude of what we face. How can we defeat the unknown?* She selfishly wonders if it would have been better to have perished with her mother and father. *There is so much uncertainty about what is to come*, she ponders.

Ashi is so deep in her thoughts that she does not realize she has instinctively walked to the shrine entrance. She stops and looks up at the gakuzuka[91] on the faded wood torii. Carved in the wooden sign is the kanji 私, which translates to Watashi (or "I am"). A memory comes flooding into her mind from when she was a shōjo. Her father once brought her up to the base of Hakusan on a Sunday. They sat together on a branch in a beech tree, looking up at the mountain and waiting for the sun to rise. She loved those moments with him. She loved that he never withheld his knowledge from her, especially regarding God. Again, his words return to her...

"Kami cannot be contained in a single shrine, Ashi-himē. All of nature is a shrine to him, a place to discover his creative majesty. Our humble shrine only helps us focus our thoughts on him and..."—he paused to look down and smile at her—"it helps us teach you and the other children about him." He exhaled as he turned his eyes back to the coming sunrise. "I cannot describe what being in Kami's presence is like. I do not possess the words for such magnificence, awe, and love."

He was silent for a moment. "Beautiful though they are, even the elaborate tea ceremonies held in our shrine cannot compare with taking tea in Tengoku either." He silently reflected on the growing amber light from the rising sun. "Hrm...I must say I miss that tea too."

"They have tea in heaven, Papa?" asked little Ashi.

"Hai, musume. It is made from the leaves of the Tree of Life. We brewed the most delicious tea from the leaves that fell from it." He looked over at Ashi and winked. "This is what gives us our long lives here." He returned his gaze to the rising sun. "Unfortunately, our quest for the perfect cup of tea also led to our banishment to earth. In our pride, we decided to make a shimmering, white tea from new leaves still growing on the tree of life. At the time, we did not understand that

---

[91] Rectangular tablet in the top middle of a torii containing the name to whom the temple is dedicated (translated from Japanese).

God caused the leaves to fall, like ripened fruit, for us. There was always just enough for tea." Her father let out a sad sigh. "We had no right to pluck still-growing leaves from the tree. We dishonored God by taking what was his and not respecting the gift he had already given us. And so, because of our pride and greed, he sent us to live here in Nihon until we are either redeemed by his Son or die in his service."

He gently tapped her on the leg with his folded fan. "Unfortunately, daughter, because you were born in this world, it will be harder for you and all our ancestors to maintain faith in our Creator. I am certain there will be challenging times when you will question your belief. When those times come, you must be still. You must seek him out in the beauty of his creation...You need only be calm and observe." He pointed his fan tip toward the brilliant golden light just starting to pierce the sky over the mountain peak. She remembers being dazzled by the rising sun's rays reaching into the sky, embracing the heavens. The light cresting the ridgeline that morning was so bright she could not look directly at it. Young Ashi closed her eyes.

It has been years since. Now, as an adult, she opens them to a dark night. She is alone and dismayed. She mumbles, "Where is the beauty now, Papa?"

Just then, something catches her eye. Ashi looks past the torii, up the path to the old ishidōrō shrine. Someone is standing near the entrance, someone she does not recognize—a tall, strong man wearing a pale blue kataginu over a soft-gray kosode with gray hakama.[92] On his head is a bright tan sandogasa, the edge of its brim glowing with white light around it. The crest on his kataginu, a simple trinitarian symbol with a circle around it, also glows with white light. Ashi recognizes it as a symbol of Kami, the one true God. The

[92] Pleated and divided skirt (translated from Japanese).

samurai stands, his hands in his sleeves, motionless in front of the shrine, staring down at Ashi as if expecting her.

She wonders if this is the same stranger who visited her father a few months earlier. Although it is a time of uncertainty and sorrow, Ashi is compelled by an overriding sense of duty. She subtly wipes any remaining tears from her youthful cheeks and pushes her fear and grief aside. She lets her uchigi down to her shoulders and stands upright. She changes the expression on her face to one of authority. It is her responsibility to find out who this visitor is. She starts up the path.

He removes his hands from his sleeves and holds them just above his waist, palms outward toward her. Though his appearance is stoic and stern, his voice is calming as he greets her, "Peace be upon you, young Ashi."

She bows and greets him, "Konbanwa.[93] How do you know me, sir?"

"All will be revealed in due time. Please, join me." The visitor invites Ashi into the shrine with a motion of his hand. Although he is a stranger, she looks deeply into his eyes and senses profound holiness. She glances into the shrine and notices a black iron teapot with steaming water inside, a long bamboo ladle, and two tea bowls on the stone altar. Guarded, she bowed again and then entered the shrine. The visitor follows her, removing his sandogasa as he enters. He sits in front of the low stone altar where the flame for the old ishidōrō once burned. Ashi sits in the seiza position across from him. Wasting no time, the stranger reaches into his kosode, removes a tiny silk bag, opens it, and upends it over the teapot. A single gray leaf falls into the steaming hot water. The stranger replaces the bag into his kosode. He smiles at her, saying, "We have much to discuss, Ashi-himē."

---

[93] Good evening (translated from Japanese).

"I must know; how do you know me?"

"My name is Præsidiel. I was with your father during his recent journey to the distant lands." While the tea steeps, he reveals the true nature of his being and that he is a servant and messenger of God. He confirms he visited her father and called him to action. Ashi sits in silent contemplation. Although she understands all he has said is true, she still feels numbness in her soul. Præsidiel senses this. He reaches for the teapot and slowly pours the tea into each of their cups. Ashi watched the vapor waft from the bowl with a trance-like stare; she could smell its delicate scent. Præsidiel picks up a cup and sets it down in front of her. "This will help," he says with a reassuring smile.

Ashi politely takes the cup; it is warm in her hands. She brings it to her lips and breathes deeply of the rich, leafy aroma before quietly sipping it. She feels it trickle down her throat to her stomach. Its warmth spreads out into her chest first and then to the rest of her body. Præsidiel hides a smile behind his bowl as he watches her; he can see the light of peace return to her face. She slowly finishes her tea and returns her cup to the low altar. "Arigatou gozaimasu,"[94] she says humbly.

"You are most welcome, Ashi-himē." The angel also places his bowl down. "You know"—he smiles slyly—"your father loves this tea. It is his favorite. He is probably drinking some right now." She looks at him with much curiosity. "Yes, yes. Although his body was broken in this world, your father's spirit, his soul, is still very much alive." He pauses, leans toward her, and looks deep into her dark, almond-shaped eyes. "Everything he taught you about God and heaven is true. Keep this faith alive in your heart, and you will see him and your mother again one day. I promise."

---

[94] Thank you (translated from Japanese).

Tears well up in her eyes. Having no words to offer, Ashi places her hands, palm down, on the ground in front of her knees and offers the angel a low, respectful bow to show her gratitude for the message. She lingers there a little longer before slowly sitting upright again.

"It is written," informs Præsidiel, "the leaves of the tree of life are for the healing of nations." He sits upright and continues more authoritatively, "To that end, I will leave a small amount of tea in the pot for you. After finishing our discussion, you will take it to Saitō, pour it into a cup, and have him drink it. The tea will heal his wing and restore his strength."

"Hai," she acknowledges softly.

"Now, for the other reason, I have been sent. The spider yōkai, Kumo." The angel's face turns solemn. "She has recruited Ishida and others from your clan, seven of the missing students. She has already managed to call upon one of the foul creatures from the abyss. It is his poison that struck down your father. Her Tsuchigumo assassinated his samurai and ashigaru, as well as your mother. Now, she seeks to release an entire horde of monsters, like the one that killed your father, upon the world. These creatures must *not* be released until the appointed time by the designated emissary," he says with authority. "Kumo is overconfident. She thinks she has eliminated your most powerful warriors and that you pose no threat. She underestimates your people." He smiles at her. "You will lead two squads to the Shrine of Ancient Behemoths. You must defeat Kumo and Ishida's traitorous Tsuchigumo, destroy the creature who escaped the abyss, and raze the shrine to the ground, forever sealing the gate there." The angel's tone softens a bit. "This is your purpose, onna-musha, to not only protect your clan and the inhabitants of Nihon but the whole world. Will you accept the will and tasking of God?"

“Hai. It will be done, mighty one.”

“Your father has taught you well, Ashi. If you are successful, Kami will bless you and your people with peace.” Præsidiel breathes deep and then exhales. “As is your custom, cremate your father’s body and bury his bones tomorrow. Then, give your people two days to mourn. You must depart on the third day. Saitō will lead you to the tree where your father was attacked. From there, you can pick up the trail to the hidden torii. This is all I have to tell you.” The angel stands. Ashi follows suit. She bows low to him out of respect, and he returns her bow. He turns and exits the shrine. As he places his sandogasa back upon his head, great white wings unfold from his shoulder blades. They are much larger than her own and are feathery. Looking over his shoulder, he offers Ashi, still standing just inside the shrine, a final piece of advice. “Those who overcome tribulation with faith in our Lord earn the right to eat from the tree of life.” He smiles one last time before taking flight into the dark, starlit sky.

* * * * *

Following the angel’s direction, Ashi gives the tea to Saitō right after he departs. While he recovers the following day, she cleans her father’s armor and returns it to his gusoku bitsu.[95] Although his sword was lost in the river, she still has his wakizashi. She spends the morning inside her shinden, cleaning, polishing, and placing it on a stand near his armor. She then prepares her jūnihitoe for the funeral. She steps back to look at it, and it triggers a more recent memory of her father.

Only a couple of years ago, she went about the castle grounds in a single white kosode without more formal layers.

---

[95] Armor display box with stand (translated from Japanese).

This is unusual, even a bit cheeky, for a young princess. She was out in the courtyard when she heard her father's voice from the veranda. "Musume!" he called firmly but without anger. "Kudasai, come here." He was standing at the top step of the veranda with a folded cloth in his hands. She obediently ran to him and stood in the gravel at the bottom of the steps. "What are you doing out here in your kosode?" he asked. Ashi had no reply. She turned her head downward in shame. "You are the daughter of the daimyō," instructed her father. "You are expected to dress in a more formal jūnihitoe." He moved down to the last step and said lovingly, "I have something for you."

Her father unfolded the silken orange and white uchigi with ornate tea leaf designs. He shook it in the summer air, then cloaked her in it. Ashi happily pulled it around herself. Takeda-san also produced the obi that went with it. He wrapped it around her and tied it properly. "Turn," he directed. As gentle as a father can, he untucked her long, black hair so it cascaded down her back, standing out against the orange silk. She turned around to face him. Gently adjusting her beauty strands, he said, "Oh, one more thing." He pulled out an elaborate fan and presented it to her. "So you can maintain your modesty in public." Ashi opened the fan and brought it up to cover her mouth. "You are beautiful, my daughter," he remarked lovingly, a soft glow of fatherly affection in his eye. "Come. Let's go to the market."

Ashi remembers their slow walk through the niwa, past the shrine, and out into the village. As they did, her father affectionately taught her, "You are grown now, Ashi-himē. You must remember your station as my daughter, onna-musha, and caretaker of our estate. Always carry yourself with dignity wherever you go." It was in those walks with him that she always learned and was comforted. She loved walking by his side through the village and visiting with all the

Hotaru-Raikō. Today, though, she makes ready for the long, sad walk to the shrine behind his body.

In the early afternoon, Ashi-himē leads the procession of villagers through the torii and up the stone path to the old ishidōrō. They follow her father's body, carried by his faithful retainers. Many Hotaru no Chikyū have come to pay their respects as well. They sit inside delicate paper lanterns lining the shrine's upward path, offering a mellow golden-yellow light in mourning for the noble daimyō and all who protect them.

Upon reaching the entrance, she noticed that all the names of the fallen warriors had been scribed on wooden plates and hung in the corners of the immaculate shrine. A single hemp rope hangs over the stone table in the middle of the shrine. At the center of the rope hang two kanji, boldly scribed in black ink on white rice paper. They say 耶穌基督 (YēSūJīDū[96]). The alpha character is on the left side of the two kanji, and the omega (Ω) symbol is on the right. Ashi slowly and somberly approaches the stone table at the center. She places her father's lightless wakizashi there, carefully pointing the blade tip to the left. She kneels at the stone table, and the musicians begin to play softly. Though she is sad, the music brings her peace as she prays for both of her parents.

Ashi genuinely loved her mother, but there is something about the father-daughter relationship she already misses. Although tough, even strict at times, he was always patient with her. He could always boost her spirits when she was down. An excellent teacher, her father taught her a great deal about nature and how to live with others. Currently, she thinks specifically of her father's teachings about heaven.

---

[96] Jesus Christ (translated from Japanese).

She was born in this world; she did not know Tengoku like her father. He would sometimes regale her with stories of heavenly life during their walks through town or when they flew among the trees. He would occasionally stop, look up, past the brim of his favorite sandogasa, and stare into the deep-blue summer sky. "You must learn to live each moment of life, Ashi, to make it worthy." He often lamented sipping tea in the soft grass under the Tree of Life, remarking, "Although the tea in this world could never compare with the tea of heaven, it is in your mother's company that I see Tokoma no Hara."[97] He loved making her mother smile regularly and even blush sometimes, in a playful way, of course.

As she prays, Ashi remembers what he taught her about Tokoma no Hara and the vertical order of realms. "You must know the truth of these things, Ashi-himē. Men of Nihon often see the angels and the yōkai as gods themselves, but they are not. There is only one true God. Angels are the servants of God, and you must always respect them and fear their power; however, they are not to be worshiped. The yōkai are like Akuma, the first to fall. Like him, they want to be worshiped as gods. They refuse to serve Kami; rather, they wish to supplant him. Tokoma no Hara is where heaven is, and I hope we all meet there again one day. Here, in Nakatsukumi,[98] you will be tested. And Yomi no Kuni, the world below, is where the enemies of God are sent."

Ashi prays to God, "I know you will give us justice, Lord. Let me be the instrument of your vengeance. Grant me the strength I need to destroy this evil, to send those who perpetrate it to Yomi no Kuni. Use me to bring peace and safety to my people and to protect man. Grant me the

---

[97] The plain of high heaven (translated from Japanese).

[98] The natural world we live in (translated from Japanese).

courage to face our enemies. I humbly ask for these things in your name, Lord."

Chapter Four

Onna-musha Rising

The day after the funeral, Ashi summons two of her fellow onna-musha, Saitō, fully recovered from sipping the tea, and another prominent young warrior to the western tainoya. They all find her standing behind a large rectangular table in the middle of the room. She appears different to them, more mature and serious-minded than they are used to seeing. Her disposition is no longer that of a young, carefree girl. Though the room is elaborate and beautifully arranged, bringing peace to their minds, her authoritative presence leads the guests to surmise this is not a social call.

Around the long wooden table are four cushions, one for each of them. A simple and rustic meal of kuri gohan,[99] miso soup, and gozen-tachibana berries is accompanied by warm tea. Behind Ashi is a six-paneled folding screen. The awe-inspiring screen depicts life near the Tree of Life in heaven and is meant to inspire and remind them who they are and where they came from. Ashi invites Saitō to sit at the end of the table to her left. Miyo, the widow of Hatano Yoshimoto, takes her place across from Ashi and next to Saitō. Miyo's daughter and one of Ashi's closest friends, Yui, moves to the next place setting. Oishi Nakamura, Sasaki's son and a fine warrior in his own right, is invited to sit at the end of the table to Ashi's right. They all bow to her, and she returns it before taking her seat.

After sitting, Saitō politely surveys the table and, his appetite fully returned, says, "I am happy to receive so much food." Ashi is grateful he has healed; she offers him a polite

---

[99] Chestnuts and rice (translated from Japanese).

smile. They clean their hands with the provided towel and then eat without conversation.

After everyone was full, Oishi said in gratitude, "It was quite a feast."

"Hai," answers Ashi, again with the polite smile of a gracious host. Her facial expression quickly turns serious, though. "Please, make yourselves more comfortable. There is much to discuss. Specifically, betrayal and war." The whole mood of the chamber instantly becomes a little tenser. Ashi informs them of Ishida's betrayal and the Tsuchigumo clan. There has been much speculation over the last year as to what happened to him and the handful of men who vanished; now they know the truth. She also tells them of the spider yōkai, Kumo, the locust-like monsters she plans to unleash, and Præsidiel, God's messenger.

After they have been brought up to speed, Ashi issues specific tasks. "Oishi-san is now samurai," she announces. Looking specifically at him, she directs, "You will recruit the ten best ashigaru for your squad."

"Hai," he says with a grateful bow.

"Yui, select the five best onna-musha. Give priority to those from the families of the fallen so they may bring honor to those they have lost. Also, select the five best kyūdōka."[100]

"Hai."

"Miyo-san, you will reinforce our defenses and oversee the security of the Raikō estate. You must protect our people during our absence."

"Hai, Ashi-sama."

"You have only today to select and prepare your troops. We depart tomorrow. Saitō will lead us to the tree where our warriors were ambushed. According to Præsidiel, the trailhead to the Shrine of Ancient Behemoths is near that

[100] Archers (translated from Japanese).

tree. We will find it and make our way to the shrine. We must be prepared for all manner of yōkai and yūrei. Once we're there, Saitō and I will confront Ishida, Kumo, and her beast. Oishi, Yui, your ashigaru will cut down the Tsuchigumo and prevent any locust from escaping the abyss. These are not normal locusts, either. Saitō was there when the one killed my father. He will instruct you and your warriors on how to fight them." The room is silent, each in their contemplative thoughts. "Iku. Prepare for war."

"Hai!" they all exclaim. Everyone, save Saitō, leaves the room. There is no doubt among them that Ashi now commands the Hotaru-Raikō. They trust her abilities as onna-musha and will readily follow her into battle.

"What do you wish of me while they go to gather their soldiers?" asks Saitō.

"Tell me everything you know of these beasts, and then spar with me for a while."

"Hai," he confirms, slightly grinning at the prospect of sparring with Ashi. "As you said, our adversary, the kaijū, has the appearance of a locust. His lengthy body is tan and speckled with black blotches. His long and rather large hind legs are lined with sharp spikes. Hidden under his wing shells is a scorpion's tail, which can curve up over his back. This is what killed Sasaki and your father." He pauses for a moment and looks down in mourning. "The monster's elongated head is almost human in appearance. His predatory black, oval eyes are right in the front, instead of on each side like a normal locust. He has a mouth full of sharp fangs resembling those of a large fox and tar-like spit. His black hair is that of a mad woman, messy and wild. And instead of two antennae, something resembling a golden crown curls up from his forehead and around his head."

"I see," replies Ashi as she stands. "Weak points?" she asks.

"None that I could see," he states as he stands. "Like any locust, the underbelly between his front and middle legs?" Saitō ventures a guess.

Ashi leads them to a small dōjō behind the screen as they talk. "Our main enemy is Kumo, the one who summoned the kaijū. Unfortunately, I know no details of her other than hearsay from men of the Nara Prefecture."

In the dōjō, Ashi turns her back to Saitō, slips her arms out of her uchigi, exposing her white kosode underneath, and then ties the sleeves around her waist. She moves over to the weapons rack, picks up her shiai yo,[101] and turns to face Saitō. He takes a wooden bokken while grinning. Wasting no time, they bow. Ashi immediately goes on the offensive, stabbing at him with her shiai yo. A bit later, Saitō disarms her, but she quickly plucks a bokken from the rack and again engages him. They frequently come to a stalemate in their practice, proving Ashi is highly skilled and exceptional with both naginata and sword.

"Had enough, my lady?" asks Saitō brazenly.

Ashi smiles and, switching to hand-to-hand combat, lunges at her betrothed. They continue to spar until Ashi flips Saitō onto his back. She quickly straddled his stomach and raised the heel of her palm over his face, signaling she could deliver the knockout blow. He looks up at her, smiles, and lets out a chuckle. Ashi reaches into her kosode and pulls out her fan. She smacks him on the forehead with it to remind him his innuendo is not appropriate but then leans down to whisper, "I love you."

"Will you still marry me if we return?" Saitō promptly asks.

"Hai."

---

[101] A practice naginata made of bamboo (translated from Japanese).

“Yoi. Now, let’s take this outside so we can see how good you are in flight.” Saitō flips her over his head, but he does not hear Ashi land on the ground. He jumps up and turns to see her hovering in the air. She smiles at him playfully, flies to grab her shiai yo, and then buzzes out of the house into the courtyard. “Hrmph,” he grunts to himself. He strolls over, grabs his bokken, and takes flight after her. Out in the sunlight, they continue to spar for a little while.

A few children watch them training from the edges of the niwa. Ashi hears them giggling and thinks of her mother, who always delighted in their presence. She does not let it distract her, though. Near the end of their practice, Ashi and Saitō land close to each other in the courtyard. Although short of breath, they bow in respect to one another. They hear the little children cheer from near the base of the shrine. It makes them both smile.

* * * * *

Later that night, Ashi bathed and dressed in a single white kosode. She wrapped the orange uchigi her father gave her around her waist. Wisps of her silken black hair dance in the evening breeze from the moat. She carries her naginata and her father’s wakizashi up the path to the shrine. She intends to pray for herself and the warriors accompanying her in the morning.

Inside, she sets her weapons on the ground and quietly sits in the seiza position before the altar. Ashi reaches for her naginata first. She raises it over her head horizontally with both hands as she bows. Offering it to God, she gently places its long pole on the altar. She repeats her actions with her father’s unsheathed sword. Once they have been presented, she bows low to pray. Unseen by her, her samurai, onna-musha, and ashigaru are beginning to gather around the shrine's base. They cannot explain why they come; they feel drawn to it. They hear murmuring prayers in the dimly lit shrine above and join in. They bow their heads and offer individual petitions to God.

A strong and unexpected wind blows through the shrine, extinguishing all the candles. Ashi stops her prayers and looks up. She hears the prayers of the warriors at the base of the shrine. The wind circles down the stone mount of the shrine and disperses into the gathered crowd. Everyone falls silent in the refreshing gust. Their attention lifts to the crisp night sky. Out of the starlit heavens, a bolt of lightning sizzles downward. Like water dropped on a stone, the lightning strikes the roof and splinters into several streams of blinding light. These streams curl out over the stone roof only to stream in through the openings of the shrine. They all meet again at the altar, striking the metal blades lying there. Sparks and embers explode into the air. The ground-shaking thunder that follows throws Ashi backward.

She quickly catches her breath, gets back on her feet, and collects herself. She is blinded by pure white light. She holds her hand out in front of her face to cast a shadow over her eyes, allowing her to see what is happening. The brilliant light emanates from the bare blades of her father's sword and her naginata. She falls to her knees before the altar.

Everyone on the ground below has witnessed this event. They see the pure white light emanating from all sides of the shrine. It illuminates the courtyard below and even the surrounding thicket. The glow dims, though, and the night sky returns to normal. It takes a few minutes for their eyesight to readjust to the night. Other villagers rush out of their homes, congregating at the southern side of the shrine mount to see what has taken place. These new onlookers point to the onna-musha and soldiers' sheaths. A curious light seeps between their scabbards and sword guards. Some pull their swords out slightly, exposing the white, glowing blades within. The Hotaru-Raikō know then that Kami has sent his blessing. In awe, they fall to their knees, bowing low from the seiza position.

Ashi hears the commotion below. She moves to the entrance and looks down at the crowd gathered there. Upon seeing her in the doorway, the people stand to greet her. A cheer erupts as Ashi emerges from the shrine. They know their onna-musha has risen. Ashi and her army are ready for tomorrow's journey.

* * * * *

The heat of summer has passed. The mornings are cool, and the afternoons are pleasant. The Hotaru-Raikō prefer to travel in the warmer afternoon. A gentle southern breeze cools them as they stay close to the foothills along the northern side of the Kuzuryu River basin. It only takes a few hours of flight to reach the beech tree on the eastern side of the Takinami River. Ashi thinks it is a good strategy to arrive just before sunset. They will have enough daylight to locate the trailhead while using twilight, when the lines between reality and the mystical blur, to cloak their movements.

Saitō has led them to a towering beech tree growing up out of the side of a large hill. It grows at the tip of a mountainous peninsula surrounded by flat river basins. They approach cautiously but find no sign of the enemy or the bodies of their fallen warriors, both mysteries they are eager to solve. Feeling confident the tree is safe, Ashi flies to the top and rests in the canopy. Her army combs the area below for the hidden trailhead. Saitō stays with his beloved, watching for the enemy; he has resolved to protect her better than her father.

Ashi has chosen to travel light, wearing only her orange chest plate, shoulder armor, and forearm guards over a single gray kosode and her favorite orange and white hakama. Her father's wakizashi is tucked securely in her obi while her naginata rests across her legs. Most of her jet-black hair is collected into a ponytail resting on her back; she leaves her beauty strands free to sway in the treetop breeze. She takes a deep breath and exhales slowly. It is a short but pleasant respite, and although she faces a great unknown, she is calm.

From their vantage point, the whole base of Hakusan is laid out before them. At first, Ashi's focus is on the mountain itself. The setting sun is warm on her back as she meditates on the beauty of the mountain's trinitarian peaks. Soon, her line of sight begins to move downward until it comes upon a wooded ravine that seems to snake through the middle of the foothill peninsula below. Not far off to the east, she spies giant spiderwebs holding back broken branches in the underbrush at the edge of a small field. She points at it and asks, "Saitō, there, in the ravine. Do the webs holding back those branches resemble those you found near the hot springs?"

"Hai." He motions for two ashigaru to join him. "I will investigate and return."

She watches her faithful samurai fly down, hand on his sword handle, ready for combat. He slows as he approaches the opening. The two soldiers fan out to his left and right. After they conduct a brief reconnaissance from the air, they return. Saitō reports, "There is a faded animal trail there. It does not appear to be well marked or often traveled. I believe this is the trailhead we seek."

"Yoi. Let's wait here just a bit longer. It's not quite time to enter yet," she patiently instructs. The sun sinks lower in the sky.

It isn't long before hues of pink and oranges fill the heavens while evening shadows creep across the land. A faint mist begins to form in the river basins around them. Ashi knows it will soon blanket the trail and obscure the old forest. "Omagatoki," she mumbles. "The end of the day when the yōkai emerge." She takes a deep breath. "Saitō-san, rally everyone to me." Her mood has changed, and her tone reflects her father's strength. "Prepare them to enter the trail."

"Hai, Ashi-sama."

Chapter Five

Revelations of the Yōkai

The Hotaru-Raikō assemble in the treetop, awaiting their commander's orders. Ashi stands in the bough of the highest branch, watching and waiting for the fog to move up the slope of the foothills. She knows it will conceal their incursion. As soon as it nears the field, she grasps her naginata in both hands and, without hesitation, flies down into the open trailhead. Her militia follows swiftly and silently. Wisps of mist swirl in the air with the beats of their wings as they pierce the webbed opening, one after another, like threading a needle.

They discover the road to the shrine has been overgrown. Unused by man, it has been reduced to the size of an animal trail. Many tracks follow the now winding path; some are clearly from the Tsuchigumo clan, but others are unknown. Yui directs her kyūdōka into the trees on each side of the path. They fly from branch to branch, forming a perimeter around those walking the trail. Their thigh armor glows white, allowing the rest always to know where they are. As they move from tree to tree, occasionally flashing their lights, they appear like normal hotaru so as not to draw unwanted attention. Everyone else is on foot, led by Ashi and Saitō.

The fog blankets the thick forest underbrush, making the trail difficult to follow. It dissipates the farther inward they travel; however, the landscape becomes darker and unnaturally silent. Then, about a kilometer down the trail, subtle *Whoosh* sounds are heard around them in the spaces between the path and the archers. Onibi burst into existence there. These blue, flamelike spirits are always thought to be malevolent, so Ashi gives the signal to stop. Everyone is still as the onibi fly about, just above the underbrush. They appear to be taunting and tempting some soldiers and onna-musha to come closer.

Ashi observes them before finally commanding, "Move forward, but stay on the trail. Keep your distance from the onibi; do not disturb them."

As they begin walking, one orb of light comes dangerously close to the trail near Yui. It manifests a face, one that she instantly recognizes. "Papa?" she asks as she unconsciously raises her hand to touch the flaming orb.

Ashi hears her. She turns to see Yui raising her hand and reaching for the orb. "Īe!" she exclaims. "Don't touch it."

Yui is shocked out of her trance. She lowers her hand, saying shamefully, "Sumimasen,[102] Ashi-sama."

As soon as she says it, taiko drums begin beating. They recognize them as the same ones they heard days ago. This time, however, the drums are loud and close. The onibi begin to vibrate and flicker. It's almost as if they were fighting against something. What they resist becomes all too apparent when suddenly pulled down the trail by an unknown force and almost out of sight.

"We must move now! Follow the onibi," orders Ashi. She runs as quickly and quietly as her waraji sandals will carry her. They follow the streaking flames until they come to an abrupt halt another kilometer down the trail. Ashi again gives the signal to stop.

The rhythm of the drums is slow and steady. Ashi watches one of the onibi get sucked into a squat stone ishidōrō hidden among the tall grass and old trees. Looking down the trail, she realizes the other flaming spirits are being pulled into other stone lanterns, which mark the right side of the ancient shrine road. The eerie lights follow the twisting and turning path into the distance. The drums boom louder, and their pace begins

---

[102] I'm sorry (translated from Japanese).

to quicken. The mist starts to thin out, pulling back into the woods.

Saitō moves up to examine the first light. The retreating fog's wispy edges lick at the ancient, moss-covered lantern. The onibi has taken the form of a man who thrashes about, seeking to escape his new prison. The spirit, now aware he is being observed, calms down, affording him a closer look. Saitō gasps. "It is Yoshimoto-san, Yui's father. These ishidōrō...they're prisons," he says, looking back at Ashi. She runs up to observe for herself. "The onibi we encountered must be the trapped spirits of those Hotaru-Raikō cut down recently. Who could have done this?" he asks.

"Kumo," replies Ashi. "If she can summon the kaijū, she can be the only one capable of this wicked spell. We must bring an end to this." She stands and motions for the rest to follow. They resume traveling the now faintly lit trail. Light from the nearly full white moon pierces the twisted canopy of leafless trees overhead. Its light casts shadows among the swaying grasses and flickering ishidōrō. The tempo of the drums quickens as they advance. Ashi felt her heart throbbing in time with the drums; it synchronized with the sound of her steps.

Always watching her kyūdōka in the trees, she notices they have stopped at the crest of a small hill. She calls her ashigaru to a halt before advancing by herself to see why they have stopped. There are only two more lanterns in the distance. A giant figure moves in the shadows past the last ishidōrō. She ducks in the foliage on the right side of the road, a few feet behind the lantern at the top of the hill. Saitō moves up and takes cover in the shadows on the left side of the trail. They wait for the figure to come into the light.

The tempo of the drums subsides a little. Something draws Ashi's eye to the ishidōrō. The figure inside is a woman sitting still with her head down. She sneaks closer for a better look. At first, the spirit barely moves. Ashi moves closer, peering into the lantern. The spirit reluctantly raises her head to look at her visitor. It is her mother, Harumi. Ashi gasped and slid back to her hiding place.

Saitō sneaks across the road to her. "What is it?" he asks.

"In the lantern..." She is saddened. "It is my mother. Her spirit is trapped within the stone prison." She stands back up and slowly approaches the ishidōrō. Saitō follows her. He can see the water collecting in the corners of her dark eyes. She peers through the flickering flame into the eyes of her mother. "Okaasama,"[103] she whispers. Harumi's spirit cannot speak; she only looks upon her daughter with love. Ashi reaches toward her mother, who immediately signals her to stop. Remembering her advice to Yui, she quickly withdraws her hand.

Saitō witnesses a change in her expression. Anger swells in Ashi for the evil done to her mother and her people. She resolves to bring this curse to an end. She shifts her body to stare down toward the cave and mutters, "Kumo." From this vantage point, she watches the figure moving in the distance.

A torii made from the cracked, bleached-white bones of prehistoric creatures stands in stark contrast to the darkness of the cave it sits in front of. Between the torii and the last ishidōrō, branches that look like twisted, bony hands reach out over the trail from each side. The roots of tall, slender trees with no foliage snake through the coarse, dark rocks where the old road ends. She notices human skulls and other bones intertwined with the roots near the base of their trunks. The trees look almost as if they were guarding the entrance. Ashi stares intently at the dark sap-like substance that glistens as it oozes down the bark in the faint moonlight. Suddenly, it dawned on her what she was seeing: jubokko

---

[103] Mother (translated from Japanese).

trees. She has heard the tale of these vampiric plants. They do not drink water, only blood. These trees look parched, too. They are positioned in this valley of death to capture curious visitors.

Just then, a tengu, the size of a human, walks out of the cave, through the torii, and into the light. The drums beat quietly enough so the talons on his black, bird-like feet could be heard clicking on the stone as he walked. He stops to inspect the wilderness, making sure those inside the shrine are not disturbed. Although details of his features are challenging to see in the low light, his red face and long, beak-like nose stand out against his white windblown hair and pointy beard. He holds his dingy, tattered, and unpreened gray wings upward like he is about to take flight. He wears maroon armor over a black kosode, with maroon hakama tucked into ebony shin guards. The only other armor he wears is maroon forearm guards. In his right hand is a spear, and a paper lantern is in his left.

The kyūdōka have observed all they can and begin to fly horizontally back down the hill toward the rest of the clan. They flash their lights regularly every few seconds, mirroring the beat of the drums. The tengu spots them and watches their movements. Soon, with a voice that sounds like the cawing of a crow, he grumbles, "*Baah!* Just firefly in the woods." He holds up a faded, old chochin-obake,[104] looking to see anything else in the forest. Two weary eyes peer out from between the ghostly lantern's old ribs near its top. Near the bottom, its internal wooden ribs have split, giving it the appearance of a gaping mouth. Thin black strands of hair hang around the face on the lantern, which resembles an old, wrinkly woman. An eerie spectral light shines out of its

---

[104] Paper lantern ghost (translated from Japanese).

yawning mouth, illuminating the old road past the two jubokko.

Seeing nothing else of concern, he plants the bottom of his spear on the stone. The tengu sets the ghostly lantern on the ground, which lets out a hissing groan of disappointment. "Stop your moaning, obake!" he caws. He then stands at rest before the gate, listening to the drums. Their tempo is picking back up.

Ashi knows the time to strike is now, but before she can give orders to her warriors, the flame of her mother's spirit crackles, catching her attention. Ashi moves back behind the lantern to look at her—Harumi's spirit motions with her hands to give her something. Ashi thinks for a second and then waves for Yui, who immediately runs up. "Give me an arrow," she whispers. Yui complies and hands her an arrow from her quiver.

Ashi gently places the tip of the arrow into the ishidōrō. "Kudasai, Okaasama, grant us use of your flame." Harumi smiles softly at the wisdom of her daughter; she knows their hearts and minds are still connected. She places her hands on the arrow tip. The blue flame of the onibi envelopes the arrowhead. Ashi bows her head reverently. "Arigatou, Okaasama." She lifts her eyes. "I will end this curse, Mother."

She turns to hand the arrow back to Yui and instructs, "Gather your kyūdōka. Spread the flame to one arrow for each of them. Two of your archers will aim for the jubokko, and three will aim for the tengu's wings. Saitō and I will fly in to kill him as he burns. Everyone else will ensure any unseen enemies in and around the cave are cut down. Iku."

"Hai, Ashi-sama!"

Ashi waits for Yui to pass the flame to the kyūdōka, who have rejoined the rest behind the crest of the hill. She watches them fan out along the ridge and prepare for the attack. Kneeling in the underbrush, the archers quietly slide their arms out of the left side of their kosode, exposing their bare arms and chests; the women archers wear muneate or leather breastplates. Undressing their arms will ensure nothing will interfere with the flight of their arrows. Slowly knocking a flame-tipped arrow, they rise in unison, stealthily draw their bowstrings, and take aim.

Ashi, Saitō, and the rest have gathered on the trail and are ready.

The taiko drums are reaching a crescendo.

* * * * *

Deep inside the cave, the flickering torchlit shrine, deep gray and black basalt columns rise straight up, curving at the top toward a central vault. Natural light does not reach this far back into the cavern. The Tsuchigumo have mounted long rust-plagued iron torches to every fourth column, which reach out into the unholy cathedral from both sides. The bodies of the fallen Hotaru-Raikō, wrists tied together, hang over the torches by their bound hands. They have been stripped of their armor, their heads hung low, and their lifeless eyes look down upon the black volcanic gravel beneath their bare feet. Strange, vile markings have been carved into their bare chests. The stench of death blankets the cavernous shrine.

The cathedral-like cavern becomes increasingly narrow as the basalt columns lead toward a colossal doorway in the back. Framed by an arch made of rib bones from prehistoric creatures, two slabs of dark-gray andesite with flecks of white crystal seal the long-hidden entrance to the abyss. Kumo stands before the stone doors with her hands raised. All eight of her hairy, black spider legs extend outward from her back. Her servant Ishida stands behind her and to her left. The locust kaijū lumbers back and forth between them and the drums.

In the middle of the cave is a small stage upon which an odaiko (or big drum) sits. Each side has a drumhead, the diameter of which is about one foot across. That means each drumhead is slightly longer than the height of the average Hotaru-Raikō. Tanned hides stretch across each head in stark contrast to the ebony wood of the drum itself. It is mounted on a rack made from the bones of the ancient behemoths. Two of Ishida's soldiers drum a side of the odaiko, producing a low, loud, and deep rhythm. Closer to the entrance, and on either corner of the stage behind the big drum, are two smaller daiko. They carry a faster, higher-pitch sound. The soldiers shout occasionally with intensity as they bang on these drums; they know they are close to breaking the door's seal and pour everything they've got into their performance.

* * * * *

Ashi gives the signal. The kyūdōka let loose their volley. Streaks of blue flame sizzle down the small hill through the night sky, each one striking its intended target. The blood-starved and dry jubokko are quickly engulfed in scorching flame, their branches creaking and cracking as they flail in pain. Other arrows strike the tengu's wings, igniting his unkempt feathers. The fire spreads quickly. He drops his spear and desperately flaps his wings while attempting to pat out the engulfing fire with his hands. Ashi grips her naginata, and Saitō draws his sword. They take flight, giving a fearsome war cry as they drive forward between the crackling flames of the burning jubokko.

* * * * *

Inside, a sudden loud crack echoes through the shrine. Eon-old dust shakes loose from the seals around the doors. The drums have worked; they have broken the seal. Ishida raises his hand in the air. Clinching a fist, he shouts, signaling the drummers to stop.

* * * * *

The drums stop, and the tengu hears the war cries of the Hotaru-Raikō. It is too late for him, though, as he realizes they are upon him. Ashi and Saitō plunge their white-bladed weapons deep into his chest, piercing his heart. The tengu lets out a loud but diminishing caw as he perishes. He falls to the ground with a thud, crushing the chochin-obake beneath his burning corpse. Ashi hears a rush of movement inside the cave; she knows the enemy has been alerted to their presence.

* * * * *

Just after the last reverberating drumbeat dissipates, the death cry of the tengu comes echoing in. Surprised, Ishida looks over his shoulder. The kaijū wheels around to face the shrine entrance. The black spittle from his putrid mouth splatters on the odaiko drum. Ishida steps to Kumo and says, "We have been discovered."

Kumo reaches to caress his scarred face with the back of her hand and says in a sweet, seductive voice, "It matters not, lover. They come to their doom."

"Hai!" exclaims Ishida. He removes the devil's mask from his belt, slides it over his distorted face, and turns toward the entrance—Kumo motions to the two odaiko drummers to attend to the doors. Ishida signals the remaining retainers to move out against the unknown enemy. The locust creature lets out a deep guttural laugh as he, too, eagerly awaits a battle.

* * * * *

Saitō signals to the kyūdōka and other warriors to create a semicircle around the cave entrance while the rest of the force moves down the trail. He joins Ashi in the middle of the old road in front of the cave. “They will be coming soon,” he informs softly.

“Let them come,” answers Ashi. There is a ferocity in her eyes he has never seen before. She hovers midair with her naginata in both hands, poised for the coming fight. Her graceful figure is silhouetted against the blue light of the flames consuming the vampiric trees at her back.

It isn't long before a small force of Tsuchigumo comes rushing toward Ashi and her Hotaru-Raikō. Their hearts, filled with a murderous rage, fuel the wicked red lights of their armor and weapons as they streak through the blackness of the cave. In their blind rage, they fly straight for Saitō and Ashi. The kyūdōka lose a volley of white-tipped arrows striking four enemy soldiers. In the middle of their formation, the fifth warrior rapidly rises into the air and then plunges downward toward them with sword drawn. Fast as lightning, Ashi streaks upward to meet him in the air. The enemy gives a loud war cry as he gets close. He strikes toward her, but Ashi swiftly spins her body to the right, avoiding his attack. She arcs her naginata downward, cleanly severing the head of the attacking traitor from behind.

She comes to an upright position, hovering high above the cave entrance as the enemy's body falls to the ground. The initial, swift, short-lived battle energizes the Raikō clan. They give a unified cheer of victory.

* * * * *

The yōkai and her henchmen hear the cheer as it echoes inward. They know it is not their own who cheer. Suddenly panicked, Kumo asks Ishida, "Who moves against us?"

"I'm not certain. We have eliminated the strongest warriors of the Hotaru-Raikō and their leadership. Only their onna-musha are left, and they are too weak, too unskilled."

"Whoever it is, they will be no match for the devil's army. Hold them off until we can open the doors." Kumo's tone has changed; she is alarmed. She turns to shout at the remaining two clansmen, "Pull, you idiots!"

A faint yellow-orange sliver of light shines through from between the doors and around its edges. Above the doors, a foul-smelling smoke seeps upward into the vaulted ceiling.

* * * * *

Ashi leaves the archers at the entrance to the cave to protect the invading force and to prevent anyone, or anything, from escaping. She and Saitō lead the remainder into the cave. Keeping the expanding, yellow-orange light in their sights, they fly cautiously into the cavern. The light grows brighter as they approach. Odd sounds echo off the stone walls. Ashi realizes Kumo has succeeded in breaking the seal on the gate, and their time is running out. They emerge into the underground chamber, lighting on the ground just behind the drums, and quickly take in the horrible scene.

Appalled, Ashi gasped upon seeing the long-dead bodies of her people hanging from the basalt walls. Kumo stands between the drums and the opening door. She keeps her back to the invading Hotaru-Raikō, her spindly legs stretched out, making her easily identifiable. Ashi assumes the warrior to the left of Kumo in the devil's mask can only be Ishida, the traitor. He has embraced the darkness she saw within him. The locust-like monster looms large in the right half of the room. He rattles his wing covers over his back in anticipation of battle. The tar-like spit Saitō previously described drips from his open maw. Two Tsuchigumo tug at the doors at the rear of the shrine.

The stone gate lurches open a bit more. A foul, stale fog churns through the cracks like the smoke from the swordsmith's furnace. It boils upward, filling the cavern vault and obscuring everyone's sight. The smog smells of death and decay. A clattering of insect wings echoes in the void beyond. Ashi can sense the contempt and the rage coming from an unseen foe. She hears the gnashing of teeth and the dripping of black spittle on smoldering stones.

"Hear that?" the beast gurgles, his gaze fixed upon Ashi. "My brothers yearn to be free." A grim smile spreads across his hideous face. “They yearn to taste your flesh. Heh-heh-heh.” He does his best to disturb and make her uneasy, but she says nothing in response.

Saitō settles his gaze upon Ishida. He wants to restore his honor and avenge the daimyō’s death. “Traitor,” he yells out. Ishida laughs in contempt, opens his wing covers, spreads his wings, and then slowly rises into the smoke collecting in the vault above. He draws his sword, its bloodred light slowly growing brighter in the thick, black haze. Saitō, his blazing white sword already in hand, lets out a loud battle cry and flies swiftly upward to engage him in combat. Their swords clang loudly; bright sparks briefly illuminate the two samurai in the hellish fog. The smoke thickens so that only the light of their swords is visible.

“Yui. Oishi. Close those doors!” commands Ashi. They immediately take flight, leading the rest of the army around the beast's right side. With a surprisingly fast and mighty thrust, the kaijū pins one of the soldiers against the basalt wall with his rear leg. Ashi knows he is off-balance and lunges toward his left and Kumo. Rapidly closing in on her target, she swings her naginata down from the right side to put an end to the villainess. The locust releases the warrior, giving him enough time to whip his tail around and stop her killing blow. He does not, however, stop her blade from slicing through one of Kumo’s spindly black legs. She screams in agony as she pulls the rest of her legs in toward her back.

Yui and Oishi rush to the doors. One of the Tsuchigumo soldiers turns, draws his sword, and, in a downward arc, cuts through Oishi’s armor and into his left forearm. Filled with adrenaline, Oishi counters, running his sword through the enemy’s chest with just his right hand. Yui pushes past Oishi and, her naginata having a length advantage, strikes the other soldier before he can draw his weapon. She looked at Oishi with concern, but he left his sword in his enemy’s body and rushed to the right door. Hitting it with his right shoulder, he grunts as he attempts to close it. Yui followed suit and leaned on the left door, pushing as hard as she could. They hear a clatter rising from the abyss like armored horses charging. A force hits the doors on the other side. The other locusts are trying to break free. The rest of the ashigaru surged to help close them. It is a stalemate.

In the smokey haze above, white and red blades continue to clash. Rising, falling, slashing, and clanging, the swords move about furiously in the air, wielded by warriors cloaked in the black fog. The red blade makes a downward strike. The white blade, moving upward, deflects it, whirls with hurricane force in the air, and finds its target. The movement of the red blade stops. It hangs tip-down in the air for a few seconds before falling to the ground with a clanking sound. Ishida's headless body lands next to it with a thud. His head lands nearby; lifeless black eyes peer dilate behind the red devil's mask. Saitō has avenged his daimyō.

Ashi, still holding down on the beast's scorpion tail, watches helplessly as Kumo casts a web upward and pulls herself to the cave vault above. The smoke hides her from everyone's view. She sees Saitō's blade in the ashen fog nearby. "Saitō!" screams Ashi. "Kumo is escaping." Just then, he is brushed aside by the hidden villainess scurrying past him. Swirls of dense smoke waft past him in her wake. He swings his blade blindly but strikes nothing.

Below, Ashi can feel the locust's tail sliding down the pole of her naginata. She knows she is no match for his strength, but she is highly confident in her speed. She spins to her left, releasing his tail. As she spins, she turns her naginata down and back up, driving the luminous blade through the exoskeleton of the venom bulb. He screams and whips his tail backward, yanking the naginata from her hands. He staggers toward the right wall, lifting the front of his body to make a lunging melee attack. Seeing the opportunity, Ashi rapidly draws her father's wakizashi and slashes downward through his chest armor. As she does, Saitō zooms below to grasp the handle of her naginata and drives the tip into the seam between two basalt columns. The kaijū is trapped and disarmed.

Ashi stands before him with the tip of her father's sword pressed against the locust's throat. Saitō stands to her left, ready to strike if necessary. The locust looks at them both and laughs. "My brothers are only permitted to torment humans. But you, little pests, you we can kill. What pleasure your deaths will bring." He coughs up vile black saliva. "Even if you stop us today, we will be rereleased and..."—he coughs again—"when we are, will seek your kind out first. We will erase you from the land. We—" Without a word, Ashi swiftly separates his head from his body. The killing stroke is so swift that tiny arcs of lightning reach out from her sword into the air around her, some connecting with the stone wall. As his long head hits the ground, his golden crown comes loose. It makes a tink, tink, tink sound as it rolls on the gravel and stone underfoot.

Ashi wipes the foul-smelling blood from her father's sword and returns it to its sheath. Glancing at her beloved Saitō, she commands, "Quickly, find Kumo."

"Hai," he answers before rushing toward the shrine entrance.

Turning her attention to the doors, Ashi walks toward them. A calmness overtakes her. Her father's voice echoes in her mind: *Our Lord once taught, "If you have faith even the size of a mustard seed, you can say to this mountain, 'Move from here to there,' and it will move. Nothing will be impossible for you." You are destined to do great things, daughter. Keep your faith in God. And you, too, will be able to move mountains.* It was one of the many lessons she learned when she walked with him as a youth. He always comforted and instructed her.

Now, Ashi fearlessly approaches the crack between the doors. The firelight piercing the doors flashes across her dark eyes. Yui, a wounded Oishi, and the rest of her ashigaru strain to close the gate. She stops a few feet in front of them. Sitting in the seiza position, she closes her eyes and places her palms together in front of her in prayer. Her warriors look at her curiously. The black fog settles to the ground while the beastly locusts rage and clatter on the other side of the doors. She begins her prayer, "Kami, my father taught me that I could move mountains with even a small amount of faith in you. I may not understand your ways, Lord, but I believe in you. I know the time has not yet come for these wretched creatures to be released upon the world. So I place my trust in you that you will help us this night. Let these doors be closed and sealed according to your will."

A stillness falls upon the room. There is silence. Then, the massive andesite slabs begin grinding slowly against the volcanic gravel floor. The doors are slowly closing.

* * * * *

Outside, the kyūdōka watch the cave entrance. Bows at the ready, they listen and observe intently, trying to discern what is happening. Thick black smoke bellows out of the cave. It hugs the entrance roof before dissipating upward into the night sky. The faithful archers hear something approaching rapidly. It stops before emerging. They train their lightning-tipped arrows at the entrance. Then, coming out slowly, holding Kumo's black and crimson jūnihitoe, is Saitō. The kyūdōka lower their arrows.

"Where is the yōkai, Kumo?" he calls. "Did she come out?"

“Īe,” responds the lead archer.

“Kuso!” he curses. He turns and, looking up, sees the smoke bellowing out of the entrance. He walks back to the mouth of the cave. On the ground, shimmering in the low light, he finds a small pool of blood just below the roof of the cave opening. He kneels to inspect it and notices a light trail of blood leading back into the shrine from the pool. A single drop falls from the roof into the pool. *Hrmm…*He thinks. *She must have returned to spider form, used the dark color of her body to blend in with the smoke, and then escaped unseen.* He motions the archers to follow him into the Shrine of Ancient Behemoths.

* * * * *

Saitō and the rest return just in time to witness the doors close with a thunderous boom. He sees Ashi on the ground before the doors and runs to her, thinking she might be injured. As soon as he is beside her, he realizes she is praying. Lightning suddenly flashes along the width of each door seal, startling the Hotaru-Raikō. God has sealed the doors. She places her hands in the gravel and gives a low bow, saying softly, “Thank you, Kami.” She gracefully rises to her feet afterward and smiles at all her exhausted warriors. A few are injured, but not one has lost their life in the battle. Though the highest goal for a samurai is to die in the service of the Lord, too many have already fallen; she is grateful none had to make that sacrifice this night.

Most of the ashigaru had witnessed her strength that night, her skill with the naginata. Only a few saw her faith. All respect her authority as their leader. She looks around at her faithful retainers, each bowing as she looks in their direction, even her betrothed when she turns to him. “Saitō-san,” she asks, “Kumo?”

"Vanished in the night. She fled under the cover of that terrible smoke."

Ashi, ever so slightly, purses her lips and lowers her head, disappointed in her escape. She takes a breath and exhales. Raising her head, she looks into his eyes. With a loving firmness, she directs, "Take charge. Lead the others. Take our honored dead down from the walls and bring them outside. Make the proper funeral pyres so we can collect their bones for burial later. Gather the remains of traitors and the beast. Pile them up in front of the doors. They are cursed and must remain here. Drag the torii down, destroy the drums, and cut down what remains of the jubokko. Bring all remnants of this accursed shrine into the cave. When done, we will raze it to the ground. The Shrine of the Ancient Behemoths is to be no more."

"Hai, Ashi-sama." He immediately sets everyone to task.

Ashi walks to the doors where Yui and Oishi are. She has noticed their lights are brighter when they are together. She calls to them, "Yui-san. Oishi-san." They bow again in respect. After they stand, she motions to see Oishi's arm. He raises it and turns it so she can inspect his wound. "Yui, take Oishi outside. Clean and dress his wound." She pauses for a second to offer them a smile. "Afterward, help the others light the pyres." They bow and then rush out into the night air together.

Ashi strides over to the locust. She yanks her naginata from his scorpion tail. Lifeless, it falls to the ground. She turns and glides just above the gravelly floor toward the entrance. Outside, her eyes follow the last putrid smoke trickling through the trees. The dark sky is filled with stars. Unable to ignore their beauty, she stares at them for a moment. Turning her attention to the old road, she notices all the ancient ishidōrō are empty; the onibi are gone. *Okaasama?* she wonders. *Have their spirits been set free?*

The Hotaru-Raikō spend the rest of the night gently removing their own honored dead, tearing down the shrine, and depositing the cursed remains near the stone doors. After everyone had entirely evacuated the cave, Ashi lit a torch from one of the funeral pyres. She then flies into the wicked domain and sets the ruins ablaze.

Saitō later watches his beloved emerge with a deep fascination. Her beauty strands sway as she flies out slowly. Though soot-covered and bloodstained, her bright orange and white jūnihitoe ripples and flows about her. Her womanly figure, again silhouetted by fire, is carried elegantly by her delicate wings. It is as though she entered a cave cocoon and emerged a woman. A shiver runs down his spine as he experiences a soul-deep attraction to her. She lands gracefully at his side and turns to watch the shrine burn. He sees only her, though; he wants nothing more than to be with her for the rest of his life.

The yellow-orange glow emanating from deep within the blackened cave is eerie. The whole clan stands in the chilly predawn air, staring into what looks like the eye of an ancient, evil goliath looking back at them. The forest is still and silent, but not for long. Ashi orders them to break the stones and fill the cavern's opening. Everyone happily complies, sealing off the accursed gate to the abyss. They leave the unmarked area, praying the forest will overgrow and hide the vile place.

* * * * *

Dirty, tired, and slightly banged up, the Hotaru-Raikō followed the faded animal trail back out of the woods. Serenity descends upon them as they move out into the open field, where they set upon their mission. The familiar early morning glow is on the eastern horizon, birdsong has returned to the woods, and a wet dew has settled upon the long grass in the field. Ashi decides to rest there before returning to their home on the banks of the Fukui Castle moat.

She flies up to rest on a large branch of the same beech tree she perched on the day before. Her onna-musha, samurai, and ashigaru sip dew from the grasses and wash their faces. Looking around for Saitō, who is strangely absent, she glimpses Yui resting alone in the long grass. She wonders where Oishi has gone off to as well.

A slight breeze causes the tree to sway. The gentle wind also takes her back to her childhood, when she sat in such a tree with her father. She recalls her father's words, "I love the beech tree. Its shape reminds me of the tree of life." This whole trial has opened her eyes to her father's positivity. No matter what danger he faced, what task, or how firm he had to be with her or his soldiers, he always saw the good in others, in nature, and in God. She reflects on how positive he was in almost every situation. She smiles, whispering, "Hai, Papa, it will be a good day."

Just then, Saitō zooms up and over the treetop. She is so deep in thought that he startles her a bit. His breath is labored as he lands, but he smiles from ear to ear. In his hands are two plump, bright-red, gozen-tachibana berries. "I thought you would be hungry," he says, offering her one.

"What about the others?" she asks selflessly.

"Ha!" He laughs. "You are your father's daughter, always thinking about others. Look." He nods his head for her to look down. Oishi takes a berry from a makeshift bag made from a large leaf and then hands the sack to one of the other warriors to pass around. He offers the berry he took to Yui. "Oishi and I thought bringing you and the others some well-earned food would be good." He presents the berry to Ashi again. She smiles at him and accepts the fruit. He sits down next to her and exhales. There is no doubt about the love they share for one another.

She and Saitō politely eat their berries and watch the yellow-orange light of the sun crest slowly over Hakusan. Once again, its glorious beams of light reach out toward the sky in many directions. Some rays stretch across the land, chasing the shadows away. The warmth of the sunlight kisses Ashi's fair skin and warms her supple cheeks; she is rejuvenated by it.

They linger for a while before she flies down to the rest, announcing, "It is a new dawn. God has blessed us. Let us return to our families and our homes." Her warriors, now rested and fed, give her a rousing cheer. Ashi takes them to the sky and leads them all home.

Epilogue

Soaring Spirits

Many miles away, on the western side of Mount Fuji, darkness settles in the Aokigahara Forest. A deposed kōgō, a seven-legged spider, haunts the once pristine forest. Harboring a profound hatred for man and hotaru alike, the yōkai named Kumo sometimes takes the form of a small woman in the trees, a beautiful fairy to man's eyes. She whispers to lost and weary travelers as they walk, tempting them to despair. She convinces weak-minded men to see no value in their lives and knows when they have fallen into her trap. For these hopeless lost, she spins the webbing for a noose and offers it as a gift, an invitation to be free of their sorrow.

Many have succumbed to her wicked and troubling murmurs, hanging themselves from the branches she sits upon. Now Kumo is never alone; she captures and keeps these yūrei, the spirits of the hanged, for herself. To this day, she feeds on their eternal souls, extending her own unnatural life.

* * * * *

In the secluded Raikō Village, a whole week has passed since the destruction of the forsaken shrine. A beautiful onna-musha and a dashing samurai have made the lengthy procession up the rock pathway into the Shrine of Watashi. There, the young couple proclaim their vows before God and then lovingly exchange cups filled with nectar with each other. They soon emerge from the old ishidōrō as husband and wife to a rousing cheer. Descending into the niwa, Saitō and Ashi are celebrated by their clan, kin, and firefly cousins as lord and lady of the Hotaru-Raikō.

After their congratulatory welcome, they return to their shinden to change into less formal attire. They hear the reception gather outside in the courtyard. It is a rare occasion for extravagance. Music, singing, dancing, firefly light displays, and, of course, Sumai no Sechi elevate the spirits of the entire village.

During a Sumai no Sechi match, which, like her father before her, Saitō is wholly engrossed in, an odd feeling comes over Ashi. She begins to look around, searching the festivities around her. Her gaze is pulled toward the ishidōrō shrine. A quiet visitor is leaning against the wall next to the door. Her dark almond eyes meet the light-blue eyes of Præsidiel. He stands upright and, with a pleasing smile, nods to her. She humbly bows her head in return. In her heart, she feels the love and affirmation of God. Having given his smile of praise and approval, Præsidiel spreads his wings and takes flight into the heavens above. Ashi happily returns her attention to her husband and the courtyard games.

* * * * *

Later in the evening, after the feasting and festivities have ended, Ashi walks with Saitō along the eastern rō leading out to the open-air pavilion. Though she is generally happy, something still weighs heavily on her mind. She hides her sadness behind the fan in her hand. In truth, she misses her parents. She desperately wishes she knew what happened to her mother's spirit. She also laments not receiving her father's blessing on their marriage. They walk the entire length of the rō silently, Saitō patiently waiting for her to open up to him.

Upon reaching the pavilion, Ashi strolls out into the middle and stares up. Something moves in the star-laden sky. Barely noticeable by Ashi at first, two bright white stars rise, fall, and encircle each other. She unknowingly lowers her fan. Saitō looks up, trying to see what has captured her attention. He, too, sees the dancing lights.

Not knowing what she is witnessing, she watches the lights intently as they descend. Their movement seemed to have a familiar rhythm as if she had seen it before. *Wait,* she thinks to herself. *I recognize that dance.* Her heart leaps with joy. *That is the way Otousama danced with Okaasama. Could it be?*

The flickering lights draw much closer. They twirl and swoop to just a few feet over the newlyweds. Ashi looks at Saitō with a joyous smile on her face. He is still staring at the puzzling lights. He looks down at his bride. She beams with an infectious smile and twinkling eyes. He has seen that look enough to know she is about to do something, but what? She opens her wing covers and spreads her wings. "Ah," he mutters, "you're going to dance with the lights." Saitō extends his wings as Ashi is lifting off the ground. He reaches up to take her hand.

They rise together into the night sky. The star-like lights spin around them both. Ashi giggles and laughs cheerfully as if she were a child again. Saitō is caught up in her delight. A feeling of pure joy and wonder fills their hearts as the dancing continues briefly. Soon, it ends, though, and the twinkling lights hover right in front of them both. Ashi hears her father's voice, "Well done, daughter...Well done." Tears of joy well up in her dark, almond-shaped eyes.

They know the time has come for her father and mother to ascend. She and Saitō humbly bow as the spirits ascend. They watch the two lights soar rapidly into the sky until they are indistinguishable from the rest of the flickering stars in the deep purple sky.

So begins an enduring peace for the Hotaru-Raikō.

MORNING GLORIES
AND
MOONFLOWERS

Contents

Chapter One

The Loss

A well-built, rustic log cabin sits at the end of a country road on the outskirts of the burgeoning town of Fort Myers, Florida. The moss has just started growing on its wood-shingled roof. A light trail of smoke rises out of the stone chimney on the left side of the house, while small green shoots have broken through the recently tilled soil in the garden on the right side. An early spring breeze blows, and the Spanish moss sways in an old oak tree out front.

Two little girls sit with their father on the front porch in front of the closed front door. Six-year-old Jamilla is nestled under her father's right arm while ten-year-old Dorinda leans on his left shoulder. Both wear plain brown dresses and are barefoot. Dorinda has her tightly curled black hair pulled back and down into two tiny braids on both sides of her head. Jamilla's loose woolen hair has not grown quite long enough to style yet and is a little wilder and unkempt.

Their father, a strong, weathered man in his early thirties, is clean-shaven and, reminiscent of his days in the army, keeps his hair short. He wears his favorite overalls, a long-sleeved denim shirt, and sturdy brown boots. They all stare off toward the South Florida sunset, desperately seeking tranquility in the pastel twilight colors.

Any other Friday evening, the girls would be swinging their legs and giggling under the orange, pink, and purple sky while Momma and Papa sat next to each other, holding hands and talking about their day's experiences. This evening, though, the painful sounds of childbirth, which pierce the solid log walls of their little cabin, have them worried.

Jamilla looks up at her father. The screams confuse and concern her. “Papa, is Momma awright?”

“Yeah, Papa,” Dorinda clutches her father’s right arm. “I never heard her yell like that ‘fore. I’m worried.”

“It’s gonna be okay, girls,” their father reassures. “Doc Howard and his missus are takin’ care of Momma.” He pauses. “She’ll be givin’ birth any time now. ’Fore yuh know it, that li’l one will be runnin’ ’round here for you tah chase.”

He offers a smile, but deep down, he, too, is worried. He’s never heard his beautiful wife wail like this, either. In his heart, he knows something is wrong. He pulls his daughters in close to reassure them. As soon as he does, he hears rushed steps behind him, and the door swings open. He looks over his shoulder at Mrs. Howard, the nurse, and the midwife who has blood splattered on her white apron. He holds his girls close, keeping them from seeing the red stains on her apron.

“Come quick, Samuel,” she prompts before returning quickly to her post inside the cabin.

“Dorinda,” Samuel’s heart beats faster, “you an’ your sister can’t see this. I want you tuh take yer sister fer a stroll. Why don’tcha go down to the picnic field ’n see if the sea grapes are a bloomin’? Don’t wander far, though, y’hear?”

“Okay, Papa,” she says with slight fear. “We’ll go down there ’til dark an’ then come home.” Dorinda gently takes her little sister’s hand while her father jumps to his feet and rushes into the cabin, closing the door behind him. “C’mon Jamilla, Papa’ll help take care o’ momma.” The two girls saunter westward down the road, each dragging their feet in the sandy wagon ruts.

They don’t have to walk far before coming to the little family picnic field on the left side of the road. A few slash pines and live oak trees grow in a semi-circle around the field. The orange needles from the pines blanket the ground around short, spotty green grass clusters popping up in the sand. Sabal palms, young sea grape trees, and other small shrubs dot the undergrowth. Their dad always thought it a beautiful spot and left the field untouched when he cleared the land to build their cabin at the end of the road. The family often brought a blanket and had picnic lunches under the shade of the trees, especially when the sea grapes were ripe. Today, however, the girls are surprised to find a stranger in their field.

A man is kneeling near one of the oak trees in the back of the alcove. The girls stop to stare at him out of both fear and curiosity. Jamilla reaches for the security of her big sister's hand. Without looking at them, the man says, "Peace be upon you, little ones. I mean you no harm."

"What're you doin' here, mister?" Dorinda cautiously inquires.

The man stands and turns to see them. He is tall and of considerable stature. He wears old dark-gray pants, brown boots (like their father's), and a lightly soiled but still white shirt with a light blue waistcoat over it. He removes his brown hat and holds it against his chest with his right hand. His facial features are unique; the girls cannot tell if he is white, black, or Seminole. His hair is dark brown and wavy, a little long, just about to touch his shoulders.

He offers a beautiful smile and a nod before announcing. "My name is Præsidiel, but you can call me Mr. Ray." He returns the hat to his head. "I received word of something terrible happening, and I came to help. I hope you do not mind me being here; I was planting some very special flowers in your pretty little field."–He motions toward two tiny green sprouts sticking out of the sandy soil.–"Now, may I ask what you two are doing here this late in the day?"

Dorinda hesitates, but eventually, her childish innocence overtakes her apprehension, and she says, "Our momma is havin' a baby, but I don't think things're are a goin' well from all the yellin' that is. It sounds like she's in terrible pain."

"Yes. Yes, I know." Mr. Ray says with a sad look on his face. "However, I had hoped planting these flowers might bring your whole family peace one day very soon." He kneels back down by the little green shoots. The girls inch closer to inspect them in the twilight. "You ever heard of moonflowers?" He asks.

Ever the bold one, Jamilla says proudly, "No, sir. But Momma an' Papa call us their li'l mornin' glories. You know, just like them li'l blue flowers."

Mr. Ray chuckles. "Well, I believe your momma and papa have picked the right nickname for you two beautiful young ladies. These here are special flowers, though a little rarer. They are found only in this country of yours and are native to the southern area where you live. When they grow up, their leaves will be shaped like hearts. Their buds will open in the evening, and their supple white flowers will reflect the light of the moon itself."

He stands slowly and turns to look closely at the girls. "Now, I have a favor to ask of you. Would you two be willing to help me feed and grow these flowers?"

There is a brief awkward silence before Dorinda says, "Mr. Ray, I'm not sure our papa would want us talkin' to a stranger. 'Sides, even if we did help, what could we do to feed 'em?" Dorinda asks.

"Well, now, that is pretty simple." Mr. Ray smiles with delight. "I will return in two weeks. If you come out and see me, I will show you a very special trick to make these flowers grow big. *But*," he emphasizes, "you each have to bring a clear bottle with you when you come back. Do not worry, though. The good doctor will leave at least two medicine bottles at your house. Medicine for your momma, as it were. When those bottles are finally empty, please wash them and bring them when you return. I will show you the rest of the process then. What do you think? Can you do that?"

"I...I guess we can," Dorinda replies somewhat hesitantly. "Whadda we tell our papa though?"

"Well," Mr. Ray pauses, "I know this will sound strange to you, young ladies, but I need you to keep these flowers secret until the time comes. This will be the only secret I ever ask you to keep. Their growth needs to be hidden from your momma and papa until the time is right. You must not worry, though. I promise no harm will come to you as we work, and when they are ready to bloom, I also promise they will bring healing and much joy to your whole family."

The night sky settles in, and from down the road, the girls hear their father calling out to them. "Dorinda! Jamilla! Where you girls at?"

"Oh. You hear that? Your papa is calling you home. It is time to go. Go on, scoot." Mr. Ray shoos them away with his hand but then waves at the girls as they run back down the road to their dad.

Samuel meets them on the road, halfway between the alcove and the cabin. He kneels, sets his lantern on the ground, and then opens his arms to greet the girls. He scoops Jamilla up with his left arm and then places his right arm around Dorinda, squeezing her shoulders and kissing her forehead. He leans down to pick up his lantern. "It's gettin' dark out here, and there ain't no moon." Turning back to the cabin, he says, "Let's get on home."

"Papa," says Dorinda, pointing toward the picnic field, "there's a man down in the field. Said his name was Mr. Ray. He's a nice man an' was friendly tuh us."

"What!" Samuel wheels around quickly. He holds the lantern above his head and peers down the road toward the field. His light shines down the tree-lined road, which appears like a long tunnel in the growing darkness. There is no movement, no sound, nor any light. He sets Jamilla down and gently moves them behind him with his free hand. He walks cautiously down to the edge of the field. He shines the lantern light around but finds no one in the alcove.

Dorinda, following close behind, speaks up, “Honest, Papa. He was here.”

Samuel turns to look at his daughters. “Come on, girls. Let’s git home quickly. It’s a bad night.” Not only does he suffer exhaustion and sorrow, but now a tinge of worry has been added. He feels some anxiety over a mysterious stranger hanging around their land.

On the way back, Samuel feels he must prepare his daughters for what is to come, so he tells them that Momma gave birth to twin girls. They look up at him with excitement but are taken aback by the tears sneaking out of the corner of his eyes. They have never seen their papa cry before, and it creates a sense of deep concern in their young hearts.

“What’s the matter, Papa?” Dorinda asks with growing concern. “Are the babies okay? Is Momma okay?”

Although he has always been genuinely forthright with his daughters, Samuel hesitates before answering. He draws a deep breath and exhales. “No, darlin’, they’re not. There was an accident, an’ yer baby sisters are gone.”

“Whaddaya mean ‘gone,’ Papa?” the inquisitive Jamilla asks. She, too, looks concerned and fearful. Dorinda knows what it means; her eyes fill with tears, and she turns her gaze toward the ground.

Samuel stops at the end of the road several feet in front of their house, which is quiet now. He squats down and sets the lantern on the ground. He gathers his girls around the light. Fighting back his own emotions and tears, he says softly, “Yer momma gave birth tuh twin baby girls. Sadly, yer baby sisters died after they was born.”

Both girls begin to sniffle.

"Momma got hurt too, but the doctor is mendin' her up. Don't choo worry now. She'll get better in time." He gently places a hand on each of their cheeks, wiping the tears away with his thumbs. He looks deep into their chestnut eyes. He gets that sting in his nose, and his eyebrow twitches as he struggles to keep the tide of emotions at bay. "We're enterin' some dark days, an' it's gonna hurt a bit, girls, but papa needs yuh tuh be strong. Ah'm gonna need yer help over the next few days, y'understand?"

Dorinda sniffles as she wipes the tears away on her sleeve. "I unnerstand, Papa. I'll try."

He looks at little Jamilla, who is speechless; the corner of her eyes and mouth are turned downward, and her eyes are full of water. "Jamilla, Ah need you tuh love on Momma for me, 'kay? Can yuh do that for me?" He asks softly.

"I try, Papa. I try," she manages to answer through the sobs.

Cupping his hands, Samuel pats them gently on the side of their heads and then pulls them both to his chest. He hugs them warmly, reluctantly letting them go after a minute. "We'll get through this, girls. Ah promise. Never forget, Ah love yuh both with my whole heart." He picks up Jamilla with his left hand and his lantern with his right. He swings the lantern around Dorinda's shoulder. "Now let's git home."

When they enter the house, Samuel notices the crib is already gone, and almost everything has been cleared from around the bed. The young girls rush to their momma's side. She is sedated and is resting as peacefully as possible. Their father stops for a second and watches with a heavy heart as Dorinda strokes her momma's hair while Jamilla holds her hand.

Mrs. Howard quietly and discreetly finishes cleaning everything up while tending to his wife's comfort. Samuel has seen many bad things in his life, but nothing can compare to the death of his children. He stares blankly in the direction of his wife and daughters, helpless and frozen by his inability to think clearly or do anything else for them. His senses return to him after a moment. He knows some things still need to be done, so he exits back through the front door so as not to disturb them.

He walks around the left side of the house to the back, where Doc Howard is standing by his horse and cart, head down, in solemn disbelief. Doc has safely bundled the lifeless bodies of the family's newborn daughters in soft blankets and placed them securely in his cart. He straightens up and humbly greets Samuel as he comes near. "You've been through a lot tonight, Samuel. I want you to rest as best as you can. We'll take great care to prepare your little ones for burial and bring them back to you first thing in the morning. Right now, though, you need to take care of yourself and those lovely ladies in there. They're going to need you." Doc pauses momentarily before trying to reassure him, "Remember, my friend, God only allows us trials we can handle. Keep your faith and pray for all your beautiful girls."

With an almost indignant look, Samuel stares him in the eyes. "Ah appreciate what yuh done here t'night, Doc. You've always been good tuh me an' mah family, but Ah don't feel as though God cares much 'bout us right now."

"Now, Mr. Samuel," comes the comforting voice of Mrs. Howard from behind him. "You know that's not true." She places her soft brown hand on his shoulder as she quietly passes him. With a slight nod, he politely and humbly smiles at her as her hand slides off his shoulder. "We know you're a good man, a good husband, and a good father in the sight of God," she says softly as her husband helps her climb into the cart. "Those girls o' yours are precious. They're takin' good care of their momma right now. I know you'll see to their and your queen's care. In the meantime, we'll pray for you all."

Samuel dips his head. “Thank yuh, Missus Howard.”

He watches Doc help his wife get settled in their cart. Then Doc approaches him once more to give him a silent handshake, to reassure him as best a man can. He then turns, climbs aboard the wagon, and, with a shake of the reigns, waves goodbye as they depart quietly.

Samuel’s eyes turn toward the soft light coming through the back door of the quiet cabin. He takes a deep breath, exhales, and murmurs, “Ah’ll do what I can, I guess. Ah’ll do what I can.” Then, he takes his first step back toward his family.

Chapter Two

Solemnity

Though exhausted, Samuel still has trouble sleeping. He rises early the following day before the sun is up. He lights a small fire in the fireplace and, from it, his lantern. He quietly looks around the silent cabin, cherishing the peaceful slumber of his wife and daughters. It is the silence that grips him, though. The sound of babies is absent from their little cabin. It makes him feel somewhat lost, unsure of what to do next. He needs something to do with his hands.

A carpenter by trade, he heads out to the small shed behind the house, where he begins building two small coffins from some good wood he was storing. He tries to keep the noise to a minimum but knows he has woken Dorinda and Jamilla because he can smell breakfast being prepared. He is grateful for Dorinda, whom he thinks the world of. He knows she will tend to her mother and little sister while he is out.

Samuel hears the door creak open, and little footprints scuffle through the sandy grass behind him. He has finished his work. He puts down his tools and buries his pain deep inside his heart. He turns to see Jamilla standing in the early morning light. Her wild, woolen hair surrounds her soft brown face like a halo. She's staring up at him expectantly. "Mornin', Papa," she says, rubbing her eyes.

"Good mornin', mah darlin'," he says.

Jamilla instinctively raises her hands toward him. Samuel squats down, and she rushes into his arms. He picks her up and holds her to his left.

"Dorinda made beckfest, Papa," she informs. "You hungry?"

"Yes, ma'am, Ah am," he says with a smile.

"Papa," Jamilla starts, "Momma said she don't wanna get up. She's sad, an' so am I."

"Me too, young'un. Me too."

The mind of a child shifts gears so fast, though, and she asks, "Whatcha doin' out here?" Jamilla looks inquisitively over his shoulder at the simple caskets. "Whad'ya make them for?"

"Ah, now don't cha go worryin' yer pretty little head 'bout that. Ah'll tell yuh 'bout it some other time."

She turns to look her father in the eyes. He sees the deep affection in her heart and smiles. She returns his grin. Still carrying her, he starts for the cabin. "Let's go check on Momma and get somethin' tuh eat."

Dorinda has set the table and is sitting by her momma, who is still in bed when they come in. Samuel puts Jamilla down. She scurries over to kiss Momma and then runs to sit at the table. Dorinda tells Momma she loves her and goes to the table too. Samuel pats her on the back as she passes. He then sits on the small stool next to his wife, Phiby.

"Mornin', mah queen," he says with a smile. He grabs the small plate of food Dorinda left on the floor and offers her a bite.

She shakes her head no.

"Okay, looks pretty good though. Sure I can't getcha tuh eat a little somethin'?" He asks.

Again, she subtly shakes her head no.

"Okay," he says as he gets up and gently sets the plate on the stool. "I'll leave it rahght here 'case yuh change yer mind." He leans in to give her a long kiss on her cheek before whispering, "Ah love you." Samuel walks to the table to sit with his girls.

He sits across the table from Dorinda and to the right of Jamilla. He offers a half-hearted blessing for the food, and they all eat in silence afterward. Dorinda finishes her breakfast at about the same time as her father. They watch Jamilla, who always eats slower, for a minute. Dorinda turns to her father and lovingly asks, "Papa, what're their names? Our sisters, that is."

Samuel turns his gaze from Jamilla to Dorinda. He is caught off guard by the bold question at first. Momentarily struck dumb, he glances over at Phiby. He can see a tear glistening in the early morning light as it rolls down her supple, light brown cheek. She stares through the open window, pretending to ignore the conversation. He turns back to Dorinda. "Well, darlin', Momma and Ah had a couple o' names picked out. Since they're twins, Ah guess we'll jus' give 'em each one o' the names. Jemima was the first one born, an' Sabina was second."

Tipping her head slightly in contemplation, Dorinda is happy with the names. She smiles at her papa. Jamilla, cheeks stuffed full of food, says, "Them's pretty names, Papa."

He turns just in time to see breadcrumbs fall from her mouth to the floor as she speaks. Samuel can't help but shake his head and chuckle at her. "You're a mess girl."

He turns back to look at Dorinda. He reaches across the table, caresses her face with his right hand, and says, "Ah love you, mah daughter. Yer a sweet girl, yuh know that?"

She leans into his hand before he slowly pulls it back. He gets up from the table. "Ah still have a lot o' work tuh do though. You take care o' your momma for me?"

"Yes, Papa. I'll do mah best."

"Whatta 'bout me?" Jamilla asks, also wanting her father's attention.

Samuel walks behind her and then, kneeling to her right, places his left hand gently on her shoulder. He leans in with a serious but loving look and asks, "Will you be a big girl an' help yer sister for me? Help her clean up and take care o' Momma too?"

"Yessir," she says confidently with a smile.

"That's mah good girl." He cups the back of her head and kisses her forehead. He then stands back up and looks at his oldest. "Dorinda, don't forget. The goat needs milkin', and you'll need tuh tend to them chickens too. Okay, darlin'?"

"Okay, Papa."

Samuel walks back over to Phiby and gives her a peck on the cheek. She offers no reaction to his kiss, which saddens him. He turns and heads out the back door. He collects the caskets and a few tools from the shed and then walks to the picnic field. He sets everything down, sighs deeply, and looks around. *Such a beautiful place. Sure hate tuh turn it into a graveyard.* He thinks sadly; *ah guess these babies deserve the best restin' spot Ah can give 'em, though.* He picks up his shovel and breaks ground on the left side of the alcove, close to the back. "Man, ground is always hard. Ah'm always amazed at how hard diggin' is 'round here!" He mutters to himself. He works to make a grave deep enough to hold both caskets but not so deep as to run into the waterline.

After a while, he eventually finishes. He climbs out and rests for a minute on the small mound of sandy dirt piles. Breathing heavily, he wipes the sweat from his brow and then leans on his shovel. The sight of the grave triggers a memory from his youth.

In his mind, he feels he is ten years old again. It's only been a few days since he was taken from his mother and sent to a plantation further south. He remembers feeling like an unwanted burden the first few days. At night, he curled up alone in the dirt corner of an unfamiliar shack. He is acutely aware of many strange noises in the darkness of night—creaking boards, tree limbs rustling and rattling outside, shadows passing by the cracks in the door and shutters. He wonders what makes those shadows and from which direction he might be attacked. Sambo, as he was known then, keeps watch until exhaustion finally carries his youthful mind off to sleep. Most nights, his thoughts dwell on his mother; he finds hiding tears in the darkness easier. Early on, he would cry himself to sleep, wondering what his future holds. It isn't long before he is taken in by the other slave families, though, and he begins to make new acquaintances as he works.

Weeks have passed since his arrival. It is the heat of the day; he's sweating profusely, making the dirt stick to his bare arms. Sambo is one of three boys; he's still getting to know the other two. They're digging a grave in the root-filled soil on the edge of the plantation. No crops could be grown in that wooded area, so the owner set it aside as a slave cemetery. None of the adults are allowed to stop working until nightfall either, so the boys know they not only have to dig the grave but also have to build a casket out of whatever scrap wood they can find, blacken it with shoe polish, and then get the body placed in it before the field workers come back. Samuel still remembers the rope burns on the man's neck and the stink of his dead flesh when they placed his body in the shoddy casket. Memories he never could quite shake.

Later that night, the rest of the slaves gather in the unmarked cemetery. Yellow torchlight flickers under the now dark, leafy canopy. This is the only time, in the dead of night, slaves are allowed to bury their deceased. It was also one of the extremely rare occasions when all of them could come together at the same time without the owners or overseers. So many emotions ebbed and flowed on such an occasion, from deep sorrow at the death of one of their own to the peace and relief of being able to speak freely without the overseers watching and listening. It was a valuable opportunity for Sambo to learn more about his new kin and their efforts to provide some dignity for their loved ones before their spirits moved on.

He remembers listening to the adult slaves' whispers that night about the man who was to be buried, how he was one of three who had tried to escape to the North where they could be free. All three were recaptured, however. He learns how the slave patrols are concentrated along the northern borders and the coast, making escape a risky venture. The man they were burying had been singled out as having planned the escape and subsequently hanged as an example to the others. That's also why the boys were tasked with digging the grave and preparing the body; it was meant to serve as a warning to them as well.

Young Sambo listens intently and observes the adults. He sees the brokenness of their wills, so many subdued and resigned to their condition. He knows deep down it's wrong. He knows he and they are destined for something better. The fire in his belly grows. He wants to escape, to be free to make his own way in life. Ever the courageous boy, he commits himself to never giving in to the brokenness and despair slavery has wrought. He remembers deciding that very night to find a way to be free and begins to plot his escape southward.

Now, as a free man, he sits on a pile of dirt, sand, and shells, carving the names of his infant daughters into the cross-shaped marker he made for them. In his youth, slaves were buried without markers; he resolved that his daughters would not suffer such indignation. They would be buried in a beautiful spot, and their names would be seen and remembered. Deep in contemplation about this and many other things, Samuel never notices the two new vines growing at the base of the oak trees in the back of the alcove as he carves his daughters' names into a wooden cross.

* * * * *

It's late morning. The warm spring sun has risen pretty high in the light blue sky. Finished with his work, Samuel removes his wide-brimmed hat, wipes the sweat from his brow with his kerchief, and exhales. He blows the curled wooden slivers away and takes a moment to examine his work. *That's good.* He thinks with satisfaction. Then, he hears Doc Howard's cart coming up the road. *Good timin'. Guess I shoulda 'xpected it, though. Doc's always been a good man.* He recalls serving with him in the army.

Although he was a white man from the North, Doc was the only officer besides the commanding officer who would come around often to check on the condition of the men. Doc was the only one who seemed to care about them. Samuel once asked him why he cared so much and still remembers his answer, "I believe what the founders knew to be true. That all men are created equal in the eyes of God. Because of that, I intend to provide you the same care I would anyone else. Moreover, I not only admire your courage to fight for your freedom but, well, let's just say I have a personal interest in caring for your people as well."

It was not until after the war ended, when Mrs. Howard, a free black woman, traveled South to be with her husband, that Samuel finally understood what he meant by "having a personal interest." With her assistance, Doc continues his profession as a civilian now, caring for all who call upon him.

Samuel rushes out to wave him down as he rides up. He directs him to pull his cart into the little field. "Ah'm glad Ah caught'cha, Doc," he says. "Now we kin take care o' things an' not disturb the girls up at the house."

Dr. Howard nods in agreement and then turns his cart around in the field so the back is toward the open grave. He hops down, ties off his horse's reins to a nearby tree, and then goes to the rear of the cart to properly greet Samuel.

Together, they then gently remove and place each baby into their tiny caskets. Samuel's heart sinks when he picks up Sabina. Both girls are wrapped in white swaddling and smell of flowers. Though her supple cheeks are pale and cold to the touch, she feels so good in his arms. He stalls, rocking her back and forth for a moment and patting her little butt, which rests in the palm of his strong left hand. He hasn't held them since the previous night and takes a moment to spend time with her. *Mah God, Ah wish Ah could hear 'em cry again. Jus' one more time*, he thinks.

Doc stands aside quietly, respectfully watching a loving father whom he knows Samuel to be. His heart breaks again for him as he watches Samuel finally kneel, gently place her in the casket, and then repeat his slow transition from the cart to the coffin with Jemima.

Samuel turns to Doc Howard, thanking him for taking such good care to prepare his baby girls for burial. He knows his wife helped and asks him to thank Mrs. Howard too. "Don't know what Ah'd do without y'all."

"It's the least we could do, Samuel," Doc replies somberly. "The very least."

He names each child before he nails their caskets shut. Doc then helps him carefully lower the coffins into the open grave. They gently remove the lowering ropes and then stand in silent reverence at the foot of the open grave. Both men have their hands clasped together in front of themselves in silence. After a few minutes, Doc Howard peeks at Samuel, whose furrowed brow and tear-stained face gazes downward. "You want to say something for them, Samuel?"

He slowly moves his head from side to side. "Ah don't rightly know what tuh say, Doc."

"May I?" his friend asks.

Samuel nods his head in approval.

Doc prays with a slow, steady cadence, "Lord God, heavenly king, we commit these young girls to your eternal love. Keep them safe in your mighty arms and grant them peace. Please help us understand this sorrow and strengthen us with hope. Help this family overcome their sadness. Give them confidence that little Jemima and Sabina are in a better place with you. May our Lord Jesus welcome them into his arms and bless them abundantly. Amen." He reaches over and pats Samuel on the shoulder, trying to reassure him.

"Thanks, Doc," is all Samuel can say. He sniffles, wipes the tear from the corner of his eye, and grabs his shovel. He stands by the pile of dirt and sand, ready to close the grave.

"Anything else the missus or I can do for you and your family right now?" Doc Howard asks.

"No, sir, not really," Samuel answers. "Doc, I...I 'preciate whatcha've done for us. I can't thank yuh enough."

Doc Howard looks him in the eyes. "You need anything, anything at all, brother, you just ask."

"Thank yuh, sir," Samuel affirms.

Doc nods at Samuel and pats him on the shoulder one more time. He then climbs somberly back up in his cart. Looking over his shoulder, he says, "I'll send the missus 'round after church tomorrow to check on Phiby."

Samuel nods in gratitude. "Much obliged."

Doc Howard nods back, gives the reigns a light snap, and slowly rolls out. Samuel looks down into the grave one last time, hesitating to fill it in. He reluctantly begins his toil anyway. Something about the sound of soil hitting the wooden caskets drives home the finality of their short-lived lives, but he doesn't stop shoveling until it's finished.

Once he's done, he drives the cross into the ground at the head of the grave with the shovel and then steps back to the foot of it. Samuel pauses for a moment, not just to catch his breath either. A trace of slight bitterness and anger settled upon him. He raises his eyes to the clear blue sky overhead. "You let 'em separate me from mah mother when Ah was a boy. Now I too must be separated from mah children?" he argues with God. "Ah thought Ah was a free man now, an' things were supposed tuh be better. I don't understand this, Lord. I jus' don't. What'm Ah supposed to do now?"

He listens for a response, but no answer comes. The only sound is the wind blowing gently through the Spanish moss. He lowers his head in the quiet alcove. Samuel lets out a somewhat disappointed sigh before picking up his hat and heading back to the cabin with his shovel in hand.

* * * * *

Sunday comes and goes silently. No one does much of anything. Phiby stays in bed all morning. The girls clean the cabin, cook dinner, and tend to their momma before walking to the river to pick flowers. Samuel feeds and brushes their horse, Micco. He knows it's selfish to leave all the household chores to his girls, but he needs some time to be alone with his thoughts. As he brushes Micco, he recalls the day they got him and how Phiby named him after one of the last Seminole chiefs to leave Florida.

Though sad, he allows himself a passing smile, especially when thinking of his beautiful queen. He cleans and prepares the wagon and tools before milling about the garden. There is some small satisfaction in watching their crops grow. He checks the lima beans, collard greens, corn, okra, and tobacco growing there. Gently touching the young leaves, Samuel quietly mumbles, again questioning God why he would allow this tragedy.

His thoughts are scattered, random, and fleeting. Though he is an intelligent and highly skilled man, deep philosophy is not his strong suit. He would much rather work with his hands and fix what needs fixing. Unfortunately, he finds the death of children to be something he cannot *fix*. He is eager to return to work on Monday. Being busy with his hands will give him the time to sort through his thoughts. He knows he can solve problems, build structures, and work out his feelings as a man should—with his hands. At home, the girls' emotions need repair, and he is unsure how to mend Phiby's pain and despair or how to teach Dorinda and Jamilla to understand what has happened.

Mrs. Howard visits later that afternoon. Samuel takes the girls out to sit on the porch, giving her privacy to conduct her physical checkup on their momma. She emerges out onto the porch after several minutes. He sends the girls back inside so he and Mrs. Howard can have a private conversation out by her horse.

"Samuel, I'm worried," she begins.

He has removed his hat and is slowly spinning it around by the brim in his hands. "'Bout what, ma'am?"

"Well, she's already begun healing physically, and that's good." She pauses. "But, Samuel, I've never seen a broken spirit like she has in her. I'm afraid it'll take a small miracle to bring her back."

There is a long silence. "Well, Ah guess me an' the girls have our work cut out fer us then 'cause we can't jus' give up on her."

"Oh, Samuel"—she places her hand on his shoulder—"my heart goes out to you all. I know you love her and that you'll all do your best. I'll continue to check in as often as I can, and I'll continue to pray for you every day, too."

"Thank you, ma'am." He places his hat back on his head, unties the reigns of her horse from the post on the porch, and holds the bridle while she mounts her steed. She touches him on the shoulder and offers a final, reassuring smile. Samuel hands her the reigns as she does. She sits upright in the saddle, tugs at the reins to turn her horse, and departs. Samuel waves farewell.

* * * * *

Much to his restrained delight, Monday morning has come. Samuel is both reluctant and happy to depart for work—reluctant to leave his family but eager to put his hands to familiar work. He kisses Phiby goodbye, though she doesn't respond. He reminds his girls of their chores and then kisses them each on the forehead before climbing up on his old wooden wagon. He gives the reins a light snap. "C'mon, Micco, let's go." Micco knows the road into town well. He plods along the sand-and-shell road.

A little way down the road, the rhythm of the wheels, the rattle of tools in the back, and the bounce of the seat lull Samuel into a sort of trance. He's haunted by a sense of uncertainty and fear, which causes his thoughts to slip back to the time of his escape, another time of fear and uncertainty.

He remembers how young he was, only fourteen, when he took flight to Seminole territory in the South. The mix of sun and shade on his face triggers eerie memories of the light of the full moon moving through the trees. Unlike his current trek into town, he remembers staying off the roads then but close enough to them to know if he was being hunted.

His food had run out two days into his escape. He was fighting exhaustion while keeping himself moving in a southern direction. Samuel had just crested a low hill and lumbered into a shallow, misty valley. His destination uncertain and his mind numb from fatigue, he pressed on with a dogged motivation. Rather unexpectedly, his mind sharpened, and his senses came alive. He stopped in his tracks and looked around. He suddenly realized there was no sound, no breeze, nothing. He became keenly aware there was something wrong in that valley. A knot formed in the pit of his stomach, and the hair on the back of his neck stood up. The still and silent night air had a palpable sense of evil. He listened for the sounds of men moving through the underbrush but heard nothing. No man, no beast, no nothing. His heart pounded, and his senses were heightened. "Mah Lord, mah Lord," he cried quietly, "lead me tuh safety. Please protect me, mah savior."

He began to walk again, quickly this time. Then, paralleling his own, the soft sound of steps crunching leafy grass came from the hushed woods. He knew someone or something was walking with him, watching. The blood drained from his extremities, and his skin turned cold with fear. He clambered up the next hill. The footsteps continued. He turned to look, straining his eyes to see anything or anyone, but could see nothing. Though it posed a significant risk, Samuel descended the hill into a tall grassy meadow. He was exposed now, out in the open. Still, the hushed footfall matched his own, and he still saw nothing around him. Profoundly disturbed and filled with dread, he continued.

This went on for a half-mile before he caught the smell of burning wood mingling with the thin veil of mist closing in on him. He spotted the orange glow of a small campfire in the distance. Samuel was almost at a full run in a near panic as he moved toward the firelight. He desperately wanted more time to inspect who might be there as he feared being chased into a trap. Then, as he drew near the camp, the footsteps behind him ended, and the low mist retreated.

He paused near the wood line to get a better look at the camp's residents. They were not white, nor did they dress like anyone he had seen before. *They must be Seminole*, he thought to himself. He approached as quietly as possible, but it was not enough. The two men sitting by the fire quickly spotted him as he neared. They jumped to their feet. One drew a tomahawk from his belt, and the other his rifle. Samuel raised his hands chest high so they could see he was unarmed. He approached slowly, cautiously. The orange light flickered in his eyes and on the palms of his hands. The two lowered their weapons. He stopped well away from their campsite. Not knowing if they would understand him, he politely asked if he could join them.

Samuel was pleasantly surprised and relieved to find out they spoke broken English. The men immediately recognized he was an escaped slave; Samuel was not the first they had ever encountered. They put away their weapons and invited him to sit at their fire. Samuel never forgot their incredible generosity in feeding him or their willingness to help him go South into free lands. As he traveled South with them and other Seminoles over the next two days, he learned about the legend of Stikini, an evil witch who could turn himself into a grotesque owl man. Samuel always wondered silently if Stikini was stalking him that night.

The two men and their tribe helped Samuel escape to Fort Myers, where he lived as a refugee. He continued to learn and develop his skills as a carpenter's apprentice there. The Civil War broke out a few short months after his arrival. He frequented the Union trading post, making friends with pioneers, ranchers, and some of the remaining Seminole who came to trade. In his off time, he found those who would teach him how to ride a horse, among many other things a slave would usually never be allowed to learn. As soon as he was of age, he enlisted in the 2nd U.S. Colored Infantry, garrisoned in Fort Myers in the latter parts of the war.

As he travels into town, he reflects on the one-day battle for the fort in 1865. In the recesses of his mind, he can still hear orders being screamed, cannon fire ringing out, and the smell of gunpowder, which billowed from their rifles, lingering in the air. He remembers losing a friend on the march to Natural Bridge and another in the short-lived battle there. Though it still compounds his current sorrow, that sadness is different. They were all men, fighting and dying for their freedom. Jemima and Sabina, however, were innocents, incapable of fighting for their own lives.

Samuel remembers being mustered out of service in 1866 after the war ended. Several of his brothers-in-arms moved back to the Fort Myers region as pioneers and homesteaders, eager to live free to make a life for themselves. Those were exciting times. The prospects of working for themselves, finding a wife, marrying, and building families thrilled them. While some of his friends settled on Sanibel Island, in Punta Gorda, and even all the way out in Alva, Samuel preferred the relative safety and familiarity of the Fort Myers area. Once there, he sought out old friendships among the tiny handful of Seminole who had remained, farmers, ranchers, and others he had easily connected with before. As the area began to settle, he found much work as a carpenter. Samuel partnered with many settlers, business owners, and even the ranchers north of the Caloosahatchee River. He helped them build homes and shops in the growing communities. In turn, they helped him with his cabin. He remembers how good it felt to see so many unite in the spirit of freedom to build their towns and neighborhoods.

Micco snorts and shakes Samuel from his reflections as he nears town. He passes a young lady walking with a gentleman on the side of the road. He tips his cap, greeting them as he passes. The young lady offers him a smile, and his thoughts immediately turn to Phiby. During the construction of his cabin, one of the remaining Black Seminole men, accompanied by his oldest daughter, came to help. He and Samuel worked hard that morning before taking lunch in the lush, shady field down the road from where their cabin now sits. Sitting in the breeze, Samuel listened to the elder's stories about how his people had moved South many moons after the attack on Angola. Although he endeavored to be a polite student, Samuel could not take his eyes off Phiby; her allure was intoxicating. They exchanged bashful glances and smiles between bites and stories. His heart would beat fast each time she spoke. There was no denying their instant connection, and they fell in love that very day.

Though Samuel doesn't smoke, he plants and continues to grow a small amount of tobacco on his modest farm to offer trade with her father. It was partly through this trade that he was able to court Phiby. In addition, he gained much from her father's knowledge of hunting, foraging, identifying medicinal plants, and learning the best crops to grow. This made the hardships of frontier life easier and helped him win his bride's hand, his queen.

He still goes hunting with his Seminole brothers while their wives visit Phiby, and their children play together. He knows he can call on them in this time of need. For now, though, there is still so much to do in town and at home. Though he thinks of his girls often, Samuel loses himself in the day's toil, trying to forget the pain and worry they are all going through.

* * * * *

At home, Jamilla helps clean the house by sweeping and putting things away. Dorinda cooks and brings medicine to her momma. They both sing sweet songs to her while they prepare her breakfast. They help her to the table, where she sits and stares out of the only window in the house. After breakfast, the girls clean up, and then Dorinda does her best to teach Jamilla what she knows about reading and writing.

In the afternoon, they feed the chickens and tend the goat. They work in the garden for a bit. The fresh sea-blown breeze stirs the Spanish moss in the surrounding trees, and warm sunshine feels good on their soft brown faces.

Once their chores are done, the girls' curiosity gets the best of them, and they sneak off to the field. They approach the freshly covered grave slowly. Except for the breeze and occasional birdsong, it is quiet. The girls stop at the foot of the grave and stare. For both, there is something amiss about the appearance of the grave. Having witnessed the birth of her little sister, Dorinda can feel the loss. She remembers the crying, the feeding, and the cleaning when Jamilla was a baby. The absence of her newborn twin sisters makes her heart feel heavy; she is unsure how to express it. She reads the names on the cross out loud for Jamilla, who sees her big sister's reaction but is otherwise confused. She empathizes with her yet doesn't truly understand or know how to react to everything that has happened.

* * * * *

Phiby is alone. The girls have gone outside, and Samuel is working in town. She gets up from the table and goes to lie on her side in bed. Still in pain from childbirth, she holds her stomach as she walks. It's not just the physical pain that hurts either, but the deafening silence stings her heart and mind. There are no infant cries, no tiny child to nurse or care for. There is no newborn-baby scent other parents enjoy. This was supposed to be a happy time, yet her joy has been stripped away. She feels utterly alone and useless.

As the desolation sinks deeper into her heart, a wicked voice whispers in her ear, "You failed. You are not a good wife. You are not a good mother or daughter."

Phiby cries. Tears roll down her cheek onto her pillow. “Yes, Ah am,” she argues weakly.

“There is not a single person who will understand your failure, your pain. You are alone.”

“That’s not true,” she murmurs to herself. “Samuel...Mah father...Dorinda an’ Jamilla.”

“They are not here. They do not understand. They will not forgive.”

“Yer wrong.” Phiby curls up in a ball. Her face contorted with both pain and sadness. “They still love me.” She pulls the blankets up to cover her mouth. “Go ’way, evil spirit. Leave me be.”

The voice is silent, but the damage is done. Phiby begins to think about what could have been. *If only Ah had known they was twins. What if they had lived? What if? What if?* She closes her eyes and cries herself to sleep.

* * * * *

Standing solemnly at the foot of their sister’s grave and observing her surroundings, Jamilla is the first to point out the oddness of the scene, saying, “It s’posed to be covered wiff grass awready?” She points at the ground with her left hand while scratching her head with her right.

Dorinda is suddenly aware that is what is amiss. “No, Ah don’t think grass grows *that* fast. Kinda odd.” She also begins to look around. “Look o’er there. Them flowers Mr. Ray planted are a growin’ too.” The two moonflower vines are already reaching for the tree trunks of nearby trees.

“Wow!” Jamilla says.

After being briefly mesmerized, Dorinda turns her attention back to the grave. Both girls stand in somber silence for a short time before Dorinda speaks up, “Papa said their tiny bodies are a restin' here, but he says their souls are up 'n heaven with God."

"That's far 'way, isn't it? You think we'll get tuh meet 'em one day?" Jamilla asks, who is innocently twisting and turning slightly as she looks around.

"I s'pose...when we get to heaven too, I guess," Dorinda answers. Reluctant to dwell on thoughts of death, she changes the subject. "We oughta be gettin' back now. Gotta check on Momma."

Jamilla nods in agreement, and both girls turn to leave. Jamilla reaches for her big sister's hand as they stroll back up the road. They return to the cabin hand in hand. There, they find their momma sleeping in her bed. The girls quietly add wood to the embers in the fireplace and stoke it into a small fire. They then begin preparing a simple dinner for Papa. They know he will be hungry after a long day's work.

*****

Though the days seem short because of all his work, it feels like time is dragging slowly on. A whole week passes. Each day, Samuel goes into town for work while the girls tend to the house and their momma, who has sunken deeper into depression. Long periods of prolonged and awkward silence interrupt the family's time together. The girls do their best to care for their momma, love on her, and cheer her up. Mrs. Howard checks in on her a couple of times. She lets Samuel know that, physically, his wife is mostly healed, but she is still concerned for her emotional well-being.

During the day and some evenings, Phiby often mills about the cabin or finds her way out on the porch. Occasionally feeling adventurous, she might walk through the garden or feed the chickens, but she prefers to sit in her rocking chair by the fire. Samuel and the girls can still see she struggles mightily with the death of Jemima and Sabina. He knows she is falling into despair. She continually turns her thoughts inward, showing no energy or zest for life around her. She withdraws further and further from them. Samuel feels her anguish in his own heart. He knows he needs to do something to bring her back.

On Friday evening, after work, he takes her and the girls on a long walk to the banks of the river to look for sea grapes and flowers and watch the sunset. The time with her family does offer a temporary respite, a reassurance that they still love and cherish her, but she quickly falls back into depression the next day. Samuel must persistently show her how much he loves and needs her.

Though most of the last few nights she has said nary a word, she sometimes lashes out at them in pain and sorrow, especially when Samuel plays with the girls. This was the case on Saturday evening; her unstable emotions came out as resentful anger toward the girls. It was raining heavily outside, so the girls were inside playing, a little too noisy as children sometimes do. Samuel had cleared the table and was starting to wash up. The girl's laughter became too loud, and Phiby barked at them, threatening to send them out in the rain. Samuel quickly intervened, drawing her ire and derision.

He knows it has been a week since the tragic night and that Phiby is likely aware of this, even if unknowingly. Although painful to hear, he humbly and quietly accepts all her insults, knowing they come from a place of loss and pain.

Finally exhausted from yelling at them, Phiby shuffles over to the fireplace and plops down in the rocking chair in front of it. She slips back into her distant, silent stare. Looking for reassurance, the girls help their papa finish cleaning up from dinner. He then quietly takes them out to the front porch to watch the rain.

Samuel sits in his chair with Jamilla on his lap. She sits on his left leg, and he has wrapped his left arm around her. She nuzzles in close, resting her head on his chest and listening to his heart. Dorinda leans her back against the house. She and Papa listen to the rain falling on the porch's roof. After a few moments of peaceful contemplation, Samuel motions with his right hand for Dorinda to come closer. "Come 'ere, sweetheart." She comes round and sits on his right knee. Still holding onto Jamilla, who has popped her head up, he gently places his right hand on Dorinda's shoulder blade. "Tomorrow's Sunday, girls. Ah think we all need tuh go tuh church, so I want'cha in bed early t'nite, okay?"

"Yes, Papa." They nod in unison.

He looks into their soft chestnut eyes, and his tone softens, "Don'choo worry 'bout what yer momma said, girls. She don't mean a lick of it. She don't mean tuh ignore you either. Deep down, she still loves yuh. Ah promise. She'll be right as this rain 'fore long. You'll see. Before yuh know it, she'll be brushin' yer hair, teachin' yuh how tuh read, and a ticklin' yuh again." He pokes at Jamilla's belly to get her to giggle. He continues to reassure them. "Ah'm proud o' you, girls. Yer doin' a great job 'round here. You keep up the good work for me?"

Both girls, smiling softly, nod in agreement again before wrapping their arms around his neck, squeezing, and heading into the cabin to get ready for bed.

Samuel lingers on the porch for a spell, staring at the dark sky. Feeling he's given his daughters enough time to change into their nightgowns, he gets up and goes into the cabin to tuck them in and kiss them goodnight. He walks toward his bed, looks at Phiby curled up there, and then decides to return to the porch for a while.

He sits in his chair, watching the rain fall and wondering if he is doing the right things. He looks skyward as if seeking an answer from God, but he doesn't say a word. A bolt of lightning, buried deep in the dark clouds, flashes, illuminating them for the briefest of moments. A low rumble moves across the sky a minute later. The floor behind him creaks in the ensuing silence. Samuel looks over his shoulder to see Phiby standing in the doorway. She looks at him with a cautious melancholy. He stands up and motions to her softly. "Mah queen, please, come sit with me?"

She moves silently to the chair next to him and sits. Samuel waits for her, and then he, too, sits. He gazes at her sad face, forgetting all about the rain while she, in turn, discovers it. She looks out into the dark, rainy night. He places his hand upon hers, but she does not acknowledge him. He sees the light from another distant lightning flash on her face; a low thunder follows again. "I don't understand why God punishes me so," she whispers. "Why does he hate me?"

Samuel doesn't have an answer, but he desperately wants to reassure her. "Oh, Phiby, God doesn't hate you." He gently pats and rubs her hand. "Ah can't rightly say why he let this happen, but Ah know God cannot hate. It's not 'n his nature." Samuel pauses. "Even if we have done somethin' wrong, yuh know Ah'll always be by your side, right? Yuh know Ah'll always love you."

Phiby doesn't respond. She sits quietly, watching the rain fall into little puddles. A few minutes pass. The distant storm has moved on, and the rain softens to a light sprinkle. "Ah guess I ought to go tuh bed," Phiby mumbles as if worn out. She slowly and quietly gets up and walks into the cabin. Samuel follows her, stopping to secure the door and shutter the windows. He slips off his boots and overalls and climbs in next to her. He snuggles close, and although she keeps her back to him, she allows him to spoon a little. The sound of light rain pattering the roof quickly sends them both off to sleep.

* * * * *

The early morning Sunday sun is just beginning to peek between the gaps in the window shutters. Samuel is lying on his back in a cold sweat. He is wide awake; the nightmares that plague him from time to time have reared their ugly head again. He woke several times throughout the night, breathing heavily and frantically looking about the cabin before realizing he was only dreaming. No bullets were whizzing by him, no cannon fire exploding, and no crack of the overseer's whip. He lies there staring at the rafters, dwelling upon the tormenting dreams of his daughters being stripped from his arms of suffering and loss. Samuel is tired; he feels empty, dazed, and confused. He wonders, returning to reality, *How could all this happen? What'm Ah supposed tuh do now?*

Bulldogged as ever, he forces himself to get up. He quietly scuffles across the wooden floor and builds a small fire in the fireplace. As silently as he can, he prepares coffee in his old metal coffee pot and sets it next to the fire. He dresses while it percolates, donning a clean white shirt, a clean pair of dark brown pants with suspenders, and his light tan waistcoat. Afterward, he pours his coffee into his little metal mug and sits at the table. First, he stares across the room at the fire, then down into his cup, and then surveys his household.

His mind slowly returns to both God and his former life. He specifically remembers the older slave who worked in the house when he was a boy. Whenever she could, she would sneak the owner's Bible out of the house in the evening and bring all the children together for a secret time of worship. She would teach them to read and write words in the dirt using sticks. A smile creeps across Samuel's face. Those memories bring him a sort of peaceful happiness. He relished those lessons. As he reminisces, he is reminded of the story of King David and Bathsheba's child who died. He thinks about how King David responded. He fasted and mourned before returning to the house of God. Samuel sees this as an example of what he must do. "Ah guess Ah oughta go tuh church too," he whispers before sipping his coffee. "Maybe, it'll get Phiby on the right path tuh healin'."

He hears blankets rustle; his girls are stirring. He sets his coffee down on the table, cupping its warmth in his palms, and watches his little ones from across the room. Dorinda rolls to her side, where she can see her papa. She slowly opens her eyes. She looks lovingly at him. Samuel smiles at her and, in a deep voice, whispers, "'Bout time yuh woke up, sleepyhead."

"Morin', Papa," she whispers back.

Jamilla unexpectedly pops up on the other side of the bed like a prairie dog. Sitting upright, she rubs the sleep from her eyes with little balled-up fists before squinting to see her papa. Her nightgown is disheveled, and her woolen hair is a mess. "Bright-eyed 'n bushy-tailed Ah see." Samuel chuckles to himself. "Welp,"—he slaps his legs—"Ah guess it's time to rise 'n shine, little mornin' glories. Gotta get tuh church t'day. C'mon now. Put on them pretty li'l blue 'n white dresses for me."

"We will, Papa," Dorinda says with a bit of excitement. She flings the blankets back, half covering Jamilla, who exclaims louder than she should.

"Hey!" Jamilla pushes the blankets off. Dorinda gets out of bed, opens their trunk, and starts laying their clothes on the messy bed. Jamilla stretches her arms out, yawns, and again rubs her eyes, saying, "Mornin', Papa." She, too, jumps out of bed, her little bare feet pattering around the bed to where her big sister is. Both girls always love dressing up and going into town.

Samuel gets up from the table and sits on the bed next to Phiby. She is already awake and has been listening passively.

"Mornin', mah queen." He gently strokes her long, loose curls. "Let's go to church this mornin'. Give our respect to the Lord."

"Ah guess." She sighs. "I jus' don't know why. I don' think he loves us no more."

Samuel leans down next to her. "Come on now, Phiby. Yuh know that's not true. He still loves us. Maybe if we go to church, he'll bless us an' heal us." Without a word, she twists to sit up next to him. He smiles at her, and she shoos him away. She gets up slowly and starts making the bed. His spirits are lifted by her willingness to get up and about. He retrieves his coffee from the table and, to give the women their privacy goes out on the front porch to finish it. Once he's emptied the cup, he goes around back to clean all his tools out of the wagon, making it presentable for his ladies. He hitches it up Micco and leads the horse and cart to the front of the cabin.

A little later, all the ladies emerge from the cabin dressed, groomed, and ready for town. They're all standing on the porch when Samuel comes around the corner. He stops Micco and the wagon and finds himself staring at them all. "Wow!" He exclaims. "Y'all are beautiful!" The girls, truly relishing their father's flattery, smile from ear to ear. They run up to the wagon, Dorinda pausing to hug her dad before jumping right up into the back of the wagon. Jamilla is right behind her. She comes with open arms. He knows she still struggles to climb in, so he scoops her up and whisks her into the back with her sister. He then turns to see his stunning bride waiting on the porch.

Samuel hasn't seen Phiby dress up for quite some time. Even after all their years together, he still looks upon her with the same breathless intoxication as he did when they met. Around the house, she usually wears a simple dress and apron with a kerchief, keeping her long curly hair behind her, and Samuel still finds her attractive in that. This morning, however, she stands on the porch in the bright sun wearing a beautiful cream-colored dress with a silky brown shawl over her shoulders. Her hair is tucked under a copper-tinted headwrap, making her smooth brown skin radiant in the sun. Indeed, he finds her most alluring.

He approaches as slowly and smoothly as possible, offering his arm to her out of gentlemanly courtesy. She takes it as she steps off the porch toward the wagon. Samuel fawns over her as they walk, using the moment to genuinely let her know how much he loves her and how gorgeous she is. "Ahh, there's mah queen." He smiles coyly at her. "You really are irresistible, yuh know that?"

She offers him a half smile that disappears as fast as it appears. He knows she's still not herself but is encouraged by her smile. He holds her hand as she climbs into the wagon and swiftly follows her. There is no denying the small joy he feels in this moment with his family heading toward the house of God.

The girls always enjoy riding in the back of their little brown wagon, giggling and pointing at things they see. That morning, Dorinda spies a Cooper's hawk staring back at them from its perch in an old oak tree near the house. She immediately points it out to Jamilla, who studies it carefully before they round the bend and are out of sight. The family enjoys a relatively silent ride with no real conversation. They go from the rutted sandy country roads to the well-laid and wide shell-ridden lanes in town. The fresh morning breezes sway the lush palms and moss-covered oaks along the way while slightly soothing their worries.

Not far from the river, sitting among the thinned-out tree line on the outer end of town is a long, simple wood clapboard church house. It sits upon short pillars, raising it above any water that might rush inland from a storm surge. Two casement windows adorn the front and back, with three more along each side. Mounted in the gable over the double-door entrance and large railed porch is an old bronze bell, pitted and faded brown with patina. A small steeple with a whitewashed wooden cross also adorns the roof above the doors. It's not a lavish building, but the congregation made it a good church.

Full of decent, God-fearing people, former slaves, soldiers, and pioneers alike, there is a true sense of community and brotherly love when they all come together. Samuel wonders if this gathering of the faithful is a small glimpse of life in heaven itself. Either way, he believes this is just what his family needs right now—to be in the house of God surrounded by people who will lift their spirits.

Upon arrival, Samuel sees his girls wave enthusiastically to friends out of the corner of his eye. He reigns Micco to a stop and then turns to see his daughters look back at him eagerly. With a smile, he nods his approval for them to jump down and play. Dorinda helps Jamilla down, and they quickly run off to spend time with the other children. Samuel jumps off the wagon. He leads the horse to a nearby hitching post and slips the reigns through the hoop. He then walks to Phiby's side and escorts her from the carriage. They arrive just in time as the preacher's son begins to pull the rope, sounding the church bell.

Although nothing is said, the absence of a baby in their presence is noted by many. Still, Samuel and Phiby are greeted warmly as they enter the church. They quietly sit close to the middle, as usual. Samuel likes to sit closest to the aisle at the end of the pew. As usual, Phiby takes her place at his side and the girls to her right.

Phiby keeps her head down after they sit. She is overcome with an unjustified paranoia, feeling as though everyone stares pitifully at her, and it makes her uncomfortable. She wonders to herself, *Ah know they saw me with child. They gotta be wonderin' where the baby is. What're they thinkin' 'bout me*? An unearned sense of shame and motherly failure dominates her thoughts. She feels outside of God's grace, even in his own house.

Service begins, and the preacher reads from 1 Corinthians 10:13, 2 Corinthians 1:3–7, and James 1:12. He gives a fine sermon on trials, faith, and resiliency before reading Isaiah 65:17–25, God's promise of a new creation. Samuel senses God is speaking to him intimately. Emotions well up within his chest, but he pushes them, along with the urge to weep, down into his chest. He retains a stoic look on his face, if only for his family and the rest of the congregation. Phiby, still questioning God's reasoning for their loss and his purpose behind it all, keeps her head down during the sermon. She uses her handkerchief to wipe tears from her cheek occasionally.

The preacher asks for prayer requests. Samuel is nervous. He twists and turns slightly in his seat, unsure of himself for the first time in a long time. He wants to ask for prayers but has never been one to ask for much from anyone, especially prayer. He generally keeps his conversations with God private for the most part. Though things have changed, he knows he could use as many prayers as possible. Not necessarily for himself, mind you; he needs them for Phiby, Dorinda, and Jamilla. He waits patiently for a time when he can stand and present his request. The preacher keeps looking in his direction while surveying the congregation as if to give Samuel a sign, an acknowledgment. "Are there any more prayers?" he asks.

Samuel raises his hand. The preacher smiles at him with a gentle, fatherly smile, encouraging his bravery. He extends his hand toward him in recognition. Samuel rises to his feet, again fidgeting with the brim of his hat in front of him. In a humble voice, he says, "I know some of y'all probably already heard this, but we lost our newborn babies a week ago. They was twin girls...Jemima and Sabina." He pauses for a moment and looks down at his own family. Phiby still has her head down, but Dorinda and Jamilla look up toward him with the purest look in their eyes. "I'd like tuh ask y'all tuh pray for them and fer us. Ah'm not sure what God's plan is, but if y'all would, please pray for his guidance in our time o' need. Thank yuh." He nods at the preacher with gratitude and then sits back down. He places his hand on Phiby's leg. She is shaking. He pats her leg and gently squeezes it, trying to comfort her. Leaning back to look at his girls, he offers them a half smile.

"Amen, brother," the preacher says. He asks all to pray for their and the other congregants' requests and then continues with the remainder of the service. Afterward, Samuel and his family are met by Doc Howard, his wife, and a handful of women at the bottom of the stairs leading up to the front door. He sends the girls off to play with the other children while he meets with them. He learns that the loss of a child is far more common in his community than he ever knew. He is slightly taken aback by his unawareness that other families, friends, and neighbors have endured the same pain. Neither he nor Phiby says much in response to their stories.

Phiby stares blank-faced out at the playing children. Quiet envy grows in her heart. She is envious that she does not have her own babies, but they all have theirs. Samuel, in contrast, receives a small amount of solace, knowing they are not alone in their suffering. They chat for a short period before Phiby calls Dorinda and Jamilla back. She tells Samuel she is ready to go home. He politely excuses himself to retrieve Micco and the wagon and then helps them all in. The girls enthusiastically wave farewell to their friends as the carriage rolls away.

The ride home is again a quiet one. Samuel contemplates the scripture while Phiby falls back into her silent depression.

As they pass by the field near the house where Jemima and Sabina are buried, only Dorinda and Jamilla notice the moonflower vines spreading. They look at each other with excitement and giggle with some anticipation of seeing whether or not Mr. Ray will actually return.

Chapter Three

Catchin' Moonbeams

Another week has grudgingly passed. Phiby is a little more active. She makes herself busy around the cabin, cleaning and cooking more often. When she's done, though, she usually sits at the table, gazing out the window or in her rocker near the hearth, staring at the fire. When she feels cooped up, she goes out to the garden or collects eggs from the chickens. She still doesn't interact with Dorinda and Jamilla as much as she used to. Friends from town, even a couple of the Seminole wives, visit them to check in on her and the girls, but Phiby always turns them away, telling them she's okay. Deep down, she still feels like no one could possibly relate to her struggles. Her silence and depression continue to bring worry to the whole family.

It's now the second Saturday since the babies passed. Neither Dorinda nor Jamilla has forgotten about Mr. Ray and his request. They have occasionally snuck down to the field to check on the moonflowers to see if they're growing. They have also managed to stash the two clear medicinal bottles left behind by Doc Howard out by the garden. That evening, Papa comes home, eats dinner, and rests for a spell before telling the girls, "Don't choo worry 'bout the dishes t'nite, girls. Ah'll wash 'em up. Besides, Ah'd like tuh spend some time with Momma. Go on out 'n play fer a while." He shoos them off with a wave of his hand and a smile. It's just what they wanted to hear. They bounce excitedly, running out the front door and toward the garden.

Phiby sits in her rocking chair, staring at the dancing flames in the fireplace. Samuel frequently glances at her while he cleans up the dishes. Once he's finished, he picks up a chair and sets it down to her right. He sits facing her, takes her hand, and does his best to love on her. Desperately hoping to bring her back to her old self, he whispers in her ear, reminding her of their courtship. “Mmmm...The scent of yer light brown skin. How yer copper eyes gleamed in the sunlight. Them dimples in yer soft, supple cheeks when yuh offered me that bright smile behind them full pouty lips.” He tilts his head and leans in to look up into her sad eyes. He offers a smile, but she does not return it. Samuel straightens back up. “From the day Ah met yuh, Ah loved yuh. Ah loved the way yuh carried yerself, strong, independent, ’n proudly free. Yet, yuh’re always humble ’n kind.” He strokes her hand. “Come back tuh me, Phiby.” He begs. “Come back tuh me, mah queen.”

* * * * *

It’s just before dusk, and it’s been two weeks since Mr. Ray planted the two flowers in the field. The girls grab their bottles stashed under the big tobacco leaves in the garden and run down to see if Mr. Ray would be there. Many emotions swirl around in their little hearts and minds. Who is Mr. Ray? Can they trust him? Will he keep his promise? How exactly are they going to feed the flowers? The girls stop in their tracks as they round the corner of the field. Mr. Ray is indeed there. He is kneeling on his right knee to the side of the small marker where their sisters are buried. A small, elegant, ornate brass lantern sits near the cross and glows a soft golden color in the evening twilight. He holds his hat against his chest with his right hand while his sizeable left hand is flat, palm down, on top of the grave. He doesn’t lift his head or turn around but greets them nonetheless. “Peace be upon you, young ladies.”

“Hello, Mr. Ray,” Dorinda says, still possessing a little mistrust in him.

“Hiya, Mista Wray.” Jamilla giggles with a more trusting innocence typical of her age.

“I must admit., I am both sad and happy to be here,” Mr. Ray says. “I lament your momma’s misery, but I am overjoyed you remembered to come and see me.” He stands gracefully, places his hat on his head, and turns to look at the young girls. Dorinda stands still with a simple smile while Jamilla twists back and forth, swinging the little bottle in front of her. “And you remembered the bottles. Excellent!” He claps his hands and presents a wide smile. “Come here and look.” He points excitedly to where he planted the two flowers. They have continued to spread and grow; their twining vines are starting to reach up onto the trunks of three oak trees.

“We saw they was growin’,” Dorinda states, “but they don’t have any flowers on ’em.”

“Well, that is why I asked you to bring those bottles. We are going to feed them,” Mr. Ray says.

“Wiff what?” Jamilla asks.

“With moonbeams, Miss Jamilla,” Mr. Ray answers with a wink. “We are going to fill those bottles with moonbeams, give them a kiss to add a little love, and then pour them out on the vines.”

“Aww, come on now, Mr. Ray. That’s impossible,” Dorinda scoffs. “I never heard such a thing.”

“Ooh! Magic?” Jamilla squeals before he can retort. “You gonna use magic?”

“No, not exactly,” Mr. Ray says. “We are going catch the beams with God’s blessing. Here, little one, bring me your bottle.” He waves for Jamilla to come closer as he kneels beside the grave. She hurries to him in the already-darkening sky. A single thin beam of light shines faintly on their baby sister’s grave. “See here, the half-moon's light is shining through the tops of those trees. Go ahead, hold your bottle out in the light. Open side up now so the bottle will fill up." The light shines into the glass container, illuminating it. "Father in heaven," Mr. Ray prays, "bless the light we collect. Help it nourish the flowers we have planted in honor of this loving family."

Jamilla's eyes grow big and round, beaming with excitement, as the bottle glows bright with white light. Dorinda's jaw hangs open in surprise as Mr. Ray finishes the prayer.

"Okay, put your hand over the top of the bottle and come over here." Mr. Ray directs Jamilla over to the vine. She stares at the bottle as she strolls over. "Now, give the bottle a little kiss. Show God and your baby sisters you love them."

Jamilla gives the glowing bottle a tiny peck on its side and then looks back at Mr. Ray.

"Lovely. Turn the bottle over and shake the light on this vine." He points to the one on the right. "You might need to give it a little shake or tap on the bottom, but do not drop it." He stands back and watches the beautiful wee girl turn the bottle over and, with both hands, give it a shake. A faint but sparkling white mist cascades from the bottle to the ground, covering the vine's dark green heart-shaped leaves. Then, as if the vine had absorbed it, the glowing mist slowly disappears.

Jamilla watches until the twinkling lights are gone, then looks up at Mr. Ray when nothing happens. He nods at her, directing her attention back to the vine, which suddenly and methodically grows a few feet up and around the tree. Her eyes light up, and taking much pride in her efforts, she dances with carefree joy.

"I told you," Mr. Ray says, laughing with her. He looks over at Dorinda, who appears to have changed her mind about feeding them and is eager to try it herself. He smiles. "You want to try it too, Miss Dorinda?"

"Oh yes, sir!" she says excitedly. She runs over to meet him near the grave. She kneeled and held her bottle out into the moonbeam like her sister. Mr. Ray repeats the prayer, and her bottle begins to glow, too.

"You know what to do, yes?" Mr. Ray asks.

"Yes, sir," Dorinda replies with humble confidence as she cautiously covers the opening with her hand.

"Let us feed the vine on the left side this time." He points to it. "Do not forget to give it a little kiss." He stands back, watches her move swiftly to the vine, and give a little *smek* to the side of her bottle. Jamilla dances over to see her big sister pour her bottle out. They again watch intently for a moment before the vine shoots up and around the other tree, just like the first. Both girls look at each other, smiling from ear to ear. They begin to giggle, then laugh, and then dance about with pure childish glee. Mr. Ray chuckles in their delight. "Okay. Now, how about you both collect some light, and we'll feed them one last time for the night."

The girls do just as they did before. Mr. Ray prays for the blessing. The girls kiss their bottles, fill the light with love and joy, and sprinkle the glittering moondust over both vines while dancing and spinning. Mr. Ray claps with rhythmic approval at their innocent merriment. "Lovely job, girls. Just lovely." The vines grow again along the ground and toward other trees.

Dorinda spins around while dancing, and the cross anchored in the ground catches her attention. Her merriment suddenly fades. She walks around to the foot of it. Mr. Ray watches silently as a slight melancholy overtakes her. She thinks about her mother, about doing her best to care for her and make her happier. She looks over her right shoulder at the visitor and says, "Mr. Ray, our momma's not feelin' well.

She's really sad." Jamilla stops dancing, too, and focuses on what her big sister says. Mr. Ray motions for her to come near as he moves toward Dorinda; Jamilla follows him.

"I know little one. I know." He squats down so he can look them both in the eyes. "I promise we are going to make her better. You will see it in time. What we are doing here, these flowers we are growing, they will help. I promise. We must let things run their course right now." He pauses for a second, puts his left hand on Dorinda's shoulder, and pokes at Jamilla's belly with his right index finger, just like her papa does. He smiles and says, "I tell you what. You girls keep coming back here the next few nights, only when the weather's nice, of course, and we will get these vines to grow tall and wide. Their flowers will be ready to bloom by the full moon. If we do that, I believe it will help make things right with your momma and papa. Agreed?"

Jamilla giggles. "Yeah."

Dorinda nods her approval.

"My darling, Dorinda, do you know what your name means?" Mr. Ray inquires a little more solemnly.

"Momma tol' me once. She said it meant *gift of God*."

"She is right. You are a gift. You are a gift to your momma and your papa. You are a gift to little Jamilla here, too." He lightly pokes her belly again to make her giggle. "You have already done so many good things for them. You are a precious gift indeed. Keep your head high, young one, and keep the same joy you had for God tonight in your heart."

"Yes, sir. Ah'll do mah best." She smiles at Mr. Ray.

"Whadda 'bout me, Mista Wray? What's mah name mean?" Jamilla asks.

"Oh, well, that is an easy one. Your name means *beautiful*. And that you are, wee girl. You are beautiful inside and out."

Jamilla, holding her jar behind her back, begins twisting side to side and smiling from ear to ear with the compliment.

Mr. Ray can't help but smile with joy at her innocence. "Now, girls, it is time for you to return home. Okay? Your papa is going to start worrying about you. So go on, scoot."

"Thanks, Mr. Ray!" Dorinda shouts as the girls start toward their little house. Her apprehension about the mysterious stranger has turned into a complete trust in Mr. Ray.

"Do not forget to say your nightly prayers. You hear?" Mr. Ray hollers out. "God loves it when you say goodnight to him."

"We will," Dorinda shouts as they turn the corner and head up the road.

* * * * *

Things go nearly the same way over the next several days. Phiby, physically recovered for the most part, shuffles around the house, straightening and cooking from time to time. Dorinda and Jamilla handle routine and daily chores in the house and the garden. During the afternoon, when it gets hotter, Dorinda sits with Jamilla on the front porch, instructing her how to read and write. *Momma is a better teacher than me*, she often thinks, but still, she does her best to teach her little sister.

Each morning, Samuel hitches up his wagon, which is already loaded with his tools, and goes to work. He earns his keep and loses himself in his work, where he subconsciously sorts through his troubles. He travels by the field each day but forbids himself to look upon his infant daughters' grave when he passes. Instead, he focuses on the day's projects, keeping the flood of emotions at bay. This self-denial means he never notices the dark green vines blanketing the ground and reaching up the trunks of several trees. For him, what was once a happy place is now a place of sorrow, and he is already fighting off a growing sense of helplessness, bewilderment, and despair. He returns home in the late afternoon each day, hungry and ready to eat. After dinner, he spends a little time with his girls, who often make him laugh and smile. He then chases them off for a time so he can make an effort to woo Phiby out of her deep depression.

That is when the girls run down to the field to meet Mr. Ray. They continue feeding the spreading moonflower vines with moonbeams they catch in their jars. Much to the delight of their benevolent visitor, they also dance and sing in the warm evening air.

Chapter Four

The Gift of Sight

It's been nearly a month now since Samuel buried Jemima and Sabina. At dusk, he sits in his rocking chair on the porch, watching the yellow-orange sunlight set one side of the sky ablaze while the indigo hues rise on the opposite side. The full moon looms low and heavy in the Saturday sky. Thinking their papa was out back, Dorinda and Jamilla come bouncing out of the cabin and off the porch with their bottles in hand. They don't notice their papa sitting in his chair. Samuel, feeling like something isn't right, like they are hiding something, stops them. "Now, where do you two think yer a'goin' in such a hurry?"

They both come to a sliding stop and turn to face their papa, swiftly hiding the bottles behind them. "We're just goin' fer a walk, Papa," Dorinda says shyly.

"Whatcha got in yer hands?" Samuel asks as he stands up. He knows his girls are not capable of lying. He leans his shoulder against the post and, placing his hands in the bib of his overalls, stares down at them with a curious yet already-knowing look.

Dorinda realizes they've been found out. She's a good girl, though, a truly honest girl, and she presents the medicine bottle. Jamilla, who watches her every move, also holds her bottle out in front of her. Dorinda, eyes moving from the direction of the field to the ground in front of her, tells her papa about meeting Mr. Ray, feeding the flowers, and everything else they have been doing the last couple of weeks. Her voice rose excitedly as she told him the moon was almost full, and this was supposed to be the last night before "the surprise" Mr. Ray had planned for them all.

At first, Samuel doesn't know how to respond to such a fantastic tale. However, his thoughts quickly turn to suspicion over the idea of a stranger hanging out in the field close to their cabin. Dred rises from his stomach to his chest. He hasn't felt fear like this since his escape. He stands upright, takes his hands out of his overalls, and spins his head to look down the road. He then snaps at the girls. "Git inside. Both o' yuh." His firm tone causes them to waver for a second. Samuel turns and sees they're still standing there slack-jawed, looking at him in bewilderment. "Go on, git!" He exclaims. He jumps off the porch and points toward the door. The girls rush back inside; Jamilla starts to cry. Samuel turns to look back down the road, walking sideways up on the porch and toward the front door.

The girls are confused and scared by his sudden change in demeanor; Jamilla is whimpering. They're not used to seeing their papa upset or behaving this way. Samuel quickly closes the shudders on the window and then secures the back door. He grabs his Spencer rifle from the mantle on the fireplace, cocks the lever, loads a round into the chamber, and cautiously goes to the front door to look around.

Standing by the foot of her bed, Dorinda meekly asks, "Papa?"

"Not now, Dorinda! You'uns git over there by yer momma an' stay there." He doesn't look at the girls. Instead, his gaze is fixed down the road. He hears their feet patter across the wooden floor and then them jumping on the bed with momma. The sky outside is darkening. The full moon's brightness helps light the sandy and grassy ground while the tree line sways gently, casting shadows. Samuel neither sees nor hears any movement. He only hears the rattling palms and tree leaves in the early evening breeze. He steps back inside, closes, and locks the front door.

Phiby, restless, uncomfortable, and annoyed, sighs before getting out of bed and going to sit in the rocking chair by the fireplace. Still carrying his rifle in his left hand, Samuel approaches the girls. He squats down in front of them. Jamilla, sniffling with tears in her eyes, leaves her bottle on the bed and jumps off it. She runs to her papa, flings her little arms around his neck, and squeezes him. Samuel wraps his right arm around her and returns her hug. She lets go after a minute and, backing up, says, "I sorry, Papa. We didn' know we was doin' anythin' wong." Samuel picks her up and sits her down by her sister, whose cheek he then caresses, reassuring her, too.

He squats back down in front of them. "Ah'm not angry with you, girls. Ah just don't trust strangers pokin' 'round our field. Momma an' Ah can't 'ford to lose you, too. Lis'en now. We're gonna stay inside t'nite. Ah'm gonna protect you an' Momma. Keep y'all safe."

"But, Papa," Dorinda begins, "Mr. Ray's a good man. He's kindly tuh us, and Ah don't think he's a bad man at all."

"Yeah, Papa. He's nice," Jamilla adds.

"That may be, hun, but Ah don't know no Mr. Ray. 'Til Ah find out who he is, y'all are gonna stay right here." He pauses for a moment and takes a deep breath. "Now, why don'choo two sit by the fire with Momma?"

Before they can get up, there is a knock at their cabin door. Papa whispers to the girls, "Hide. On th' other side o' the bed, girls." He motions with his hand for them to go. "Now." He stands, places his right hand close to the trigger, and slowly approaches the door. "Who's there?" he asks firmly.

"Mr. Ray," comes a muffled answer.

The girls pop up from behind the bed like prairie dogs. Samuel turns and motions for them to get back down. Gripping the rifle in his right hand and ready for anything, he opens the door slowly with his left and then backs up. He places his left hand on the rifle grip but lowers the barrel. Mr. Ray is standing in the doorway with his hat in his hands. The luminescent glow of the full white moon highlights his grand stature. The girls again jump to their feet in excitement. Their father glances back at them with both surprise and scorn.

"Hello, Samuel, my name is Præsidiel, but please, call me Mr. Ray." He pauses, allowing Samuel to get a good look at him. "May I come in?"

Samuel can see that he is alone and bears no arms. Although he doesn't quite understand why he feels compelled to approve, he reluctantly nods, inviting him to enter. Being tall as he is, Mr. Ray ducks under the doorway. He raises his hands as soon as he crosses the threshold, saying, "Peace be upon this house."

Dorinda and Jamilla cannot stay hidden. They run out excitedly from behind the bed, around their papa, and up to Mr. Ray. Dorinda hugs him around his waist while Jamilla hugs his leg. "We're so glad tuh see yuh, Mr. Ray," Dorinda says.

"Thank you, girls. I am delighted to see you, as well." With a grand smile, he pats Dorinda on the back and Jamilla on the head. They release him and stand staring up at him. Mr. Ray looks at Samuel and points to his rifle. "You will be needing that, Samuel. You have nothing to fear from me."

There is something in his voice as if Samuel has received a command he cannot disobey, yet, at the same time, it pleases his ears and comforts him. A little perplexed, he lowers the barrel of his gun.

Mr. Ray offers a smile of gratitude. "May I greet the mother of the house?" Samuel, still cautiously observing the stranger, silently nods his approval again.

Mr. Ray purposefully but slowly strides to Phiby's side and kneels, facing her. Utterly uninterested in everything transpiring, she continues staring at the fire. Her eyes are dilated and glazed over; there is a sort of incoherence in them. It's as though her heart and mind have retreated to the deepest part of her soul. Mr. Ray places his hand on the bare skin of her forearm, which rests upon the arm of the chair. "Blessed are you who mourn, for you shall be comforted. Peace be upon you, daughter of Eve."

His words call her back from her distant, withdrawn state. Her eyes focus. Phiby turns her gaze from the fire. A look of wonder for Mr. Ray resides in her eyes.

He smiles at her. "There you are, sister."

She looks around the room at her family as though she has just awakened from a deep sleep.

The girls run to her. "Momma!" they say in unison.

Samuel has no words.

Mr. Ray stands and returns to the still-open front door. Awestruck, Samuel watches him like a hawk. He turns to address Samuel. "Will you bring your family and visit me in the field? Again, I assure you. You have nothing to fear. I promise only healing."

"Ah don't know you, sir," Samuel says cautiously.

"But I know you, Samuel," Mr. Ray answers.

"How can that be?" he asks puzzled.

"Visit me in the field, and all will be revealed. Please bring your queen and your lovely daughters." He winks at the girls. "Dorinda, Jamilla, bring your medicine bottles with you. You will need those." Mr. Ray walks outside onto the porch, puts his hat on his head, and then walks purposefully toward the field.

The girls help their momma up. "C'mon, Papa. Let's go."

He looks at the three of them, disbelieving in what he has just witnessed. Dorinda reassures him, "It'll be all right, Papa. Please, just come with us."

Little Jamilla chimes in, "Yeah, Papa, we got somepin' tuh show yuh. Pwease?" She tilts her head, her wild woolen hair shifts to one side, and she gives him that smile that always melts his heart. Although he knows his daughters are a bit naïve, he sees their deep trust in Mr. Ray. Something within his own heart also tells him he can trust this stranger.

"Okay," he reluctantly agrees.

The girls walk Momma over to Papa. He offers his left arm, and Phiby slides her hand around it. The girls grab their bottles from the bed, run through the door, and bounce off the porch into the sandy front yard. A thin, deep crimson stripe highlights the blackened tree line in the west. The sun has set, and amber and purple hues give way to a dark indigo sky. The stars are beginning to appear in the eastern sky.

Samuel pauses by the table, which is near the door. He sets his rifle down, taking a doubtful second look at it and wondering if he should leave it here. Even though the moonlight illuminates the ground outside, he reaches for the flickering lantern on the table beside his rifle. He then leads Phiby through the door and helps her off the porch. The girls start for the road, but their papa calls to them, "Stay close, girls." They heed his call and dance in the moonlight in front of them with their shiny glass bottles.

The family meets Mr. Ray a couple of minutes later on the road near the field. The girls run up to him again, and he bends to greet them. "Dorinda, Jamilla, you have done well. Thank you." He points to the east, and they look to see the full moon rising just above the tops of the trees. A slight spring breeze stirs the palms and Spanish moss, making them dance in the white light. "You know what the full moon means?" he whispers to them.

"The flowers?" Dorinda asks excitedly.

"Yes. They are blooming right now. But," he cautions, "we must wait for your momma. Remember, all our work was to help her be better."

He stands, holds up his left hand, and greets their parents. "Now, before we go any further, I must ask you a question." An awkward silence replaces the breeze and rattling leaves. "Do you believe in God's love for you?"

"Now that there's an odd thing tuh ask, Mr. Ray," Samuel says.

"Still, do you believe God loves you?"

Phiby has heard the question. It has gone straight to her heart; tears stream uncontrollably from her eyes.

Samuel glances over at her, "Mr. Ray, yer upsettin' her," Samuel retorts anxiously and defensively.

"Samuel, do you believe God loves you?"

Samuel looks at his wife and his children and then lets out a sigh. In his heart, he cannot deny the answer. "Yes. Yes, sir, Ah do believe God loves us." He pauses and then continues, "I jus' don't understand why he took our babies. Why we have tuh suffer like this."

"Samuel. You know scripture, yes?"

"Ah like tuh think Ah do, Mr. Ray."

"Well then, do you remember what Jesus said when his disciples rebuked those who brought little children to him?"

"Yes, sir," Samuel answers humbly. "The Bible tells us Jesus said, 'Suffer little children, 'n forbid 'em not tuh come untuh me: fer such is the kingdom o' heaven.' He then dips his head down, acknowledging the truth of things.

"Very good. Come then," Mr. Ray says in a more cheerful tone. He motions with his hand to follow. "Bring your bride. The girls and I have something for you. Something to brighten your spirits." He smiles at the silent and tear-filled Phiby. The couple respectfully follows.

As they near the edge of the field, they all see a strange glow emanating from it. They round the sabal palm at the corner of the field and observe a blanket of velvety white flowers covering the ground behind their daughters' grave.

The vines' dark green and heart-shaped leaves have grown into the semicircle of trees, setting a backdrop for the reflected light of the circular flowers growing in the moonlit alcove. The entire family stops at the entrance to the field. They are amazed by the sheer beauty of it all. Then, as if on cue, tiny golden lights begin to twinkle in the tree line around the edges of the moonflowers.

"What're those?" Dorinda asks, pointing to the blinking lights in amazement.

"Those, child, are fireflies." Mr. Ray kneels between the girls. "They are small beetles whose bellies light up so they can find each other in the dark. Girls, I know darkness can sometimes be scary, but if you carry the light of our Lord in your hearts, you will always be able to find one another in the dark."

"Can Ah catch one?" Jamilla asks playfully.

"Yes. That is why I asked you to bring your bottles." Mr. Ray laughs. "Go ahead. Be gentle when you catch them, though. We have to set them all free before you go back home." Bottles in hand, the girls run about, skipping and jumping around the field, giggling and collecting the blinking fireflies in their bottles. Mr. Ray stands and laughs before turning toward Samuel and Phiby and more serious matters.

As he approaches them, he notices a childlike glimmer in Phiby's eye. He nods at her with a slight smile and motions toward the girls. "Please, daughter of Eve, dance with your children."

She lets go of Samuel's arm and runs past Mr. Ray into the middle of the field. Holding hands, she dances with Dorinda and Jamilla for a bit before unexpectedly flopping down upon a lush patch of grass in the middle of the field. Samuel starts for her after she flops down, but Mr. Ray holds up his hand, stopping him.

She sits quietly, inspecting the entire field. She sees the grave to her left. Her eye follows the curtain of delicate round flowers, glowing white in the moon's reflection, from the grave to her right, where her girls are catching fireflies. She places her hands behind her, leaning backward and propping herself up. She lifts her head to the large full moon, rising between the oak trees and the tall, skinny pines in the indigo sky. Phiby then turns, looks over her left shoulder at Samuel, and smiles. He sees the life in her again, and his heart leaps with joy. She sits back up and turns to watch her girls dance in the garden.

Mr. Ray now stands to Samuel's right, who is putting his hands into the sides of his overalls. Samuel's brow furls: he is having trouble understanding what is happening. "How?" is all he can get out.

Mr. Ray looks over at him. "Samuel, I asked your daughters this same question: do you know what your name means?"

He keeps his gaze on his wife, children, and the incredible scene unfolding before him. "No, sir, not really. No one ever told me such."

"It means *God has heard*. You were once called Sambo, were you not? That was your slave name, yes?" Samuel snaps his head quickly, looking with fear and astonishment into the blue eyes of Mr. Ray. "I told you, Samuel. I know you. You have forgotten who *you* are, son of Adam? You prayed often when you were a slave, knowing deep in your heart that God would one day be the source of your freedom. Just as he helped the Israelites escape their captivity, you believed he would help you escape too, and so you did."

Mr. Ray turns to look out upon the field. "Instead of fleeing to safety in the Islands of Bahama, however, you stayed here. You joined the Union Army and risked your life to free your brothers and sisters. You served and fought here in this very land. After your service ended, you came back here as a pioneer with other emancipated men, helping to build this community. You have always lived in peace with those native to this land. You have been a devoted husband and a doting father." Mr. Ray pauses for a moment. Letting a grand smile bring slight wrinkles to the corners of his eyes. "Raising two wonderful, innocent, and loving young ladies, I might add."

Mr. Ray turns to look back at Samuel. His eyes are wide and full of water. A single tear breaks free and runs down his weathered ebony face. "How...How do yuh know so much 'bout me, sir?"

"Because I have watched you your whole life."

Samuel is stunned. He cannot grasp how this is possible.

"Samuel, God gave you a strong will, a courageous heart, and a mind anchored in his truth. There is much evil in this world. You know this. You have witnessed its cruelty firsthand. You have been stalked by it and experienced its malevolence. You have been tested as a slave, as a soldier, and now, as a father. You have tasted the bitter fruit of the loss of a child. Through it all, you upheld your oaths to God, your family, and your country. And, though you have suffered much already, you *will* be tested again. When you are, you must accept it courageously and joyfully as you have before. You must be better than those who would persecute you."

Mr. Ray places his left hand on Samuel's shoulder. "Samuel, you once possessed a deep longing for freedom. Freedom from slavery, from tyranny. This is the same freedom the founders of your great country sought. Freedom to speak, worship God, our Father, and travel throughout this gifted land. You wanted to be free to pursue life, liberty, and happiness as they did. You cannot let suffering of any kind harden your heart. Instead, you must be free of the guilt, regret, and despair you carry. You must never forget these things. Our Lord Jesus was also beaten. He, too, stands against the tyranny and oppression of sin. Our Father has felt the sting of having to give his only son up to the cross. There is nothing you have experienced that God has not shared through Jesus, and your faith in him will deliver you and lift you."

Mr. Ray turns again toward the garden, lifting his right hand as if presenting the joyous scene to Samuel anew. Mr. Ray continues, "Besides, God has answered many of your prayers. Look at the gifts you have already been given. You are not alone in your struggles. See, your queen returns to you. You must rediscover the splendor of her heart. See the majesty of this simple garden? You must never overlook the magnificence of Our Father's creation. See, too, your children dance with delight. Savor the simplicity of their innocent joy. Dwell not on the wounds of your past or the present. Instead, live in the moment with them all." Mr. Ray motions. "Now go. Be with your family in this moment, my friend."

Samuel removes his hands from his overalls and walks swiftly to Phiby's side. He kneels and looks at her soft brown face, which shimmers in the bright moonlight. She meets his gaze, their eyes lock, and their love is rekindled. Phiby smiles again. Genuine peace and happiness shine forth from her copper eyes. Samuel cannot help himself. A smile breaks through his rugged features in response.

He looks about their former picnic spot turned cemetery. It had become a place of mourning and sadness for a time, but the love of his daughters and the kindness of the strange

Mr. Ray have transformed it into a place of unbridled splendor.

Jamilla comes running to them, bottle full of fireflies in hand. She holds them up proudly. “Look what Ah caught, Momma!” she exclaims, short of breath.

Samuel chuckles, and Phiby smiles at her.

“You like them moonflowers, Momma?” she asks with a big grin. Jamilla can see the happiness on her mother’s face and knows her pain is gone.

“Oh, mah darlin’, yes. Yes, Ah do,” Phiby says softly and lovingly.

Dorinda hears her momma’s pleasant voice and comes running. She falls to her knees on the grass in front of her. Phiby reaches out to them both and embraces them. “Mah beautiful babies. Now Ah have mornin’ glories an’ moonflowers. Yuh know Ah love yuh both. Ah’m so sorry for what Ah put y’all through.”

“S’okay, Momma. Me ’n Dorinda, we knew you wasn’t feelin’ good. That’s why we helped Mr. Ray grow them flowers. He said they’d make yuh feel better,” Jamilla says. Dorinda sniffles and wipes a tear away with her sleeve while still holding her bottle of flashing golden fireflies.

“Ah know, girls. Ah’m so grateful. Yuh’ll never know jus’ how proud momma is of you.” Phiby looks upon them with renewed love.

From behind them, near the entrance to the alcove, Mr. Ray speaks, “It is time for me to go. Before I do, though, I have one more gift for you.”

Samuel helps Phiby up, and the whole family stands and faces him. As he approaches them, his appearance begins to change. “I offer you the gift of sight.” A bright white light burns away the appearance of the road-weary traveler, revealing his true angelic form. The light subsides, and his brilliant white wings spread upward behind him. He is wearing deep blue Romanesque armor over a light gray tunic. His belt and sandals are gold in color. At his side is his gladius in a golden sheath. A golden-colored halo around his head replaces the hat he wore.

Samuel and Phiby instantly kneel. Dorinda sees this and also kneels. “Ah knew it!” Jamilla exclaims, still standing. She takes her right hand off the bottle top to point at Præsidiel, and two of her fireflies escape. “Ah knew you was an angel.” She jumps up and down, squealing with giddiness before realizing the rest of her fireflies are escaping.

Præsidiel smiles warmly at her and lifts his hands upward and outward as he nears them, instructing, “Rise. Please, stand. You need not kneel to me, only to our Lord Jesus.” Then, he smiles, placing his left hand on Samuel’s right shoulder and his right on Phiby’s shoulder. “Samuel, I have always known you because I am your guardian angel. I look forward to keeping you and your beautiful family safe in the coming days. That said, I know you are not without grief; you both have much healing to do. However, the Lord sends you this gift. He knows this will bring you peace in your moments of sorrow.”

A vision appears in their minds. Two baby girls, wrapped in pure white swaddling clothes, rest in the arms of Christ Jesus. He is seated with them on his lap. He looks upon them with great love while they coo in response. Their chubby, light brown cheeks reflect the light of his face. He gently kisses each child on the forehead. A booming yet soft voice reverberates through their hearts, minds, and entire beings. “Do not worry. You will see them again. Until then, no harm shall ever come to them. They will be safe and loved forever.”

The vision ends as swiftly as it came. Their hearts pound within their chests; both exhilaration and peace overcome them. Their eyes glaze over with tears. Neither Samuel nor Phiby will ever forget hearing the Lord's sweet, powerful voice. The sight of his radiant face, as he blessed Jemima and Sabina with a kiss, will neither be erased from their thoughts.

Their worldly sight returns, and Præsidiel is standing in front of them again. He smiles at them all. "Remember, trust in the Lord. Rejoice and be happy. Have courage. Be bold. Forgive those who cannot see beyond your skin into your blessed hearts. Build a better future for yourselves and your children, and never forget to love." He begins to beat his wings, slowly lifting himself upward into the night sky. "Farewell, my friends. We shall meet again." The angel waves a final time before rising slowly into the night sky. Then, as swift as a streaking star, he blazes out of sight and into the heavens.

Laughter, forgotten over the last few weeks, returns. Samuel once again sees the spark of life in Phiby's chestnut eyes. Mother and daughters celebrate their beautiful garden of lights. Dorinda and Jamilla showed their momma how to catch moonbeams in their bottles and how they fed their twining vines. They teach their papa the blessing Mr. Ray taught them. Parents and children alike laugh and dance in the moonlit garden. The family is reborn in majesty, happiness, and love that night.

Epilogue

God Will Hear

Summer has come and gone; it's now early fall, and although it's late morning, it is still a bit hot outside. Nevertheless, the South Florida weather is still beautiful. Phiby has fully recovered and is back to her happy, hardworking self. She and the girls have thoroughly cleaned the cabin and helped grow a fruitful garden nearly ready for harvesting.

It's Saturday, and Samuel has a rare day off. Most of his chores are already done, so he takes a break in the porch shade. Phiby steps out through the front door and calls back to their daughters, "You young'uns keep grindin' up all that allspice. When yer done with that, Ah want yuh to start churnin' that cream. Papa 'n Ah are goin' for a walk. Stay in the house 'til we get back."

"We are?" asks a surprised Samuel.

Phiby gives him a coy glance and smiles. "When we get back, Ah promise we'll all go for a carriage ride in tuh town. Maybe get some fresh bread tuh go with that butter yer churnin'."

"We will?" Samuel rebuffs quietly.

"Okay, Momma!" the girls shout excitedly.

Phiby struts over to Samuel and playfully takes his hand. She leads him off the porch and starts down the road to the field, continuing to hold his hand as they go. "You seem quite happy today," Samuel remarks.

"Oh, Ah am, mah love. Ah am." A sort of mischievous smile spreads across her beautiful face. Once they round the corner from the cabin and are on the open road, Phiby releases Samuel's hand, picks up her dress, and starts to run.

She glances playfully over her shoulder at him, laughing. He smiles grandly and begins to pursue her. He quickly catches up to her, grabbing her by the waist. They both laugh as young lovers would. They stop for a kiss right before they enter the alcove. The expansive growth of the moonflower vines, which now cover the back of the field like a rich, dark green blanket, never fails to mesmerize. Samuel looks around while Phiby keeps her gaze on him. A light breeze moves through the treetops, and the late morning sun makes the shadows dance on the field.

"You 'member that day, Samuel? When we was young? When we took our lunch in this field?"

"Yes, ma'am, Ah do." He pauses. "Seems even more beautiful now."

Phiby moves in front of Samuel and rests her arms on his shoulders, clasping her hands around the back of his neck. There is a twinkle in her eye that Samuel hasn't seen for some time. "More beautiful than me?" she asks seductively.

"No, mah queen. Nuthin's more beautiful than you."

She raises to kiss him on the lips. Samuel places his hands on her hips and returns her kiss. A loving fire is ignited. Their kisses become deeper, more passionate. Phiby pulls away slightly. Keeping her hands on his shoulders, she walks backward, slowly leading him toward the moonflower vines. Eventually, seeing them at her feet, she stops. She begins to sway her hips, dancing and coxing Samuel to swing around to where she is. Once his back is toward the vines, she slides her hands from around his neck down to his chest and unbuckles his overalls. She lets them go, and they fall to the ground. She then playfully pushes him down on the thick blanket of moonflower vines. There, resting on his elbows, he watches his seductive wife.

Phiby undoes the buttons on the front of her dress. She slowly removes her arms from the dress and then lets it fall to the ground. With her eyes fixed on Samuel, she steps over her clothing, displaying both the naked, natural, and utterly vulnerable beauty to her beloved. He is captivated by her soft curves and delicate brown skin. With slow, seductive movements, she approaches him, lowering herself over him. Samuel's passion swells. With the lightest touch, she invites him to enter. She envelopes him, and he embraces her. In the late afternoon summer sun, on a bed of moonflower vines, husband and wife consummate their love with a burning passion unfelt for some time. The two once again become one in body, mind, and soul. They give themselves to each other, without reservation, until they are both entirely spent.

Exhausted and out of breath, they fall back into the lush vines. Lying side by side for a time, they feel a deep connection that goes beyond the physical body. A unifying love for one another that comes from deep within their souls. The love, the passion, the unending possibilities of a life bound together as soul mates surge within their beating hearts.

Phiby rests her head on Samuel's right shoulder. He gazes skyward, watching small white clouds move across the bright blue sky while running his fingertips up and down Phiby's naked side. He delights in the softness of her bare skin. That moment reminds him of the day they were united in marriage and when they made love for the first time. He never felt more complete that day. So many past fears and trials were behind him, and with her at his side, a bright future lay before them. He knew he could not be without her from the day he met her. Now, once again, she lies on her left side with her arm draped across his broad chest.

Phiby reaches up to touch his face before sliding her right leg over his. She lets out a sigh and a moan. "Mmmm...Samuel, Ah love you."

"An' Ah love you, mah queen."

"Thank you, mah love," she whispers in his ear. "Thank you for never givin' up on me."

Samuel turns his head to look into her chestnut eyes. "Ah never will, Phiby. Ah never will."

She tilts her head up. His lips met her full, soft lips in a slow, lasting kiss.

* * * * *

A few weeks later, Samuel is reclining at the dinner table, staring at his beautiful bride and darling daughters as they prepare Sunday dinner. He sometimes sits and watches them; he is reminded of all he has come through and is thankful for all he has been blessed with. He focuses on Phiby. Something is different. She has let her loosely curled hair down with only a kerchief, keeping it out of her face. She is leaning over, happily and patiently instructing Dorinda and Jamilla how to make one of Papa's favorite meals. When she stands upright and turns, he suddenly realizes what is different about her. He sits up promptly in his surprise, lovingly calling to her. "Come 'ere, Phiby."

She glides across the cabin with that playful grin on her glowing face and, in a fluid, graceful motion, wraps her right arm around his shoulders and sits on his lap. "Yes, mah love?" she says with a twinkle in her eyes.

Samuel gently but firmly places his open palm on her belly. It feels bigger and rounder. He smiles and looks up at her. The radiant glow from her soft brown face seems to brighten. "Is this...?" He begins.

Phiby nods yes. "Yes, it is." She smiles. "God has blessed us again."

Dorinda knows that look; she's heard those words before. She leans down and whispers something to Jamilla. Then a sudden squeal erupts from Jamilla, "Eeeeeeee!" Both girls run toward their momma and papa, throwing their arms around their parents. Jamilla, possessing no subtlety, blurts out, "You gonna have another baby, Momma?"

"Yes, mah li'l mornin' glories. Yer gonna be big sisters again."

A sudden and unexpected sting of apprehension clouds Samuel's mind. A voice, whispering and malevolent, tries to implant fear in his mind. "Do you think this child will survive? Can you be sure it will not suffer?" Samuel quickly rebukes the voice. *Ah, have no fear,* he thought to himself. He knows he can trust God in all things; he has faith in his divine providence. The voice and doubt leave him. A sense of peace falls upon his heart, and another firm, familiar voice speaks softly, "Do not worry, Samuel. Do not fear. Everything is going to be just fine." He looks at his bride's glowing face and his daughters' beaming smiles, and he believes it to be true—that everything will be okay.

* * * * *

Winter has passed. A small gathering of friends and neighbors is in the spring air outside a simple log cabin. A crowd of different people has come together: carpenters, nurses, merchants, farmers, ranchers, and even a few remaining Seminoles. They have come together for a family they love and respect. All their children play in the grass on the side of the cabin with the girls who live there. There is much excitement, anticipation, and cheer in the air. The people happily converse with one another while awaiting a big announcement.

A newborn's cry pierces the cabin walls, spurring the crowd to a hush. Minutes later, a strong, weathered man in his early thirties moves toward the front door. This man was once a fearless slave who became a courageous soldier and then a bold pioneer. Now, he lives life as a well-known and trusted carpenter, a loving husband, a doting father, and a friend to the community. The man crosses the threshold out onto the porch. He walks with a slow, confident demeanor, that of a free Christian man secure in his faith. Although he usually walks with his head and back upright, today, he walks with his head down. He whispers to a small swaddled bundle warmly cradled in his arms, "Oh, mah precious son. How long Ah have waited for yuh. Because Ah know God will hear you as he heard me. Ah give yuh the name Ishmael."

Samuel raises his eyes to see his friends who have gathered to welcome Ishmael into the world.

The Journey's End

Contents

Chapter One

Alexander the Great

Alex lies in bed with his eyes closed. *It has to be a dream.* He thinks to himself over and over. Then, finally, the sickly youth opens his eyes, and seeing the familiar sights of his hospital room; he sighs loudly with disappointment.

"You okay, son?" asks his father. Alex turns his head to the left to see his mom and dad sitting next to him. Both are happy he is awake.

"I guess, dad." He says, turning his head back to the right to stare out the window. "I was just hopin' it was all a dream that I'd wake up in my own bed." There is a long pause. "Just kinda tired of bein' in this hospital."

"I know, Alex, I know. But, believe me, son, your mother and I would love to get you back home." He pats Alex's arm.

The boy skylarks out the window. "Sure looks nice out there. Wish I could go outside; play pirates, fight dragons, you know, go on an adventure or something?" He feels his mother's gentle touch on his left hand, the one with the I.V. in it.

His father stands and leans over him to brush his hair back. "Me too, son, me too. You have the best imagination of any kid I know. Your mother and I always love watchin' you play."

Alexander McBain is nine years old. He has a head full of wavy brown hair, dark green eyes, and a few freckles running across his nose. A typical boy from a small, midwestern American town, he was bold, adventurous, and highly imaginative. He has spent many summer afternoons playing with the other boys in the neighborhood. He and his friends enjoyed playing hotbox in the vacant lot down the street and riding their bikes to the public pool on the outskirts of town. When they weren't doing that, they would go on 'expeditions' in the creek behind their house and shoot their bows and bb guns in the field beyond. Alex also enjoyed catching tadpoles and crawdads in the brook or playing with his action figures and toy cars on the banks. Unfortunately, he hasn't been to the creek for some time now. Instead, he's been bedridden in the hospital, suffering from a disease that weakens him.

His dad sees the despondent stare in his son's sunken eyes, so he decides to break the uncomfortable silence with a story. "Son, you know why I gave you the name Alex?"

Alex turns to look at his dad; his curiosity is peaked. "No, dad. Why?"

"As a boy, I was fascinated by Alexander the Great's conquests. Do you know who he is?"

"No."

"Well, he was a great warrior from Greece. He fought many battles in many countries. From Persia down to Egypt."

"Where the mummies are?" Alex interrupts excitedly.

"Yes. He even won lands from Mesopotamia all the way over to India. He conquered the known world as a young man only in his 20s."

"Wow!"

"That made me want to go into the world and make my mark. Until I met your mother, that is." He turns to smile at her. "A Mediterranean beauty herself." He turns back to his son and winks.

"C'mon, Dad. No mushy stuff."

"Anyway, she gave me you. Ever since then, **you** have been my greatest adventure. I have always been amazed by you."

"Is'at why you call me Alex the Great sometimes?" he asks with a smile.

“No, I call you Alex the Great ‘cause you are the greatest gift I’ve ever been given. You have always brought me great joy.” He places his hand on his son’s shoulder and looks deep into his eyes. “I have and always will be proud of you, son. And I’m sure you’ll conquer this illness too.”

“I’ll do my best, Dad.”

“I know you will, my boy.” Alex’s parents know that what he suffers from is terminal. But, whether out of hope for a miracle or a desire to keep his spirits up, they have agreed not to discuss it with him yet. His dad works daily and can only be by his side evenings and weekends. His mother is with him most days. Alex is delighted when they are both with him, like today.

Aidan and Abila’s marriage is somewhat unique. Neither of their families saw it coming; an American Protestant man marrying a Lebanese Catholic woman. It certainly stirred some heated discussions among family members. Even now, Alex has noticed his grandmother, Sitti, as she is affectionately known, scowling at his dad occasionally. His youthful naivety prevented him from understanding why, but he always shrugged it off because he loved his parents as equally and unconditionally as they loved him.

Aidan will often leave the room when Alex sleeps. He usually finds a secluded place outside the hospital to discuss his son’s condition with God. On the other hand, Abila stays by his side and prays her rosary unceasingly. Alex has woken to her beautiful prayers before, which always lifts his spirits.

This Sunday is no exception, either. It has been a fantastic day for Alex. He enjoyed the company of his parents, grandparents, and friends who stopped by. He watched cartoons on the TV while his mom fed him lunch. “Hospital food can be so gross.” He sometimes protests. Yet he always eats as much of it as possible, especially when Sitti has smuggled in a sweet treat. Of course, nothing to upset his vitals, just something to let him know she cares.

It's growing late, though, and they have all departed for the night. Alex is tired after such a busy day. He nods off while his favorite nurse, Mrs. Bonnie, takes his vitals and completes her paperwork. He knows she won't be back for quite a while after this, so he has grown accustomed to falling asleep then. What he doesn't know is that this night is different.

Hospital nights are never truly quiet. Monitors are beeping; nurses are coming and going, and cries and conversations from neighboring patients have woken him before. Tonight, however, an unknown sound startles young Alex awake. His room is dark and still, more silent than he is used to. He looks around and is shocked to discover a stranger sitting beside him. The man has a peculiar glow about him, like he makes his own light, which causes Alex to study him briefly. The man appears tall, seated with his elbow on his knees and leaning toward Alex's bed. He is clean-shaven and about the same age as his dad. The visitor is wearing a clean, dark-blue suit with a gray waistcoat and gold-colored tie. His shirt is probably the brightest white Alex has ever seen. His facial features are unique; Alex can't tell what race he is. His hair is dark brown, wavy, and a little long, just about to touch his shoulders. Regardless, the stranger waits until he knows the boy has finished inspecting him before saying, "Peace be with you, young Alexander."

Alex has deduced where this man has come from somewhere in the deep recesses of his young mind. "Are...are you an angel?" He asks nervously.

"Yes. How very perceptive of you," He says as he stands. "My name is Præsidiel. I am here to...."

"Wait," Alex interrupts, "does this mean I'm dead?" he asks in a panic as he pats his body and visually examines himself.

Præsidiel chuckles. "No, young Alexander, you are not dead yet."

"Phew." He pushes himself up in bed. "I'm sorry, Mr. Præsidiel, I didn't mean to interrupt. Yuh just caught me off guard there."

The angel smiles. "It is forgiven. However, I am here with a message. First, may I ask, are you aware your illness is terminal?" He questions with a somber tone.

"I, uh. What's 'terminal' mean?"

"It means your illness will claim your life; sadly, you will die."

Alex slumps his shoulders. "Well, no one has **actually** told me that before. But I could tell it wasn't good by the looks on everyone's faces and some o' the talk I've overheard."

"Are you prepared for what is to come, Alexander?"

"Can I tell you the truth?" Alex thinks about his question for a split second and mumbles, "What am I thinkin'? You're an angel; you'd know if I was lying anyways." He looks to the angel, "No sir, I'm not ready for what I think happens next. Oh, uh, don't get me wrong; I'd be excited to meet Jesus an' all. It's just...well, I'm a bit scared." He begins to wring his hands. "See, I don't want to make my parents sad or anything, neither."

"Alexander, our Lord has heard your mother's prayers, your father's ... opinions, and even your desire for a backyard adventure too." The angel pauses. "You know the story *A Christmas Carol*, yes?"

"Oh, yes, sir." Alex's eyes light up. "Mom 'n dad watch the cartoon movie with me every year. I like it when Scrooge turns nice. I sometimes feel like Tiny Tim without the crutch. Unfortunately, I'm stuck in this hospital too."

"Good. You will appreciate this then. Our Lord has sent me to take you on a different quest for the next few nights so you might live life to the fullest before joining him for the greatest of all adventures. This will also afford you more time with your family before you depart."

"So, I still have tuh die, then?" Alex asks sadly.

"Yes, child. Everyone must." Alex turns his eyes downward. "However, Our Lord awaits you; nothing is greater than being with him in paradise."

Alex exhales a deep breath. "Okay, Mr. Præsidiel, I trust you ... and God." He looks back up at the angel. "So, z'is mean you'll be back tomorrow night, then?"

"Yes."

"Can I tell my mom 'n dad you came to see me?"

"Yes."

"Gotta tell yuh, sir, I don't know how you're gonna do it, but I'm kinda excited about gettin' out o' this bed and goin' on an adventure. So where're we goin' first?"

"All in good time, young Alexander. All in good time. For now, you must rest."

"Okay. I am kinda tired anyway." Alex says, sliding back down into the hospital bed. "Do I need to say my prayers again?"

"No." says the angel. He pulls the boy's blanket up, covering and tucking him in. "Our Lord has heard your prayer and intends to take and keep your soul." He grins at Alex. "He has sent me to guide your ways until then." Alex returns his smile before falling fast asleep. It will be the deepest sleep he's had in quite some time.

* * * * *

Alex wakes the following day to the sound of his parents whispering. "Morning, Momma. Morning, Dad." He says, carefully rubbing his eyes and avoiding tangling the I.V. tube.

"Good morning, my darling," his mother sings.

"Morning, son. How'd you sleep last night?" Asks his dad.

"Great!" exclaims Alex bolting up in his bed. He extends his scrawny arms, stretching in the morning light beaming through the window.

"Wow." His dad chuckles. "You sure are bright-eyed and bushy-tailed this morning."

After a prolonged yawn, Alex begins to chatter, "Mom, Dad, you won't believe it, but an angel came to see me last night. Said his name was Pra...Pray...sidiel? Cool, huh? Can't believe I got to meet a real angel."

"An angel, huh?" Aidan asks with skepticism. Alex's mother slaps her husband's arm, scolding him with a look.

Alex is unphased. "He said he was gonna take me on a different adventure each night this week before...." Alex's voice trails off when he suddenly realizes he is about to confess his fatal prognosis. Sadness overwhelms him. Alex's mother reads his sudden emotional change; tears well up in her eyes. She knows her son all too well and can see he understands his fate.

Aidan, contrarily, grows angry. He thinks someone has informed his son without consulting him. "Son, who told you this? Was it a doctor, a nurse?"

"No, Dad, it was the angel. We talked about things, and he said it was almost time to go see Jesus."

"I'll find out who was in here last night." He growls before abruptly departing the room.

Alex feels like he has done something wrong. "You believe me don't you, Momma?"

"If you believe it's true, Alex, then yes, I believe you." She tries to be more encouraging and comforting. She leans over his bed and hugs him. "Please forgive your dad and me. We're scared and don't want anything more to happen to you." A tear escapes down her cheek. She stands back up and discreetly wipes it away.

"It's true, Momma. It really was an angel."

Aidan returns a short while later. His quest to find the one who revealed the horrible truth to his son was unsuccessful. However, his conscience drives him back to visit his only son before he must head off to work. Abila stays by her son's side most of the day. She comes and goes as necessary but is always there to help Alex eat and speak with the doctor when he checks in.

The day eventually closes out in the usual silence. Nurse Bonnie left the curtains half open so Alex could fall asleep on his side while staring out at the night sky.

Chapter Two

Alex the Firefighter

Alex feels someone grasping his left shoulder and gently shaking him. "Come on. Wake up, Alexander! There is no time to waste." The boy rolls over to see a fully dressed fireman staring at him. "Get up. Get dressed. Can you not hear the alarm bells?"

Dazed and confused, Alex looks around. He is not in the hospital anymore. Instead, he's in an upper room with a brass pole in the corner and bunks on either side. "What time is it?" He rubs his eyes. *That's strange*, he thinks. He has grown used to I.V. tubes getting stuck in a blanket and pulling at his arm, but he doesn't feel that. He looks down and sees he's in his pajamas, not the hospital gown. There are no tubes or wires connected to him, either.

"Hurry up and get your gear on!" Yells the man who woke Alex up. "We will be in fire truck number one." He jumps to the pole and quickly slides out of sight.

"Is this the adventure Præsidiel promised?" He wonders out loud.

A few moments later, Alex comes sliding down the pole. Running in boots two sizes too big, he clomps toward the firetruck. A firefighter's coat drags the ground behind him while he keeps shoving the oversized helmet up on his head so he can see where he's going. Then, finally arriving at the truck, he recognizes the person holding the door open for him. "Mr. Præsidiel!" He exclaims.

The angel chuckles at the boy's appearance.

"What? This's the smallest I could find back there."

"I guess it will do, young Alexander. It will do." The angel approves. Alex shuffles up into the truck. "By the way, you may call me Mr. Ray for short."

"You got it, Mr. Ray." Replies Alex as he slides over in the seat.

Mr. Ray climbs in and settles on the seat. He leans to Alex and asks, "I heard this fire is hellish; are you ready for it?" The truck lurches forward. The sirens begin to wail while red and blue lights illuminate the night.

"Yessir. Jus' hand me a hose when we git there and point me in the right direction." He answers boldly. "I'll put that fire out, fur sure."

Mr. Ray looks heavenward and grins widely.

* * * * *

The driver turns off the sirens just before they arrive. He slows the truck to a crawl before stopping on the side of the house. Alex gets his first, up close, and personal look at a real-life inferno. Fire belches from a broken window, curling up and around the roof line in a steady stream. Vinyl siding melts away while wood buckles. Flames dance on the roof as they turn the house to smoke. He can see through the wall studs in one area. He mumbles, "Boy, looks hot as a pizza oven in there."

"Again, are you sure you are ready for this?" Mr. Ray asks one more time.

The fight-or-flight urge battles deep within Alex's rapidly beating heart. Though fear grips him, he thinks, *I gotta be brave. God gave me this adventure, so I gotta show Him I can do this*. He swallows hard. "Yessir,"–his voice cracks slightly–"I'm ready." He flings open the door, jumps out, and asks, "Where's the hose?"

Mr. Ray leads him to the side of the house, untouched by the fire. There he unreels a garden hose and hands the business end to Alex. "Here you go. You are the lead nozzleman."

Alex eagerly takes it without hesitation, rounds the corner, and points it at the burning building. He twists the nozzle back and forth, but no water comes out. He looks behind him at Mr. Ray, who shrugs his shoulders. "Little help," Alex yells. One of the other firefighters turns the spigot on while a playful sigh slips past Mr. Ray's lips.

Mr. Ray nudges Alex to move into the burning building. A thick, black smoke greets them when they enter the front door. Flames climb the walls and lick at the door jam. The boy can barely see the hallway past the living room through the smoldering fog. They move forward. Alex is indiscriminately spraying everything around the living room. Mr. Ray pats him on the shoulder and shouts, "Make a path to the hallway. We must check the rooms for survivors."

"Okay." He begins soaking the area directly in front of them and cautiously following his stream of water.

Upon reaching the hallway, something at the end of the hall catches his eye. There is a giant face within the flames. It is a red, snarling, devilish face. Spiraling horns of fire protrude from it. Its mouth opens, and it appears to be screaming something, but whatever it's yelling goes unheard. Alex tries to focus on spraying the walls, floor, and ceiling in front of them while cautiously approaching the terrifying face.

The boy stops within a few feet of the thing on the wall. The heat in the confined space is intensifying. He stands upright and cocks his head to the side. Though he listens intently, he still can't understand what the face is saying. "Psshh!" He says in a dismissive tone, "I don't have time fer you." He turns the hose nozzle straight into the mouth of the flaming face. It sputters and gurgles, dissipating into a cloud of white steam. The bulk of the fire sizzles away with it. "Cough…cough." Alex waves his hand in the air trying to dispel the sulfuric fumes. "Man, it smells like rotten eggs." He yells while turning to look at Mr. Ray. He laughs before saying, "Just like them clowns at the fair. You know, yuh squirt 'em to make the balloon fill up an' pop?"

Mr. Ray shakes his head and smiles. Then, turning more serious, he points to the closed door next to them. "Go on, kick in the door," he shouts. "We must clear the house."

"I don't think I'm big 'nough for that."

"Yes, you are. God has given you the strength you need. Quickly, kick down the door! Get in there and clear the room."

"Oookay." Alex kicks as hard as he can at the door with his oversized boot heel. To his surprise, it cracks around its edges and falls to the ground. Smoke billows out of the dark room, filling the ceiling overhead. Alex looks down at his feet. *Wow, can't believe that actually worked*, he thinks.

"Alexander." Prompts Mr. Ray.

"Oh, yeah." He turns and hands his nozzle to his partner. Taking out his flashlight, he shines it around the smoke-filled room. He spots a man lying on the floor. The man is weak but conscious. Without a second thought, Alex rushes to his side. He lifts the man's arm over his shoulders and pulls him out. The man regains enough consciousness to stagger alongside Alex.

Together they make it back through the smoldering hallway and out the front door. Alex helps the man sit on the edge of the porch and then rushes back into the house. He yanks on the hose and yells, "He's out. Let's go."

"Roger, backing out." Responds Mr. Ray. Alex helps walk the hose back, leading his nozzleman out of the burning house. Once outside, Mr. Ray shuts off his nozzle while Alex helps the man stand. Another group of firemen rushes in with hoses to contain the flames erupting from the charred home. Paramedics receive the man from Alex, escorting him to an ambulance.

Mr. Ray pats Alex on the back, "You did very well, young man."

Alex removes his oversized hat and wipes the sweat and soot from his forehead. "Thank you, Mr. Ray." Out of breath but very excited, he exclaims, "You see me kick that door down? That was awesome!" Alex and his angel rest long enough for the boy to catch his breath.

"We have a few moments, Alexander; maybe you better check in on the man you rescued." He nods in the direction of the ambulance.

"Oh. Yessir. I'll go check in on him."

Alex walks over, his coat tail dragging behind him. Then, bashfully, he approaches the man sitting in the back of the ambulance. "Uh, hi. My name's Alex. What's yours, mister?"

"Alasdair." He coughs. "Al...cough, cough...for short." The man takes a good long look at the boy. "Aren't you...cough...a bit young to be a firefighter?"

"Yessir, I probably am. I've pretended to be one many times before, though, so it's okay. I knew what I was doin'."

"Well...cough, cough...you did a great job, son. Thank you for savin' me."

"No problem, Mr. Al." The paramedics return to treating the man. "Well, sir, I better get back with my teammate. The paramedics'll take good care of you." Mr. Al nods his gratitude. "God bless you, sir." A tear appears in the corner of the man's eye. Alex nods back and then heads toward the fire truck.

"Woo, it was hot in there, huh?" Mr. Ray asks. "A real baptism by fire."

Alex sits down and places his helmet on the ground in front of him. "Yessir, it was." They watch the rest of the firefighters tamp down the blaze until the half-standing house is a smoldering, black mess. The young firefighter has a bit of a confused and worried look. "So, what was that...thing? In the fire?" He asks, his voice trailing off at the end.

"That was the face of the evil one, Alexander, the adversary."

"Oh." Alex grows silent for a moment. "Then how...?"

"Good thing I was holding on to the hose, huh? The devil cannot stand holy water." Mr. Ray says with a wide grin.

"Wait, what?" Alex looks up at Præsidiel, who winks and smiles at him.

"Never forget, young man. I am your guardian angel."

"Oh. Oh yeah." He smiles to himself. "You holding onto the hose turned it into holy water. Huh."

"We saved more than a man's life tonight, my young friend. We may have just saved his soul as well." Alex scratches his head in confusion. Mr. Ray slaps the tops of his legs and says, "Well, we cast out the most unclean and saved a soul. All in a good night's work, yes?" He lets out a deep sigh. "Unfortunately, it is time to get you back."

"Back? To the hospital?" Alex turns his head downward. "Aww, man. Do I have to go back?"

"Yes, I am afraid you do...for now." Mr. Ray motions to the red pickup truck. "We will take the truck back while the rest finish up here. Come on, get in."

Alex reluctantly climbs in. He takes off his coat and wads it up. *I am feeling kinda tired after all that,* he thinks. He places the coat between his head and the door and then leans against it. It's surprisingly comfortable. Mr. Ray drives them toward the hospital while the boy quickly falls asleep.

Chapter Three

Sir Alex, the Brave

The next day he wakes in his hospital bed. He is sad at first. All the tubes and wires have been reconnected to his body; he hears the familiar beeping of the heart monitor. Sitting in his bed alone, he thinks about how he will explain everything that happened. *How in the world did I get out of these tubes and wires? Who put 'em all back in? I sure hope Mrs. Bonnie won't be mad at me for that.*

His mood brightens, though, as soon as his parents arrive. He tells them about the burning house, the scary face, squirting water in its mouth, and saving Mr. Al. He is so excited about telling the story that his heart monitor beeps faster. Concerned, one of the nurses charges into the room mid-story to check on him. Then, realizing he is okay, she stays to hear how his tale ends.

"Wow, that was some dream." She states.

"No, ma'am. That wasn't a dream. That was real. I was sweating and everything." Alex looks down at his dry robe. "Huh. Must've changed when we got back." He mutters.

"Mmm, hmm." The nurse doubts. "I'll be back in a while with your meds, Alex."

"Mom. Dad. You believe me, don'tcha?"

"I don't know, son." Hesitates his dad. "How'd you get the I.V. out or fool the monitors? Not to mention getting out of the hospital." He smiles at Alex. "You've always been a very imaginative boy, so I think you had a fantastic,"–he nods, trying to reassure him–"and very realistic feeling dream. And that's great. I'm glad you did, right, mommy?" She smiles.

Deflated, Alex's expression turns downward.

"I'm sorry, son."–his dad says, looking at his watch–"I wish I could stay longer, but I need to get to work." He steps to his son's side and caresses the side of his head. "I do love you. Be brave, like the time you pretended to be a knight exploring that old dungeon. You remember? The basement?" He winks at Alex. "I'll see you as soon as I get off work." He kisses Alex on the forehead and then leaves quietly.

Alex looks at his mother, sitting calmly with her hand on his shin. "Mom?"

"Yes, honey."

"Do you think it was real or a dream?"

"Oh, my darling. I want so much for it to be real. I'm just not sure." She rubs his shin before stepping closer to him. She spots soot on his earlobe on the other side of his head. "Alex,"–she licks her thumb and reaches to clean it off–"how in the world did you manage to get dirt on your ear?" She stops her line of questioning when she remembers the story he just told.

"Told yuh, Mom, I really did help fight a fire last night."

At first, Abila doesn't know what to say. She thinks quietly for a moment. "I know. I'll ask nurse Bonnie to keep an extra eye on you tonight to check on you often. She'll find out if you're being whisked away or not. Okay?"

He perks up a little. "Okay, Momma."

* * * * *

As usual, Aidan returns in the evening to spend time with Alex. Unfortunately, the evening passes quickly. It isn't long before nurse Bonnie reminds everyone that it's quiet time. She completes her checks as the little family says their goodnights and goodbyes. "I'll be back to check on you soon." She assures. "Your mother told me to keep both eyes on you tonight, Alex. Mmm-hmm." She gives a playful nod to Alex, who gives her a 'thumbs-up.' Weak and tired, the boy slips into a deep slumber after she is gone.

"Wake up, Commander! You must wake up."

Alex bolts up in his bed. His head is spinning; he feels like he just closed his eyes. His body also feels extraordinarily heavy, weighted down. He lifts his hands and again notices all the tubes and wires are gone, but to his surprise, he realizes he is wearing a suit of chain mail. He looks to his left. Præsidiel is there. He wears a black surcoat with a white Hospitaller cross over his chest. He holds a black helmet with a white cloth turban around its crown. Alex looks down to find the same tunic adorns his chest.

Before he can ask any questions, Præsidiel debriefs him, "We have little time, Commander. A serpent has trapped the princess and several fair maidens in the hospital tower."

"A serpent?" He asks, flinging the blanket off his legs.

"Yes."

"Does it have wings and claws like the ones I've seen in books?"

"No. However, this serpent is still as fierce as the ones you have read about."

Alex jumps to his feet and searches for his sword. He spies it leaning in an old wooden chair. He grabs his sword belt, secures it around his waist, and inspects his stone-walled chamber, lit by torches. *Not in the hospital anymore*, he thinks as he smiles to himself. He grabs his round and somewhat battered shield. "Where is this snake then?"

Præsidiel continues to brief Alex as they make for the door, "It surrounds the tall spire next to the keep. The princess is trapped there."

"Well, let's go rescue 'em." Alex grins with excitement before dashing out of his chamber. His heart beats with excitement as he runs down the torchlit passageway. The chinking sound of his armor echoes off the stone walls. He feels his sheathed sword banging against his thigh. He can't wait to draw it against the serpent. It isn't long before he rushes beneath a stone archway and out into the courtyard. There he stops and takes in the scene.

The serpent's long, scaly body slithers slowly around the central spire, ascending to the enclosed parapet. Dark red spots run down its rust-colored back. Its scales shimmer eerily in the morning light. Two long, ebony horns curve upward from its skull behind its eye sockets. A short row of smaller horns juts from the top of her viper-like head. A long, forked tongue darts in and out of its mouth as it tastes the air.

"The wicked serpent seeks to devour them, commander," Præsidiel informs before slipping his helmet on. He looks over at Alex, who is setting his shield on the ground. The young knight begins tip-toeing toward the tower. "Wait. What are you doing, Commander?"

"Shhh." Alex makes a swatting motion toward the angel. "I'm gonna yank on its tail to get its attention."

"Will that not make it angry?"

"Course it will. S'what I'm countin' on. Gotta get its attention somehow. Once it finds out we're here, it'll come down after us. When it does, I'm gonna whack it on the head."

"Alexander, this is **not** an ordinary garter snake."

"I know. Still, we gotta get it away from the ladies up there, right? Just be ready." He continues to sneak up to the serpent's tail. He cautiously grabs hold of the tip of it with both hands. "Ooof. It's as heavy as those logs dad made me carry that one time." He whispers. Once he has a good grip, Alex positions himself. He takes a deep breath and then yanks the tail with all his might. He lugs it a couple of feet backward before slipping and falling on his rear end. He looks up to see the serpent whip its head around, gazing at them. "See. Told ya." He grins at Præsidiel, pointing to the serpent's head.

The beast glares down at the young knight with black eyes and piercing white pupils. Then, it slowly turns to slither back down the tower toward the knights. The boy knight's ploy worked. The serpent opens its gaping maw, hissing loudly. A smoky, fog-like mass bellows forth from its pitch-black mouth—two rows of needle-shaped fangs spring forward.

"Oh, snap!" Exclaims Alex. He jumps back to his feet and runs toward Præsidiel so fast he kicks up a dust cloud. He picks up his shield and, breathing heavily, says, "I think I cheesed it off."

"You certainly got its attention." Confirms the angel.

Alex draws his sword, which is a wooden picket, from a fence. He tightens his grip on the handle of his shield, a dented round metal trash can lid. He spreads his feet and crouches slightly. "You ready?" He asks, slightly bouncing in place.

"I am, commander." Præsidiel draws his glimmering crusader's sword slowly.

Eyes fixed on its enemies, the serpent's head barely moves as it slithers slowly toward the ground. Its darting, forked tongue tastes the air again and again. The giant snake stops as it nears them and rears its head. It knows Alex is the weak one, and quick as lightning strikes at the boy knight. Præsidiel deflects the blow with his crusader shield. Alex jumps to the side, narrowly dodging the poisonous bite.

Man, this thing is fast. He thinks. *I'm only gonna get one shot at this.* Though scared and wanting to run deep down, he stands his ground. The serpent raises its head to strike again. The boy throws down his shield and doubles his grip on his wooden sword. The serpent's tongue tastes the air while his body coils beneath him. Alex knows he's about to strike again.

Anticipating the beast's attack, Alex swings his weapon like a bat, landing a mighty blow to the side of the serpent's mouth. The impact hurdles the snake's head to the side and breaks one of its long fangs. Unfortunately, the shock of the strike breaks his sword and sends Alex flying sideways.

Præsidiel uses this opening to pierce the serpent's hide behind its jaw. He removes his blade, and it hisses and writhes in pain. Then, knowing it is beaten, the serpent spews forth a dark fog to conceal his escape. It turns and slithers away rapidly.

"Ow, ow, OW!" exclaims Alex, sitting on his bum and looking at his stinging hands. "Man, that hurt!"

Præsidiel runs to his side. "Are you okay, Commander?"

"Yes, sir. My hands are stinging, though."

"Well, I must say, your plan worked." Præsidiel sheaths his sword and extends his hand to the youth. "Forgive me, Commander."

"Course it did." Alex takes his angel's hand, who helps him to his feet. "Snakes are scared of you more than you are of them. You hit 'em in the head with a stick, and they'll always run." He makes a wiggly motion with his hand before dusting himself off.

"Yes, well, very courageous of you, Sir Alexander." The young knight nods in gratitude. "Now, we must call upon the princess and her maidens."

Alex blushes slightly. "I guess we should." He picks up his broken sword and dented shield. "You think God'll be mad I broke this sword."

"No, Commander. I do not think he will."

"All right then. Let's go check on the princess." Alex smiles and blushes again. "I hope she's pretty."

The two warriors climb the tower's stairs until they reach the apex. They knock on the door—the sound of a steel bolt sliding free echoes in the stairwell. Then the door is flung open by the beautiful princess. "Our heroes!" She exclaims. Embarrassed, Alex lowers his head. She continues, "We witnessed your valor from our window. Truly, we are pleased to receive such brave knights. Please, come in. Rest." She motions with her hands, and her handmaids rush to prepare places for them to sit comfortably. "What is your name, good sir knight?"

"I'm Alex," he proclaims proudly, "and this is Præsidiel. He's a real live angel."

"Oh!" Answers the princess. "We are honored to welcome you, Sir Alex, the brave, and Sir Præsidiel, the holy." She curtsies and asks, "Please, may we offer you something to eat?"

"Thank you, your majesty." Alex makes a slight bow. The two take a seat at a small table. "I am kinda hungry."

The princess looks a little sad. "I'm afraid all we have to offer is bread and cider." One handmaid pours the cider into a cup while the other breaks a chunk of bread off for each.

"Most gracious. Most gracious indeed. Thank you." Says Præsidiel. He motions to Alex to take the cup.

The boy knight takes it. He sniffs at its contents before sipping it. "Oh,"–his words muffled by the cup–"this is delicious!" Alex sets the cup on the table and takes the bread. "Thank you." He noisily munches on the bread and, talking with his mouth full, says, "Did you see me yank on the snake's tail?" The princess smiles, and the maidens giggle as Alex regales them with his exploits. The angel watches and takes joy in the boy's happiness.

The conversation dies down soon after the young knight finishes his snack. "Don't know why, but I'm really tired all of a sudden. Must be that warm cider. You mind if I rest my eyes for a minute?" He asks, laying his head on the table. Alex is clearly exhausted.

"Please do, good sir knight." Says the princess. A hush settles over the tower. All is quiet as Alex falls asleep on his forearm.

Præsidiel stands. “Thank you, my lady, for your hospitality.” He gently scoops up the wee knight in his sturdy arms. He unfolds his brilliant wings. “If you will pardon us, I must return the lad to his chambers.”

“Of course,” she says. The princess curtsies, and her servants bow. “It was our pleasure, o holy messenger. We will pray for the boy and you. May God bless and keep him.” The angel nods before gently taking flight out through the window.

Chapter Four

Cap'n Alex

Alex wakes to the sound of whispering voices. At first, he's unsure if he's still dreaming or awake, so he lies still. It doesn't take long to feel the discomfort of the I.V. or realize the voices are not of the princess or Mr. Ray. Finally, he identifies the doctor's voice as he asks, "Has Alex been baptized?"

Lying still, Alex listens to his father's response, "No, but doesn't he already belong to God? I was always taught that a boy should be old enough to decide whether he wants to be baptized or not, that he must reach the age of discernment first. Why do you ask, anyway?"

"It is your decision, Aidan, but the boy's condition is deteriorating...rapidly." The doctor pauses. "Sadly, I don't think he will be with us much longer."

There is a silent pause after this statement, but Alex remains motionless, waiting, listening for more of the conversation. He doesn't realize his father dwells upon a memory of Alex. Aidan recalls a day not too long ago in his garage. Alex is picking up a piece of wood and some tools, distracting him from his work. "Alex, please put those down. What are you looking for, son?" Alex hastily put the tools back in place but unconsciously hung onto the wood. He remembers the innocence in the boy's eyes when he said, "I jus' wanna help dad." The youth's purity was not lost on his father either. He remembers smiling at him and saying, "Okay, son, hand me that piece of wood you have, and I'll show you what we're going to build."

Alex hears the voice of his mother call out, "Aidan." The boy opens his eyes slowly to see what is happening. He witnesses his dad looking deep into his mom's copper, tear-stained eyes. "Please, Aidan," she pleads. "We need to baptize Alex. We cannot put it off any longer. I know you believe it must be the child's choice to accept Jesus as the savior and be baptized, but isn't it our responsibility as his parents to ensure we have done everything to remove any sin? To prepare him as a gift to God?"

Aidan relents. He lets out a deep sigh. He takes her hands, "You're right, my love." He caresses Abila's face, wiping away her tears. "You're right. Call Father Soutane and ask him to come."

The doctor has noticed Alex is watching them. "Good Morning Alex." The doctor's voice catches his parents off guard. "I just popped in to see how you are doing today. You know, the nurses are still talking about your dream? Don't suppose you had another amazing adventure last night, did you?"

"Morning, Mom. Morning, Dad." He greets his parents as they regain their composure. Abila moves to his side. "I did go on another adventure last night." He states with muted excitement.

"Really?" asks his dad.

"Yessir. My angel," he pauses for a second, "you know, Mr. Ray? We had to fight a really big and scary serpent. I yanked on his tail and then whacked him in the snout. He slithered off, and we saved the princess." Alex smiles. "She was pretty and nice. We ate some yummy bread and drank some cider. It was delicious. I guess I fell asleep at the table, and Mr. Ray must've brought me back here."

"Wow! Now that is a dream." The doctor responds. "I bet the nurses would love to hear about this one too."

Just then, nurse Bonnie, Alex's favorite, enters the room. "Good morning Mr. Alex. How's my young adventurer this morning?" She winks at him before acknowledging his parents. "Mr. and Mrs. McBain." The family always enjoys her smiling face. "If you all will excuse me, doctor, may I speak with you for a moment?"

"Sure. By the way, wait until you hear Alex's latest dream." He nods at the boy and then follows nurse Bonnie out.

They pass through the door. Thinking they're out of earshot, nurse Bonnie says, "We have a small issue. The data you requested is incomplete. There was a 30-minute lapse in all our monitors last night." The door closes on their conversation.

Abila notices Alex has a few tiny breadcrumbs sprinkled on his blanket. "Sweety," she begins while brushing off the crumbs, "how did you get crumbs all over you?

* * * * *

As usual, the day came and went. After another day of unpleasant naps, hospital food, and uncomfortable silence, Alex finally got to sleep for the night, which was challenging considering his excitement at the prospect of a new adventure. However, tonight, Alex is finding it hard to remain asleep. It feels like his bed is moving, as though the ground is undulating beneath him. Furthermore, a strange light warms his face instead of the hospital lights' soft, cold glow.

Alex takes a deep breath and exhales. *I can't sleep*, he thinks. He slowly opens his eyes to find daylight beaming through oddly slanted oaken windows. He sits up, taking in his unfamiliar surroundings. There are cabinets next to shelves that have stacks of airtight bottles containing scrolls stored on them. A small desk and chair sit right in front of the windows. An hourglass, a feathered quill seated in an old inkwell, and paper are on the table. A dressing table sits in the corner, upon which a blue frock coat, gold waistcoat, and sword belt. Resting atop it all is a painted newspaper hat, which he instantly recognizes as the captain's hat he made last summer.

He looks down at the little twin bed upon which he sits. He's covered with a gray wool blanket. *Mmmm, warm but super itchy*, he thinks. There are two drawers underneath his thin mattress; one is halfway open. In it are another blanket and a brass spyglass. The headboard behind him is decorated with knotted rope and decorative lines. There is no doubt now. He has awakened aboard an old ship and is pleased to do so.

There is a rap on his cabin door, followed by, "Captain Alexander? Are you awake, sir?"

Happy yet groggy, Alex shouts back, "I'm up! I'm up." He rubs his eyes and smiles. Then he spins to his side to let his feet dangle off the bed. "Come on in."

A tall man bursts into his quarters. He is dressed in a similar, but less ornate, coat, tan pants, and white waistcoat, with a black kerchief tied around his collar. His hat is a short stovepipe shape with a flat and round brim. "We are in danger, Captain."

"Oh!" Exclaims Alex. "Mr. Ray. Good morning, sir." He greets while slipping on his stockings.

"Good morning, Captain. I have disturbing news."

"What's going on?" He asks, standing up and sliding his feet into his deck shoes.

"A pirate ship is gaining on us." He points out the window to a ship on their stern. "No doubt those scurvy buccaneers seek to board or sink our vessel."

Alex finishes dressing and quickly straps on his sword belt. He picks up the paper hat, sets it on his head, and smiles, "Ahhh. Still fits." Looking at himself in the mirror, he tugs at his coat. He thinks, *Now I look like a proper captain.* Then, satisfied he is ready for the battle, he turns to his first mate,

"Show me the way, Mr. Ray." A giggle slips past his lips at the rhyme he just made.

The first mate escorts his captain topside. Together they rush to the helm of the 3-masted gunship. Alex looks over the main deck in awe at the HMS St. Michael, a First-Rate ship of the old British Navy. Ocean spray sprinkles his face, and the cooling wind refreshes him—the invigorating and overflowing energy of 9-year-old boy surges in his heart. Uncharacteristic of a regular sea captain, he looks out to his crew and enthusiastically salutes them by waving his paper hat in the air while shouting, "Ahoy, shipmates!" They erupt with a hearty cheer.

"Cap'n! Cap'n!" comes the call from the crow's nest. Alex looks up at the seaman there, who is pointing astern. "There, Cap'n, the ship what's 'bout to overtake us."

Alex turns and runs up to the quarterdeck railing. He produces a spyglass from his overcoat and looks astern at the ship. It's smaller, more maneuverable, and faster. He spots the Jolly Roger flying high and bold from the main mast. Scanning down the tattered and filthy sails, he finds a beastly man at the helm. He wears a black frock coat with silver buttons over a blood-red waistcoat. His dark gray pants are tucked into his black boots, with a cutlass on one hip and pistol on the other.

The pirate captain sees Alex looking at him. He momentarily steps to the side of the helm, removes his black and tattered tri-corner hat, and offers a sarcastic curtsy. Alex suddenly notices two horns protruding from the pirate captain's head as he stands back up. He places his hat back upon his head, covering them. His scraggly black beard blows in the wind as he parts his chapped lips in a wicked smile, exposing the rotten teeth behind them.

"Boy, he's ugly." The words slip unconsciously past his lips.

Mr. Ray whispers in his ear, "Aye, Captain, tis the devil that pursues us."

Alex lowers his spyglass. "Mr. Ray, ready the guns on the starboard side." He looks up at his first mate with a resolute grin. "We're gonna sink that mean ole' devil."

Cap'n Alex turns to his crew, pulls out his wooden sword, and, raising it in the air, shouts, "Prepare the guns!" Another rousing cheer goes up. "Always wanted to say that." He says softly to Mr. Ray, who winks back at him.

"By your leave, sir, I will take it from here." Alex nods his approval. Mr. Ray begins barking orders, "Gunners, prepare the cannons on the starboard side. Master-at-Arms, Bo'sun, make ready the crew."

"Aye, aye!" They respond.

"Helmsman, starboard 20 degrees." Mr. Ray turns to Alex, "That should slow them down enough for the crew to make ready, Captain."

It isn't long before the devil's ship begins to pull alongside. Alex first notes their ship's blasphemous figurehead. He has seen many beautiful statues of the Mary, but this ship's insulting depiction of the Virgin Mother deeply offends and angers him. "Nobody mocks our Blessed Mother. We'll send 'em down to Davey Jones for that!" He mutters. He observes the motley crew. The devil's band of misfits swear and curse while waiving their cutlasses about. Some are shirtless, wearing only striped pants and black boots, with red sashes around their waists and bandannas covering their heads. Most are in tattered clothes and tri-quarter hats. Cannons thrust out through open portholes as the devil's ship swiftly pulls alongside.

Everything grows eerily quiet for a few seconds before thunder and smoke fill the air between the ships. The crew of the HMS St. Michael duck and dodge as cannonballs whoosh overhead. The projectiles pass cleanly between the masts and rigging of the HMS St. Michael. Miraculously, the ship takes no damage. An unexpected wave caused the sea to swell at the right time. The crest raised the pirate ship just enough to make its cannons miss. However, the patience of St. Michael's gunner pays off. "FIRE!" he yells while they're in the trough of the wave.

Again the roar of the cannons shudders the air. Their volley strikes the pirate ship lower than planned, just above the waterline. The adversary's ship is rocked to the right before rolling back. It begins to list to the port side. "They are taking on water!" exclaims Mr. Ray.

A raspy and guttural voice carries across the water from the pirate ship, "I'll keel haul yuh from yer own vessel, yuh landlubber."

"Not today, you scallywag!" Cap'n Alex shouts back, shaking his sword at the adversary.

"Keep a sharp eye, me hearties!" cries the Bo'sun, pointing toward the adversary's rigging. "Scupper those bilge rats!"

Alex quickly glances out over the main deck to see what's happening. Several buccaneers swing on ropes from the pirate ship's rigging, trying to board Alex's vessel. One pirate swings across no man's land unseen, landing with his feet on the quarterdeck railing. He catches Alex by surprise. "Gotcha now, lad," snarls the dirty pirate staring down at him.

Alex freezes for a second. Mr. Ray realizes the scoundrel is still holding onto the rope he swung over on and is off balance. Alex snaps out of his fright and looks down to draw his sword. Mr. Ray leaps unseen toward the pirate. With a swift stroke, the first mate slices clean through the rope. Alex, not very tall, yanks his sword from his scabbard and smacks the feet of the would-be pillager, who falls backward into the ocean without the support of the rope.

He knows his senses are dulled, but he spied something odd as the raider falls backward. Alex quickly peers over the railing, sword still in hand, and notices a slender red tail with a point on its end swishing about just before the pirate plunges into the briny sea with a loud 'KER-SPLASH'!

Alex looks out over his ship to see what is happening. First, he witnesses his stout and steadfast crew repelling the enemy's boarding crew. A cutlass repels some, some are thrown over, and even one is blasted with a blunderbuss. Then, as the last one is kindly escorted off his ship, Alex points to the helmsman and yells, "Hard to port!"

"Aye, aye, Cap'n!" He confirms before spinning the ship's wheel.

Wind fills the sails of the HMS St. Michael. She pulls gracefully away from the sinking pirate ship. The devil curses and yells with fury. Again, in the very uncharacteristic manner of a naval sea captain, Alex turns aft and sticks out his tongue. "Nyah!" he exclaims. Afterward, he offers a cold shoulder to the would-be plunderers. He knows they're sinking, and their cannons cannot reach him. Cap'n Alex raises his sword high in the air in full sight of his crew, yelling, "Well done, me buckos!"

The crew throws up their arms and shouts in victory.

"Mr. Ray."

"Aye, Captain."

"Best adventure yet! However," Alex exhales deeply, "I'm feeling really tired all of a sudden." He sheathes his sword just in time to cover a giant yawn with his hand. "Let's find a port. I'm sure the crew could use some shore time." He adjusts his hat, informing, "Think I'm gonna go back to the cabin."

"Aye, aye, sir. Helmsman, steady as you go until we can get the proper bearings."

"Aye, aye," the helmsman acknowledges.

Alex stops at the top of the ladder to witness the HMS St. Michael sailing into the expanding amber and vermillion sky. The sun is setting. The smell of gunpowder and the sounds of battle fade in their wake. The smell of the sea, the sounds of the ship plying its waters, and the rocking motion soothe the young captain. The Bo'sun sings a shanty while the crew works in rhythm, cleaning the boat, handling lines, and returning her to good order while others keep watch. The Quartermaster takes new bearings and gives commands to the helmsman. Though tired, Alex feels a deep sense of satisfaction and joy.

He starts down the ladder toward his cabin. Mr. Ray accompanies him. "You have accomplished much as a brave young sea captain." He opens the cabin door. "Forgive me for reminding you, but Captains must log their day's activities and seal them in a bottle."

"Uhg!" Alex rolls his eyes. "Seriously! Homework?"

"I will prepare your desk while you get comfortable, Captain."

"I'm sorry, Mr. Ray. I'm just tired, is all." Alex says while sluggishly undoing his sword belt and kicking off his shoes. "You're my new best friend. You know that, right?"

"It is my pleasure, *Captain* Alexander." Mr. Ray picks up the parchment, grabs a bottle, and places everything on the desk. "A thought before you make your logs." Alex throws his frock coat on the dressing table and turns to listen respectfully to his angel in disguise. "Life ebbs and flows on a tide. Some days the swell will raise you, and others, you will find yourself down in the trough. Either way, my good friend, you must be thankful to God and sail ahead boldly."

Alex rubs his eyes. "That's pretty deep there, Mr. Ray." He gives a sudden coy smile as he sits at the desk. "Just like the ocean."

“Aye, captain.” Mr. Ray chuckles. “That it is. That...it...is.” He grabs the blanket from the bed and gently lays it over Alex’s back. “To keep you warm, sir. Now, by your leave, I will see to the crew.”

“Thank you, shipmate.” Alex smiles as his friend departs.

“Aw man, why do I have to do this?” the boy grumbles. “After an adventure like that?” He grudgingly takes the quill in hand, dips it in ink, and begins to write. He’s only entered a few words into his log before exhaustion takes hold. He places his arm on the table and lays his head on it. He tries to keep writing, but his eyes are too heavy. Moments later, a child’s snore can be heard coming from the captain’s quarters.

Chapter Five

Sheriff Alex, the Kid

Sunlight warms his face, and a subtle chatter fills his ears. A groggy Alex wakes in his hospital bed. He is not alone. There is a small crowd in his room. His mother, father, and Sitti are there, as always, but so are a couple of first responders, nurse Bonnie, her husband, and a man in a black cassock. His grand tales of fighting fires, defeating serpents, and hanging out with an angel are reaching the ears of many. Inspired by the joy with which he faces a life-threatening illness, they have come hoping to hear another grand tale.

Alex, emaciated and weak, struggles to sit up in bed. Bonnie moves swiftly to adjust it, so he doesn't have to labor. "Thank you." He says before rubbing his eyes. It takes him a second, but he finally recognizes the man in the black robe. "Father Soutane?"

"Ah, you do remember me. God bless you, lad."

"Course I do. You're my mom's favorite priest. She says good things 'bout you." Father Soutane glances at Abila and smiles. His mother blushes. "They tell yuh about Mr. Ray; I mean Præsidiel? That's his real name. How he's a real angel?"

"Yes, they did." He says as he moves to Alex's side. "Sounds like you're in good company." He winks at the boy. "And I'm guessing you've been on another adventure?"

"Oh, yes, sir. You wanna hear about it?"

"Yes, of course, but in due time, my young explorer." The priest's tone takes on a more serious tone. "First, do you know why I'm here?"

"Well, I heard my mom 'n dad talkin' about baptism yesterday, so I'm guessin' you're here to baptize me."

“You are a smart young man, Alex. That is precisely why I’m here.” He leans closer, “I’m sure your angel, Præsidiel, will be most happy when it’s done too.” He winks at him again.

“Okay, father. I’m ready then.”

“Well then,”–he lightly claps his hands together–“let’s get started.” Father Soutane greets everyone present officially. He briefly reminds them of the joy with which the parents welcomed this child as a gift from God and then moves on to the ceremony. “You have named this child Alexander. Now, what do you ask of God's Church for him?

“Baptism.” Aiden and Abila reply in unison.

“And the grace of Christ and eternal life." Add Sitti and Alex’s mother.

Father Soutane turns toward nurse Bonnie and her husband. “I understand you are to be his godparents. Are you ready to help his parents in their Christian duties?”

“We are.” They also state in unison. Based on his surprised yet happy look, they could tell Alex was surprised by the announcement. He likes nurse Bonnie, who has become a close friend of their family over the last few weeks. Tilting her head slightly, she offers Alex a warm smile.

“Alexander, the Christian community welcomes you with great joy. I claim you for Christ our Savior by the sign of his cross. I’ll trace the cross on your forehead and invite your parents, your Sitti, and your Godparents to do the same.” The priest signs the child on the forehead. The rest follow his example.

“Due to the circumstances, we will celebrate with an abbreviated reading from the apostle Mark.” Father Soutane motions for everyone to sit and be comfortable. He reads from Mark 1: 9-11 (the baptism of Jesus) and Mark 10: 13-16 (let the little children come to me). Next, he gives a short homily on Luke 2:21-40 (the presentation of Jesus in the temple) and the trust the Blessed Mother and St. Joseph had in God. He notices Alex's heavy eyes and says, "Let us profess our faith." Everyone in the hospital room recites the Apostle's Creed in a low, whispering tone.

"Now, let us prepare for Alex's baptism." The movement in the room reinvigorates the boy. Father Soutane readies the holy water he brought. Abila moves to the boy's side to help lift him while his dad stands near the head of his bead. Nurse Bonnie slightly lowers his bed, gathers a towel, and stands beside his mother.

Once they're all in position, Father Soutane begins the baptism from the opposite side of the bed. "Alexander, I baptize you in the name of the Father," the priest gently pours the water over Alex's head. He stops momentarily as some of the water runs down his forehead. A nervous giggle slips out of the boy. "and of the Son,"–He pours the water a second time and again pauses–"and of the Holy Spirit."–He pours the water over his head a third and final time.

Alex is wide awake now. His new Godmother raises the bed while Father Soutane puts away the water. His mom dries his face and head with the towel, and his dad helps him get comfortable.

The priest returns to the bedside with a bottle of oil. He says, "God the Father of our Lord Jesus Christ has freed you from sin, given you a new birth by water and the Holy Spirit, and welcomed you into his holy people. He now anoints you with the chrism of salvation. As Christ was anointed Priest, Prophet, and King, so may you live always as a member of his body, sharing everlasting life."

Everyone in the room responds, "Amen."

Father Soutane dips his thumb in the bottle of olive oil mixed with balsam. Its fragrance immediately fills the room as he again traces the Sign of the Cross on the boy's forehead, saying, "Alexander, be sealed with the gift of the Holy Spirit."

Though he's only a boy, Alex feels a sense of relief, of peace. An effervescent thought fills his young mind; *Everything is going to be okay*. He knows his life's story will end happily, and his heart soars with joy. He understands the gift he has just been given, enthusiastically responding, "Amen."

His response is received with light applause from everyone in the room. Family and visitors crowd around to congratulate him while Father Soutane packs the ceremonial items. Then, as things settle down, he returns to Alex's side. "Now," he says with a wink and a smile, "how 'bout that adventure?"

Rejuvenated, Alex scooches up in his bed and tells the tale of his battle at sea, the roar of cannon fire, and fighting off scurvy pirates. He beautifully describes sailing into the setting sun. He expresses his awe of the ship and her crew. He even laments being tasked with homework.

"My goodness, lad!" Father Soutane says, jumping to his feet. "I wish I could've been right there with you." The priest, acting as though he had a sword in hand, waves his hand, saying, "I'd've helped you scupper those brigands too." Alex giggles. The priest suddenly realizes he's probably a little too excited. "Ahem. Well then." He pauses to regain his composure. "How did you get back here?"

Alex shrugs, "I guess the angel keeps bringing me back after I go to sleep."

"Hmmm..."–Father Soutane glances toward Alex's parents and then back to Alex–"Let's hope he keeps bringing you back to us." He gives the boy a fond smile, which Alex happily returns, nodding. "It has been a pleasure, young man. However, I must get back to the parish and God's work." He collects his things and prepares to depart. He pauses as he passes the foot of the bed, asking, "May I come back to hear more of your stories?"

"Yes, please." Alex delightfully confirms.

"I look forward to it. Until then, Alex, may God bless and keep you, always." He waves and smiles at all those present. Aidan rises to escort him out. They whisper as they exit. Alex hears something about reconciliation and sacraments.

Afterward, the day's routine slowly returns. Visitors and nurses come and go. His dad comes back for a moment before heading off to work. Abila feeds her young adventurer lunch, though he is only capable of eating half of it. However, he saves just enough room for the sweeties Sitti sneaks him when nobody's looking. Alex slides in and out of catnaps over the course of the day. Unfortunately, his discomfort and naps are noticeably more frequent than before.

Alex's parents return in the evening to find him staring out the hospital window. Typically, the evenings grant father, mother, and son quiet solitude from the rest of the world. They would much rather be gathered around the kitchen table instead of eating supper around Alex's bed. Regardless, they usually discuss the day's happenings, but tonight there is a palpable and uncomfortable feeling of numbness in each of them. The encroaching finality renders them silent for most of the evening. Nevertheless, for now, there is a simple unspoken pleasure in being in one another's company.

Alex groans with discomfort as he turns to lie on his side for a bit. As he does, Bonnie returns. She has started her shift and wants to check on her new godson. Her heart breaks at seeing the pain behind his heavy eyes. She kneels between his parents, "Mom, Dad, I hate to say it, but it's getting late. Visiting hours are almost over. We need to take his vitals and make Alex comfortable for the night."

"C'mon, Bonnie. We still have time." Aidan protests.

"S'okay, Dad," Alex interjects before letting out a big yawn. "I'm really tired anyway. 'Sides, I wanna get some rest before Mr. Ray comes tuh get me."

Parental love and instincts create a reluctance to leave, even now. However, the deep trust they have in their nurse assuages their fears. "Okay, little buckaroo. You get some sleep. We'll see you in the morning. Until then, I know Mrs. Bonnie will take care of you."

He hasn't heard his dad call him that for some time. A contented Alex sleepily grins. "Love you, Dad. Love you too, Mom."

"Oh, my sweet darling, I love you. You mean the world to me. Sweet dreams." Abila leans over and kisses her son softly on the cheek.

"Love you too, Son." His dad winks. "Be safe on your next adventure."

Nurse Bonnie politely ushers mom and dad out of the room. When she returns, she finds the brave young boy fast asleep. She quietly sets to the work at hand. She straightens his room, checks his I.V., inspects the monitors, and tucks him in. As she does so, she accidentally kicks something under his bed. The distinct 'clink' of a glass bottle rattling there perks up her ears.

Hmmm, she thinks, *I wonder if Father dropped his bottle of chrism oil*. She stoops to look under the bed. She finds an old bottle, not at all like the one the priest used. It's a little misshapen, like it was handblown. It's a sea green color with an old cork in the end. "Now, where in the world did this come from?"

She notices a piece of old parchment inside the bottle. She removes the cork, which makes that familiar 'pop' sound, upends the bottle, and shakes the note to its mouth. "Aw, c'mon," she mutters when it doesn't come out. She pinches at the message with her fingertips. Finally grasping enough parchment to pull, she gently removes it, turns it over, and quietly reads the child-like scribble, "Thank you God for." The sentence ends abruptly.

She looks at Alex. *It can't be*, she thinks to herself. *How'd he get out of the bed, much less the hospital?* She stuffs the note back into the bottle. After replacing the cork, she slips it into her pocket. "Someone's havin' a laugh at my expense." She scoffs.

* * * * *

Alex wakes to someone nudging his arm. "Sheriff. Wake up. There is trouble." He slowly stirs. Unable to see, he realizes there is a hat over his eyes. His feet slip off the desk they once rested on, and his leaning chair flies forward, landing on all four legs. Wide awake from the sudden lunge forward, he grabs the hat off his head and inspects it. It looks like the one his dad brought back from a trip to Wyoming once. He always loved it when his dad would place it on his head. It's one of his favorite hats. He smiles and puts it back. A little oversized, it falls to his ears.

He looks around and realizes he's in some old west jailhouse. Two cast-iron cells on either side of the jail's half-open front door stand out against the simple, wood-clapboard walls. Before he can finish checking his surroundings, the man beside him says, "Sheriff. We have trouble." Alex looks up, immediately drawn to the silver, 5-point badge on his tan waistcoat. He turns his gaze back to his own coat. He slides his thumb behind the lapel and lifts it to inspect the circular badge surrounding a 5-point star pinned there. "You hear me, Sheriff?"

"What? What's all the fuss about?" Asks Alex.

"El Diablo and his gang are down at the Bartlett Inn. They have come for old Polly's soul." Deputy Ray points to the apparition floating in the cell on the right. A transparent, gaunt-faced woman with black hair is in the middle of the cell.

Her once-white dress and dark blue, button-downed shirt fade and shimmer. The woman's spirit sways and moans.

"Yikes! Is that...a real ghost?" Alex exclaims as he jumps to his feet. "Never seen a real ghost before." He adjusts the oversized hat on his head, peering at the specter from under its brim. "She sure is creepy."

"That is the ghost of Polly Bartlett. She murdered many men in her day. Her soul is trapped here, awaiting judgment. El Diablo has come to claim her." Mr. Ray pauses briefly before repeating, "He and his gang are at the Bartlett Inn. I must warn you, Sheriff; he is mean enough to steal the coins off a dead man's eyes, as they say."

"I know. I've heard he's one mean hombre, but I ain't 'fraid of him. You know why Mr. Ray?" Alex pats the receiver on his lever action BB gun. "'Cause I got Ole Betsy with me. I'm a pretty good shot too." He then points to Deputy Ray's side arms and continues, "Besides, you got them Colt peacemakers. 'Tween you and me; we can take 'em, pardner."

At that very moment, a deep, raspy voice echoes through the dusty western town, "Sheriff Alex! I'm a callin' you out, boy!"

"Welp,"–Alex clacks the lever on Ole Betsy, cocking the gun–"guess it's time we mosey on out there and face the music." He winks at Deputy Ray. "Let's run that varmint outta town."

In agreement, Mr. Ray tugs at the brim of his hat, "I am with you, Sheriff."

Alex pulls the door open and walks out into the hot summer sun. He stretches in the warm light. "Man, I'm sore." As he walks into the town's main street, his boots crunch on the dry, dusty ground. A tumbleweed blows past, and the silence becomes deafening. Then, finally, he stops to observe his surroundings. "Where is everyone?" He mumbles.

"This is a ghost town, Alexander." Confirms the angel.

As his friend speaks, Alex notices a single man standing in the middle of the street. The young sheriff turns to stare him down. A wide-brimmed black hat shades the man's dark eyes. His pointed beard and handlebar mustache hide the scowl of his curled lips. His deep crimson waistcoat stands against the foil of his long black duster coat. He wears a full bandolier over his shoulder with another gun belt on his hips. He has two pistols holstered there. Alex instinctively raises his blue-steeled BB beauty to his side.

"Whaddaya think you're gonna do with that li'l pea shooter?" The desperado turns his head and spits on the ground.

"Maybe I'm gonna shoot yer eye out."

The bandit gives a hearty laugh.

Mr. Ray leans toward Alex, "Watch out, sheriff. He's got one on the roof of the old General Store and one hiding by the Inn." Alex nods his gratitude but keeps his focus on the outlaw.

El Diablo slowly reaches for his guns. "You have one of mine in there, Sheriff, and I aims to bust 'er out." Then, he growls, "No yellow-bellied, snot-nosed kid's gonna stop me, either."

"Hold it right there,"–Alex raises his rifle and aims–"you old son of a gun," Alex commands. Although he has a firm grip on his pistols, El Diablo hesitates to draw them. It's a standoff. If it wasn't for the light wind stirring up the dust, Alex swears he could hear showdown music from some old spaghetti western playing in his ears.

Flinching, El Diablo moves to draw his revolvers. Alex squeezes the trigger of Ole Betsy. Two sounds break the peace, 'KA-PAP,' followed by a light 'thunk.' The devil drops his guns and clutches his face. "Holy @#$%*! He shot my eye out!" He kneels in the road, screaming with rage, "Get 'em, boys!"

Deputy Ray pulls his Colt peacemakers with lightning speed and jumps in front of Sheriff Alex just as two bullets strike the dirt on either side of the boy. He fires a round from each of his pistols, hitting the would-be assassins with deadly accuracy. El Diablo's assassins burst with an ectoplasmic explosion when struck by the bullets.

Just as fast as it began, the shootout is over. Alex and Mr. Ray run toward El Diablo with their guns trained on him. Alex cocks his trusty sidearm again. Deputy Ray kicks the outlaw's guns out of reach.

"Go on. Git!" Alex shouts before mumbling, "You old sidewinder." He raises his voice again, "Less you wanna lose the other eye!"

Clutching his bad eye with one hand, El Diablo points to the lawmen, "I'll be back to get her one day 'n there's nothin' you can do about it."

"I said, go on."

The devil looks at Mr. Ray, who motions for him to go with one of his pistols. "You heard the sheriff. Depart from us." El Diablo turns and grudgingly leaves town. The two lawmen watch him until he disappears over the hillside. Once he is out of sight, the angel holsters his pistols and turns to his young friend. "Well, I do not think he will return for some time. You did a great job, Sheriff."

Alex lowers Ole Betsy. "We sure showed him, huh?" He raises the brim of his hat. "Yessir. I've been enjoying these adventures with you, Mr. Ray. But, I gotta tell yuh, it's getting harder and harder to do 'em. I just keep getting so tired so easy." He takes a deep breath and exhales. "I feel so weak all the time."

"You are tired because your journey is nearly at an end." There is an uncomfortable silence as they stroll on.

"Are you ready, Alexander?"

"Whaddaya mean? To go back to the jail and check on ol' Polly?"

Mr. Ray stops and turns to face his ward. He shifts his form, losing his western attire and taking on his angelic appearance. "No, Alexander, are you ready for what is to come?"

"Oh," Alex says sadly. "That."

The two turn back toward the Old Sweetwater Jail. "You are weak because the illness has taken its toll on your body and mind. As such, this was our last earthly adventure," states Præsidiel.

"I understand." Alex drags his boots on the dusty road. The little sheriff looks up at his angel, the brim of his hat almost covering his eyes, "Do I still get to see my mom and dad one more time?"

"Yes."

The young man quietly smiles as he turns his gaze back to the ground before him. Upon entering the old jailhouse, Alex notices the bed in the empty cell has been turned down with lush sheets and blankets not found in the wild west. He doesn't care that it's out of place, however. Instead, the boy lumbers toward it and sits down on the edge of the bed. He leans Ole Betsy against the headboard, takes his hat off, and places it over the barrel of his trusty BB gun. Then he kicks off his boots and crawls under the covers. "Sure am...tired." He is unashamed about not covering his big yawn. "But I do wanna see Mom & Dad again."

Alex's guardian angel tucks his special ward in. "Sleep well, Alexander, for the next time I am sent to you...." his voice trails off.

Chapter Six

A Warrior's Welcome

Alex hears his mother's quiet prayers. Lying still with his eyes unopened, he feels the weak heartbeat in his chest. It's weird, but he could swear it beats in cadence with his mother's prayers. He feels the I.V. in his vein and the chill of the solution running up his arm. The sensors on his chest itch and pull at his youthful skin. He doesn't want to move because he knows it will be painful if he does, so he slowly opens his eyes. His mother stops praying.

"Good morning, my beautiful boy." She greets.

Alex exhales before saying, "Good morning, Mom." He smiles at her. "Where's Dad?"

"He stepped out for a few minutes but will be right back."

"Momma?" Alex asks with a weakened voice.

Abila wraps her rosary around her wrist and approaches her son. "Yes, my darling?" She gently takes his hand.

"Mr. Ray said last night was my last adventure. I...I think...it may be time for me to..." Alex passes out.

His mother frantically pats the boy's hand. "Alex! Alex!" she screams. His heart monitor beeps in an odd pattern. "Nurse. Nurse." Her cries escalate.

A nurse rushes into the room, quickly assesses the situation, and hits the call button for help. "What happened?" She asks.

"I don't know. He was talking and then just passed out."

Another nurse and a doctor rush into the room. Abila is gently squeezed out of the way by the tending physician. They administer oxygen and check Alex's vitals, among other things, to stabilize him.

Aidan bursts into the room and quickly envelops his wife in his arms. "What happened?"

"Alex just collapsed while he was talking." Tears stream down her face. "Oh, Aidan. I'm not ready to lose him yet. I'm not..." she sniffles. He offers no words, for he has none himself. So instead, she turns her face into his chest, hiding within his strong embrace.

* * * * *

When Alex opens his eyes again, he sees Father Soutane before him. He is groggy and unsure. He looks slowly around to discover his mom and dad next to him. Extremely weak, he lifts his hand, which his mother readily takes in her own. "Sorry...Momma."

"Oh, baby, it's okay. I'm here. I'm here."

His dad brushes Alex's hair back and caresses his head. "You gave us quite a scare."

Alex sees the restraint in his father's eyes. "Dad?"

"Yes, Son?" He continues to stroke his hair.

"I...I think it's time...time tuh go meet Jesus."

Aidan can no longer hold back the tears; they flow freely. He chokes back his emotions. "That's why we asked Father Soutane to come." He glances in the priest's direction. "He's here to offer you viaticum, last rights"–he sniffs and wipes his eyes–"so you can go to Our Lord."

Alex shifts his head slowly to the right, turning his attention to Father Soutane. "Whadda I gotta do?"

"Don't worry, young Alexander; I'll take care of everything." He moves to the table set up at the foot of the bed. There are two small candles, a vase, and a small cloth. Father Soutane solemnly removes a pyx from the burse around his neck. He gently places it on the table, genuflects, and rises again. Then he takes a rod with a ball on the end of it out of the vase.

"What's that?" Asks Alex.

"An aspergillum. We use it to bless with holy water." The priest sprinkles first the boy with the shape of a cross. Alex smiles briefly when the cool water lands on his cheeks. Then he sprinkles some on the floor around his bed, the room's walls, and those gathered around. When he is finished, he returns the aspergillum to the vase. Then, turning to everyone else, he informs, "I am truly sorry, but I have to ask everyone to step out of the room for a moment so I can hear Alexander's confession."

Though it was expected, everyone reluctantly exits into the hospital hallway.

Father Soutane pulls up a chair and sits next to Alex. He wants to be at eye level with the boy. He looks into Alex's sunken eyes and gaunt face. He knows his time is limited.

"Father, I don't know how this works."

"It's okay, Alex. All I want to ask is if there is anything you might have done in your life that you are sorry for. Get into a fight? Disobey your parents? Things like that."

"Well...there was one time when I pulled Suzie's hair. I felt awful bad 'bout that. I punched Tommy once too. He broke my favorite action figure. I lied to Momma when I took some cookies, and Dad too when I broke his tape measure and hid it."

"Are you sorry you did those things?"

"Yessir. I love my momma...and my dad. I wish I could take back what I did tuh my friends, too."

"Is there anything else?"

"No, sir. Not that I can think of."

"That was a good confession, Alex. For your penance, I want you to say a Hail Mary."

"Like my mom says?"

"Yes, dear one, like your mother says." The priest grants him absolution, "...through the ministry of the Church, may God give you pardon and peace, and I absolve you from all your sins in the name of the Father, the Son, and the Holy Spirit."

Alex joins Father Soutane in saying, "Amen."

"You have been forgiven, Alex. Now, you say your Hail Mary, and I'll call everyone back." He gets up, moves the chair back, and goes toward the door. He takes much delight in hearing the lad repeat the prayer from memory.

Aidan, Abila, Sitti, Bonnie, and a few of the hospital staff re-enter. Mom and Dad immediately go to his side.

"Momma, I said the same prayer you say all the time, the Hail Mary." She smiles at him. "Maybe I'll meet her too when I get up there."

"Oh, my darling, I hope so." Tears stream down her face. "I hope so." She caresses his sunken cheeks.

Once everyone is settled, the priest goes to the table, genuflects again, rises, and then uncovers the pyx. He picks up the open pyx and carries it to stand next to Alex's bed on the opposite side of his parents. There he prays before taking out the consecrated host. Then, holding the pyx in his left hand under the eucharist, he offers the consecrated host to Alex.

Alex's eyes dilate immediately after he consumes it. The room changes. Several angels appear around the room, each standing behind those who came to see him. He recognizes their faces. They were the EMTs on the scene in his first adventure, the two servants in the tower, and his faithful shipmates on the ship. The walls beyond alsobegin to fade.

In the distance, a tan and white stone wall gradually materializes. In the middle of it is a fifty-foot tower extending into a pre-dawn sky. At its center are two arches, one external and one recessed. Two elegant stone lions are carved on either side of the archway. Massive oak doors, ornately decorated, seal the entrance. Small shrubs and grasses spring up around his former hospital room. Hints of a vast wilderness between the wall and a gleaming city on a faraway hill tease his curiosity.

His distant stare scares his mother. “Alex. Alex, baby. What are you seeing?”

“Mom. Dad.” Alex's voice grows faint, but his eyes refocus. He turns his head toward them. "Don’t be ‘fraid. You...you gotta let me go.” His eyes dilate again, and he returns his view toward the distant wall. “See...there’s a...a great expedition for me...in heaven. One to ‘scover Jesus.” Although his parents try to hold back their sobbing, their tears flow freely. “He’s waitin’ for me, Momma. We get to explore together...Him ‘n me."

The angel Præsidiel appears at the foot of the bed. Only Alex can see him and hear his call. Alex lifts his hand to wave. Those gathered look around, trying to see whom he’s waving at. "Are you ready, Alexander?" Asks the angel.

The dying boy nods slightly, "Yessir, Mr. Ray." His voice is fading to a whisper, "I'm...ready." Alex's eyes close slowly.

The heart monitor flat lines. The room grows silent.

* * * * *

The remnants of the hospital, the world itself, disappear. It takes a moment before Alex's eyes adjust to the blinding white light. Appearing before him is a small group of people. Beyond them is an endless and vibrant wilderness waiting to be explored. Still coming into focus is a great, shining city that rests on a distant mountain. Alex turns his eyes back to the group forming a semi-circle before him.

The two men on the left wear light blue tunics with white linen togas. To their right is an American Indian Chief dressed in tan animal skin pants, and a pale-blue shirt, with a large, feathered headdress on his head. Sitting on his shoulder is a curious little man. Alex has seen pictures of Japanese warriors wearing the same clothes, but this man is much smaller, about a foot tall. Next to the chief is a black man wearing blue denim coveralls over a white linen shirt. On his head is a faded blue forage cap with a black brim, like the Union soldiers wore in the civil war. They're all smiling at Alex, who looks curiously at the angel beside him.

Two more small, winged Japanese warriors fly toward the group. One is a man, the other a young woman wearing an ornately blue kimono. The man lands on the Chief's other shoulder while the young woman lights gracefully on the Præsidiel's shoulder. She smiles at the angel and then turns to offer a polite bow to little Alex.

"Please, Alexander, allow me to introduce you." Offers the angel with an open palmed point. "This is Ioannes, Cælius, and Hania. On his right shoulder, Takeda-san, and on his left, Hasegawa-san." Præsidiel looks down at Alex and says with a wink, “We sometimes call him ‘Wrestles with Hare.’” The others chuckle. “To their right, Samuel, a patriot from your own country. He, of all these fine warriors, knows exactly what your parents endure, but that is for another time. And lastly, but certainly not least, here on my shoulder, the brave Ashi-hime. These Alexander, are some of my friends. Each a warrior in their own right.” Alex politely nods and smiles at them. “Everyone,” continues the angel, “this is Alexander ‘the great’”–he winks at the boy–“our newest, and youngest, warrior.” They gather around to pat him on the shoulder, say hello, or offer a bow, welcoming him.

After the warm welcome, the angel puts his arm around Alex and leads him through the group. “Now, my young friend, you see what lies at your journey’s end. However, before we go any further, there is one you must meet.” As everyone makes way, Alex is unexpectedly met by a man and a woman. The tall, strong man stands slightly behind and to the woman’s right. He has the appearance of a wise and gentle father. He gives Alex an affirming nod. The woman is dressed in a flowing, silken white gown. Over that is a royal blue mantle trimmed in gold and adorned with golden floral patterns. A white veil, trimmed in lace, cascades from her head past her shoulders. Around her waist is a gold belt and cincture. On her head is a crown with 12 stars. She radiates light as bright as the sun. Alex instantly recognizes her.

“Mother Mary?” Alex asks shyly, unconsciously twisting his bare toes in the dirt.

“Yes, child.”

“I knew it was you.” Shouts Alex. “It just had to be.” He runs to her exuberantly.

She squats down, spreading her hands wide to embrace him as only a mother can. Alex rushes into her arms. “Oh, my child, I am so happy to see you.” She pats him, “You are such a brave young man.” She holds him out to look at him and smile. He sees the same deep love in her eyes as he has always seen in those of his earthly mother.

"Hope you don't mind me sayin', but you're way more beautiful than I imagined." Alex's cheeks flush.

Joseph pats Alex on the shoulder and smiles warmly at him while Mary continues, "We are only here to welcome you briefly." Alex cocks his head at the curious statement. She gazes over his shoulder, looking beyond him. "Even now, I hear your earthly mother's cries and your Sitti calling out to me." She returns her eyes to the boy and smiles. "They call to me on your behalf."

Though he is reluctant to turn away from her majestic and loving beauty, Alex looks over his shoulder. He is surprised at the sight of his mother holding tightly to his hand and weeping. His earthly dad stands beside his body, looking down at his only son with tremendous sorrow. Alex turns back to the immaculate face of Mary. "I don't understand." He says with curiosity.

"Oh, my child. It is not your time," Mary answers lovingly. "Your earthly journey is not quite at an end."

* * * * *

Though the sun blazes through the hospital window, the otherwise silent room is filled with weeping, sobbing, and sniffling.

Abila feels an unexpected twitch in Alex's hand. She raises her eyes in shock. "Beep, beep...beep, beep," the heart monitor sounds again.

Aidan looks at the machine first, then at Alex, whose eyes open slowly and blink. "Mom? Dad?"

Chapter Seven

Astronaut Alex & the Space Ogre

Alex's mother stands at the kitchen sink, doing some dishes and looking out the window into their lush backyard. There is a raucous racket upstairs. Her mother, Sitti as she is known, sitting at the table with her tea, inquires, "Abila, what in the world are those two doing up there?"

"If I know Aidan, he's probably roughhousing with Alex." Then, a deep-throated "RRROOOAAARRR!" reverberates through the house, immediately followed by a boy's scream, "Ahhhh!" Next, they hear the sound of small footsteps pattering quickly across the floor above.

Young Alex comes thundering down the stairs, bounds over the ottoman in the living room, and rushes into the kitchen, where he is confronted by his mother, "Whoa, whoa, whoa there!" She exclaims. Alex's sneakers screech to a halt on the linoleum floor. An oversized space helmet bobbles around on his head. "Who do you think you are, Spaceman Spiff?" She asks with a grin. "What planet do you think this is?"

Sitti is doing her best not to snicker at his appearance.

Alex lowers the ray gun in his right hand and lifts the visor on his helmet with his left. "I'm not Spaceman Spiff, Mom. I'm astronaut Alex!" He declares. "I've gotta get back to the moon base and protect it from the space ogre who's chasin' me."

The sound of purposefully heavy footsteps falls on the treads in the stairwell, followed by another loud "RRROOOAAARRR!"

"Goodness me, what is that?" Asks Sitti.

“That’s the space ogre I was warnin’ yuh ‘bout, Sitti. He’s chasin’ me and is gonna attack the moon base,” exclaims Alex. “I gotta get outta here.”

“Well then, I guess you better hurry. On your way, Astronaut Alex,” Says his mom.

“Yes, ma’am.” He slams the visor shut on his helmet and bolts for the back door. He opens the door and warns, “Y’all better find a place to hide, too, or he’ll getcha!”

Just then, Aidan stomps into the kitchen. His arms are raised like Frankenstein’s monster, and he is wearing a pair of old springy antennae on his head. He bellows, “I’m gonna eat yuh, scrawny spaceman.”

Alex takes aim with his ray gun and says, “Nuh, uh! Take this! Pew pew!” He then runs out the door toward his backyard treehouse. The screen door slams closed behind him.

Aidan lowers his arms and laughs. “Ladies,” he greets them with a smirk. Sitti smiles, shakes her head, and sips her tea. Then, he raises his arms back up and grabs Abila. “Grrrr. Pretty spacewoman.”

She squeals and smacks playfully at him. “Don’t you have a moon base to attack…space ogre?” She laughs.

Aidan dips his wife, and the antenna on his head bounces. He kisses her. “Don’t you worry, fair space maiden; I’ll destroy that base.” He stands her back up and releases her. He looks over at Sitti and smiles mischievously. “Ma’am.” He nods.

Sitti rolls her eyes, smiles, and says, “Boys….”

Aidan walks over to the back door. He throws it open and yells, “RRROOOAAARRR! Must destroy moon base!”

A faint voice calls back from a distant treehouse, “No, you won’t!”

Space ogre roars again before stomping out into the backyard, letting the door slam behind him. Sitti takes her tea and joins her daughter at the sink. “It was so good to see **all** of you at Mass on Sunday." She says, standing next to her daughter.

"Yes. Yes, it was." Abila drapes her towel over the edge of the sink and opens the kitchen window. The fresh air wafts in. She takes a deep breath. "Mmmm," she exhales with a contented moan. Placing her hands in front of her on the sink, she stares out the window at her boys. Together, she and her mother watch the legendary battle for the moon base unfold.

"So, his illness is completely healed?" Sitti asks before taking a sip of her tea.

"Yes. The doctors have no explanation for it either, Mom. It's just...gone."

"A miracle then," Sitti states with certainty.

"It would seem so." A deep sense of peace enters her heart as she stares out the window. Bright-colored flowers dot the verdant landscape. She watches a breeze move across the grass and then rustle the leaves in a tree on its way toward the kitchen window. The gentle wind caresses Abila's skin and brushes her hair. It also causes a bottle on the sill to wobble.

Sitti sets her tea on the counter before reaching for the sea-green container. "Where'd you get this?" She inquires, gently taking the bottle in hand.

"Bonnie gave that to us on the day we checked Alex out of the hospital." Abila looks at her curious mother, who is inspecting it. "She found it the night before Alex...." She doesn't want to finish the sentence.

"There's a note inside." Sitti rotates the bottle. "It's kind of scribbly." She gasps when holding it up in the light. "Is this Alex's handwriting?"

"Yes." Abila's eyes fill with tears. "Go ahead, read it."

"Thank you, God, for." She turns it looking for more. "It just trails off," she notes.

A teardrop escapes from the corner of Abila's eye. "Yes." She sniffles before continuing, "Thank you, God."

"Yaaarrrg!" Alex's fearsome scream interrupts their moment of peace.

The ladies turn their attention to the backyard. They look out just in time to witness Astronaut Alex leap fearlessly over the railing into the space ogre's arms, who subsequently, and overdramatically, falls to the ground.

Unscathed, Alex jumps to his feet, "That'll teach yuh to invade my moon base, ogre!"

"Aahhhk! You got me, spaceman!"

Mother and daughter giggle at the boys playing in the backyard. Sitti replaces the bottle on the windowsill. She wraps her arm around her daughter. "Yes, Abila, God is good."

A loving family has been made whole, and once again, all is right in the world.

"But Jesus looked at them and said, "With men it is impossible, but not with God; for with God, all things are possible." Mark 10:27

The Father Soutane Essays

Contents

Essay One

Gehenna's Wordsmith

A secret forge burns brightly in the depths of Gehenna. A weaselly little soul once called Ygor works the tanned-hide bellows, fanning the flames. Billowing black smoke swirls around a monstrous daemon's arm as he slams his hammer down upon an anvil. Sparks and embers burst from the three-letter word he strikes and scatters through the smoke-filled air. A childish taunt echoes over and over in his mind, filling him with hate. Sticks and stones may break my bones, but your words will never hurt me. He responds by pouring his malice, fury, and disgust into each subsequent hammer blow.

An upstart dæmon named Wormword paces back and forth in front of the smithy, his footsteps in rhythm with the clang of the hammer fall. "I know. I know." He affirms. "You would much rather be on the battlefield, but your skills are needed here. Remember this, oh great wordsmith, Cain listened to the words of our father below and then killed his only brother with a stone. Our job here matters. We must control the language of men. We must forge new words and reshape others." He stops in his tracks. "Yes," he says, as he contemplates, "the original temptations are still the best."

Straightening his back and holding his finger high, he continues his villainous monologue. "My uncle once told me how our father below convinced the first man and woman they could be like God. Now I shall convince this new generation they can become gods; that they can transform themselves." He strokes his Billy goat bearded chin. "Yesss, I like that prefix. Transss." He says with a hiss. "I will convince them they can transcend their bodies. They can transform their gender. They can merge their minds with machines and become transhuman." He grows quiet for a moment. "But where to start? Where to start?"

"Master." Calls Ygor in his nasally, wheezily voice. "What about educators? That is where my former master got his ideas."

"Ah. Yes. Very good, Ygor." Wormword pauses. A malevolent giggle slips past his lips. "Of course, we will begin in academia. That lovely brood of vipers is always ready to inject their venom. Their ideology will course through the veins of the young. It will cloud their vision, and a veil of ignorance, relativism, and atheism will blind them to the hereafter." He wrings his hands, saying with a scowl, "We will replace the repugnant word of the enemy"–suddenly perking up with a joyful sarcasm–"with beguiling and benign terms." A self-approving smile creeps across his face. "Terms that will cause those lost in the fog of war to declare good evil and evil good."

The smithy's hammering stops. The bent and twisted word claimed from the battlefield is finished. The brute has taken perverse pleasure in reshaping what was once a word that conveyed happiness and joy in literature, songs, and expressions. He has warped it, filling it with sadistic and domineering wickedness. He drops his hammer on the ashen ground, reaches for his tongs, and grabs the word with them. He holds the glowing multi-colored word up briefly to admire his work. Then he turns to the cauldron-like crater filled with a bitterly cold mire nearby. With a salacious moan, he thrusts the word into the sludge, where it hisses, bubbles, and smolders.

"Yes. Yes." Wormword pats his closed fingers together. "Many sinners will share the same short-lived ecstasy when they live by that word's new meaning. All the while, it will corrupt their souls. Now," he suddenly commands, "we must work on creating a thick fog of war. Let us work on ambiguity, indifference, and obtuseness." He smiles at Ygor, "Three of my favorite words."

Wormword snaps to attention and points his finger at Gehenna's wordsmith. "We don't need any new names or accusations. We already have so many." The wordsmith groans in disappointment. "Yes. Yes, I know they are useful, but we must forge words that distract the enemy's creation from His truth. Let us redefine a few for good measure, too; words we can use to corrupt the souls of the weak and lead them astray. Our hordes will collect their self-mutilated bodies in the aftermath of our verbal onslaught." He begins to chuckle. "I will make my uncle proud; I will." His maniacal laughter, muffled by smoke from the forge, is joined by Ygor.

* * * * *

Elsewhere, an unwavering man in a long black cassock moves about the skirmish. He is called simply Soutane by many and is one of several brothers on the battlefield of ideas. These men, this black robe brigade as they are sometimes called, do not consider themselves warriors; they prefer the title of servant, servants of the trinitarian God. Soutane himself is a servant leader who seeks to inspire faith and courage on behalf of the Lord. Presently, this man in the black cassock rallies the king's troops. He does so with a story.

"There is one who scatters seeds of truth in this world. Some of his seeds fall upon well-trodden paths where they cannot take root and are carried away by the servants of the adversary. Some seeds fall on the barren battleground, where there is very little earth to take root in. These seeds are easily trampled underfoot or swept away in battle. Yet more seed falls in the wilderness, where the thicket prevents them from rising. But" Soutane encourages with a smile and a finger pointing skyward, "other seed falls on fertile ground. Their roots go deep. They grow strong, producing much fruit."

Soutane extends his hand to those who had lost the will to fight when the names and insults were cast at them. He lifts them to their feet and encourages them with a pat on the shoulder. "They are only words, sisters and brothers." Raising his hands, he stops another who broke and ran out of fear of being called a bigot, a racist, or some kind of 'phobe.' "Stop, young man, do not fear the names hurled at you, for they have no power." For yet another, he clears the entangling brambles of social media and washes the muck from a youth's eyes and ears. "There, child, let us clear away that which confuses so you may grow upright and strong."

The black-robed leader steps out past the frontline. With pity, he witnesses traitors who fell prey to the diabolical propaganda flee gleefully into the adversary's camp. He has arrived too late to stop them. Sadly, Soutane knows he will see them again, and when he does, they will return with the adversary's words in their mouths.

Soutane turns to face those courageous souls on the frontline. "Fear not," he proclaims! "The numbers of the just,"–he lowers his tone and winks at everyone–"that is you, brothers and sisters,"–he raises his tone back up, "are far greater than one might imagine. Remember, "In the beginning was the Word, and the Word was with God, and the Word was God. The Word became flesh, dwelt among men, and was full of grace and truth." The battle-weary look to their leader. He continues, "I know the fog of war the enemy generates is thick. Combined with treacherous terrain, it can be hard to navigate. Some of our own have betrayed us and joined them. It is true; they lie in wait, hoping to cut us down and destroy our resolve and faith. But we, the faithful militant, know that we will be justified or condemned by our words." He points to those fleeing toward the adversary. "It is what comes out of the mouth that defiles a man."

"The word of God is alive and will return to us one day." Reminds Soutane. "He who is the Word wields truth and commands the armies of heaven. Out of his mouth will come the double-edged sword of truth, able to pierce and cleave body and soul alike, able to both bless and curse. With it, he will strike down the most foul."

The rest of the gathered faithful rise as their leader inspires them. "Until then, humble warriors, we must withstand the poisonous words of Gehenna's foul wordsmith. Let not the slings and arrows of the adversary discourage you, for they are merely words and cannot destroy your flesh. Now is the time to go forward. The King of Kings has already won the great battle; we must only finish our march and rescue those poor souls overtaken by the adversary. Let God's truth, which is sown in your hearts, grow and flourish."

Essay Two

Madrecita's Angel

A young woman lies in a cold, sterile room. She stirs to a whisper in her mind, *Wake up, Madrecita. Wake up.* She opens her sleepy eyes and is unsure of her surroundings. Through the haze, she remembers coming to this place out of desperation. She believed in her friend, who brought her to this nondescript building before speeding off. She remembers the man she thought she loved, the father of the child in her womb, who abandoned her after she confessed her pregnancy to him. Regret fills her slow-beating heart. She wishes she could be with her mother and father; they would know what to do and how to help, but they are too far away now. She is alone, confused, and genuinely fearful of what will become of her.

As she comes to, she thinks of the woman at the counter's words, "We can help you. It's a short and painless procedure. After it's over, you can return to work, school, you know, your normal life." Another fuzzy memory fades in, "Just through here, dear. Your private room. I'll be back with the doctor shortly." Although blurry, she recalls the nurse helping her prepare for the procedure and the anesthesiologist giving her something...something which made her dazed and confused. Their voices change to a low murmuring in her mind. It sounds like an unholy chant.

The room begins to change before her eyes. *Am I hallucinating*? Madrecita wonders. She feels something grasping her ankles and looks toward her feet. Two hands of black smoke hold her bare legs in the air. More smoldering hands hold down her shoulders and hands. She cannot touch her belly and feel for signs of life in her unborn. She starts to panic.

The walls of the room morph and change to stone. A dark fog billows up from the floor around her. Looking to her left, she sees two towers. She squints to see if they are in the shape of leaves or the letter 'P.' A deathly fear grips her when she looks closer at them, however. Hundreds of tiny skulls, no bigger than newborns, fill each P-shaped tower. "No." She whimpers, "This can't be real."

She closes her eyes and whips her head to the right. She hears a stone door grinding open and slowly opens her eyes again. A stairwell descending into a black abyss materializes in the floor below—the sacrificial blood of the innocent stain its steps. From the blackness, she swears she can hear a baby's cry. Madrecita thrashes weakly on a stone table as the fullness of Aztec temple imagery comes to life around her. The drug has done its work; she is too weak to escape. "This is a mistake." She whimpers. "I don't want to sacrifice my child. Please, God, not like this."

A beam of brilliant white light cuts through the murky fog behind her. Its warmth caresses her tear-stained face. She strains to see the light's source but cannot turn her head far enough. "Quickly, Madrecita." Comes a compassionate voice. "Get up and leave this place of death." Her legs fall, and the pressure on her shoulders and hands is lifted. The Aztec temple dissipates in a flash as though it never existed, and the room returns to a plain doctor's office.

The young mother sits up, her head still spinning. She turns to see an angel standing in the light. She can feel his pale-blue eyes peering into her heart. He is wearing a white cloak over sky-blue armor with a wide, golden belt around his waist. The angel tucks his enormous, luminescent wings behind him, and they blend into his cloak. He removes his right from the handle of his gladius long enough to point to

Madrecita's clothes draped across the chair, "Put on your clothes and sandals."

She follows his direction without hesitation and clumsily dresses. After slipping her sandals on, she asks, "Am I dreaming? Who…?"

The angel produces a light gray cloak while interrupting her, "Here, wrap this around you and follow me." Madrecita does as the angel says. He turns, and the door to the room opens. He moves swiftly but slowly enough that she can keep up in her weakened state.

The two move, unseen, down the hallway, out into the lobby, and past the receptionist, who has her head down reading paperwork. The exterior doors open of their own accord, ushering Madrecita and her escort into the cool city air.

The young mother follows her silent liberator down the sidewalk. No one seems to notice either of them. She continues to wonder, *Is this all just a dream?* It is nearly dusk, and the air is crisp, causing Madrecita to pull her cloak closer around her. The streetlights are blinking to life. As they do, her full faculties return; she becomes keenly aware of herself and her surroundings. She looks up at the back of the angel, who suddenly fades before her eyes. As he disappears, she notices a man walking straight toward her in a long black cassock.

A priest? She asks herself—childhood memories of going to church with her mother flood her consciousness. A sudden sense of shame overwhelms her. She tries to pull her cloak over her head and conceal herself from him, only to find she is covered with a simple blanket.

"Oh, daughter." The priest greets compassionately with his hands extended. Madrecita looks left and right, thinking he is speaking to someone else. "Yes, child. I am here to meet you." He affirms, stopping in front of her.

She tugs at the blanket, trying to hide within its folds. "How would you...me? You came for me?"

"Yes." He says simply as he moves to her side. "Come, let's get you to safety." He raises his left arm behind her and motions to proceed further down the sidewalk with his right. Aware that she has nothing, no shelter or food, she decides to go with him. She knows she should be able to trust this man of God.

He introduces himself only a few paces into their flight to safety, "I am Soutane." He says, offering a reassuring smile.

"Madrecita." She whispers meekly.

"May I tell you a story Madrecita?" She turns her head toward him and nods her approval. Soutane walks with his hands clasped in front of him. "Earlier this evening, while in prayer," he begins, "God blessed me with a vision of a new mother. A young woman escaping that...that temple of death"–he says with slight disdain–"with the aid of an angel." His voice changes to a more reflective tone. "Much like St. Peter escaped his prison cell, you see?"

Madrecita offers no reaction.

"Anyway, I knew it was my duty to rise at once and go to help this young mother. As I walked, I saw your guide, your angel, disappear before you. That is how I knew you are the one I sought, the one in need of sanctuary"

Still, she walks silently beside him.

Soutane understands there will be no conversation right now, so he makes a final reassurance, "The church is just up ahead, Madrecita."

They walk together in silence until they near the church. "We're here." Says Soutane. Madrecita exhales a sigh of relief as she gazes up the stairs at the wooden doors in the recessed archway. "Please, come in." Soutane invites as he pulls open the door.

Madrecita enters slowly. Peace fills her heart. Everything she sees starkly contrasts with what she experienced just minutes before. Pillars and arches rising into the vaulted ceiling lead her eyes heavenward to God. The setting sun casts its final golden rays through stained-glass windows on the western side. She has not been to church for some time, but she feels at home here. She is surrounded by beauty and warmth. Here life is welcomed and supported.

She unconsciously lowers the blanket from her shoulders, letting it drape across her arms. Placing her hands on her lower belly, she rubs her tummy. Tears fill her eyes. As only a mother can, she feels the life inside. She has kept her unborn child safe from those who would take its life, which stirs a motherly satisfaction within her. With renewed vigor, she moves swiftly down the center aisle, kneels near the middle of the nave, and takes a seat in the nearest pew. Madrecita begins to solemnly yet joyfully repeat prayers she learned as a little girl.

Soutane approaches and quietly kneels in the aisle next to the young mother. He offers a quiet prayer of gratitude before going to retrieve the little sisters who reside across the street from the church. They will provide her with a bed for the night and nourishment. There is great joy in God's house this evening.

* * * * *

The next day, Soutane introduces her to a young man named Joseph, who regularly volunteers at the church. He is only a year older than Madrecita. He is kind, gentle, and devoted to God.

Upon meeting her, Joseph is immediately taken aback by her beauty. He sees wonderous things in her copper-colored eyes. More than physical beauty, he sees fear and ferocity, bashfulness and boldness, and above all, an unfathomable love and devotion about to emerge. The young woman captured his attention with just one look and rendered him speechless.

"Joseph?" prompts Soutane.

"Yes, father." He stammers out of his daze. Madrecita grins at his awkwardness.

"I have called ahead to the pregnancy resource center. They are expecting our guest; you really must be going."

"Oh, uh, yes. I guess we should, huh?" He offers his arm to Madrecita, who gladly accepts it. His cheeks flush at her touch, and a broad smile grows uncontrollably. They leave the church arm in arm. Joseph walks upright, exuberant in his task at hand.

Slightly shaking his head, Soutane looks skyward, "You were right, Father. Joseph is perfect for her."

* * * * *

After her check-up and all the resources have been presented, Joseph and Madrecita depart the center. They fall into a blissful conversation on the way back, which causes them to forget they must walk by the other place. Madrecita becomes all too aware of her proximity to it as they approach. She prompts Joseph to cross to the opposite side of the road.

As they pass warily by, they witness a woman being ushered out of the building and off the property by another woman. They discretely engage in a dispute. Madrecita recognizes the one who is led out as the receptionist. Curiosity prompts her to stop to listen. She unintentionally lets go of Joseph's arm and stands staring at them.

"I can't believe you're firing me over this!" exclaims the receptionist.

"You let a young woman under the influence of anesthesia leave the facilities."

"But I have no idea how she got out or even where she went. She left of her own accord. How is that my fault?"

"Regardless, you must find employment elsewhere."

Madrecita hears her name whispered in her ear, calling her attention away from the dispute. "Come on. Let's go." Joseph says softly. "Leave them to their bickering."

The young mother glances up at his face. His compassionate smile warms her heart.

"So, they think it's a boy?" He asks, offering her his arm yet again.

She smiles. "The nurse said she's pretty sure it is." She informs as she wraps her hand around his forearm.

"I would love to have a boy one day." He says with excitement. "What will you name him?"

"I haven't decided. I'm thinking maybe Salvador,"–she looks bashfully at Joseph, trying to gauge his reaction–"for my little savior, or maybe Alejandro, my little warrior." She hesitates momentarily before asking, "Which one do you like, Joseph?"

"Hmmm…" he contemplates as they walk.

The two stroll on. Deep in their hearts, each feels the unexpected connection they share, blossoming into something greater.

Essay Three

Soul Affirming Care

Joseph is walking to the local grocery store, desperately trying to recite his shopping list. "Eggs, bread, and uh, um...what else did I need?" He mumbles. Thoughts of the beautiful girl who works there continually interrupt his train of thought. "Ahhh, Madrecita," he whispers. "I need to see her." A growing commotion down the street disrupts his daydreams.

He slows his pace. Observing from a distance, he immediately recognizes the cluster of multi-colored flags and realizes it is a protest. The flags represent a subject he vehemently disagrees with, so out of caution, he decides to cross the street and avoid the mob.

However, one of the demonstrators catches his eye as he skirts by. A young man he thinks he recognizes but cannot place from when or where. The young man sees him and makes a beeline toward him, waving and shouting, "Joseph! Hey, Joe!"

Joseph stops and waits for the young man to approach out of politeness and curiosity. Joseph stares at him intently, mentally grasping for a name to match the face.

"How you been, buddy?" The familiar guy asks.

"I apologize, but do I know you?" Joseph inquires.

"It's me. Mel." He tilts his head a bit. "From high school." He suddenly realizes how much time has passed since they've spoken. "Oh, sorry. It's been a while; you probably don't recognize me now."

"Mel?" Joseph glances down briefly. He recognizes the voice. Then, a name materializes in his mind. "Melissa?" He asks cautiously.

“Yes! You do remember me.” There is a brief, awkward silence. “That’s my dead name, though. I go by Mel now; he/him.” She searches his face for validation, for acceptance of her as a man.

Joseph’s heart sinks. He remembers Melissa being a rather pretty young girl. Now she has a crew cut, piercings in her lip and nose, and a flat chest. “What... what happened?” He asks as he looks her up and down.

Mel’s face immediately flushes with anger. “Whaddaya mean ‘What happened’?”

“Oh, I’m sorry. I didn’t mean to...,” he stammers. “It’s just... You were so pretty the last time I saw you. Now you look like... like a boy.” Mel’s face contorts with rage, and Joseph suddenly realizes he has offended her.

“Wow! Talk about rude. You’re a real jerk, you know?” Mel screams. She curses at Joseph. She insults him, calls him several names ending in ‘phobic,’ and bestows many other derogatory titles on him.

Other protesters gathered around, screaming and shouting at Joseph. In his heart, he senses an evil within his former friend. His conscience shocks him with the thought that they are possessed by unclean spirits, which saddens and enrages him. His temper flares, which is entirely out of the ordinary. He screams, “You’re all stupid, misguided, and mentally disturbed!”

His grocery list forgotten and his emotions in turmoil, Joseph escaped the scene as quickly as possible. He headed straight for the church where he sits now, bathing in the warm glow shining through the stained glass. His head down and fingers tightly intertwined, Joseph fervently prays, “Have mercy on me, O Lord. Forgive me for my outburst.” He pauses, laboring to overcome his reluctance. Finally, he offers, “Father, forgive Melissa, too.”

He asks God to quell the anger in his heart, but the altercation continues repeating in his mind. "How could this happen?" he mumbles. Though he works to let go of his resentment, his heart still swims in anger. There is also a deep sorrow for Melissa. "What did she do to herself?" Shaken and disturbed, he pleads with God for mercy, peace, and wisdom. Not just for himself but for his former friend as well.

Immersed in his thoughts and prayers, he does not see Father Soutane enter the church from the Sacristy. The reverend observes the young parishioner and sees he is distressed. He sets his things in the chair next to the Sacristy and then approaches Joseph, saying, "Good morning, Joseph." He offers kindly. "You look troubled. May I ask what brings you here?"

"I had a bad incident a little while ago, Father. It's really thrown me for a loop."

"You want to talk about it? May I sit with you?"

"I guess," Joseph answers meekly before sliding over.

Father Soutane faces the altar and genuflects before sitting beside his young friend. "I can see something has upset you."

Joseph recounts the conflict and his response to it. He expresses remorse for his outburst before finishing, "Honestly, Father, I just don't know what to do about all this."

Father Soutane takes a deep breath and exhales. "I believe this 'trans' movement is sinister. The diabolical seeks to distort and pervert all things. It is a distortion of the 'trans' word that truly matters, transubstantiation."

"Father," Joseph interrupts. "How can this be a perversion of the Holy Eucharist?"

"Bear with me, Joseph. I'm getting there." He continues, "A man named Julian Huxley once claimed it was possible to take over 'human evolution' by refining and improving man through social and cultural change. Transhumanists thought scientific advancements like computer technology, cryo-technology, you know, preserving human eggs and embryos, nano-technology, and other stuff would enable people to transcend their bodies. They believe humans with augmented capabilities will evolve into a "posthuman" species. I believe transgenderism is an extension of this thought. If they can augment their bodies with technology, then why can't they change their sex? Either way, it's man's or woman's attempt at placing themselves ahead of God. Transgenderism is propagated by both social institutions and technology. It's another route to garner acceptance of the posthuman ideology."

"Okay. I get it, but how do I respond to all this?"

"Unbridled rage and name-calling do us no good. After all, this is a battle for their souls as much as it is for ours. We must pray for internal peace and discernment in every situation. We should use clarity, concern, and cleverness to counter the diabolical. It is not for us to condemn those lost in the fog of these modern movements, like your friend...?"

"Melissa."

"Like Melissa, whom I will pray for." Father Soutane reassures. "Instead, we must be like our Blessed Mother, pointing these lost souls toward the light of our Savior, who is always with us in the Eucharist. Receiving the Blessed Sacrament fills us with grace and prepares the body and soul for the resurrection. Transhumanism and transgenderism break down the body and poison the soul. Sure, they may lead to slightly longer lives or some level of pleasure; however, neither leads the individual toward God. So, at the risk of being yelled at or 'canceled,' we must use the three 'C's' to share the gospel and call those lost in the fog to repentance and redemption."

"So, instead of gender-affirming, we should offer soul-affirming care."

Father Soutane grins widely. “Yes! Very good.” He winks at Joseph as he taps his nose. “I’m going to steal that slogan.”

Joseph smiles. “S’all good, Father. I feel much better now. Thank you for visiting with me.”

“No. Thank you for listening to me ramble.” Father Soutane stands and steps out into the aisle. Facing the altar, he genuflects again before asking, “You have prayed for Melissa?”

“Yes.”

“Good.” He pats Joseph on the shoulder. “You’re a fine young man, Joseph.” He turns to leave but suddenly wheels back around. “Oh, by the way, how’s Madrecita?”

Joseph blushes. A large smile erupts from the young man’s face. “She’s glowing, Father. Only a couple more months before the baby comes.”

“You ask her to marry you yet?”

Joseph digs into his pants pocket and pulls out a simple ring with a tiny diamond. Inspecting it in the glow of the stained-glass windows, he answers, “You know, Father? I think I may head over to the grocery store when I leave here.”

Father Soutane smiles and nods. “Godspeed, lad. Godspeed.”

Essay Four

The Last Time

The old man leans on an old wooden table, his head in his hands. Lifting his graying eyes, he raises his head, and his hands fall upon the rickety table. The simple hourglass resting there shakes. A snake hisses in protest as it tightens its grip around the base of the timepiece. Placated by its dissent, it continues devouring its tail. The man slumps in his chair, his calloused fingers sliding off the table's edge.

The day's last light shines through the dirty window of the shack upon the hourglass. The sand glints as it slips through its glass neck. The top bulb is almost empty, and the sands of time have nearly run out. He covers his bearded face with his weathered hands and recalls the devil's words.

"It has been a thousand years since I was bound, you miserable, old bastard," he said when he slammed the hourglass on the table. "There is no babe for the new year. You are the last of your kind, and your end is nigh. When these sands run out, so too does your existence."

In arrogance, the devil bent the old man's sickle over his knee before throwing it in the corner. "There is a time for everything...bah! Time marches on...indeed. Time heals all wounds...bleck!" sneered the devil, sticking his tongue out. "I can **easily** tear open old wounds. The season is mine now."

The old man remembers the black scythe in the fallen one's hands. "Now watch, ancient Kronos, as I march to war!" He exclaimed before storming off into the darkness.

The ancient one, once called Kronos, has spent the last hour locked away in his dilapidated cabin, set in a desolate wasteland, consumed by regret. The sound of war rages around him. The smell of sickness wafts through his dingy window. Cries of starvation echo in his ears. Death rides freely through the world, his scythe severing the tethering cords of millions of souls.

"Ole Scratch knows how to torment," he laments. "Especially here at the end."

The room darkens. The sounds of destruction fade. Eerie quiet creeps in as the coldness of night envelopes him. His ears tune to the final passage of sand through the hourglass in the silence. Then, speaking into his palms, his muffled voice meekly asks, "What becomes of me, Creator?"

An unexpected light peeks through the gaps between his boney fingers. A stunning warmth drives the chill from his shivering body. Slowly, he lowers his hands from his face. Squinting through bleary, tear-stained eyes, the old man inspects the hourglass. It has run out of sand, and the serpent at its base has devoured himself. His vision focuses, and he suddenly realizes he is not alone.

The ancient one jolts up in his chair, startled by an angel beside the table. The tips of his primary feathers nearly touch the ground, while the alula feathers of his wing joints rise high above his hooded face. He holds a simple, battle-scarred spear in his right hand. A bright, blue-white flame dances freely in his extended left hand. His wings' cup shape reflects the flame's warmth and light, illuminating the room. The angel wears a light-blue chest plate over a soft gray tunic with a golden sash tied elegantly around his waist.

"Who...Who are you?" stammers time immemorial.

The angel looks down at the old man. "I am Præsidiel."

"Is this the end of me, Præsidiel?"

"Yes."

"What becomes of me as the eternal is ushered in?"

The demeanor of the stern-looking sentinel relaxes. He offers a comforting smile. "You are to be freed of your burden. There is no further need to measure His creation. Oblivion awaits."

Præsidiel turns his head to look straight ahead. Then, without losing his grip on his spear or extinguishing the flame in his hand, he kneels and bows his head.

The Word made flesh steps into His creation once more. Time pushes his chair back, steps to the side of the table, and kneels fastidiously. "My Lord, your servant is here."

The Master of all creation stands before his servant and calls him to his feet. His presence warms the old man's heart. The Messiah turns his gaze to the hourglass on the table. He reaches for it, and the eyes of old Kronos follow his hand. Jesus grasps it, turns it over, and sets it on the table. No sand passes through the glass neck; time, it appears, no longer flows. Eternity has come.

He bows to the Creator. When he stands, he discovers only he and the angel remain. The hourglass, the table, and even the walls of the desolate cottage dissipate like dust in the wind. A widening gap, void of light, is revealed. It separates two dimensions, and the massive gates slowly close on each one. One realm is glorious and bright, full of song and feasting in honor of the Creator. The other is dark and firelit, full of wailing and gnashing of teeth; he glimpses the fallen one chained in its depths.

Time immemorial looks to Præsidiel. The angel extinguishes the flame in his hand. The creature once known as Father Time fades peacefully into oblivion.

About the Author

John Eudy is a 26-year military veteran. He was both a soldier in the Army National Guard and a 'shallow water' sailor in the U.S. Coast Guard.

Admittedly not as well-traveled as the wayfarer rat, he has at least been up and down the river a time or two. Additional expeditions include cautiously wandering the lava fields of Kilauea, snowshoeing to the summit of Cadillac Mountain, strolling among giants in King's Canyon, and swimming with wild dolphins in the Gulf of Mexico (which he embarrassingly thought were sharks at first sight). John even traveled through time once... by crossing the international date line to visit Guam.

These days, John and his family reside smack-dab in the middle of the country, not too far from the river, though. He has been married to his lovely wife of 30 years, and they are the proud parents of four daughters, two of whom are already with God in heaven.

Inspired by faith and scripture, he enjoys weaving history, cultural legends, personal life experiences, and Christian morality into fictional novellas.

Matthew 8:5-13

www.ingramcontent.com/pod-product-compliance
Lightning Source LLC
Chambersburg PA
CBHW070644310726
48982CB00001B/408
* 9 7 9 8 9 9 2 7 1 5 9 0 3 *